HAUNT ME STILL

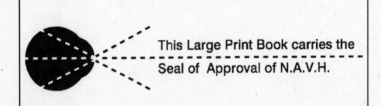

This Large Print Book carries the
Seal of Approval of N.A.V.H.

HAUNT ME STILL

JENNIFER LEE CARRELL

THORNDIKE PRESS

A part of Gale, Cengage Learning

GALE
CENGAGE Learning·

Detroit • New York • San Francisco • New Haven, Conn • Waterville, Maine • London

GALE
CENGAGE Learning

Copyright © 2010 by Jennifer Lee Carrell.
Thorndike Press, a part of Gale, Cengage Learning.

Thorndike Press® Large Print Mystery.
The text of this Large Print edition is unabridged.
Other aspects of the book may vary from the original edition.
Set in 16 pt. Plantin.

LIBRARY OF CONGRESS CATALOGING-IN-PUBLICATION DATA

Carrell, Jennifer Lee.
    Haunt me still / by Jennifer Lee Carrell.
        p. cm. — (Thorndike Press large print mystery)
    ISBN-13: 978-1-4104-2742-7
    ISBN-10: 1-4104-2742-0
    1. Shakespeare, William, 1564–1616—Influence—Fiction. 2. Shakespeare, William, 1564–1616—Authorship—Fiction. 3. Shakespeare, William, 1564–1616—Dramatic production—Fiction. 4. Scotland—Fiction. 5. Large type books.
    I. Title.
    PS3603.A77438H38 2010b
    813'.6—dc22   2010010946

Published in 2010 by arrangement with Dutton, a member of Penguin Group (USA) Inc.

Printed in the United States of America
1 2 3 4 5 6 7 14 13 12 11 10

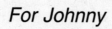

For Johnny

I can call spirits from the vasty deep.

Why, so can I, or so can any man;
But will they come when you do call for
them?
— William Shakespeare

An it harm none, do what ye will.
— The Wiccan Rede (or Witches' Counsel)

PROLOGUE

November 1606
Hampton Court Palace
Wrapped in a gown of blue-green velvet trimmed with gold, a queen's crown on his head, the boy sat drowsing on the throne near the center of the Great Hall, just at the edge of the light. Tomorrow, it would be the king who sat there. Not a player king, but the real one, His Majesty King James I of England and VI of Scotland. Tonight, however, someone among the players had been needed to sit there and see just what the king on his throne would see as Mr. Shakespeare's new Scottish play, blood-spattered and witch-haunted, conjured up a rite of nameless evil.

The boy, who was not in this scene, had volunteered. But the rehearsal had been unaccountably delayed, stretching deep into the frigid November night, until it was almost as cold inside the unheated hall as it was in the frost-rimed courtyards below. The heavy gown, though, was warm, and as the hours crawled on, the boy found it hard to keep his eyes open.

Well out of the torchlight illuminating the playing area, a grizzled man-at-arms in a worn leather jerkin, gaunt as a figure of famine, leaned against the wall at the edge of a tapestry, seeming to drowse as well.

At last, movement stirred in the haze of light. Three figures, cloaked head to toe in black, skimmed in a circle about the cauldron set in the center of the hall, their voices melding into a single chant somewhere between a moan and a hiss.

"What is it you do?" rasped the player king as he entered, eyes wide with horror.

The answer whined through the echoing hall like the nearly human sound of the wind, or maybe the restless dead, seeking entry at the eaves: *A deed without a name.*

Not long afterward, a phalanx of children, eerily beautiful, drifted into the light, gliding one by one past the throne. In the rear, the smallest held up a mirror.

On the throne, the boy-queen sat bolt upright.

Against the wall, barely visible in the outer darkness, the old soldier's eyes flickered open.

A few moments later, the boy slid from the throne and melted into the darkness at the back of the hall. Behind him, the man followed like an ill-fitting shadow.

Robert Cecil, earl of Salisbury, was wakened by his manservant in the small hours of the morning. Behind him in the darkness, two more faces floated in a double halo of candlelight, one slipping from black hair toward gray age, and the other just rising into the fullness of his prime, but both Howards and both smug. The earl of Northampton and his nephew the earl of Suffolk.

Salisbury was instantly awake. He did not know what the Howards had to look smug about at such an hour of the morning, but anything that happened in the palace without his knowledge disturbed him. When it involved the Howards, it invariably meant danger.

"It's the boy, my lord," said his manservant, coughing discreetly.

"The players' boy," Suffolk specified.

"He is missing," purred Northampton. "Along with the mirror."

Wherever that boy is, Salisbury thought with an inward sigh, *the Howards know about it.* Aloud, he said, "rouse Dr. Dee," and painfully sat up, aware of Northamp-

11

ton's stare aimed at the hump on his back. "And send for the captain on duty."

To the captain, he simply said, *"Find him."*

Half an hour later, Salisbury led the way, splay-footed and limping, toward the waiting chamber off the Great Hall, aware at every step of the proud, straight stalking of the tall Howard earls flanking him. He did not like working with either of them, especially Northampton. Generally speaking, Salisbury was fastidious about his person and his apparel, small and misshapen though he was, but not about people, whose talents he assessed with a cold, accurate eye and then used as necessary. But the Howards curdled something within his soul, making him long to step out into the nearest rose garden, whatever the weather, to rid himself of some not-quite-detectable stench. The king, however, had fallen under Northampton's spell and had made the occasional partnership unavoidable. Witness this unsavory business of the boy. When it came to the kingdom's safety, Salisbury was not above using anybody, but he did not enjoy baiting traps with children.

Dr. Dee was waiting for them, his dark robe and long white beard fairly shaking with indignation. "You told me you were keeping them here for their safety," he charged. "The boy and the mirror both."

Salisbury sighed. Not for *their* safety. For the king's. For the kingdom's. Why couldn't men as undoubtedly brilliant as Dr. Dee make that distinction?

The earl did not give much credence to such things as magic mirrors and conjuring spirits. But just in case, he kept his finger on the pulse of what was happening among the kingdom's conjurors, John Dee foremost among them. His brilliance as a mathematician and navigator was, after all, unmatched, and he had done Salisbury's father and the old queen good service in the field of cryptology. If even a fraction of Dee's claims about conjuring angels or transmuting base metal into gold turned out to be true, Salisbury wanted a handle on the old man.

So when Dee had come running, spouting a wild tale of blood and fire seen in one of his show-stones, Salisbury had listened with a seriousness that had shaken Dr. Dee even as it gratified him, and then he had interviewed the boy who claimed to have done the actual seeing. For, as Salisbury already knew, but Dr. Dee did not, there were indeed plans afoot among some renegade Catholics to blow up Parliament and, with it, the king.

To Dr. Dee's chagrin, however, Salisbury

had kept the boy, who seemed to have foreseen not only the Gunpowder Plot but also a mysterious woman holding a knife. And he had kept, too, the mirror the boy claimed to have seen them in.

That had been a year ago. The Powder Plot had not come off, as Salisbury had all along known it would not. The plotters had been caught and either killed in the capture or executed with the full ferocity of the law. Only one figure was still at large: the king-maker who Salisbury was certain had been behind the plot from the beginning, but whom he had never been able to identify. Someone among the great of the kingdom who had meant to take the reins of rule amid the chaos. Someone who was most certainly among those who fawned daily on the king he had plotted to kill.

Salisbury had naturally assumed that this person was a man, but the boy's vision of a woman with red hair and dark eyes, holding a knife engraved with letters the boy could not read, had brought him up short. If the earl had believed in ghosts, he might almost have said that the boy had seen old Queen Elizabeth. But the enemy he sought was surely still among the living. The old queen's blood ran in other veins, though — thinly, to be sure, but there. Women with Tudor and Plantagenet ancestry, and the telltale red-gold coloring to prove it, were not hard to come by at court. The king's widely scattered family of Stewarts among them.

When it came to these royal families, that touch of flame in the hair often came with a Machiavellian ruthlessness that made the Howards, dangerous as they were, seem as innocent as kittens. It was one reason the Plantagenets, Tudors, and Stewarts had occupied thrones for centuries, Salisbury reflected sourly, while the Howards had lost the lone dukedom that had been their pinnacle of achievement — unless you counted the two queens whose crowns Henry VIII had cut off, along with their heads. Tudors and Stewarts, though, had produced women of more formidable mettle, Queen Elizabeth and her cousin, the present king's mother, Mary, Queen of Scots, prime among them. So why not a woman?

Or a woman in concert with a still unknown man.

So Salisbury had set out to discover the identity of the face in the mirror. He'd tried the boy in various positions at court — but there were limited opportunities for a young boy to observe great ladies unnoticed, and the child had never encountered her. In the end, it had been another of Mr. Shakespeare's plays that gave the earl the idea of installing the boy among the King's Men, giving him both a perfect excuse and a prime vantage point from which to observe the courtiers drawn around the king. He'd had to use Suffolk, the lord chamberlain, whose job it was to organize the king's palace and all the entertainments within it, for that. But he'd bypassed the Howards when commissioning a play to touch on plots against a king's life; that he had done himself. It wouldn't be only the boy, of course, scanning the crowds for reactions. But only the boy could identify the particular face of his dreams.

Except that now, on the eve of the performance, the young idiot had gone missing. If it hadn't been for the Howards, he'd have concluded that the young rascal was in the kitchen pinching puddings, and gone right back to sleep. As it was, he listened wearily to the tramping feet of soldiers fanning through the palace.

An hour later, the captain skidded back into his presence. "We've found something, Your Lordship," he panted. But when asked what, he just shook his head. "I think, sir, you had better come and see for yourself."

And so they had marched through long winding ways back into the oldest part of the palace. The chamber where they stopped was marked as unassigned on the lord chamberlain's list, but the door was locked from the inside. Stranger still, several of the captain's men swore up and down that they had heard an ungodly cry from somewhere in this corridor — though all the other rooms were open and empty. Grown men, all of them, but Salisbury could sense the ooze of fear on their breaths.

"Break it open," he said shortly, aware of the Howards clenching in anticipation beside him.

It took axe-work; Hampton Court had been made to last. With a wrenching groan, the door at last split down the center and the soldiers stood aside, allowing the earls to pass.

Even from the threshold, it could be seen that the room was empty. There were no rushes on the floor, no hangings on the walls, and no furniture cluttering the space. A fire, however, had recently warmed the grate, though it had been allowed to die out. The air still bore faint traces of some stew or broth that had seethed there. In the midst of this emptiness, the only object to stop the eye was a body lying stretched out on the flagged floor in front of the hearth.

Draped over it was a heavy gown of peacock blue.

Dr. Dee darted forward, plucking a small slice of darkness from a fold in the velvet. With precise fingers, he held up a dark disc of polished stone: his missing mirror. The old conjuror rubbed it with his sleeve, peering into its depths as Suffolk leaned forward with unseemly eagerness. "What do you see?"

Dr. Dee looked up, the skin below his watery eyes sagging, and shook his head. "There is a dark veil drawn across it." A shudder passed through his entire body. "Whatever this mirror has seen, it is evil."

A boy is dead, thought Salisbury. *We need no magic to tell us that.* In a flicker of irritation, he twitched the gown aside.

Beside him, Suffolk and Northampton went preternaturally still. Their surprise was momentary, so quickly smoothed over that they would have fooled almost any other man, but Salisbury could often tell what a man was thinking before he was aware of the drifts of his own thoughts — to the point that some men muttered that it was Salisbury, not Dr. Dee, who bent strange spirits to his will. Now, beneath his rigid mask of revulsion, he felt a sly curiosity waken and stretch through every vein and

18

sinew. Whatever the Howards had been expecting, this was not it.

The body at their feet was naked and strangely bound. But it was not the boy.

■ ■ ■ ■

Blade

■ ■ ■ ■

Is this a dagger which I see before me,
The handle toward my hand?

1

It's the oldest temptation. Not gold or the power it can buy, not love, not even the deep, drumming fires of lust: What we coveted first was knowledge. Not just any knowledge, either, but forbidden, more-than-mortal knowledge, as seductive and treacherous as a will-o'-the-wisp glimmering like unearthly fruit amid dark branches.

At least, that's the tale that Genesis suggests. Not that I believe everything the Bible says. But it's a good story, and I love stories. Besides, whether or not knowledge is the oldest temptation, it's beyond doubt one of the most dangerous. Spellbinding in the full, old sense of the word. That much I can swear to. I've felt the pull of it myself and come closer than I like to admit to being lured into the abyss.

For me, it was a voice, low and musical,

that first enthralled me; at least, that's how I remember it. I can see her still, crossing to a tall window, throwing back curtains of pale blue silk embroidered with Chinese dragons, opening the casement to the chill Scottish night. The sharp scent of pines swept through the room, stirring the silk, so that the dragons seemed to writhe and coil around her.

Lady Nairn was nearing seventy, her face lined with the fine-china crackling of very fair skin in old age. Awash in moonlight, with her hands thrust deep into the pockets of her jacket, a gauzy scarf at her neck, and hair of the palest gold swept up in a graceful French twist, she seemed to be shining with a light of her own.

"It's one of the Sidlaws," she mused, staring out the window at the hill that dominated the landscape. A strangely shaped hill sitting apart from its fellows, capped with a turret-like top. *"Law,* from Old English *hlaew,* meaning hill, mountain, or mound, and also the hollow places inside them, like caves or barrows. And *sid,* from the Gaelic *sidhe"* — which she pronounced like "she." "The Good folk," she said without turning. "The fairies . . . It's a fairy hill."

She was tall, taller than me, and still imposing — not someone you expected to hear musing about fairies.

She shrugged slightly, as if brushing off my thoughts. "People have disappeared from it, from time to time. Caught up by the Good folk riding out on one of their hunts and swept off to feast in enchanted halls where time passes differently, and the golden air is laced with laughter and song. Most never return. Those who do come back touched. Fairy-stricken, as it's said around here. That's what the old legends say, at any rate." She glanced around. "Not the gossamer-winged flower mites the Victorians liked to draw, mind you. The Scottish fairies, I'm talking about. Sometimes confused with the weird sisters or with witches — but not hags, as Shakespeare makes them. In Scotland, the fairies are bright and beautiful and fey. Dangerous."

It struck me suddenly that standing there silvered with moonlight, she looked like one of them herself.

"We have one rule in this house. *Don't go up the hill alone.*"

I'd met her for the first time earlier that evening. It was Athenaide who engineered it, of course; who else?

Athenaide Dever Preston was a small, white-haired woman with an outsized personality more in keeping with the expanse of her ranch than with the diminutive scale of her person. The ranch encompassed a wide swathe of southwestern New Mexico; she lived there in an improbable palace modeled on Hamlet's Elsinore, concealed within a ghost town by the name of Shakespeare. Since the death of her cousin Rosalind Howard, once my mentor at Harvard, Athenaide had decided that I needed a family and that she was the best candidate for the job.

That morning, the phone had pulled me from a deep blanket of sleep in my flat in London.

"I have a friend who wants to meet you," she said.

"Athenaide?" I'd croaked, sitting up. I peered at the clock. "It's five A.M."

"I don't mean at this instant, *mija.* Tonight. Dinner. Are you busy?"

All week, I'd been looking forward to a rendezvous with Chopin at my piano, a velvety glass of cabernet, and maybe later some mindless TV. But I owed Athenaide more than I could ever count up. "No," I said reluctantly.

"Not even with the redoubtable Mr. Benjamin Pearl?"

I swallowed hard against a pang of irritation. Ben Pearl and I had met two years before, trying to outrun a killer while tracking down one of Shakespeare's lost plays — an experience that might as well have been a lightning bolt fusing us together. At first, we'd met whenever we could, with a fizz and sparkle that felt like champagne and fireworks. For a week or ten days, we'd be as inseparable as we were insatiable. But then one career or the other would come calling, pulling us down separate paths. In the end, the strain was too great. Six months earlier, we'd parted ways for good, but Athenaide stubbornly refused to absorb that fact.

"Ah, well," she clucked. "As some bright young thing once said, the course of true love never did run smooth. Now write this down: Boswell's Court, off Castle Hill."

I was halfway through scribbling out the address when I stopped. London had no Castle Hill that I knew of. "You mean Parliament Hill? Tower Hill?"

"No, I mean Castle Hill, *mija*. Edinburgh."

"Edinburgh?" My uncaffeinated voice cracked.

"How far is that from London — three hundred miles?" she sniffed. "Wouldn't get you from the ranch up to Santa Fe. A jaunt, not a journey."

27

"But —"

"Boswell's Court at eight-thirty," she said firmly. "There's a train from King's Cross at three-thirty. A ticket will be waiting for you. Gets in at quarter past eight, I'm told. Just enough time to get up the hill."

"Athenaide —"

"Bon appétit, Katharine. Lady Nairn is quite possibly the most glamorous person I know. You'll have fun." Laughter burbling through the phone, she hung up.

I stared at the phone in mute disbelief as its blue glow faded to darkness. So much for Chopin and *Project Runway*. I collapsed back in the bed with a groan that sputtered into laughter. Athenaide, whose parents had been costume designers for the likes of Bette Davis and Grace Kelly, and who had since made herself a billionaire, had spent her life running in glamorous circles. If this woman was at the pinnacle of Athenaide's league, she was way out of mine.

After a few minutes, I threw back the covers and padded toward the kitchen and coffee. I'd signed up for Athenaide's ride — or at least failed to throw myself off. I might as well enjoy it. Even without the redoubtable Mr. Benjamin Pearl.

By the time the train pulled into Edinburgh,

darkness had long since fallen. Across the wide boulevard of Princes Street, the New Town paraded away in neat, if rain-swept, Georgian elegance. On the other side of the station, the medieval town jostled stubbornly up a steep hill, crowding toward the castle perched atop its summit in brooding golden defiance against the night.

Minutes later, I was in the back of a taxi winding up the hill, the street a dark chasm between tall houses of gray stone slick with damp. Just before the buildings fell away into the open space in front of the castle, the taxi drew to a stop. "Boswell's Court," the driver said, pointing to an open doorway.

Overhead, a placard like an old-fashioned inn sign glistened in the rain, sporting two goats rampant and a leering devil's head above gilded letters that spelled out THE WITCHERY.

Beneath this, a low stone archway led through to a small courtyard. At the far end sat a little wooden house dominated by a great black door; just inside, a wide stair led down into an opulent fantasia on a Jacobean palace. Mute courtiers hunted stags across tapestries, heavy furniture swelled with dark carving, and, everywhere, candles flickered in iron stands that looked to have been riffled from either cathedrals or dungeons.

Making my way through the restaurant in the wake of the hostess, I wound toward a back corner. *Quite possibly the most glamorous person I know,* Athenaide had said, but through some trick of the shadows and flickering light, I did not see her until I was very close. And then I found myself face-to-face with a legend.

"L-Lady Nairn?" I'd stammered in confusion.

"You must be Kate Stanley," she'd said, rising. She extended her hand. "Yes, I'm Lady Nairn. Better known as Janet Douglas," she added with a disarming smile. "Once upon a very long time ago."

Janet Douglas had once had beauty to make Helen of Troy burn with envy. In the 1950s, she'd had a meteoric acting career, coming to the world's attention as Viola, the silver-tongued heroine of *Twelfth Night.* After that, she'd made five or six films in quick succession, all of them classics. But it was her live performance of Lady Macbeth, Shakespeare's fiend-like queen, in London's West End, that had seared her face into the consciousness of a generation. If Lady Macbeth had been her greatest role, it was also her last. In the audience at the premiere, a

Scottish lordling had fallen in love with her — nothing unusual in itself. What set his passion apart was that she returned it. A month later, she'd abruptly left stage and screen to marry him. From that day forward, her disappearance from the world's stage had been more mysterious and complete than any other since Greta Garbo's.

Yet here she was, shaking my hand with an amused look on her face. "I've been looking forward to this moment for a long time," she said, her voice just as I remembered it from films and interviews, husky for a woman, with a honeyed golden timbre. "I saw your *Cardenio*. And your *Hamlet*."

The plays I'd directed at London's Globe Theatre.

Disbelief jangled through my bones. *Janet Douglas had been in the audience at the Globe, and nobody noticed?* In London, tabloid capital of the universe?

But then, nobody seemed to be noticing her here, either. I glanced around. Not a single diner or waiter appeared to have registered her presence, needling our table with sidelong glances and surreptitious whispers.

And then I saw that I was wrong. From a booth across the room where he sat alone, one man gazed steadily in our direction. I'd

31

noticed him as I walked in; an impression of height and dark hair had made me think, for a fleeting instant, that he was Ben. I'd stopped and glanced back, but his face was thin, with a long, patrician nose and eyes so pale they might have been silver; he was nobody I knew. Now he sat staring in our direction, a half smile playing on his mouth, but there was no amusement in his eyes — only something feral and hungry that had nothing to do with food.

If Lady Nairn noticed, she gave no inkling of it. "Thank you for coming such a long way, on an old woman's whim."

I smiled, thinking of Athenaide's acid tongue: *A jaunt, not a journey.*

"I'd like you to meet my granddaughter. Lily MacPhee. Though perhaps I should say I want her to meet you." She spread her hands in mock dismay. "Fifteen going on twenty-five. She's at rehearsal at the moment, but I'm to walk up and collect her after dinner. . . . She's had a hard year of it, as have I. Her mother — my daughter, Elizabeth — and dad were killed in a car crash six months ago."

A jagged sorrow ripped through the universe. I laid my spoon down; it was shaking. "I lost my parents at about her age," I said carefully. What was wrong with me? That grief was fifteen years old, yet it had washed over me with the raw intensity of newness.

Lady Nairn nodded. "Athenaide told me. It's one reason I pushed for this meeting."

"And the other?"

She sighed. "It's been a gloomy year in the Nairn household. Our own annus horribilis, I suppose. I also lost my husband recently."

It dawned on me that she was wearing her black silk dress as if it were armor. "I'm sorry," I said.

Those famous turquoise eyes grew bright, but she did not look away. "It's not well known, but Angus — my husband — spent his life collecting all kinds of flotsam and jetsam to do with . . . well, with the Scottish Play."

Macbeth, she meant. In the theatrical world, there was a strong taboo against naming it. The Scottish Play, the Plaid Play, even MacDaddy and MacBeast, it was called — but somehow it surprised me that forty years after she'd walked away from the theater, the worldly woman sitting across from me would indulge in the old superstition.

"He was fascinated by both the historical king and Shakespeare's play," she went on. "Anything to do with the story. Including,

I'm afraid, me." She glanced down with a self-deprecatory smile. When she raised her eyes again, though, they were dark with worry. "I sometimes wonder whether the curse is clinging to me."

I frowned. In the theater, the spiraling evil of Shakespeare's witch-haunted tragedy is held to be so strong that it cannot be contained by the frail walls of the stage but spills over into reality. By long tradition, it may not be quoted within a theater beyond what is necessary for rehearsal and performance. Even the play's title and its lead characters' names are forbidden. Lady M, she is, while her husband is the Scottish King. Or just the King and the Queen, as if no other royalty, imagined or real, matters. There are elaborate rites to exorcise the ill luck of violating that taboo.

Anthropologically, I found it intriguing. Practically, I found it absurd and even irritating. "I'm sorry. I can't believe that."

"No." She sighed. "Nor do I, most of the time." She took a sip of wine. "We'd been planning to put his collection on exhibit. I'd like to go ahead with it, as a memorial of sorts. And I'd like your help."

I shifted uncomfortably. "Sounds like you'd be better off with a historian. Or a curator. Someone from the British Museum, maybe."

She shook her head. "Not that kind of exhibit." Her voice slid into the cadence of poetry. *"How dull it is to pause, to make an end, to rust unburnished, not to shine in use. . . .* I want Angus's collection burnished, you might say, in performance. In a production of *Macbeth*. And I want you to direct."

In the midst of a sip of wine, I spluttered and set down the glass.

"I haven't yet set a date," she was saying. "But it's to be a one-off, by invitation only, at Hampton Court. Sybilla Fraser has signed on as Lady M. And Jason Pierce has agreed to play the King."

I knew Sybilla by sight; everybody did. She was the UK's latest "it" girl, a rising star — or diva-in-training, said some — with deep golden skin and dark golden hair that cascaded around her in luxurious ringlets. Even her eyes were amber, as aloof and inscrutable as a lioness's. Jason, though, I knew personally. He cultivated the aura of an Australian bad-boy film star, but he was a more serious actor than he liked to admit, with a hankering for proving his dramatic chops onstage, through Shakespeare. I'd directed him as both Hamlet and Cardenio, and both times, he'd often seemed more

35

like my nemesis than my colleague.

I raised an eyebrow, and Lady Nairn sighed. "He's the inveterate philanderer, you know —"

"Epic," I interjected.

"But as I understand it, she's the one who's already got someone new on the line. With luck, they'll channel their tension into the fire and ice between Macbeth and his lady."

"And without luck?"

"Free fireworks, I suppose."

"So, Jason and Sybilla —"

"And myself," said Lady Nairn. I did a double take. "One last time," she went on, "I mean to take the stage. Not as the Queen, obviously. At least, not the Scottish Queen. Bit past the expiry date for that." She set her wineglass down with a small click. "I mean to play Hecate, queen of witches."

So withered, and so wild in their attire, Shakespeare had written of his hags, *that look not like the inhabitants of the earth, and yet are on it.*

"Hecate doesn't suit you," I said suddenly.

"A backhanded compliment if ever there was one," said Lady Nairn with a smile.

"Athenaide told me that you're the most glamorous person she knows."

"Did she, now?" She raised one brow. " 'Glamour' is an old Scots word for magic. In particular, the power to weave webs of illusion. *All was delusion, nought was truth,* as Sir Walter Scott put it."

This entire evening was beginning to feel like a delusion. Janet Douglas was returning to the stage in *Macbeth*? And she wanted *me* to direct?

"Why me?" I blurted out. "You could have anyone you ask."

"I'm asking you. Or do you know another director with expertise in occult Shakespeare?"

Hell and damnation, I thought. *So that's it.* What now seemed like a lifetime ago, I had written a dissertation on that subject, by which I meant the codes and clues that various people believed were hidden in the Bard's works. The twisting meanings of that small word, "occult," it seemed, would haunt me as long as I lived.

"Lady Nairn, don't get me wrong, I don't mean to disappoint, but by 'occult' I mean —"

She waved me off. "You mean the old sense of the word: hidden, obscured, secret. *Not* magical. Yes, I know. I've listened to your interviews. But it's not magic I want you for." She leaned forward. "I told you that my husband collected anything and everything to do with *Macbeth.* Well, a week or ten days before we lost him, he grew tense and excited in a way that meant one thing. He was closing in on a find."

Somewhere within, a small seed of misgiving sprouted warily into life. "What kind of find?"

She sat back, eyeing me in silence. Then she rose from her chair. For a moment, her hand rested lightly on my shoulder. "Come to Dunsinnan."

I didn't recognize the word.

"Better known as Dunsinane. Macbeth's castle of evil. Surely you remember that," she said with an elusive smile. "I live there." Turning abruptly, she headed for the stairs.

Knowledge, the oldest temptation. Caught in the tug of curiosity, I rose and followed her out.

2

Outside, the rain had stopped, but the air was still damp, thick with the sharp bracken scent of autumn, even up here in the old stone heart of the city. We turned left, up the hill toward the castle.

Lady Nairn had invited the entire prospective cast up to her house for a weekend of "atmospheric research," as she put it, with the intention of carting them back down to Edinburgh, two nights hence, for the Fire Festival of Samhuinn, the old Celtic holy night that Christianity had co-opted and turned into Halloween. Pronounced "Sowen," more or less, by English speakers, *Samhuinn* means "summer's end" in Scottish Gaelic, she explained. It was the turning of the year, when the door between the living and the dead was said to thin to a transparent veil. The Edinburgh festival was a winter carnival, a street pageant in which masked players mimed a modern version of the ancient pagan myth of the Summer King meeting the Winter King in battle.

Her granddaughter, Lily, had a part in it. "As a torchbearer," she said. "More or less the Shakespearean equivalent of a spear carrier. Necessary, but nearly invisible. Someday, though, I expect she'd like to be the kayak."

That's what I thought I heard, at any rate.

Lady Nairn laughed at my confusion. "Cailleach," she explained. "Not 'kayak.' Another Gaelic word. Sounds to English ears like an Eskimo canoe, but it means 'old woman.' The old woman of winter, who comes into her power as summer wanes and dies." She wrapped her coat closer around herself. "The queen of darkness and death," she went on quietly, "but also of renewal. Most people forget about that part. But there is no life without death, and no spring without the great die-off of winter. . . ."

For a moment we walked in silence, our footsteps ringing against the pavement. "The old myths personify that conundrum," she said. "And the festival dramatizes the myths. The Cailleach chooses the Winter King as her champion and eggs him on into battle against the old King of Summer. All in mime. So archetypal, really, that words are superfluous."

40

The image of a terrible queen urging a warrior in his prime to kill an old king and take his place skimmed through my head. "But that's the story of *Macbeth*," I said slowly.

"It's the myth behind it," she specified.

"But *Macbeth* is based on history," I protested. "Scottish history."

She sniffed. "History rearranged — cut and pasted — to fit myth. Scholars have forgotten that part, if they ever knew it. But myth is not so easily cornered and tamed into neat academic fact."

In all the years I'd spent in the ivory tower, working toward being a professor of Shakespeare before falling in love with the Bard onstage and running off to the theater, I'd never heard any version of Lady Nairn's theory. But it fit. It fit with the simplicity of truth. "You think Shakespeare knew?" I asked quietly.

She looked straight ahead, a mischievous smile upending the corners of her mouth. "I think he knew a great deal more than we credit him with."

The buildings fell away as we came to the dark emptiness of the Esplanade. At the far end, the castle reared into the night. In the center of the parade ground, a crowd roiled and milled. Under a loose netting of laughter, torches flickered here and there, and somewhere in the middle, someone in a stag mask was tossing his head so that antlers reared into the night. Now and again, unearthly howls rose in waves of loneliness toward the moon.

The crowd shifted and for an instant I saw the dark-haired man from the restaurant. His eyes met mine, and then the crowd shifted again, and he disappeared. A girl detached herself from the outer fringes, loping over to us with adolescent gangliness.

Lily MacPhee had her grandmother's wide-set eyes and high cheekbones, though her coloring was entirely different. Flame-red hair spilled in waves past her shoulders. Her milk-white skin was scattered with freckles like stars, and her eyes were a pale sea-green. A small jewel winked in her nose. The Pre-Raphaelites, I thought, would have fought bitter duels among themselves for the right to paint her as Guinevere or the Lady of the Lake.

"You said yes!" she said with girlish pleasure.

"She said maybe," said her grandmother. "More or less."

Dunsinnan Hill, Lady Nairn told me as we

drove, lay fifty miles ahead, just north of the Tay. It had been fortified since the Iron Age, but a thousand years ago, the old histories said, the historical King Macbeth had rebuilt it.

For a generation, he'd ruled Scotland from its heights, until his young cousin Malcolm had come north in the year 1054, at the head of an army of the hated Sassenach — Anglo-Saxons from northern England — along with a fair few Vikings. Charging up the hill, Malcolm's Saxons had clashed with Macbeth's Scots in a pitched battle that raged from sunup to sunset, leaving the slopes scattered with crow's bait. It was not the end — though Macbeth lost both the battle and the hill, he lived to lead his battered men in retreat — but it was the beginning of the end. Two years later, Malcolm finally caught up with him, and this time the knife went home. Malcolm had mounted Macbeth's head on a pole and claimed the kingship of Scotland for himself.

Macbeth had been a good king, famed for both generosity and bravery — by some reckonings, the last truly Celtic king of Scotland, ruling in the old ways. But among the most lasting spoils of victory is the right to write history, and Macbeth's legacy had quickly darkened. It was Shakespeare, though, who'd made him a byword for evil.

It was a tragic arc, I thought as Lady Nairn's voice faded away: to fall, after death, from hero-king to reviled tyrant. At least Shakespeare's fictionalized Macbeth made the plunge during his life, of his own accord.

"There," said Lady Nairn presently. She pointed to a rounded hilltop with a small turreted summit, set a little apart from the others. We'd left the main roads and were hurtling south on a narrow lane across fields and through hedgerows. The road led straight for the hill, veering at the last minute around the western slope, plunging into a pine wood and past a quarry, and then left along the south side of the hill. Soon after that, we turned off the lane, away from the hill, and into a gravel drive.

Dunsinnan House stood in a high saddle, looking north across the road to the hill for which it was named and south to the glimmering waters of the firth of Tay. At its heart, the tall rectangle of an old Scottish castle could still be seen, though in ensuing centuries it had sprouted several new wings, not to mention towers and cupolas, balconies and bay windows, seemingly at random, giving it the air of an aged grande dame proudly squeezed into a gown from her youth, now haphazardly adorned with gew-gaws and baubles collected from every period of her life.

Lady Nairn led me swiftly up four flights of stairs to a bedroom in a high corner. Its walls were covered in watered blue silk; along the northern wall marched three tall windows curtained in more blue silk embroidered with Chinese dragons. "I thought you might like a view," she'd said, crossing the room to throw open the middle window, so that both the sound and the scent of pines blew through the room. Beyond, the hill was visible mostly as an absence of stars.

Don't go up the hill alone. The sentence hung on the air between us.

"I told you I lost my husband," she said. "I meant it more literally than you perhaps realized." She looked back toward the hill. "He disappeared up there one night three months ago. We went to the police, of course. They poked around a bit but didn't find anything. Suggested, in a roundabout way, that maybe he'd gone off for a bit of something on the side. He was not that sort of man.

"Auld Callie — a woman from the village,

someone he'd known from childhood — found him the following week, sitting on the hilltop, dangling his legs like a child over the ramparts. He was rocking back and forth, muttering one phrase over and over: 'Dunsinnan must go to Birnam Wood.' "

"Macbeth's riddle," I said quietly.

"No," she said with a slight shake of the head. "The witches' riddle." She launched into the Shakespeare:

Macbeth shall never vanquished be, until
Great Birnam Wood to high Dunsinnan
    Hill
Shall come against him.

In the play, King Macbeth assumes the riddle is a metaphor for *never,* only to learn, when confronted by a forest on the move, that the witches meant it literally. *"The equivocation of the fiend that lies like truth,"* I murmured.

She gave me a sad smile. "I'm not sure it counts as equivocation if there's no clear answer at all, rather than too many. And in any case, Angus reversed it: *Dunsinnan must go to Birnam Wood.* His title, you know, was Nairn of Dunsinnan, so I thought he was referring to himself. And you can see the wood, or what's left of it, from the hilltop, so it seemed to me that he was saying that *he* must go to Birnam. I took him there. . . . He'd known the place since childhood, but he didn't recognize it. Stood there turning round and round beneath the great oak, looking bewildered."

Her voice dipped into bitterness. "He died a fortnight after that. A month ago, that was. Blessing, really. His mind was gone, or mostly so. Just enough left to understand that he wasn't right. Made him desperate, near the end."

Her voice had begun to waver, and she paused to steady it, turning to the window and brushing damp cheeks with the back of one hand. "I'm sorry," she said, giving herself a little shake and going on. "The doctors said he had a stroke. No doubt they're right. But that isn't the whole story. When we found him, he'd been missing for a week, but he was clean-shaven, and his clothes were immaculate." Her chin went up. *"As if he'd just left."*

She pinned me with her gaze. "Do you know Aleister Crowley's definition of magic? It's 'the science and art of causing change to occur in conformity with will.' "

I frowned. It was a famous — and famously baggy — definition. By its lights, just about everything was magic. Crowley himself had included potato-growing and banking in the list, along with ritual magic and spells. Where was this going?

She leaned forward. "There were those who wished Angus ill," she said with quiet intensity. "Mostly, I'm afraid, for my sake."

"Wishing doesn't make it so."

"Perhaps not."

Beyond her, through the window, I saw something — a weasel or a stoat, maybe — undulating across the corner of the lawn, a furtive shadow in darkness. Almost in rhythm with it, a prickle of foreboding crept across my skin. What was she suggesting? That someone had murdered Sir Angus by magic?

"Lady Nairn, if you suspect foul play in Sir Angus's death, you should go to the police."

"I think it must be dealt with by other means." She cocked her head. "How much do you know about the writing of *Macbeth*? Not the story. The writing of it."

I frowned. "There's not much to know. It's Shakespeare's shortest tragedy. Published posthumously, in the First Folio."

"The first collected edition of his works," she said, nodding. "Dated 1623, seven years after Shakespeare's death. But that's about its printing. Not its writing."

"We don't know anything about the writing of any of his plays."

"There was an earlier version." She said it defiantly, a gauntlet thrown down.

"Many scholars think so," I said carefully. That much was true, mostly because of the witches. Eerie and terrifying at one moment, they are, and broad comedy at the next — not to mention Hecate, queen of witches, who seems to have been pulled wholesale from another, later play by Thomas Middleton and slapped down haphazardly into Shakespeare's play, for all that her brand of gleefully cackling evil would be more at home in a Disney film. "But there's no real evidence one way or an—"

She cut me off. "As a child, my husband's grandfather met an old woman on the hill. She told him that long ago, Shakespeare had come here with a company of English players and met a dark fairy — a witch — who lived in a boiling lake. She taught him all her dark arts; in return, he stole her soul and fled.

"She searched high and low, but he had hidden it well. It was not in a stone or an egg, a ring or a crown: not in any of the places one normally hides such a thing. She found it at last, though, written into a play, mixed into the very ink scrawled across the pages of a book. Snatching up the book, she cursed his words to scatter misery rather than joy, and then she vanished back to her lake.

"Some time earlier, the boy's grandfather had vanished on the hill, so when the old woman told him her tale and made him repeat it back to her, he decided she was the dark fairy of her own story, and the book, if he could find it, was her payment for his grandfather. . . . In later years, he — Angus's grandfather — came to believe she had been talking about *Macbeth*."

I gazed at her in silence. How could I put what I had to say tactfully? "Lady Nairn — with all due respect to your husband's grandfather, as wonderful as his story is, it's a child's half-remembered tale, a hundred years old. It hardly counts as evidence for an earlier version of the play."

"Not by itself. But it fits with this." She went to the desk and opened an archival folder, handing me a Xeroxed page. "From the old Dunsinnan House account book," she said. "Half ledger, half diary."

Under an entry dated 1 November 1589, someone had written, "The English players departit hence." But it mentioned no names.

"Read the next sentence," said Lady Nairn.

The same day, the Lady Arran reportit a mirror and a book stolen, and charged that the players had taken them. But they could not be found.

I looked up quickly. I knew of Lady Arran. Elizabeth Stewart, Lady Arran, her contemporaries had sneered, was a greedy, avaricious, and ambitious woman. A Lady Jezebel who consorted with witches. For a time, young King James had been besotted with her and her husband both; there had been whispers in some corners that she was the reason the king would not take a wife. Other whispers charged that she'd kill him if she could, that she desired, above all else, to be queen. She was, said some, the historical figure standing in the shadows behind the character of Lady Macbeth.

Lady Nairn smiled. "I thought you might recognize that name. So you see, we do have evidence."

"Of what?" It was all I could do to stay calm. "That Lady Arran was here, yes. That Shakespeare was, no. He knew *of* her, almost surely — almost twenty years later. But we don't know that he ever knew her in person. We don't know anything at all about him in 1589, actually, beyond the fact that he was alive. That's right in the middle of what's called his lost years. No record of his whereabouts whatsoever."

"Unless he was here. You might at least be gracious enough to admit it's suggestive," she said reproachfully. "As it happens, it also dovetails with my family legends." She looked out at the night. "I am descended, in a direct mother-to-daughter line, from Elizabeth Stewart. From Lady Macbeth."

I must have been gaping in disbelief, because she shot me a wry smile. "My husband found my heritage quite alluring. Lily, on the other hand, doesn't know, and I'd like to keep it that way. It's not information that's necessarily . . . *useful* to a fifteen-year-old."

"You have family legends about her?" I asked, feeling a little faint.

"Elizabeth Stewart didn't consort with witches. She *was* one. Not a devil-worshipping crone but a serious student of magic. As my mother and grandmother would have it, the Bard once saw her at work and later put his recollections — quite accurately — in a play. It was not easy to dissuade him from performing it, but it was done. And the manuscript made to disappear."

I groped my way to a chair, my mind reeling.

"You can make of the witchcraft whatever you like, Kate. It's not the magic I'm trying to interest you in," she said patiently. "It's the manuscript." She drew the archival folder off the desk, holding it out to me. "Three days ago, shuffled among Angus's papers, I found this."

I opened the folder. Inside were a postcard and a single sheet of heavy ivory notepaper. The postcard was a copy of one of my favorite paintings in Britain, John Singer Sargent's portrait of Ellen Terry as Lady Macbeth. Terry had been one of the three or four all-time great Lady Macbeths. The last before Janet Douglas. Sargent had somehow made her gown shimmer between blue and green. With her long red braids, a gleam of gold low on her waist, and the blue-green gown accentuating the curve of her hips and then narrowing as it cascaded toward the floor, I'd always thought she looked more like a mermaid than a queen.

Behind the card, the notepaper was covered with writing in a large looping hand of confidence and passion, and something stubbornly childlike, too. I glanced at the signature. *Nell,* it read, with a long tail like a comet.

The pet name used among family and friends for Ellen Terry. I glanced up.

"As much as can be discerned from a fax, both signature and letter are genuine," said Lady Nairn. She turned to look out the window. "Read it. Take your time."

It was dated 1911. "My dear Monsieur Superbe Homme," it began. *My dear Superb Man. My dear Superman.*

My dear Monsieur Superbe Homme,

I am forwarding to you a curious letter I have recently received from a fellow denizen of the drama whose personal tale is as tragic as any role she might encharacter on the stage. Indeed, I am not at all certain that her long woes have not in the end loosened her hold upon sanity. As you will see, she believes, poor soul, not only that Mr. Shakespeare first circulated a version of Macbeth substantially different from the one that has come down to us, but that this earlier version has survived (!) — and that she is the guardian of its whereabouts.

"Surely you don't bel—"

"I think my husband believed that his grandfather's mysterious old lady and

54

Ellen's 'poor soul' were one and the same."

Our eyes locked in silence. "Go on," she said presently. I looked back down.

> I would conclude out of hand that she is lunatic, were it not for the enclosure which she gave to me along with her tale, and which I now send on to you. I think the book queer enough, but it is the letter inside that you will find most curious. Unfortunately, all it conveys about the nature of this supposed earlier version is that its differences lie chiefly with the witches, especially Hecate, who is said to be "both there and not there."

I glanced up. "Thus Hecate?"

"I'm an actress," she said with a small shrug. "I learn characters by playing them. *Finish it.*"

There wasn't much more:

> A riddling sentiment of an appropriately Shakespearean fashion, I suppose, but exasperating all the same. I cannot make head or tail of it.
>
> As it is, I am hoping that you can glimpse the Forest through the Trees.
>
> Nell

I lifted the letter, but there was nothing

else in the folder. "The enclosure?"

"Missing." She sighed. "And no indication where, when, or how he acquired the letter, either. So you see, I don't know what Angus found." She cocked her head. "But I know what he was looking for."

For a moment, I sat in stunned silence. Someone — a real woman, not a witch or a fairy — had believed not only that an earlier version of *Macbeth* had existed, but that it had survived to the dawn of the twentieth century. And while Ellen Terry had been skeptical, she had not been able to dismiss the woman's tale out of hand, either. On top of that, it was the witches — and their magic — that were said to be different: the very aspects of the surviving play that bothered scholars most.

A tremor of excitement, or maybe it was dread, went through me. What if it were true? The *Cardenio* manuscript I'd helped to find had had cachet as a lost play . . . but this . . . we were talking about one of the great plays. One of the most profound explorations of evil in all human history. A play most people could quote, even people who'd never seen it — or any Shakespeare at all, for that matter. *Double, double toil and trouble, fire burn and cauldron bubble . . .*

Lady Nairn cut into my reverie. "What do

you suppose it would be worth?" she asked.

Cardenio had gone at auction for many millions; a lost version of *Macbeth* would very possibly fetch more. A *Macbeth* that linked Shakespeare to magic actually practiced, not just cackled on a stage . . . I shook my head, running my tongue around dry lips. "I have no idea."

"Surely it would reach to a sum worth frightening an old man to death for, at least in some quarters."

I looked up sharply. *"You think . . . ?"*

"I don't know what to think. But I would like to know what happened to my husband. And if he did find what Ellen Terry was talking about — *I want it.*" She drew about herself all the hauteur of a queen. *"I want you to find it. And then I want you to stage it."*

She straightened, erect as a queen heading for execution. "I loved Angus, Kate. I left the stage for him, the adulation of the world. . . . And he was enough. He was worth it. You, of all people, might understand the measure of that. I am not asking you to find his killer. I am asking you to find the manuscript. Will you help me?"

Something about her strange mix of pride and fragility tugged at the heart. And however disturbing her charge of murder might be, the manuscript had just enough plausibility to pluck at my curiosity.

"Dunsinnan must go to Birnam Wood," I said quietly. "You took him there?"

She nodded.

"I had no idea it was a real place — at least, not one that still existed. . . . I suppose we should start there."

She let out a long, slow breath, bowing her head with relief. "Thank you." Straightening, she rose to leave. "I'll take you there first thing in the morning." At the door, she turned back, her eyes gleaming, though whether with tears or with triumph it was hard to say. "Meanwhile, don't go up the hill alone."

My head still spinning, I changed into a pair of striped silk pajamas laid out for me and climbed into bed. On the bedside table was a copy of *Macbeth*.

I sat for a moment with my arms wrapped around my knees. My agreement to help Lady Nairn was already beginning to look like folly. Her charge of murder, for one, was a dark return to superstition, the sort of stuff that had spawned witch hunts. Even the more rational parts of her story were dubious. For all I knew, Terry's letter was a forgery. Nobody could authenticate something like that by looking at a fax; I doubted that reputable experts would even consent to try.

How had the grandfather's story gone? That a dark fairy had told him that Shakespeare had learned magic here, from a witch who lived in a boiling lake?

I want you to find it. And then I want you to stage it. Out of her presence, Lady Nairn's demand seemed little less lunatic than the old fairy's geography. A task set by an angry and sorrowing goddess: find what her husband had found. Or hadn't. More likely, she'd set me to catch a dead man's dream.

And she wasn't a goddess. She was Lady Macbeth, in a deeper way than anyone imagined. What would it be like to have that past running through your veins?

I sighed and opened the play. It took a scene or two for the rush of adrenaline to clear from my head. A scene or two after that, I was nodding. Before I reached the end of the first act, I was asleep.

Aware that I was walking through a dream, I picked my way up a steep hill that leveled off into a wide field. In the distance rose a castle. High on its battlements, a woman with red hair stood staring into the night, ignoring a jeering crowd below, her gown whipping about in the wind as if she were riding out a storm on the prow of some immense ship. Around her, I sensed malice closing in so thickly that it became hard to breathe.

I woke in darkness, gasping for air, and for a moment I had no idea where I was. Then I remembered Lady Nairn's voice: *Dunsinnan . . . Dunsinane, Macbeth's castle of evil.*

I rose and filled a glass of water from the bathroom tap. On the way back to bed, I passed the dressing table, its mirror reflecting the three tall windows, the middle curtain still drawn open to the sky. I stood there a moment, watching the reflection. I could still see a faint glow from the moon in the west, though the moon itself had set. As I watched, though, a yellow star winked into being. I whirled to the window. *Not a star.* Across the road, high up, flames kindled and caught, blossoming into what must have been a great bonfire atop the hill.

I stood there rapt, staring at it for I don't know how long. All around that point of light, the night was dark and still. Then I glimpsed movement closer in. Peering down, I saw a shadow striding across the grass. A woman in a short coat and trousers, a pale scarf fluttering at her neck. Twisted into a neat knot, her hair was paler still.

Lady Nairn crossed the lawn and disappeared into the shadows of the drive. Going where at this time of night — alone?

Maybe half an hour later, I saw movement again, but this time it was high and farther away. Perhaps it was the wind and some odd trick of the damp Scottish air. Perhaps I was dreaming. But I could have sworn that silhouetted against the fire I saw the shadowy form of someone dancing with arms outstretched to the moonless night.

3

I watched as long as I could, but sleep eventually dragged at me and I stumbled back to the bed. I curled up facing the window, propping myself up with pillows, watching the hill until I could stay awake no longer.

When I woke again, much later, the fire on the hill had gone out. Suddenly, both mirror and window seemed ominous staring eyes. Rising, I drew the curtains and cast my robe over the mirror. Then I lay back down and slept till morning.

I woke late but did not feel rested and dressed in a hurry, eager to be off to Birnam Wood. Downstairs, I had the dining room all to myself. Breakfast — though by rights it was closer to lunch — was served by the cook. I poked at oatmeal and an egg and tried to finish reading the play, but both my mind and my stomach were jumping around like excited rabbits. On the subject of the whereabouts of either the lady of the house or her granddaughter, however, the cook was polite but noncommittal, and I saw no one else about.

I had no choice but to wait; I might as well make use of the time. Leaving my breakfast half-eaten, I took an apple and let myself out into the garden. The morning was unseasonably warm; surely there would be a bench someplace where I could tackle *Macbeth,* which I hadn't read all the way through in a long time.

On either side of the drive that swooped up from the road to the house lay thick lawns bordered by tall conifer woods. On the left a Renaissance knot garden had been laid out, its gravel paths and low hedges marking out beds shaped as lozenges and triangles and filled with lavender, rosemary, thyme, and many more herbs I couldn't name. I wandered for a while, not seeing a soul, and eventually I found a bench at the bottom of the slope. Once again, I sat down to read the play from the beginning.

When shall we three meet again,
In thunder, lightning, or in rain?

On the other side of the road, Dunsinnan Hill loomed over the words. It was thrilling

63

to read the play in its shadow, but surely it would be even more stirring to read it at the summit where Macbeth had battled all those years ago.

Suddenly, I remembered Lady Nairn saying, *You can see Birnam Wood, or what's left of it, from the top.* As if the hill itself had pulled me up, I rose and took two steps toward it, and then stopped. *Don't go up the hill alone,* she'd also said. *People disappear from it, from time to time.* Her husband among them. I shuddered, thinking of the fire I'd seen in the night. But that had been well past midnight, I told myself firmly. Probably a dream from beginning to end, for that matter. Surely on a bright warm day, more like August than October, there couldn't be any harm in a short hike — if one could even call it a hike. More like a walk.

Across the road, the slopes were sheer exposed rock. There was no climbing the hill from this direction. But as we'd driven in, I'd seen a stile over the fence and a path winding up the northern slope. It had been a short drive from there to the house. It wouldn't be a bad walk. I hesitated, glancing back. The windows of the house stared back blindly.

I'd like your help, Lady Nairn had said.

Well, she would have it. Shoving the play in my coat pocket, I stepped purposefully down the drive and out into the lane.

It took twenty minutes to reach the stile. Beyond it, the path led up along the edge of a steep grassy field and past a thick plantation of pine. The grass gave way to heather clumped with gorse, and then even the gorse disappeared, leaving russet brown waves of heather unbroken by anything but wind. Topping a rise, I heard the grind and clatter of the quarry splattering through the morning. At my feet, the heather ended abruptly at the edge of a large meadow. To the west, it was edged with a fence labeled DANGER; all that was visible through the fence was sky. To the south, though, the meadow lapped against the sheer grassy slopes of the hill's strange cylindrical summit, rising into the sky like an emerald ziggurat. All that was left of the ancient fortress at its top were the worn tracks of its earthen ramparts, visible in outline as terraces circling the hilltop like a road spiraling into the heavens.

I caught my breath. Macbeth, the real Macbeth, had stood atop that summit.

Ten minutes later, I scrambled over a slight lip and found myself at the edge of a shallow grassy bowl on top of the world. A sweet wind swept endlessly up over the edge, and for a moment I stood looking about me, breathing it in.

I stepped down into the bowl. It was instantly quieter and warmer, almost as if I'd stepped into a different place and time. I walked toward the cairn, meaning to use it as a backrest, but a few steps on, I stopped. Just beyond, hidden from first sight by a small hummock, was a ring of fire-blackened stones. As if pulled against my will, I drew near it and bent down. The ash in the middle was still warm.

I jumped back, my heart thudding in my chest. So there *had* been a fire up here last night. And from the grass beaten down in a circle just outside the fire ring, a dancer, too. For a moment, I stood poised to run.

But the day was bright and beautiful, and I was clearly alone. Besides, I told myself, there's nothing inherently ominous about a bonfire atop a hill on a clear autumn night. No need to bolt like an addled antelope, at any rate. I'd come this far — I might as well look at what I'd come to see.

I turned and looked northward. Far across the valley, the Highlands rose in waves of deepening purple. Somewhere out there, fringing the feet of the mountains, lay Birnam Wood. *Dunsinnan must go to Birnam*

Wood, Sir Angus had said. What the hell was that supposed to mean?

The reverse had not been good news for King Macbeth, at least in Shakespeare's telling.

For a while I stood roiling with frustration, staring across the valley. At last, though, I made myself sit down in the grass with my back to the cairn and pull out both my apple and the book. If Sir Angus's words were any indication, the play itself worked in some manner as a clue. I couldn't reach Birnam Wood without wings, but there was no better place to read *Macbeth* than here.

When shall we three meet again,
In thunder, lightning, or in rain?
When the hurly-burly's done,
When the battle's lost and won.
That will be ere the set of sun.
Where's the place?
Upon the heath.
There to meet with Macbeth . . .
Fair is foul and foul is fair,
Hover through the fog and filthy air.

Even read silently, the words had the eerie rhythmic quality of a spell. In the distance, I could still hear snatches of the tractor's droning, its sound winding around the clank of the quarry closer to hand and the trill of birds swooping overhead. Somehow they all seemed to twine together in a rhythmic accompaniment to the Shakespeare.

The birdcalls grew harsh and more insistent. Lower down the hill, I heard the whinny of a horse and then a sound I knew only from the stage: the clash of swords.

I woke with a start. How long I'd dozed before tipping over into dreams, I had no idea, but it must have been some time, because the warm afternoon had dissolved, leaving behind a world swathed in a cold gray blanket of mist. Low in the southwest, the sun had become a silk-wrapped pearl. By its position, the time looked to be late afternoon. If that was right, I'd slept a long time. I was gathering up my book and my half-eaten apple when I heard the whisper drifting on the wind, so that I couldn't even tell from which direction it came: *"Thou shalt be queen hereafter."*

I froze. But all I heard was the wordless sweep of the wind up over the summit. *I still have one foot in my dreams,* I thought. Gingerly, I stepped toward the path leading down through the old ramparts of the fortress. And stopped. At my feet was a gleam of metal.

I bent down for a closer look. A long

single-edged blade of blue-gray steel lay half-hidden in the grass. The hilt, lying toward me, was black with glints of silver. I was reaching out to grasp it when I saw the foot.

At the edge of one of the old trenches, someone lay stretched out in the grass, covered by a heavy blue-green gown shimmering like peacock feathers, except that it wasn't feathered. It was scaled. I stepped closer. It looked like Ellen Terry's gown, the one she'd been painted in as Lady Macbeth. It seemed to ripple in the grass like a long serpent, draped lengthwise, as it was, over — over whoever it was. By the narrow delicacy of the foot, a woman, and young.

Instinctively, my fingers wrapped around the hilt. Sliding the knife from the grass, I stepped closer. She didn't move.

I lifted a corner of the gown and saw a fall of flame-red hair. Aware of a dull thudding that must be my heart, I lifted the gown farther. What lay beneath I glimpsed only for an instant, but it is branded in my memory: her hands bound behind her back, a length of cloth passed lengthwise around her torso, passing through her groin and knotted around her neck, smeared thickly with blood.

It was Lily, and she was dead.

Floating on the wind came another whisper. *She must die.* And then, drifting closer, a third: *Nothing is but what is not.* Whoever they were, they were closing in.

The blue gown slipped from my grasp. Tightening my grip on the knife, I backed slowly for a few paces, and then I turned and ran.

4

Still gripping the knife, I stumbled through the mist, slipping and sliding down the ramparts and on down through the heather. A gorse bush loomed out of the swirling grayness. As I swerved to avoid it, someone grabbed me from behind. I swung around with the knife, but it was knocked from my grasp, thudding off into the heather. A broad hand clapped over my mouth, and I was forced to the ground and dragged from the path.

"You've kent what you shouldna," whispered a voice in my ear. Broad Scots for *You have known what you should not.* Twisting around to look at my captor, I saw a wild-eyed, gray-haired woman, broadly built, at least twenty years my senior.

I lunged away, but she jerked my arms back so expertly that the pain nearly knocked the wind from me.

"Lie still," she said, "if you don't want to

get the both of us killed."

A few seconds later, I heard what she must have sensed earlier: hoofbeats coming fast down the hill. I twisted around to face the path, just in time to see a white horse emerge from the mist not five feet away. Spooked by the gorse, the animal whinnied and reared. The rider threw his weight forward, fighting for control, his focus so intent on the horse that I don't think he ever saw us. But the horse did.

Its hooves crashed down no more than a foot from my head. Backing a few paces, it bolted. But not before I'd seen the rider's face. He was the dark-haired man.

For what seemed like eons, my captor and I lay in silence beneath the bush. At last, she raised her head. I sat up, but she shook her head. "Hush," she said, her head cocked, listening.

Footsteps were coming back toward us, up the hill. Footsteps, not hoofbeats. This time, she did not have to pull me down; I crouched next to her, as small as I could make myself.

Bent low to the ground, the man ran right past us. Then he stopped and looked back, reaching down to pick something up.

My book. Hot panic flooded through me. Stealthily, he crept toward us and then stopped. *Go,* I prayed with every sinew of my body. *Go, and don't look back.*

He turned and took one step away, and then another, and then without warning his hand darted out, grabbing me by one wrist.

Behind me, the gray-haired fury cried out. Shoving me forward so that I stumbled right into his arms, she darted across the heather, flapping like a broken-winged bird as she disappeared into the mist.

I jerked away from the hands grasping me, but he held tight. "Hello, Professor," said a voice I knew, and I realized that his hair, though dark, was curly, and his eyes were green. It was Ben Pearl, and he was laughing.

"You!" was all I could manage to croak.

Something in my voice cut through his hilarity. "Are you all right?"

My breath came out in a sob. "Lily," I gasped, pulling free at last.

"Your friend?" He nodded in the direction the old woman had run.

"*No.* Lady Nairn's fifteen-year-old granddaughter. On the hilltop," I said. "Dead." I bent down, scrabbling through the heather for the knife.

"Whoa," said Ben, crouching down with me. "Slow down."

I sat back on my heels, brushing away a

hot squeeze of tears. "Up on top of the hill. I found a knife. And then Lily, lying there dead, with her throat cut. And a voice, or maybe two voices. Whispers. I don't know. So I ran. The woman you saw, the gray-haired woman — I don't know who she is — knocked the knife away and dragged me off the path, and then the dark-haired man nearly rode me down on a spooked horse. . . ." I waved wildly in the direction of the hilltop. "And now I can't find the knife." The last sentence was nearly a wail.

Dropping to his hands and knees, Ben began combing the heather for it.

"Did you hear me? She's fifteen. She's *dead.*"

"I heard you." Two minutes later he plucked the knife from a clump of heather. It gleamed darkly, a pattern of whorls in the steel catching the strange gray light, so that the blade seemed to ripple and undulate almost as if it were alive. "Jesus, Kate," he said, staring down at it with a low whistle. "Where did you say you found the girl?"

"On the hilltop."

He was suddenly terse. "Show me."

"We need to call the police."

He was gazing upward through the mist. Slowly, he shook his head. "Are you sure she's dead?"

"I saw her."

"Did you check her pulse?"

"She's dead."

"You said her throat was cut. But there's no blood on this knife."

"So maybe the killer used another. . . ." My voice trailed off. There hadn't been enough blood around the body, either.

I began running back up the hill. Ben followed.

It didn't take long to reach the summit. For a moment we crouched just below the rim, listening, but all we heard was wind in the grass. Silently, Ben eased out the sharp-edged black pistol I had never seen him without and cautiously peered up over the edge. After a moment, he jumped up and strode over. I followed.

The cairn was there, and beside it the fire ring. But where the body had lain, nothing was visible but grass.

Other than Ben and me, there was no one, living or dead, atop the hill.

5

"But she was here," I said. "I found her. Over there. By one of the pits. It was only a few minutes ago." I pointed toward where I had seen her.

His gun drawn and ready, we slowly circled the hill just below the rim, Ben bending to look at the grass as we went. When we'd come full circle, he peered over the edge once again. "Stay here."

Bent low to the ground, he slid silently across the grass, glancing into each of the pits in turn. At the last one, he straightened, motioning me over. They, too, were empty of everything but grass and wind.

"She was here," I insisted.

Ben crouched down to the ground, scanning the grass with a tracker's fine eye. "I see no sign of it," he said after a while, sitting back on his heels. "A few footsteps — but nothing like the weight of a body."

"She was here," I said again. "It was Lily.

She was dead." I glared at him for a moment in silence, and then, feeling the hot swell of tears, I turned on my heel, speeding back down the hill.

"Where are you going?" he asked as he caught up with me.

"Back to the house," I said shortly. Lily would be there, or she would not. "And you?"

"I was looking for you. Now that I've found you, I don't exactly know."

I stopped. "You knew I was up here?"

"Lady Nairn told me that she'd told you not to come up the hill. So it was the first place I looked."

"Not funny."

"But accurate."

Trained in some branch of the British special forces that he'd never identified to me in all our time together, he'd left it to found a high-tech security company. "As in guns," he'd told me when we first met. "Not stocks and bonds." That Lady Nairn would need someone like Ben made sense. The moment the merest hint of her show got out, she'd be hounded by paparazzi. No doubt she'd worried about Sir Angus's collection as well, at least the part that she meant to move down to Hampton Court and back.

But it was Lily who had needed protection, I thought. And had not had it. Ben hadn't even known who she was.

By the time we got down to the lay-by, dusk was quickly fading to dark. Ben drove me back to the house in silence.

I leapt out of the car as soon as it came to a stop and raced inside, taking the stairs two at a time, up one flight and then down a wide passageway toward the sound of the party. *I'd completely forgotten about Lady Nairn's dinner.*

The company had already gathered in the old great hall, now laid out as a comfortable drawing room, filled with sofas and chairs, a fire of some sweet-smelling wood crackling in the immense fireplace. I scanned the room for Lady Nairn; she was holding court among three men in front of a long bank of windows. *"Where's Lily?"* My voice felt ragged in my throat.

Around the room, conversation faltered and the clink of glassware and ice stilled as everyone turned to stare.

Lady Nairn's eyes flickered across the room in the direction of a grand piano in a far corner. A man bent over it, laughing. Jason Pierce. Registering the silence, he straightened and turned, revealing Lily in

78

green velvet at the keyboard, flushed with delight. "Oh," she said. "It's you."

I felt a wash of loose-limbed relief, followed by a flush of confusion. The dead girl wasn't Lily . . . but in that case, who was she?

At the piano, Lily launched into the dark, downward sweep of Bach's Toccata and fugue in D Minor. *"By the pricking of my thumbs,"* she chanted, *"something wicked this way comes."*

Flat-footed and heavy, silence smothered the room. "The play," gasped a small white-haired woman, clutching at a silver cross on a chain around her neck. "You've quoted the play."

"Worse than that," said Sybilla Fraser, her fingers wrapped gracefully around a champagne flute. "She's quoted the witches." Sybilla was draped in fiery silk that set off her golden hair and skin; her eyes were smoldering. She was, if anything, more beautiful in person than on-screen.

But I could not get the girl on the hill out of my head. Neither Ben nor I had found any trace of her. Maybe she'd been a dream. Or maybe I'd left someone up there, dead or dying, alone on the hill as darkness fell.

I turned to leave, only to find that someone had stepped into the doorway behind me, blocking my way. The gray-haired fury from the hill. In dark accusation, she raised her arm to point at Lily. At least, most people in the room seemed to think that she was pointing at Lily. But from my vantage, she was pointing straight at me. "You've brought evil into this house," she said, her voice a low rumbling growl.

For a moment, no one moved.

"The curse only works in a theater," said Lily, rising. When no one answered, her bravura faltered. "Doesn't it?"

"As of today," said Sybilla, "this house *is* a theater." She pointed at the door. *"Out."*

"Christ, Syb," protested Jason. "She's just a kid. And it's not like we've started rehearsals. You don't have to do the bloody fiend-like queen thing yet."

Sybilla's eyes flashed. "You, too. Out."

"Fiend-like queen?" he scoffed. "You think that counts?"

Behind Sybilla, a large man with a paunch and grizzled ginger hair balded into a tonsure rose to his feet. "A quote's a quote, laddie. And as the lady says, I gather we're to rehearse in this room. Informal-like, but, still, rehearsal's rehearsal. So out with the both of you."

"Hell," said Jason. Brushing by me and then past the gray-haired woman, he flung himself out the door. Eyes spitting fire, Lily followed.

The gray-haired fury never moved. With Lily gone, she was now clearly pointing at me.

"Does either of them ken the ritual to counter the curse?" asked the ginger-haired man of no one in particular.

It seemed an easy way out of the room. "I'll show them," I said. As I came to the old woman, she leaned in close. "Put it back," she said in my ear.

Put it back? Did she know about the knife? And if she knew about the knife, did she know about the body? "Did you see anyone on the hill this afternoon? A body?" I asked, low enough that no one else could hear.

She shook her head. "It's the blade you should be worried about," she said, and then she scooted me through the door in Lily's wake. Behind me, it closed with a resounding thud.

"You *believe* all that voodoo twaddle?" growled Jason out in the passageway.

"It's about respect, not belief," I said shortly.

"Tell that to Medusa in gray," Jason retorted.

"Auld Callie," said Lily. Standing there in

a green dress with faux-medieval trumpet sleeves, her flame-red hair floating about her face, she was near tears of fury. "She's playing one of the witches. The kids in the village think she *is* one."

Auld Callie, I thought suddenly. *That's the name of the woman who found Sir Angus.*

"I thought I saw you this afternoon," I said to Lily. "On the hill."

"Well, you didn't. You just saw Sybilla make a fool of me. And my grandmother *let* her."

Had I been dreaming? Or was there someone else out there? The only way to find out was to go back. I started down the passage.

"Oh, no," said Jason, grabbing my arm. "You're not going anywhere till you get us out of this."

His grip tightened. It was going to be faster to give in and show him how to exorcise the curse than to argue. Under my terse direction, Jason turned three times clockwise and then pounded on the door to the hall, asking to be let back in. Sybilla opened the door. *"Fair thoughts and happy hours attend on you,"* he said as he stepped back through it. Sybilla gave him a smile of incandescent triumph, and then, without acknowledging Lily at all, she shut the door behind him.

"Cow," shot Lily. She spun around three times and crossed to the door, her knuckles pausing a few inches out. "What should I say?"

I glanced anxiously down the corridor. "You have to quote from one of the lucky plays. Jason went with *Merchant of Venice.* Why don't you do *Midsummer?*"

She shrugged. "Sure."

"An old standby is *Hand in hand with fairy grace, will we sing and bless this place.*"

She looked back, her sea-green eyes alight with mischief. "You should have said that up on the hill. It's a fairy hill, you know." Before I could respond, she rapped sharply on the door, which opened to reveal Lady Nairn.

"Enter, Lilidh Gruoch MacPhee," said Lily's grandmother, and Lily stepped through the door, pulling me with her. Around the room, the gathered company strained forward to hear.

Exhaling sharply, Lily blew a strand of red from her face, fixed Sybilla with her gaze, and began to speak:

What you see when you awake,
Do it for your true love take;
Love and languish for his sake.
Be it lynx, or cat, or bear,

83

Leopard or boar with bristled hair:
In your eye, whate'er appears
When you wake, it is your dear:
Wake when some vile thing is near.

Whirling on her heel, Lily strode from the room, slamming the door so hard that the antlers rattled on the walls.

The company stood stunned. She'd known, of course, what to do, I realized. One would, growing up in this house. Her question to me had been no more than a tease; she'd known exactly what she meant to say. She'd altered a few bits here and there, remembering sense rather than exact phrasing, but the words were recognizably Oberon's — the king of fairies to his sleeping wife, Titania, the fairy queen. A love trick, you could say, if you were in a charitable mood. A magical practical joke with razored humiliation at its core, though, would be more accurate.

"But that's not a blessing," quavered the woman with the silver cross. "That's another curse."

Sybilla rose, coolly surveying the company, her eyes coming to rest at last on Jason. "And how does the curse end? Oh, that's right: *Titania waked, and straightway loved an ass.*" Sweeping across the room, she disappeared through a narrow door onto a balcony.

With a groan, Jason strode after her.

"Gallus lass," said a deep Scottish voice. The ginger-haired man.

"Sybilla or Lily?" snapped Lady Nairn. She wore her hair swept back again today, and she was again in black, this time in a pantsuit.

"Take your pick," the man said with a grin. " 'Gallus,' from 'gallows,' " he said in my direction. "A compliment in Scots. Cheeky, mischievous, daring."

"As in 'worthy of hanging,' if you want to be literal about it," said Lady Nairn darkly. "I will be raising gallows myself if we begin shedding actors before we ever get to rehearsals. . . . Kate, meet the gallus Eircheard." His name sounded like Air Cart, though with the breathy back-of-the-throat "c" at the end of *loch* and *Bach.* "The king's loyal servant Seyton in our production. And also the doomed King of Summer in the Samhuinn festival. Emphasis on 'doomed.' "

He winked at me. "Marching merrily — if a wee bit hirplty-pirplty — to the sacrifice." He took a few steps toward me, extending his hand, and I saw that he had the rolling gait of someone with a lifelong limp. One foot was encased in a strangely shaped and heavily built-up shoe.

"Eircheard," Lady Nairn went on, "meet Kate Stanley. Whom you may *not* monopolize until you have given her the chance to escape upstairs and freshen up." To me, she added, "I laid something out on your bed. I hope it fits."

He raised his drink in my direction. *"Slàinte mhath,"* he said. "When you're suitably tarted up to be given a drink, you can toast me back. I'll teach you how." His eyes bright with laughter, he turned away.

Before anyone else could stop me, I slipped out, running downstairs and out into the night.

6

I'd just reached the lane when a car turned into it up ahead and drew alongside me. It was Ben.

"She's not there, Kate."

I started walking again, and he jumped out of the car and caught me by both shoulders, spinning me around to face him.

"I *saw* her," I said stubbornly. "Not Lily, obviously — but that doesn't mean she wasn't somebody else."

"That's why I went back."

I blinked. "You . . . ?"

"Went back," he said. "Checked every inch of the hilltop and as much as I could of the surrounding slope, just to be sure. She's not there. . . . She was a nightmare, Kate."

"She was real. And the gown that was draped over her was real, too. I touched it. . . . It was blue. It had weight. It had *sound,* for Christ's sake." It had cascaded back over her with the dry, rattling sound of rain in the desert.

"They do, sometimes."

I let him drive me back up to the house, watching him as he drove. He'd battled demons of his own, once, in the aftermath of some operation-turned-bloody-fiasco in Africa. I'd never learned the full details, only bits and pieces as his worries about me had come out, after I'd seen a few gruesome sights myself in the wake of searching for a killer two years before. I caught my breath. Was that what he was worried about? That this was some kind of delayed reaction to that experience?

"It wasn't a hallucination," I said defensively as we walked across the terrace. At a bench near the door, I stopped and sat down, blinking back tears. "I mean, the knife is real."

"Another reason I went back." He pulled the blade from his knapsack and laid it on the bench. Its pattern of coils and scrolls gleamed in the moonlight. "You have no business going up there alone, Kate. No jacket. No flashlight. And no weapon. For Christ's sake, if she *is* real, there was — and maybe is — a killer up there. If you want to go back, at least ask me to go with you."

"Where I need to go, actually, is Birnam Wood."

He sat down on the bench, the knife between us. "Kate — we need to talk."

I stiffened. "Not now." I'd been afraid this was coming.

"I —"

"Not now." I wanted to think about the knife. About the girl on the hill, dreamed or real. About the manuscript and Sir Angus's mysterious death. About anything but our parting. "What are you doing here, anyway?"

"Consulting."

I was used to the half truths and tangents that were all he could or would tell me about the black hole of his career. The secrecy at the center of his life was the only thing I'd hated about him, even though I understood it. "For Lady Nairn," I said, working it out for myself. "Did Athenaide put you up to this?"

He smiled noncommittally.

Just then a slim figure walked around the corner of the terrace. Lily, still mad at the world, by the look on her face. "Hullo," she said sourly. "Didn't expect to find you two out here."

"We were just going in to dinner," I said.

"Then I hope you're quick-change artists.

Gran's a stickler for dress in the evening. Show up in jeans, and she'll turn you away hungry at the dining room door." Catching sight of the knife glinting on the bench between us, she sucked in a quick breath. "Bit Tristan and Isolde, don't you think?"

Ben sighed and rose. "Would you like me to keep it under my wing?" he asked me with a nod at the knife. "Or do you mean to wear it in to dinner? Presupposing that there's not a weapons check, along with a dress check, at the door."

"This is Gran's house," said Lily. "Jeans, no. Daggers, yes. Though that's usually with kilts."

"I think the company's jittery enough," I said, handing the knife back to Ben, "without giving them reason to wonder whether they've got a mad slasher in their midst."

He dropped it back in his knapsack. "See you inside," he said, striding up the stairs and into the house.

Lily plopped down beside me. "So tell me . . . why do you even *like* this stupid play? I mean, all Shakespeare does is rip off the old myths, stain a good king's reputation, and shove a really interesting woman out of the way." She kicked at the stone pavement. "Who in their right mind would just let a creature like Lady Macbeth fade out, offstage? I get my grandparents' obsession, living where they do, and with Gran's past on the stage and all. But why you?"

I took a deep breath and forced my thoughts in her direction. "I've loved Shakespeare since childhood, I suppose. Loved the stories. And it was mostly encouraged by my family. But *Macbeth* — that was different. That was rebellion. My mother hated it. Wouldn't allow a copy of it in the house. So I went looking for it. Naturally."

Lily threw her head back and laughed. *"That's* the way to get kids to read Shakespeare. Tell them they *can't."* She rose, dusting off her hands. "Are you coming in?"

"In a few minutes."

With a shrug, she flitted up the stairs in Ben's wake.

I leaned back against the wall, watching the moonlight play in the trees. *Tristan and Isolde,* she'd said, likening us to guilty lovers eager to proclaim their innocence with a symbol no one could mistake, laying a sword between them on the bed just before spies burst into their love nest. The reference attested to some fine schooling, probably private and outrageously pricey, but as for Ben and me, the kid was so far off base it was laughable. Epic lovers didn't let oceans or deadly feuds, or even death, come between them. Ben and I had let the small twists and tugs of two careers pull us apart.

An American freelance theater director with a specialty in Shakespeare and a home base in London, I went wherever the jobs were — and in the wake of finding *Cardenio,* they were scattered all over the globe. As for Ben, it wasn't easy to explain what he did, especially since the word "mercenary" made him snort in derision. Before we'd met, he'd left whatever special-ops part of the British military or secret service had trained him and formed a private security company whose bread and butter was protection of the sort he was probably discussing with Lady Nairn. But he also had a quiet side-specialty in missions too delicate or dicey for politicians to stomach. Missions that, being his own commander in chief, he could accept or decline at will. I thought of him as a modern-day Drake or Raleigh. "You think I'm a pirate?" he'd asked, his voice cracking in amusement, when I'd told him that once, as we lay in bed one rainy afternoon.

"Not a pirate. A privateer."

He'd shrugged off the distinction. "What's a swash? Perhaps I should know, in case I ever need to buckle one."

"I like you unbuckled, thank you very

92

much," I'd said. He'd risen over me, naked and beautiful, and I'd sunk back into the sheets, laughing. A week later, he had disappeared, and I had not known where he was — or whether he was still alive, for that matter — for two months.

In atonement, he'd arranged a week in a cottage in Ireland, overlooking the sea: just the two of us, he promised, some friendly horses, and a long unspoiled stretch of beach. And then I'd had a call from my agent.

"Coriolanus?" Ben had said in disbelief when I phoned to cancel the trip. "In Saint Petersburg? Nobody even likes *Coriolanus.*"

And so it went, growing increasingly hard to make time for each other, and increasingly easy to chafe at the other's absence. In the calendar year and a half that we'd been together, I figured that we'd actually been in each other's company for two months. Three, tops.

Then, on a bright morning in June, I'd walked to Ben's flat through showers of birdsong to find him staring absently out the big front window overlooking the Thames. He was wearing jeans and a green T-shirt that made his eyes look like a malachite sea.

"Do you want this?" At first I'd thought

he was talking about breakfast. "Us," he'd specified in a voice that canceled my hunger.

"Of course," I'd said, swallowing hard. "Look, about last night, I'm sorry. But I'm not the only one to —"

"God knows I'm no model of steady presence. But I miss one date for every three times you stand me up." It wasn't an accusation, just a fact stated with a flat calm that I found far more frightening than recrimination or clever retort.

"At least you know where I am." I'd tried for insouciance, but it came out with a peevishness that made me wince.

"Not here." He'd given me a wry smile.

"But I'm starting to get really interesting work," I protested. "Chances that won't come around twice. In a few years, I might be more established. Able to line more things up in advance." *Able to say no to the stray, wind-borne chance.* I'd left that last thought unsaid.

He'd watched the sunlight rippling like scales of gold on the river. "What you and I have, Kate, it's . . . unusual. I'll wait, at least for a while, if you can tell me that you'll be there at the end of this tunnel — if you can tell me that there'll *be* an end."

But I could not give him a date, and I would not make up the false specter of one.

In truth, I wasn't even sure I wanted one to exist. In perverse stubbornness, I stood mute, and in the silence, something snapped, sending a million invisible cracks spidering across the sky.

It was an amicable, if bittersweet, parting. Very adult. I walked home in a small gray shroud.

"How long is 'a while'?" Athenaide had asked when I reported the rift.

I didn't know. I'd thrown myself into my work, which was thankfully plentiful all through the summer. I'd had no more than a few days of downtime when I'd had to fend off the foreboding that I'd made a terrible mistake.

Until now.

I rose and went upstairs to dress.

Laid out on my bed was a deeply V'd halter dress in silk of peacock blue. I very nearly turned around and went down to dinner in my grass-stained khakis. Only the notion of trying to explain why I'd done so made me shed them and slip the dress over my head. Pulling on the black heels I'd worn the night before, I smoothed down my hair and glanced in the mirror.

I was no majestic beauty like Ellen Terry, but given the afternoon I'd had, I was fairly presentable. In my mind's eye, though, the image that floated up to cloud the mirror wasn't the mermaid painting of a ferocious queen, but a girl with flame-red hair and a red slash across her throat, naked and bound beneath a fall of blue silk.

Tossing a bathrobe over the mirror, I went downstairs to dinner.

The crowd had filtered into the dining room, but people were still milling about, finding their places. At the door, Lady Nairn introduced me to Effie Summers, the white-haired lady who'd protested when Lily quoted the play. Effie's eyes widened. She looked from side to side, as if my presence might make someone else burst into dangerous quotation, and scuttled away.

The table, set for well over twenty, was a Victorian fantasy of china and crystal, with a pyramid of sugared fruit as a centerpiece. Before each plate a small enameled bird held a card with a name in its beak. I found mine in the beak of a swan near the center of the table; Jason was to my right. Eircheard was down at the end of the table, near a mutely sullen Lily. So much for learning to toast in Gaelic from Eircheard; I'd be toasting in Australian instead.

"Where am I to sit?" Sybilla asked with a pout.

Lady Nairn motioned to a still vacant place across from me. Frowning, Sybilla picked up the bird — a raven — with the card in its beak, turning it around so the whole table could read the neat black lettering:

HAL BERRIDGE.

"Who's Hal Berridge?" asked Jason.

Down near the end of the table, Effie Summers rose. "The boy," she gasped, clutching at her throat, finding the cross that hung on her necklace. *"The boy who died."*

7

A cry of surprise rose and then died over the table.

"The first Lady M," said Effie, her voice edging near hysteria.

Lady Nairn had been staring at Sybilla's card in consternation, but eyeing Effie's panic, she cut in briskly. "He was a boy actor with Shakespeare's company, when women were banned from the stage and boys played all the female roles. The night before the premiere in front of the king at Hampton Court, he took ill and died."

Effie leaned across the table toward Sybilla, her eyes wide and dark. "Mere hours before the show was to start, this was. Only one other actor knew the role well enough to step into it: Shakespeare." Her hands scrabbled like claws across the table. "Don't you see? The death of Hal Berridge is what started the curse. *It's a warning.*"

Still holding the raven with the offending

place card in its beak, Sybilla was within a breath of tossing it into the fire and making a grand, irrecoverable exit.

"Who put it there?" asked a slightly amused Jason Pierce. No one answered.

With a sigh, I put down my napkin and rose. "I'm sorry to have to disagree with Ms. Summers, but that tale is — and was — no more than a hoax."

All eyes swiveled to me. Even Lady Nairn looked confused.

"I have no idea who's to blame for its appearance tonight," I went on, "but the name Hal Berridge was first dreamed up at the end of the nineteenth century, by a theater critic named Max Beerbohm."

"The cartoonist?" asked Lady Nairn, her face pinched with concentration.

I nodded. "Caricaturist, critic, novelist, man-about-town. A satirist at heart and a brilliant wit. More in demand to liven up London dinner parties than Oscar Wilde. Shakespeare bored him. One night, he balked at picking apart a production he disliked and devoted most of his review to anecdotes about Shakespeare. Including Hal Berridge. Larded the whole thing with quotations from obscure historical sources, which made it convincing. So convincing that his stories were swallowed whole by generations of actors, unchallenged by scholars. Problem is, he made them all up."

"Do you mean to say that the curse — the whole history of it — is based on a lie?" asked Sybilla.

"A jest." I smiled. "I don't discount that some productions have been dogged by terrible luck. My personal favorite involves Charlton Heston's tights. But the bad luck did not have its origins in the demise of Hal Berridge."

It was a strange prank, I thought as I spoke. Not in good taste, for starters — mean-spirited, really. But obscure as well. So obscure that it failed the first test of a good joke: that its audience should get it without reference to footnotes. The jester had surely been counting on someone to explain the joke, but in which direction? Effie's superstition or my skepticism?

The small enameled bird trembled in Sybilla's hand. She was not yet ready to give up her grand scene.

Ben walked over and plucked the card from the raven's beak. Pulling a pen from his pocket, he turned it over, scrawled *HM the Scottish Queen* across the back, and tucked it back into the bird's mouth. "Your Majesty," he said to Sybilla with a little bow, holding out his arm.

Thank you, I mouthed.

She gave him a smile of such radiance that I winced. And then she reached up and ran a hand down the side of his face. "Thank you, darling," she said in a voice purring with satisfaction and promise.

Darling?

Small details of the past few days floated loose from their moorings and fell back down to earth in a new arrangement. I heard Lady Nairn's voice, as if in an echo chamber: *She's the one who's already got someone new on the line.* And Ben — he'd tried to talk to me, but I'd refused to listen and then ducked behind Lily.

Bit Tristan and Isolde, she'd said, peering at the tableau of the two of us separated by the knife. Had she known? Had everyone known but me?

I felt myself flush and looked down. If I could have, I would have fled to upper Siberia, to cool off in the permafrost. But I was hemmed in by the ritual of a formal dinner. If I left, I'd only make the scene worse, and my part in it more pathetic.

"So what happened to Charlton Heston's tights?" asked Lily from the far end of the table.

"Somebody doused them with kerosene," I heard myself say, as if from far away. "He was in an outdoor production that involved riding a horse. It can't have been very far, but the combination of friction and horse sweat heated up the tights to the point that Heston had to dash offstage crying, 'Get them off me, get them off. . . .' Not very nice for Heston, I suppose, but it makes for a mental picture that sticks."

There was some laughter, and blessedly the focus drifted elsewhere. Normally, the nervous chatter about strange happenings during *Macbeth* productions would have fascinated me, but tonight the various Macbeths who'd accidentally stabbed Macduffs, and vice versa, the Lady Macbeths who'd taken tumbles during the sleepwalking scene — even the patron who'd committed suicide by diving headfirst from the balcony of the Met during a performance of Verdi's Scottish Opera — it all sounded dull as dust. At one point, Jason — not the world's most sensitive man — leaned over and asked whether I felt all right.

I could not look at Ben, but I couldn't keep myself from stealing the occasional glance at Sybilla. She had eyes only for Ben, whom she proceeded to monopolize all the way through dinner, without once acknowledging Jason's existence.

Or mine, for that matter.

■ ■ ■ ■

I excused myself at the first possible moment, stumbling blindly down the corridor, finding myself in the deserted drawing room. I stood there for I don't know how long, numb and hollow, the very air scraping my skin raw. After a while, I heard voices approaching. Footsteps and laughter. The company coming back in for after-dinner coffee, no doubt.

I wanted neither coffee nor company. A small door near the front of the room led to a steep spiral staircase. I took it. It wound up and up through what I supposed must be one of the corner towers to a cramped landing and from there into a circular room. I stopped just inside. The whole room seemed to be singing. Directly across, a large window perfectly framed the hill. To the right, another window was open to the night, hung with wind chimes that gave the room its voice, from a high silvery ring to a rich dark bass. A wall fountain added the quiet laughter of water. Before a small fireplace stood two comfortable armchairs and a small table, and an antique carved chest sat beneath the hill-filled window. Other than that, the room was empty of furniture.

It was the chest that riveted my attention. Centered atop it sat an immense silver bowl, flanked on one side by a small rectangular standing mirror in an ornate carved frame, the glass spotted and dim with age. On the other side lay a knife with a black hilt and strange undulating whorls running through the steel of the blade.

From even a short distance, it looked exactly like the knife I'd found on the hill. Had Ben given it to Lady Nairn?

I stepped through the room and bent close. Only then could I see that this knife had no runes running down the blade, and its edge was rounded and smooth. Oddly thick, too. It had never been honed.

"You've found my inner sanctum," said Lady Nairn over my shoulder, and I jumped. "The pieces at the heart of our collection. Cauldron, mirror, and blade. The inspiration for the production, too. The cauldron is Iron Age Celtic. At least the original is — dug up out of a bog in the Highlands in the eighteenth century. Too fragile for use, though, so what you see is a reproduction. The mirror is Elizabethan. Said to have belonged to the King's Men."

"And the knife?" I asked, my breath tight in my throat.

"A modern copy."

"Of what?"

"Of one found on the hill."

"Tell me about it," I said.

She was watching me as if she could see through me to the past and maybe also the future. "I had it made for the stage —"

"The original."

Crossing to the chest, she set it in my hand and motioned me to one of the arm-chairs by the little fireplace. Turning to sit, I saw on a hook by the door a shimmering length of blue silk, scaled like a dragon. Knife in hand, I stared at it as if at a ghost.

"Ellen Terry's Lady M costume," said Lady Nairn with some amusement. "Or an approximation thereof. Made of silk embroidered with beetle wings. How perfect is that, for a queen who was a witch in all but name? Though perhaps the beetles would disagree."

I was still staring at it, openmouthed, remembering the peculiar dry pattering sound of the gown over the body on the hill, when she started her tale. The knife had been found at the end of the eighteenth century, she said, during the first archaeological dig on the hill. It had not turned up in a spadeful of earth, though. Instead, it had been plucked, early one morning, from the grass, where it lay gleaming in the weak sun. How it got there was never discovered. Even to amateur eyes, though, it was clearly ancient, fitted with a black hilt and etched with letters no one could read.

"What happened to it?" I asked, my mouth dry.

"Evil rumors gathered around it — mostly whispers that it was the blade that had killed Macbeth. The real one. Grim, but it made it valuable. For nearly fifty years, it passed from father to son, as one of the great treasures of the house. Then it was sold to pay a gambling debt. Soon after that, the family very nearly lost the entire estate."

She cleared her throat. "Coincidence, no doubt, though not everyone thought so. By the time a son of the house tried to trace the knife, however, it had passed beyond reach. Then, in 1857, William Nairn, my husband's great-great-grandfather and the paterfamilias at the time, claimed to have found it, once again, just lying in the grass on the hilltop. This raised some eyebrows — not least his wife's — even at the time, but he never wavered in his story.

"However he came by the knife, thereafter he would not let it out of his sight. By the following summer, when his son — my husband's great-grandfather — was born, the knife seemed to have taken an uncanny hold over him that not even a new child could shake. He spent his days watching the play of light across the blade. At night, he grew restless, walking the battlements at all hours, knife in hand, looking toward the hill. His wife began to wonder whether the thing had bewitched him.

"On the eve of Samhuinn in 1859, he disappeared in a gale. A young servant girl later claimed she had seen him struggling up the hill, though how she could have seen through the lashing rain that night put her story in some doubt. In any case, neither William Nairn nor his knife was ever seen again.

"To the end of her days, his wife believed that he had been taken by the Good Folk, who had reclaimed the knife as theirs and had taken him along in the bargain."

The tale faded slowly, lingering long after her voice had stilled. "It was William's grandson who met the dark fairy on the hill," she said presently.

The old woman who Sir Angus believed had sent something along to Ellen Terry. The phrases I'd heard whispered on the wind swirled around in my head. *You shall be queen hereafter. . . . Nothing is but what is not. . . . She must die.* Chased by a few

107

clearer phrases: *Evil rumors gathered around it. . . .* Most strident of all: *You have brought evil into this house.*

I shifted uncomfortably. "Lady Nairn . . . do you think the knife could have anything to do with whatever Sir Angus found?"

"I shouldn't think so. Why?"

I looked up from the knife in my hand. "I found a knife very like this today."

Her eyes narrowed. "Where?" Before I could reply, she answered her own question. "You went up the hill."

"I'm sorry." I swallowed. "It — the knife wasn't all I found. I also found a body, or at least I thought I did. I thought — at first — it was Lily."

"My God, Lily?"

"Obviously, it wasn't," I quickly explained. "It must have been a dream or a nightmare."

She drew in a sharp breath. "That explains some of your rushing about, I suppose."

"There was no body." I got up and went to the window. "Ben went back to make sure."

"And the knife?"

"He has it."

"Is that where you met Auld Callie?"

I nodded. "Lily says the kids in the village think she's a witch."

"As the saying goes, you say witch, I say

wise. . . . If she's a witch, she's a white one. Caledonia Gorrie is worth heeding."

"Where did you get this?"

She put out her hand for the knife, and I gave it back. "My husband had it made for me. It's a copy of the original."

I frowned. "But if the knife was lost in 1859," I said slowly, "how could he have had a copy of it made?"

"We still have the dig notes from 1799. There's a full-scale drawing."

My heart turned over. "May I see it?"

"Come," she said, heading swiftly out of the room.

8

As we neared the foot of the stairs, we heard a strange, almost inhuman keening, and every hair on my body rose. Ducking back into the hall, we found that most of the company had drifted off to their rooms and the lights had been dimmed. Those who remained had gathered at the French doors, thrown wide open to the night. The sound was drifting in from outside.

Among them was the white-haired woman who'd been so nervous about the curse, Effie Summers . . . another of the witches. She was looking back at us, her mouth shaped into a long narrow "o" of fear; a low, whining sob laid a line of guttural bass under the strange song filling the air.

"Effie," said Lady Nairn, "what's happened?" Gripping my wrist, she drew me through the room.

Shaking her head, Effie pointed at the doors.

I eased forward to look outside. The moon had set, leaving the night sky awash in stars. The pines ringing the house seemed to scour the horizon as they swayed in the wind. On the lawn below, candles marched in a flickering circle, and in its midst stood a woman.

No — a girl. Lily, her dress rippling in the wind. Slowly, she began to raise her arms skyward, and I realized that the keening was swelling from her throat. At her feet lay what looked like a small gleaming fountain. I stepped onto the balcony, squinting through the darkness. It was a mirror, laid on the grass.

Behind me, a voice cracked into prayer. *"Our Father, who art in heaven, hallowed be Thy Name."* Gripping her cross before her, Effie sank to her knees. Beside her, Lady Nairn raised one hand to her mouth and went still.

On the lawn below, Lily swayed a little. Her arms, still rising, had reached shoulder height, the long sleeves streaming behind her. Still singing her wordless song, she began to spin.

"Thy kingdom come, Thy will be done, on earth as it is in heaven . . . ," Effie growled.

Lily's spinning quickened, her feet stamping the ground.

All along the front of the house, other windows were thrown open, filled with dark figures staring into the night. Still others, I realized, were gathering in the hall behind us.

"Deliver us from evil," whispered Effie. *"For Thine is the kingdom, the power, and the glory, for ever and ever. Amen."*

Down on the lawn, Lily noticed neither Effie nor the gathering crowd. Her voice had lost all contact with individual sounds, stretching into an inhuman whine, a moaning of wind or of ghosts. Arms stretched high over her head, she was spinning so quickly that she'd become a blur.

Holding the cross out before her, Effie suddenly rose and strode to the balustrade, lifting her voice with all the wrath of a prophet. *"Thou shalt not suffer a witch to live!"*

A gust circled the lawn, rattling the windows, and most of the candles went out. With a great cry, Lily flung down her arms and fell to the ground.

For a moment, there was no sound but the wind roaring in the trees. Her face taut, small flecks of foam caught at the corners of her mouth, Effie turned to Lady Nairn. "Thou shalt not suffer —"

Lady Nairn rounded on her, cutting her off. *"Effie!"*

She blinked. Her voice had dissolved to a dry whisper. "This is what comes of allowing satanic rituals under your roof."

"Wiccan, not Satanic," said Lady Nairn shortly. "There's a difference. As for 'allowing,' I wasn't consulted, and, technically speaking, she's not under my roof."

Still clutching the crucifix, Effie was panting a little. "Pray for her," she said quietly. Turning around, she glimpsed the gathered crowd, scanning it from one end to the other. *"Pray for her,"* she said again. *"Pray for us all."* With one last glance of reproach at Lady Nairn, Effie stumbled back through the room, the crowd parting to let her through in silence.

"Puts the 'effing' in 'complete effing lunatic,' " said Jason as she disappeared through the door. Around him, the silence splintered into nervous laughter.

Down on the lawn, Lily stirred. Lady Nairn had seen it, too. "Exhibitionist little fool," she said under her breath. "If I ever get my hands on Corra Ravensbrook, I'll bloody well throttle her." She glanced at me. "Meanwhile, if you run across Ben, tell him I want to see him. And that blasted knife." With that, she hurried out.

So much for seeing the drawing of the original knife, I thought with irritation. And

113

who the hell was Corra Ravensbrook? Not knowing what else to do with myself, I wandered back up toward my room.

"Kate," said Ben as I reached the top, and I stopped as if I'd run into glass. He was perched on a sofa in a small sitting room just off the landing. He'd changed back into jeans and a sweater. Resting his chin on both fists, he was staring at a low table before him.

I went to the doorway and stopped again. Sybilla was nowhere to be seen. He rose. "I'm sorry."

"You're a colossal bastard, you know that? You should have told me."

"I tried."

"You should have made sure."

"Fair enough." He eyed me in silence for a moment. "Look, I didn't know you would be here, or I wouldn't have come. I won't stay."

"Surely we can both act like professionals for the length of one weekend," I said stiffly.

"In that case, you want to take a look at this?" He motioned toward the table in front of him. On it lay my knife, his BlackBerry, and a pad of paper crossed with a line of bold lettering. He'd transcribed the runes from the knife onto the paper.

I crossed the room and looked down at the pad:

RIꓷꓘ✝ꓕꓘR

"You read runes, Professor?" His old nickname for me, from my roots in academia, though I'd left the ivory tower for the theater long before I'd achieved that exalted status.

"Two R's, a couple of slanted F's, and some butterflies," I said shortly. "In other words, no."

"Thank God for Google," he said, handing me the BlackBerry. On the Web, he'd pulled up a table of runes and their modern equivalents. In spite of myself, I was interested. Staring at the small screen, I lowered myself onto the arm of the sofa. "The F's turn out to be A's," he said, "and the butterflies are D's."

Letter by letter, I translated the word into the modern Roman alphabet, and he wrote them in large block letters beneath the runes:

R I A D N A D R

"Make any sense to you?"

115

I shook my head. "Couldn't even tell you the language."

"Bloody useless. Don't you at least know a bona fide professor of runes we can call?"

"Past midnight?"

"How about Eircheard?" asked Lady Nairn.

I jumped. She was standing right over us. Next to her stood Sybilla, in jeans and a jacket, her hair floating about her face in wild ringlets. She was impossibly, preposterously beautiful. I could have throttled her.

"Is that it?" Lady Nairn asked with a glance at the knife.

I nodded and Ben held it out to her, but she just stared, as if it might bite. It was Sybilla who reached for it in the end, her fingers drifting across Ben's.

"Eircheard is a professor?" I asked.

"He'd find that amusing," said Lady Nairn. "No. He's a swordsmith. Which means he actually *uses* runes, in addition to studying them."

"What does it say?" asked Sybilla, looking wide-eyed at Ben.

"That, *bella donna,* is what we're trying to figure out."

Bella donna? I got saddled with "Professor" and she got *"bella donna"*? Okay, so it meant "beautiful lady" in Italian. Like it or

116

not, that was accurate. But I had a sudden savage jolt of pleasure that "belladonna" was also the name of an ancient and potent poison.

Lady Nairn touched my arm. "It was Eircheard who made the stage knife. The one you saw downstairs. My husband let him refit an old byre down the road into a smithy, and took the knife in payment. Eircheard researched it for months, poring over every bit of knowledge he could glean about the knife William Nairn found on the hill. He must know as much about it as anyone."

"Do you think he made this one?" asked Ben.

Lady Nairn tapped her chin with one finger, thinking. "Do you know, I believe a late-night visit to the gallus Eircheard is in order."

"I'll come too," announced Sybilla.

The house was quiet and dark. On the lawn, the candles still stood in Lily's circle, though their flames had long since blown out. Leaning at crazy angles, some of them had spilled wax onto the grass.

It was one of those startlingly clear nights of late autumn, hushed as if waiting. A faint scent of woodsmoke, thin as a dim memory, haunted air otherwise clean and crisp.

Something about the star-scattered depth of the blackness overhead squelched small talk. I tried not to notice Sybilla holding Ben's hand.

We stepped quietly down the drive, footsteps crunching on the gravel, and into the road. With the hill looming over us, we turned left, skirting its steep slopes. Five minutes later, we came to the road that we'd driven in on the night before, leading off around the hill to the right. Crossing it, we stayed on the lane, which plunged straight ahead into thick woods on either side.

We heard the smithy before we saw it, the rhythmic clank of steel hammering steel gradually separating itself from the measureless moan of the trees. *Clang, clang, clang.* Pause. And then again.

I glimpsed lights through the branches, and then the trees fell away. In the midst of a wide field sat a low stone building with only three sides; the fourth was open, like a doll's house, to the Scottish elements. Inside, the forge glowed white, yellow, and orange in the night. Eircheard, in a leather apron, gloves, and goggles, was hammering a long rod of white-hot steel against an anvil.

We strode up to the edge of the smithy. Though the night was crisp and the building was entirely open at one end, the heat coming off the forge made the whole place uncomfortably warm. "Eircheard," called Lady Nairn, but got no answer through the hammering. With every stroke, bright burning flakes of scale scattered around the anvil like falling stars, as if we'd walked unawares into the midst of some creation myth, watching a squat god forge new constellations for the deeps of space. "Eircheard," Lady Nairn called again. Still no answer.

Taking the knapsack from Ben, I drew out the knife, brushed past Lady Nairn, and slid it onto the anvil alongside the long piece of steel he was shaping into a sword. The whorls and curls in the finished blade undulated like a living thing in the firelight.

For a split second, the hammer stilled in midair before clattering to the ground. Pulling me close, Eircheard wrapped an arm around my neck. Something flashed in his other hand, and I felt the prick of cold steel against my throat.

"Where'd you come by that blade?" he demanded.

9

Against my back, I could feel Eircheard's chest heaving for breath, the dry skitter of his heart. He gave me a quick shake. *"Where?"* he growled.

Before I could answer, Lady Nairn stepped into the light. "Not from me," she said.

"Fegs," said Eircheard, dropping me so quickly it almost felt like a shove. "It's yourself. Why didn't you say so?" Tossing his knife on a large round table, he stared at it, panting. Then he turned to me. "Saw the knife, lassie, not yourself. Thought you'd taken what wasn't yours to take. No harm done, though, eh?" He extended a meaty hand, now empty.

Still dazed, I shook it.

Ben had seized the rune-engraved knife from the anvil the moment Eircheard grabbed me. With a nod at him, Eircheard pulled out a handkerchief and wiped his brow, beaded with sweat. "I'd still like to hear where you came by that blade, though."

"On the hill," said Lady Nairn. Behind her, Sybilla was pale.

The handkerchief stilled in the middle of Eircheard's face. He peeped out from under it. "Dunsinnan Hill?" When Lady Nairn said nothing, his glance slid to me.

"I fell asleep. It was there when I woke."

"You ken it's a fairy hill?"

I nodded.

"Then you're either gallus, lass, or goamless. Foolhardy, or just plain foolish." He shook his head, thrusting the handkerchief back into his pocket. His eyes flashing, he thrust out his other hand. "Let's have a wee look at it, then."

Ben glanced at Lady Nairn, who nodded. Reluctantly, he set the knife in Eircheard's hand.

Eircheard moved so that the blade caught the firelight better. Pulling off his goggles, he drew a pair of wire-rimmed glasses from another pocket and shoved them on his nose, which he put right down near the blade. He looked, I couldn't help thinking, like some young, ginger-bearded Santa Claus.

His eyes locked on Lady Nairn, his breath exhaling in a long, whistling sigh. "I'd like

121

to say I made it, but no. I've made another very like it, but mine has no runes. Nor an edge, neither."

"Edges can be honed," said Lady Nairn softly, "and runes can be added."

"So they can," he replied, "but the pattern in the blade is forged into the steel in its making and cannot be changed. And that pattern's not mine. You ken your own, see, like you ken your own bairns."

"Can you read the runes?" asked Sybilla.

He ran a stubby finger down the center of the blade. Almost a caress.

"We tried," I said, "but all we came up with was RIADNADR. Which I can't make heads or tails of."

Eircheard cocked his head, his eyes suddenly twinkling, the way they had when he'd teased me before dinner. "So that's what the delegation's about it, is it?" His gaze rested on me. "Don't sell yourself short. You've used Norse instead of Anglo-Saxon runes, but other than that, you've got the tail — the last half of the word — right. It's the head, I expect, where you went wrong. The first three letters are worn, see, and you missed some strokes." Handing me the knife, he went to a workbench and rustled about, returning with a rag and a can of some kind of grease. As the four of us leaned in around him, he dipped the rag into the grease and passed it over the bright surface of the blade. As if he'd revealed invisible ink, other lines appeared, faint but there, so that

ᚱᛁᚠ

became

ᛒᛁᚠ

In other words, he explained, RIA became BLO, so that the inscription read not RIADNADR but BLODNÆDR. "Runic shorthand," he said, rubbing his chin thoughtfully, "for *Blod Nædder.* Blood Adder."

"Blackadder's vampire brother," quipped Ben.

Eircheard looked up in reproach. "You can say 'Blood Serpent' if it'll keep you from laughing like a daftie at what's not funny. Likely it's the knife's name. A common kenning — poetic metaphor, that is — for 'sword.' " He ran a finger along the back of the knife. "Makes sense. It's a classic Sassenach shape, this. Called a *seax.* A single-edged short sword or long knife, often with this angle along the back. Terrible fierce cutters, these are." He glanced up at Ben. "Nothing funny about the damage they can do."

"Whoever made this knife," I said slowly, "must have seen Lady Nairn's."

"Or the dig notebook," said Lady Nairn.

With a grunt, he limped into the shadows at the far end of the building and rummaged about, returning presently with a roll of photocopies on oversized paper. Dropping it on the table, he thumbed through the pages and drew one out, unrolling it and weighting its corners with an old coffee mug, a small hammer, and two twisted bits of steel. It was flecked with burn marks and ringed with coffee-cup stains. "Working copy," he said sheepishly, smoothing a hand over the stains, as if he might wipe them away. "Never left this building."

The drawing was life-sized, delicate lines done in pen and ink, and though the ink had faded a bit, it was a near photographic copy of the knife in my hand. The runes were smudged, as if someone had rubbed them out. But the pattern in the blade was remarkably exact.

"But that's a drawing of this knife," I said slowly, "not the other way round."

Eircheard sat down suddenly, running a

hand over his bald head. "So it is, lassie, so it is."

Lady Nairn frowned. "That drawing was made in 1799. Are you suggesting that this is an eighteenth-century knife?"

A grumble of dissent rose from deep in Eircheard's throat. "Cannot be," he said, shaking his head. "It's pattern-welded, like I said. A process that was lost for centuries before archaeologists and smiths put their heads together in the twentieth century and worked it out again." He touched the knife with one finger, as if it might disappear. "So you see, it's either under a hundred years old, probably well under — or nigh on a thousand."

The fire had cooled from white and lemony yellow to richer oranges. In the silence, the whole room seemed to flicker. The knife, too, seemed to be flickering.

"So if it's the original of these drawings —" I swallowed hard.

"Then nigh on a thousand would be right."

I stared at the blade, its strange markings exactly mirrored in the drawing. "That's impossible," I said slowly. "Isn't it?"

For a moment, all of us stood in a circle staring down at the knife.

"Could a blade survive that long in this

condition?" asked Ben. "Still bright, still holding an edge?"

"I don't ken of any," said Eircheard. "But I don't ken any reason why one couldn't, were it taken care of properly. Not on a Scottish hill, mind. Or *in* one, at any rate. Our hills are a wee bit damp, if you haven't noticed, and damp's no friend to a bonnie bright blade such as this. But taken care of — well, steel's wonderful strong stuff."

The heat of the forge was suddenly making me dizzy. The battle in 1054 had pitted Macbeth's Scots against Malcolm's invading army of Sassenach Northumbrians — a combination of northern Anglo-Saxons and Viking mercenaries. Had one of them carried this knife?

Nigh on a thousand years old. I found myself staring at a corner of the drawing. In a fine copperplate hand, someone had written a few lines of description. I read them aloud: *Black hilt of fine-grained wood. A polished steel guard. Barbarian inscription down the center of the blade, and another around the hilt.*

I looked up. "Another inscription?"

"Well, now," Eircheard said, stroking his beard. "I'd forgotten about that."

I picked up the rag and dipped it in the oil, brushing it around the metal ring at the base of the hilt, where it joined the blade. Very faintly, runes appeared, running around the perimeter in an unbroken ring. No beginning, no end — not even any divisions between words. "It's a round," said Eircheard softly. "A phrase that begins and ends with the same word or syllable. But on the blade, see, that word'll only be engraved once. So that the phrase runs round and round in a never-ending circle. Strong magic, that was thought to be."

Pulling a pad of paper toward him, Eircheard turned the knife slowly until he found a word he recognized and began transcribing, first dividing the runes into words and then putting them into the modern alphabet:

ᛒᚢᛏᚠ ᚦᛏᛗ ᛏᚠ ᛏᛗ ᛒᛁᚦ ᛏᚠᚹᛁᚾᛏ ᚠ

BUTO THTE NANE BITH NAWIHT A

He bit his lip, concentrating. "*Buto* plus an abbreviation for *thætte,* 'Except that,' " he murmured. "Northumbrian dialect. Then you skip to *bith,* or 'is,' negated by *na ne,* or 'not.' Then *nawiht,* 'nothing,' and *a,* or 'always.' " He scribbled out the whole sentence in block letters:

127

"Sounds more Eeyore than warrior," said Ben.

Eircheard ignored him. "Like I said, it'll make a phrase that begins and ends with the same word. Let me think. . . ." He sat staring at the blade, his fingers rubbing his temples.

"Jesus, Mary, and Joseph," he said after a few minutes, his breath coming out in a long whistle. "It's *bith.*" Hunching over the pad, he wrote out another line, rearranging the words:

BITH NAWIHT A BUTO THÆTTE NA NE BITH

"What's it mean?"

It was Sybilla who'd asked the question, but it was me he looked at as he answered it. "Nothing ever is but that which is not," he translated.

"Begins and ends with 'not,' " said Ben. "I like it. It's even a round in modern English."

The whole smithy seemed to be rising, spinning around me.

"You know it in its shorter form, lass, no?" Eircheard asked softly.

128

I nodded, and my throat moved, but no words came out. It was Lady Nairn who spoke, her voice no more than a dry whisper. *"Nothing is but what is not."*

Ben frowned. "Sounds familiar."

"It's Shakespeare," said Lady Nairn.

"It's *Macbeth,*" I said, the words seeming heavy, slow, impossible, as they floated away from me.

Sybilla glanced at all of us in turn, frowning. "But I thought you said the knife was a thousand years old. How can it quote *Macbeth* if it's a thousand years old?"

"It can't," I said. "It would have to be the other way around."

"Runes can be added," Lady Nairn said again, her voice harsh as a crow's.

"In Old English verse?" shot Eircheard. "Complete with alliteration, correct stress, and decent meter? Possible, not likely."

I ran a hand through my hair. "But that means swallowing the notion that Shakespeare not only marched up to Scotland and saw this knife, but that he could read Anglo-Saxon — in runes, no less. It's absurd."

The blade winked mockingly in the light. *Nothing is but what is not.*

Eircheard went to a cupboard, where he drew down five mismatched tumblers and a squat, wide-shouldered bottle of single-malt

Scotch. "A blade called Blood Serpent, ringed with an unbroken verse about the intertwined web of being and not being — that's a blade that has killed plenty," he said as he splashed a finger of amber whisky into each glass and shoved them around the table. "But Ben's right. The inscription doesn't read like a warrior's thought." His eyes met Lady Nairn's.

"It reads like magic," she said.

He nodded. "I think you've found a ritual blade. Never seen one, mind you, but there are whispers of them in the old stories. If that's the case, maybe it wasn't this blade that Shakespeare somehow knew. Maybe it was the ritual it was used for.

"Religious rites have longer lives and a wider reach than any single object used within them. If you found a thousand-year-old chalice engraved with a line from the Latin Mass, should you infer that someone who'd quoted the Mass in English yesterday, or four hundred years ago, for that matter, had seen that particular cup? Or only that they both knew some form of the same rite?"

The fire in the forge had cooled even further, to a simmering red that brought the pattern of the blade to life. It seemed to writhe and undulate, coiling and uncoiling like the creature for which it was named.

"What ritual would require such a blade?" Sybilla's eyes glittered.

He shrugged. "Hard to say." He poured out another splash of whisky and wiped his forehead with his arm. "Neither the Anglo-Saxons nor the Celts were shy about sacrifice, though. There's a Roman account of Celtic priestesses dressed all in white, moving through sacred groves dispatching victims with sacred blades, cutting their throats and letting the blood run into a cauldron." He drained his glass, sucking the last drop of whisky through his teeth. "Like I said, I haven't seen a ritual blade. But I've handled a fair few that've seen hard use in battle. Something strange happens to blades that have drunk a fair lot of blood. They wake. Not quite alive, but, still — sentient, somehow. And some of them grow to want more. Blood, I mean."

For a moment, there was no sound between us save the guttering of the fire. Then, from the back of the smithy, came a shrill cry. We turned to hear a grating sound floating in through a narrow window high up in the wall. The noise grew into a rumbling, rattling slide like a sudden fall of rock and then faded to silence.

For an instant, no one moved. Then Eircheard and Ben sprinted out of the open front and around the corner toward the rear of the building. Snatching up the knife from the table, I followed close behind. A stack of crates and pallets under the window had collapsed in a heap that was still groaning and settling. Just beyond, what looked like a small shed clung to the back wall. The door was ajar.

"Come out, you wee rotten scunner," growled Eircheard.

Inside, nothing moved.

He yanked the door open and shone a flashlight inside, revealing a bedroom, neat as a monk's cell and as small — barely big enough for Eircheard to lie down in. It was empty.

"Can't've gone far," said Eircheard.

Ben turned and shone the flashlight about the area around the back of the smithy. Patiently, he and Eircheard began scanning the ground for clues.

They'd just disappeared around the far corner, heading into the field beyond, when something caught my eye off to the right. Someone moving stealthily back into the woods that divided the smithy from the hill, and from Dunsinnan House.

If I yelled, the intruder would take off. If I waited for Ben and Eircheard, or went to fetch them, the intruder would be long gone.

My grip on the knife tightening, I slipped into the woods in the wake of the shadow.

The woods turned out to be a stand no more than ten feet thick, after which they opened up again. At the edge of this clearing, I paused. It was not a work of nature. It was a carefully shaped circle, lined on the inside with a ring of immense old beech trees, the last of their leaves rustling like dry paper. Inside the trees hunched a circle of standing stones. Not as tall or as massive as Stonehenge. Lumpier, somehow. Older and less refined. And in the darkness, far more powerful. A brooding, ancient power.

Wind swept through the treetops. I glanced up, watching them bend and lash against the star-scattered circle of night overhead, their moaning rising from a low murmur to the howl of an oceanic gale. Leaves floated downward in large, eddying flakes, as if the sky were snowing darkness. I shivered and drew my jacket closer around me.

When I looked back down, a figure stood in the center of the stones. The silhouette, black on black, of a woman from an earlier century, her long hair and gown stirring in

the wind. A dry hiss left her lips, and she
began to glide toward me.

10

The blade in my hand burned with a cold fire; it seemed to buzz at a pitch so low that I felt rather than heard it, as if it were resonating with some strong source of energy. Backing a few paces, I turned to run, but her arm whipped out and gripped my wrist. I yelped, but only a squeak came out.

"It's me, Kate," she whispered. *"Lily."*

Lily alive, or Lily dreamed and dead? My heart thudding hard in my chest, I slowly turned around.

Her face was pale in the faint light, her wide-set eyes large and dark. What had looked like the gown of a renaissance lady resolved into a coat with a tight bodice and long flaring skirt. Above the coat, her throat was a pale column, unmarked.

"Do you think it's true?" she asked in a low voice. "Do you think that's a ritual knife?"

I glanced down at the dagger and then back up. "How much did you overhear?"

"All of it." She grinned sheepishly.

From over at the smithy came a shout. *"Kate!"* It was Lady Nairn.

"Damn," said Lily. Her grip on my arm tightened. "Please don't tell her I was here. I'm already entry A-one on her shit list."

I was staring at her wrist gripping my arm. On it was a small tattoo I hadn't noticed before. A delicate five-pointed star. A pentacle, the symbol of witches — of Wicca, the neo-pagan religion of witchcraft.

Lady Nairn called again. "Please," whispered Lily, her eyes pleading. "I won't tell a soul."

Fifteen going on twenty-five, Lady Nairn had said of her. In the days following my parents' death, I'd been very like her. Unpredictable and a little wild. But she was, at heart, a good kid. "Go on, then," I said with a wave of the hand.

She flashed a wide smile. "Thanks. You're awesome." She dashed across the circle, in the direction of Dunsinnan House.

In a bright, evil flare the image of her body, bound and naked on the hilltop, flashed across my mind. "Lily," I said, stepping after her. At the far edge of the clearing, she looked back. "You'll be all right?" I

136

asked, feeling suddenly both frightened and foolish.

"No worries. We're practically in the back garden. Besides, we're too bloody far out in the sticks for a bogeyman to bother in the first place." And then she was gone, her passing barely stirring up a rustle amid the deep bracken.

I was turning to head back to the forge when a voice whispered out from the woods at my back. *Why did you bring the dagger from that place?*

I whirled. "Who's there?"

Another voice snaked from the right. *It must lie there. . . .*

And a third voice came from the left. *Dunsinnan must go to Birnam Wood.*

The wind tossed in the trees, and I thought I saw shadows glide in toward the stones as all three voices spoke at once: *She must die. . . .*

Gripping the knife close, I turned slowly about.

"Kate!" This time, it was Ben's voice. Flashlight beams crisscrossed the night, and footsteps pounded across the field toward the woods.

Thirty seconds later, a flashlight beam strafed the clearing. Eircheard and Ben crashed through the trees in its wake.

Ben took one glance at the knife and looked up at my face. "Are you all right?"

"Someone was here." I swallowed hard.

"What happened?" asked Eircheard.

I shook my head. "Nothing. Voices. I saw nothing but shadows."

Ben was scanning the ground around the stones.

"Kids," said Eircheard with contempt. "At a certain age, the village kids love to scare themselves silly telling ghost stories in the circle. Make a night of it, they do, by heading over to snoop about the forge. A few of them, you can see their eyes all starry with dreams of lame smiths forging magic rings and dragon chains. Most of them, though, are just idling, hoping to see me burn the place down, maybe the woods with it. Sodding little pyros."

"Not kids," I said. Lily had been here, only moments before. Was I sure of that?

I looked at Ben. "They were the same voices I heard on the hill this morning." That time, there had also been a body.

I told them what I'd heard, thinking through the words as I did. *Why did you bring the dagger from that place? It must lie there. . . .* Lady Macbeth's cry to her husband after he's killed the king, with the dagger made singular. "Put it back," was the gist of it.

Auld Callie's words exactly.

But the voices had stolen Sir Angus's words, too. *Dunsinnan must go to Birnam Wood.*

All in all, a fairly clear message: Drop the dagger, go after the manuscript — or whatever it was that Sir Angus had been after.

Who would need to tell me that in the guise of ghosts in a stone circle? And tack on a death threat, besides.

She must die.

Who must die?

"Jesus," said Eircheard. "No, not kids."

Lady Nairn and Sybilla walked into the clearing. "A stone circle," cried Sybilla, clasping her hands in delight. "I knew it. I *knew* there was a place of power hereabouts."

"Everything all right?" asked Lady Nairn.

"I'd like to go to Birnam Wood," I said.

She looked from me to Ben and Eircheard and nodded. "I've organized a reading of the play on the hill at sunrise," she said. "To begin the celebration of Samhuinn. We'll head to Birnam directly after that."

It would do. It would have to.

Sybilla was standing in the middle of the circle, swaying a little. "The knife belongs here," she said. "I can *feel* it."

Irritation suddenly overwhelmed me. "The stone circles of Britain — and I am assuming this is one of them — are Neolithic," I said crossly. "Stone Age. The druids were Iron Age Celts. And if Eircheard is right about the knife, it's late Anglo-Saxon, which makes it medieval, at least five hundred years after the fall of Rome. So where that knife belongs is anybody's guess, but it isn't here."

Sybilla wasn't fazed. "It's a sacred knife, and this is a sacred place. *It belongs.*"

I gave up. "I'm heading back to bed."

"High time we all followed suit," said Lady Nairn.

At the smithy, Eircheard gave me a leather scabbard for the knife, and then we made our way back to the house in silence. Orion the hunter, his star-studded knife at his belt, was just rising into the southeastern sky. To our left, the hill seemed to lean down over us, heavy with menace. Or maybe it was just mockery.

We said good-night to each other at the upstairs landing. Sybilla's hand lingered on Ben's arm in unspoken invitation, but he discreetly disengaged himself and walked me down the hall. Just outside my door, he stopped.

His clean, slightly spicy scent sped through me until my whole body ached for him.

Nothing is but what is not.

"Hide it," he said with a glance at the scabbard in my hand. "Are you okay with that? Or would you like some help?"

"I can take it from here, thanks." *Bastard.*

He opened his mouth to say something but thought better of it. "Good-night, Kate." Turning the corner, he walked ten feet down the corridor. Lady Nairn had given him the room right next to mine.

In that, I thought I saw the long hand of Athenaide.

Just inside my room, I leaned back against the door, wondering whether I was about to cry or scream. In the end I did neither, splashing water on my face at the sink instead.

A small fire was burning cheerily in the fireplace; the luxuries of life with a staff, I thought. Toweling off, I sank into one of the armchairs before the fire and drew the knife out of the sheath, watching it ripple in the light. My outburst in the circle had left me shaken. Not just because it had been childish, but because for all that my facts were right, it was Sybilla who had hit, however

141

messily, upon some truth. Not about the knife, but about the place. There *was* something strange about that circle in its clearing in the woods. *A place of power,* she'd said. And she was right. I'd felt it too. But I wasn't as sure as she was that the power there was entirely benign.

She must die, the voices had chanted. *Who must die?*

The phrase was Shakespeare's, I was certain of that. But not from *Macbeth.* On my phone, I pulled up the Web and entered the words into a Shakespearean search engine. *Othello, Julius Caesar,* and *Henry VIII,* came the answer. Spoken about Desdemona, Portia, and Queen Elizabeth.

I frowned. It had been an old jest between my mentor Roz Howard and myself that my auburn hair, dark eyes, and the tiniest hint of a hook in my nose made me look like Shakespeare's queen, in her days as a princess. It was a jest that Ben had kept alive. But the voices couldn't have known that. Could they?

I clicked on *Henry VIII,* pulling up the phrase in its context.

She must die:
She must, the saints must have her; yet a
   virgin,

A most unspotted lily shall she pass
To the ground, and all the world shall
     mourn her.

Lily, I thought raggedly. They hadn't
threatened me; *they'd threatened Lily.* And
I'd let her walk out of that circle alone.

I stood up, filled with sudden dread. I had
no idea where her bedroom was. On this
floor, I thought. I had to find it — and her
— if it meant knocking on every door in the
goddamned house. I was already striding
for the door when I heard a quiet tap from
the other side and flung it open.

11

Lily stood in the hall in loose flannel pants and an old black Belle and Sebastian sweatshirt, a book and a small wooden box under her arm, her face bright with excitement. "I couldn't sleep. I've had an idea, and, well, I saw your light on, so I thought I might as well run it by you." She bounded into the room. "You aren't angry with me, are you?"

In my confusion, I felt as if I'd been bounced by Tigger. "For listening? I would've done the same thing at your age. Maybe at my age."

"I'm not normally so nosey. Only, I saw the knife out on the terrace before dinner, and afterward I heard you talking about it in the little sitting room, and I was so curious. . . . Is that it?"

It lay where I'd left it on the table, shining in the firelight. "Yes." Setting the book and the box on the table, she caught it up, hefting it in her hand.

I glanced at the book. The cover showed a tall stone standing alone in a green field under lowering clouds, a single bright ray of sun illuminating the scene. It was titled *Ancient Pictland,* by Corra Ravensbrook.

Using both hands, Lily began waving the knife in slow motion, almost like she was doing Tai Chi. "Do you think it's really a thousand years old?"

"I don't know." How could it be? How could it *not* be?

"It'd be really cool to use this in the festival, don't you think? For the fight between the kings."

"For a stage fight?"

She smiled. "You heard Eircheard. It's a ritual knife. And it's an old ritual we're staging."

"Lily — it's a *real* knife. An edged weapon."

"I know. But it's a king-sacrifice we're staging, just like the one that killed Macbeth."

" 'Staging' being the operative word."

"It would be *authentic.*"

"It would be insanely reckless," I said incredulously. She was from a theatrical family, for heaven's sake.

"You know Eircheard and Jason are taking those roles? If anyone could handle a real knife, it'd be those two." She gave me a wicked smile. "And there'd be those who'd be happy enough if Jason came out a little worse for the wear, I can tell you that. It's one thing for Sybilla to have been asked to be the Cailleach; she's been a member of the Beltane fire Society — the festival organizers — since long before she hit the big time. It was idiotic, though, when Jason was cast as the Winter King. That role has always been cast from members of the fire Society before. Like Eircheard as the Summer King. Amateurs who really care about the show and the myths behind it. But Sybilla wrote a big check, and voilà, we're saddled with Jason. Bit uncomfortable, now that they're not speaking. On the other hand, there's no speaking in the show, either, so maybe their feuding won't matter a toss."

She blew a strand of coppery hair from her face. "But I'm in no position to complain, or even say 'I told you so,' because I'm an exception to the rule myself. Too young, you know. Gran pulled some strings for me."

Holding the knife tightly, she raised both hands toward the ceiling, as she had out on the lawn. "I'd like to be the Cailleach one day. Ever so much more than Lady Macbeth. I mean, the Cailleach's, like, the real thing, isn't she? It's her show. She chooses the champions who will be kings, and she sets them against each other. They're fighting for the right to marry her, at least in her young person of the Bride, as much as anything else."

She brought her hands down to her hips. "Do you know what the name 'Dunsinnan' means?"

"No."

She marched over to the windows. I'd drawn the curtains wide, letting the windows frame the hill. "Fort of the Nipple," she said with a flourish. "*Dun* means fort in Gaelic, and *sine* means nipple. You can't really tell from this side, but next time you drive in from the main road, have a look. The whole hill looks like a woman's breast." She threw open the middle window and leaned out into the night. "Weird name for a military hill."

I had my doubts, having met a few of Ben's friends. Some of them were capable of seeing breasts and penises in the void of outer space. But I held my tongue.

"The archaeologists all say that the ramparts on the hilltop are the remains of an Iron Age hill fort . . . but there's no evidence of that. I mean, buildings, yes. But not of a fort or castle specifically. And it doesn't seem, militarily speaking, the best place around. I mean, the hill just to the east, the King's Seat, is higher. So if the point is really male and military, like all the histories say, don't you think you'd build your fort next door?"

Privately, I doubted her expertise in judging suitable spots for fortification from an Iron Age perspective, but it didn't seem the right time to point that out.

"But they didn't." Pulling back inside, she turned and hopped up to sit on the sill. "For over a thousand years, the stronghold was on Dunsinnan. Which would make all the sense in the world if it were less a fort and more, say, a *spiritual* stronghold. Especially given its shape and the stone circle at its base." She crossed her arms in triumph. "I think it was a temple complex."

She was looking at me as if daring me to disagree. As I made no move to shout her down, she went on. "There are records, you know, of Macbeth coming here to consult with witches. But, like, change that title to 'priestesses,' and you've got a Stronghold of the Lady. The great Goddess worshipped in this land for millennia before the coming of Christianity. . . . I'm not talking about *Scot*-land, mind you." Her nose wrinkled in contempt. "The Scots are newcomers, invaders from Ireland." She threw her arms wide. "This — the whole of central Scotland — was Pictland, the kingdom of the Picts. That's what the Romans called them. The Priteni, they called themselves — or something like it. Their actual language is lost. Celtic, but closer to Welsh than Gaelic, apparently. In any case, it's where we get the word 'Britain,' " she said proudly. "Dunsinnan — or the stretch of country from Dunsinnan to Scone — was once the spiritual center of Pictland, the land of the Priteni. The spiritual center of *Britain*. Ground zero for Goddess worship, right here. How cool is that?"

How much of this was being regurgitated from Corra Ravensbrook, whoever she was? No matter — Lily was clearly very taken with her version of history. If I wanted her to consider another viewpoint — a sane one, say — I'd have to proceed with caution. "But isn't Dunsinnan where the battle was?" I asked aloud. "The great battle between Malcolm and Macbeth in 1054? Sounds military to me."

She shrugged. "Wouldn't be the first battle fought at a temple. Think about it: Malcolm's army came down from Birnam, just this side of the river from Dunkeld, where his grandfather had been the lay abbot. Even then, way back in the eleventh century, Dunkeld, see, was a bastion of Christianity." She jumped down from the sill and began to pace before it. "Don't you see? They weren't just fighting for the throne, Malcolm and Macbeth. It was a holy war. A Christian crusade against the old faith. Against the Goddess. A war to enforce Christianity and disinherit women. To banish the old Pictish ways that properly belong to this place."

She pointed at the book with the knife. "That's where Ravensbrook's so interesting. The usual Wiccan stuff — well, it tends to be airy-fairy. All about how gentle and good Wicca is, in tune with the earth and the natural rhythms of life, you know? Which is fine — more than fine. But the old Goddess religion, it could be *fierce*. It didn't just pay lip service to the notion that death is a part of life. It embraced that fact fully. If you know what I mean."

I frowned. "You mean sacrifice?"

"*Blood* sacrifice," she said with teenage relish. "Sacrifice of the king. There are a lot of stories about king sacrifice, you know," she babbled on, "the Samhuinn Fire Festival among them, but they weren't always just stories. Corra says the myths are memories of old rites."

She held up the knife. "According to Eirc-heard, this is a ritual knife. And it's also the knife that killed Macbeth. *King* Macbeth." For a moment, we both stared at the firelight and moonlight playing on its surface. "Ergo, the knife killed Macbeth in a ritual killing. *Macbeth was killed as part of a ritual sacrifice of the king.*" She let one finger stray across the runes on the blade. "I mean, what is a ritual knife *for* but ritual?"

Who was this Corra Ravensbrook, I wondered again. The ideas of king sacrifice she seemed to have planted in Lily had been discredited among academics long ago. A growing number of neo-pagans, especially the more intellectual sort, dismissed much of it as wishful thinking. But Lily, I realized, was in no mood to hear the voice of reason.

"Seems like rotten timing," I said mildly, "to slice up your leader and feed his life-blood to the gods just when you're on the run, looking for a place to make a last desperate stand."

"King sacrifice would never have been common. Performed only in times of great need, to settle some extraordinary debt with the gods. And what greater need than the destruction of your whole civilization?" She grinned. "Hey, apocalypse threatens, you'll do anything. Reason goes right out the window."

It was the most sensible thing she'd said in some time. I sighed. "All the old histories say that it was Macduff, fighting for Malcolm, who killed Macbeth and set his head on a pole. Not priestesses. Even Shakespeare used that part of the story." It was one of his most blunt stage directions: *Enter Macduff with Macbeth's head.* So preposterous that it was a dicey moment onstage: Audiences had been known to laugh.

Lily waved off the authorities. "And who wrote those histories? Monks! Christians. Busily writing the Goddess and her priestesses out of existence. I imagine Macduff found the pole, all right, and took it up as a trophy, waving it about. But it was the Celts, not the Christians, who worshipped heads. Decorated their sacred spaces with them. Submerged them in wells, boiled them in cauldrons, believed they could speak. It would have been Macbeth's own people who wanted his head as a talisman. By taking it, I reckon Macduff ripped the heart out of whatever will to fight they had left. A sort of grim Capture the Flag, if you like."

"If you're right, it didn't work out any better for them than for him, did it?"

"No," she said sadly, "not much." She

crossed the room and set the knife back down on the table and stood with her hands on her hips, staring into the fire. "He was the last Celtic king. The last king of the Priteni. But because of him, not everything was lost."

She was starting to make Macbeth out to be a Scottish King Arthur.

"The old religion survived, you know. It just went underground. Really deep. Especially in places like this. Out in the sticks now — think what it would have been like in the eleventh century." She turned to me, her eyes gleaming with excitement. "So . . . imagine Shakespeare coming through with a troupe of traveling players. Imagine him glimpsing, somehow, a rite preserved from the old days by women descended from the priestesses of the ancient Pictish Goddess. What would he do with it, do you think?"

Presupposing all her ridiculousness was true, I knew exactly what Shakespeare would have done with it. He was a magpie, a pack rat, when it came to plot, borrowing and stealing from everywhere. And magic made good theater. Spectacular.

"He would have written it into a script," I said quietly.

"Now, *that* would make your bloody play interesting," said Lily.

No, I thought, *that would make it explosive.* It was titillating enough to suggest that he'd put in a real spell or some rite of casting a circle — at least one that people once thought was real. But those could be found on the pages of grimoires and witch-hunting manuals. They weren't entirely lost. Putting in a rite of sacrifice preserved from an otherwise lost pagan religion — hell, if we were talking about the Picts, it was pretty much a lost civilization — that was something else entirely. Never mind the obvious fascination for Shakespeareans. Every neo-pagan, every Christian, every scholar of Britain's history, every journalist who wanted to sell papers or airtime, would be salivating over it.

I cleared my throat and said aloud what a responsible adult ought to say. "That's a lot of ifs."

"And one cold, hard, thousand-year-old piece of evidence," she said with shining eyes.

Nothing is but what is not.

"I'll tell you one thing," she said, "even if he got it wrong — painting something as evil that wasn't, really — I'd still want to read it. I'd even forgive the irritating old git for tormenting every schoolkid in modern Britain, just for preserving it at all." She turned to me. "So, what do you think?"

"That I need to think." I felt as if she'd just gone after me with a baseball bat.

Picking up the wooden box she'd brought along, she opened it. Inside was something covered in black silk. "I brought my tarot cards," she said. "Want a reading, while you think?"

I glanced over at the clock. I'd have to be up in three hours. "Could I take a rain check on that?"

She jumped up. "Oh, Lord. So sorry. You've got to get up for Gran's early morning hike up the hill, haven't you?"

"You're not coming?"

She snorted. "Let's see. *Macbeth* and a cold walk up the hill, or my warm bed and a nice morning's lie-in. No bloody contest. But I don't think you have a choice. So of course we can do it later. . . . Just as long as you let me corner you at some point. I bet your cards will be really interesting. Besides, you'll like my deck. It's a *Macbeth* deck."

She started for the door. "Lily — what were you doing out on the lawn tonight?"

Halfway across the room, she stopped. "Charging the mirror."

The mirror that had been in the middle of her dance. "What does that mean?"

She sighed. "I'm trying to learn to scry.

155

To see things in a mirror. But you have to learn how to empty your mind first. And also charge your mirror. Fill it with energy. Kind of like you'd charge a mobile phone, but the energy's different. Natural. Mostly, you charge them with moonlight." She turned back with a mischievous smile. "Like I said, Goddess worship had to go underground. But it never entirely died out. Not through all the battles, not through all the burning years. And now, it's coming back. People are returning to the old ways."

"Including you?"

"Among others."

"What do you want to see?"

She shrugged. "Same as everyone else. My first love. My future." Her eyes met mine. "My parents."

I took a deep breath but said nothing. There was nothing useful I could say.

"I heard you lost yours," she said in a small voice. "What happened to them?"

I sighed. "They were diplomats. A small plane and bad weather in the foothills of the Himalayas. A lethal combination. I was fifteen."

Her eyes were growing glassy. "Better than the motorway outside Preston."

In the fireplace, a log disintegrated in a

shower of sparks. "There's no good place for it."

Her voice shrank. "They were driving home from visiting me down at school."

I locked my eyes on hers and held them. "It wasn't your fault, Lily."

After a moment she shrugged. "I *know* that. Lots of expensive therapy." She gave me a watery smile and looked away. "But sometimes it's hard to feel it. When did you stop missing them?"

Was this it? Was this why she had sought my company? A toxic combination of guilt and longing. Poor kid. No wonder she was acting out. "Never."

She looked back sharply.

"Only, the hurt loses its sharpness, gradually," I said more gently. "And other experiences collect and change the balance of things. It doesn't go away. But it does become bearable. Does that make sense?"

"Thank you for not saying it will all be fine."

"You're welcome."

"Did I tell you that you look nice in that dress?"

I'd followed her to the door. Having entirely forgotten what I was wearing, I looked down and saw Lady Nairn's peacock-blue silk. "Thanks. Your grandmother lent it to me."

"It was my mother's."

I looked up, aghast. What the hell had Lady Nairn been thinking? "I'm so sorry. I had no idea."

She smiled. "It's okay. You look a little like her. Besides, she'd have liked you. I like you, too." Squeezing me in an impulsive hug, she opened the door and pattered off down the hall.

And I like you, I thought, staring after her.

I was turning back into the room when I heard another door open and glanced back. Sybilla emerged from Ben's room in a flame-colored kimono. Seeing me, she nodded, her eyes sly with triumph as she swayed silently down the hall. As if the flames from her kimono had brushed me with kerosene, I felt waves of heat sweeping around me, the blue silk disappearing in a whoosh of yellow and red, my skin liquefying, melting into puddles at my feet.

I looked up to see Ben standing in the doorway, watching me, his face a blank.

12

I closed the door and shut my eyes, squeezing Ben from my thoughts.

Imagine Shakespeare coming through with a troupe of traveling players, Lily had said. *Imagine him glimpsing, somehow, a rite preserved from the old days by women descended from the priestesses of the ancient Pictish Goddess. What would he do with it, do you think?*

Now, that *would make your bloody play interesting.*

That was the understatement of the season.

Her notion echoed the Nairn legends but one-upped them.

It was plausible, or at least possible, that Shakespeare had at some point come north. It was plausible that had he ever glimpsed a real magical rite, some hocus-pocus current during his lifetime, he would have slipped it into a play. But a survival of some pagan

159

sacrificial rite, kept alive by a secret line of priestesses?

That was entirely fucking preposterous.

Except for the knife gleaming on my table.

A knife that was, according to Eircheard, a thousand years old.

Nothing is but what is not.

It would make sense of the manuscript's disappearance, I thought. Had anyone recognized it for what it was, it would have been deemed demon worship in those days.

Which made hash of putting such a thing in the script in the first place, even if he had it at his fingertips. Why court such disaster with a king who fancied himself both a target and a skilled hunter of witches?

And in any case, he wouldn't have had such a thing at his fingertips, because it didn't exist. It couldn't.

And besides, a cook wanting paper to line a pastry tin or start the day's fire made equal sense of the disappearance. . . . Except that in 1911, Ellen Terry had written about evidence that the manuscript still existed.

Dunsinnan must go to Birnam Wood.

I looked out the window, willing day to come. But the moon just hung there in the west, a wide teasing smile in the night.

Suddenly exhausted, I slipped the knife in

160

its scabbard under my pillow and fell instantly to sleep.

I woke with a shriek to find myself on my knees in front of the mirror, the drawn blade in my hand. I dropped it, and it fell to the deep-carpeted floor with a soft thud.

I scooted back, staring at it as I might stare at a snake.

It must have been five minutes before I could move.

What was it Eircheard said about blades that had killed? *Some of them grow to want more. Blood, I mean.*

When I finally dressed, I walked in a wide circle around it.

Only at the last minute could I bring myself to touch it. I couldn't just leave it there, after all, lying in the middle of the carpet.

I threw a towel over it, scooped it up, deposited it in the bottom drawer of the dresser, and shoved a small pillow on top of it. And then I fairly ran down the stairs.

We'd been told to gather in the hall at six-thirty sharp, ready for a brisk walk. Auld Callie, who lived in the village on the other side of the hill, was meeting us at the top. Everyone else had wandered in by 6:35 —

except Effie Summers. A check of her room revealed a bed that hadn't been slept in. "I thought I calmed her down enough to at least stay the night," said Lady Nairn in irritation.

"Gone off to pray for all our sins," said Jason.

"God knows you could use it," snapped Sybilla.

Ten minutes later, we left without Effie.

In the gray light of dawn, the hill was quiet. In wellies and an old green Barbour jacket, Lady Nairn led the way. The rest of us straggled behind her in a long line. Laughter rippled up the hillside. It was hard to reconcile this slope, quietly drowsing, with the menacing creature that had loomed over us in the night, much less the mist-shrouded nightmare I'd traversed yesterday afternoon.

The Fort of the Nipple. The Stronghold of the Goddess.

The only goddess around this morning was Sybilla, who looked as if she'd just walked off a Ralph Lauren shoot, with high caramel-colored boots, khaki trousers, and a short tweed jacket that fit so well it appeared to have grown on her. She'd pulled her thick curls back into a ponytail.

Why couldn't it have been her, I thought

savagely, *whom I saw dead on the hill, instead of Lily?*

I strode forward to catch up with Lady Nairn. "I had a talk with Lily last night," I said, panting a little. She'd meant it when she'd said the walk would be brisk. "After everyone went to bed."

"Oh?"

"I hadn't realized she was Wiccan."

"Wiccan, my foot," said Lady Nairn, stabbing the hill with an ivory-handled walking stick. "She's read a few books. Lit some candles. Had that ridiculous tattoo incised into her wrist." She looked sideways at me. "If she'd done that on my watch, it would've cost her a month of Sundays in grounding, but that was when her parents were still alive. Did she show you the book?"

"If you mean *Ancient Pictland,* yes."

She snorted. "Wretched woman. Here Lily is, having barely outgrown Harry Potter, reaching for something else in the weeks after her mum and dad died. Lights upon Corra Ravensbrook." She said the name as if it were poison in her mouth. "Next thing I know it's Corra this and Corra that. Equally fictional as Potter, you know, but a lot less amusing. And pretending to be *history.*"

We'd reached the base of the final summit, and she stopped to rest, letting the remainder of the company catch up a bit. "She has glamour, though. I'll give her that. In her prose, at any rate. No idea what she looks like."

She gave me another sideways glance. "*All was delusion, nought was truth.* One might be able to forgive it as a dram of piss-poor scholarship and a whole damned cask of wishful thinking, except that it's not — *she's* not delusional. It's deliberate. She's making money, hand over fist as I understand it, off people who are . . . are reaching out for something. And more than the money, I suspect, she's feeding on their admiration. Which makes her, in some ways, frankly vampiric. I'm not coming from the same place as Effie, you understand. I'm not equating what Ravensbrook does — or Wicca proper, for that matter — with demonic evil. I'm speaking about misleading vulnerable people, many of them still half-children. A much more mundane, infuriating, and hard-to-pinpoint evil. You can't exorcise it. You can't prosecute it. You can just hope the child comes to her senses."

We crested the summit and stood watching the straggling line of people below. Beyond, the sun slowly crept across the valley. "It's not that people shouldn't yearn for something more. Especially young people who are hurting, like Lily. It's that Ms. Ravensbrook offers easy, pat answers. Recipes, really." She turned and wiggled her fingers, her voice taking on the witchy tones of a Disney fortune-teller. "Take a pinch of dragon's blood, add a little nakedness under the full moon or the dark of the moon, and throw in nine knots in a red thread, and *poof,* you will tap your true power. And find wealth and happiness, too." She sniffed. "It doesn't work like that. No religion works like that." She stopped again, hands on her hips, the walking stick jutting out at an awkward angle. "If you want the truth, I suspect Ms. Ravensbrook isn't much of a Wiccan herself. Probably a bored housewife."

She took a deep breath and forced a smile on her face. "Apologies for the rant. You hit a sore spot, as you might have guessed by now." The others were catching up, filing into the bowl of the summit in ones and twos.

"You said she feeds on her readers' admiration," I said. "How?"

Lady Nairn groaned. "She has a Web site, with an e-mail address. You can write to her. So Lily did. Or does, I should probably say."

"They have a regular correspondence?"

"God, no. Or I *would* be ballistic. But I know Lily's written to her more than once. And that she's responded. Wouldn't surprise me, you know, if Lily's antics on the lawn last night were Corra-directed."

"Why?"

She looked out over the valley below. "I've read a little about Wicca myself. And what Lily was doing, it was sloppy. Maybe that's just a teenager improvising. On the other hand, Lily also improvises her clothing. That should give you a good indication of her style in general."

"Sloppy" was not a word that went with her fashion statement. "Romantic," one might say. But not "sloppy."

Lady Nairn pointed northwest across the valley. "Birnam Wood. Right about there."

What had drawn Sir Angus there?

Behind me, I heard shouts of laughter. Ben and Sybilla were playing some private game of tag. Bright-eyed and golden, Sybilla was running, I realized with sudden misgiving, straight toward the pit where yesterday I'd seen Lily lying dead. Or thought I had.

Glancing back like some eager Daphne luring on her Apollo, she did not see the hole opening just in front of her. Ben shouted, and she caught herself right at the edge. She looked down, and her mouth opened wide in surprise, and then horror; a cry caught in her throat. A swarm of flies rose around her like dark thoughts, and Sybilla took one step back and simply wilted.

Ben, already running, reached her first, catching her mid-faint. *"Jesus God,"* said Eircheard. Behind him, a scream rose in waves of panic.

I knew before I got there what they were seeing. A naked young woman, strangely bound, with her throat cut. Surely the body by now beginning to decay. Steeling myself, I walked forward and looked down into the trench.

But there was no body, naked or clothed. There was only blood, curdling from red to brown, filling the trench like a shallow bath. Next to me, Lady Nairn's face was taut with revulsion. *"Blood will have blood,"* she murmured.

INTERLUDE

April 30, 1585
Dirleton Castle, Scotland

The countess had the English lord shown up to her in her private aerie in the old lord's hall, a circular room beneath a vaulted dome high in one of the oldest towers of the castle. The servants were terrified of the place, thinking it haunted, and she'd made no effort to combat that fear, finding it useful. She was content, up here, to be served by her old nurse and one faithful manservant, both of whom would die for her.

Lord Henry Howard was dark of complexion and stealthy in demeanor, a battle between disdain and hope permanently etched in his face. On one finger he flaunted a signet she recognized: a phoenix. The emblem of Mary of Guise, the mother of Mary, Queen of Scots.

It was both unmistakable and deniable, and she admired its combination of cleverness and discretion.

For it was unsafe, most decidedly unsafe, to carry a token pointing to Queen Mary, the king's mother, who'd been forced to abdicate the throne of Scotland in his favor when he was thirteen months old. Eighteen years ago, that had been, or nearly so. Long imprisoned in England and persona non grata in Scotland, the queen remained a focus of rebellion in both kingdoms at once.

"A true king of Scotland would not balk at delivering real support to the rightful queen of England," said Lord Henry. Setting down his wine, he rose to go. "The throne, of course, must belong only to Stewarts, and of royal blood." He cleared his throat. "Such a king, the queen would back." He looked at the countess with mocking eyes, but hers could be as cold as his were.

He had left soon after, and she'd watched him go with a coolness that belied the froth boiling in her blood. *Stewarts of royal blood:* It described both herself and her husband, another Jamie Stewart, older and braver than the pigeon-hearted boy who occupied the throne. And yet a man whom she had, more or less, under her thumb.

The message, of course, had been from Queen Mary. *Support me, and I will support you.* Or at least, *I will not contest you, if you can win and hold the crown.* The countess had little sympathy for the queen languishing in comfortable imprisonment in a remote English castle. The woman had just signed her son's death warrant, so badly did she want a crown — and not the Scottish one, which she had always thought beneath her.

It was less the queen's ruthlessness than her incompetence, however, that irritated the countess. For it was the countess's misfortune to have been born with the capacity to rule that Mary lacked but a lineage that gave her no real road to power: Her Stewart blood, though royal, was bastard, and through the female line. Even so, in her youth in her father's Highland strongholds, she had listened more than once as old powers of darkness decreed that one day she would be a queen. She had exulted at the thought, even at the age of ten or twelve, and she had been doing her best to help fate along ever since.

Now she went to a chest and pulled from its velvet wrapping a dark mirror. This she fixed to the end of a long leather strap hanging down from the apex of the dome, allowing it to twirl a little, this way and that, over the center of her worktable.

She had taken the mirror, long ago, in payment from the English wizard Dr. Dee. unknown to her parents, who thought she was frequenting warehouses full of the world's silks and jewels, feathers and spices, she'd spent that cold February in Antwerp working her fingers to the bone, helping Dr. Dee copy a rare manuscript of angelic magic. But when she had finished, he'd refused to pay the price they'd agreed upon: knowledge. She'd wanted teaching: to learn the Great Art. What he offered, in the end, was a purse of silver. As if she were a whore. She, an earl's daughter.

She'd burned the pages she'd copied one by one till he was on his knees and weeping. And then she'd tossed the rest into the air above the hearth. As he hurried to pick them up, she'd taken the mirror and left.

She did not know what it was made of, or who had made it. It seemed a work of magic in itself. But she'd taught herself to scry in it. Quite a feat, as Dr. Dee had told her it was known to show fire and blood to those who could not wrest it to their will.

At a nod, the old nurse banked down the fire, moved one chair near to the table, and left. Palms down on the table, the countess sat still before the dangling mirror, gazing obliquely at its surface, barely brushed by firelight and moonlight, letting her mind touch upon Lord Henry and then drift. Letting the question form and shift like clouds: *Is he the one? Is he the man who will make me, at long last, a queen?*

Clouds misted the surface of the mirror though she knew there were none, or few, in the sky. And then they dissolved and she saw, quite clearly, a face with dark half-moon brows and a high forehead. A pointed chin. Delicate features and pale skin. What made this face arresting was a luminous, yet precise, quality of eye.

A young man, barely more than a boy. The king's age, or thereabouts. Perhaps a year or two older. He was not a face in her mind, she realized suddenly. He was a reflection of flesh and blood, caught in the mirror.

She turned, and he froze, caught stepping from the space between tapestry and wall. He'd thought her sleeping, perhaps, or entranced. How long had he been there? How much had he heard and seen? The consequences of treason, which the conversation with Lord Henry most certainly was, were unspeakable. The consequences of witchcraft, which is what the mirror-gazing would be counted, were worse.

If he'd run, she'd have called the guard and had him killed before he could say a word. But he stepped out and bowed with a brash flourish and a flush in his cheeks that was oddly beautiful. One of the English players, she saw.

Young, expendable, and eminently unbelievable in his word against the countess, a favorite of the king.

She summoned him forward with a crook of one finger, and obediently, he came. Diane de Poitiers had been only a year or two younger than she when she'd first seduced her king, twenty years younger than herself. This boy, common though he might be, looked to be the same age, or thereabouts, as James. Hitching the king to her skirts as her lover was not, at present, the likeliest road to consolidating her power, but the countess believed in keeping all roads open. A little practice with a boy would do no harm, and it might cool the sudden burning in her blood.

She ran a finger down his cheek. He trembled under her touch, and not from fear. She untied one lace of his plain doublet, and then another. Saw a sardonic brow half-lift. He would neither fight nor flee, then. But would he rise?

She was down to his fourth lace before his hand closed around her wrist, and he drove her back against the wall, the tapestries billowing out from the force of it as young, strong hands slid up around her.

He pulled her back to the table, clearing it with one arm, lowering her on her back before him. Even now, in the twilight of her beauty, she knew she was resplendent, showed to best advantage in low firelight and candle flame. She let him watch, savoring for a moment the appreciation in his eyes, and then, beneath the dark mirror now swaying above them like a pendulum, she pulled him into her.

She saw, once, much later, their reflection in the mirror. A beast with two backs. She said as much, under her breath, and he looked up and laughed. And then they rolled to the floor.

She lost count, after a time, of the rising carillons of pleasure that beat through her blood at the insistence of fingers and lips, eyelashes and tongue. He was a master of tension and release. He was not, as she'd thought, inexperienced at love.

As the first traces of dawn lightened the horizon, even he lay sated and spent. Standing at the window, she could see the Beltane fires kindling in the distance on the low rises that passed for hills in this flat land bordering the sea. The preachers could thunder all they liked, but even when the farmers listened to them quaking in fear, when it came to the fertility and well-being of their land, their crops, and their herds, they feared to break with tradition more. No matter how pious they might be at other times, on two nights of the year, Samhuinn and Beltane, they kept stubbornly to the old ways. Older, in fact, than all but a very few could possibly imagine.

There was a knock at the door. She nudged the boy with her foot, and he grunted and pulled himself behind a tapestry. A messenger stood just outside, the sheen of sweat from a hard ride still glistening on his face. "My lady," he said with a quick bow. "The king comes here tonight."

She caught the tip of her tongue between her teeth in her excitement. "Madness," she said under her breath. "You're mad to say it."

"The plague has broken out in Edinburgh; His Majesty rides hence with His Lordship, your husband."

As she dismissed the man, a wild surge of elation coursed through her. By nightfall, the king would ride under her battlements, but if she had her way, he would not ride out again. At least, not this king.

The king is dead, long live the king.

She hardly noticed as the player picked

up his doublet and, with a sly smile, bowed
and left.

■ ■ ■ ■

WOOD

■ ■ ■ ■

Who can impress the forest, bid the tree
Unfix his earth-bound root?

13

Yesterday there hadn't been enough blood; today its thick, metallic scent was suffocating. No one could survive the loss of that much of it. Whoever I'd seen the evening before, she was dead now. But where was she? And who?

Whoever she was, I'd left her alone, dead or dying, on the hill as dusk fell. And now she was gone.

I glanced from the blood-spattered trench back to Sybilla lying on the bank. On the grass, for a moment, she lay like the body I'd seen the day before. But she was dressed, her arms and legs unbound, her neck intact, and her chest rising and falling. She was coming to, Ben right beside her. I felt a twinge of regret. *Why couldn't it have been Sybilla?* I'd thought, as we started up the hill: something one shouldn't wish on anyone, even in passing, even in a private moment of sarcasm.

"We need to find Effie," Ben said quietly.

I did a double take. I'd been thinking of the unknown woman seen at the edge of a dream, but Effie was also missing.

Her voice shrilled through my memory: *Thou shalt not suffer a witch to live.* I'd assumed — I think we all assumed — that her words were aimed at Lily. Maybe so. But suddenly they seemed a double-edged sword. Effie, after all, had been set to *play* a witch.

Next to me, Lady Nairn said, "Oh, dear God." She tried Effie's cell, but it went straight to voice mail. Her next call was to the police.

My eyes drifted back down the trench. On the far side, a bit of paper fluttered in the grass. Stepping around, I bent down to look at it.

It was a playing card. No — too long and thin. A tarot card. One of the major arcana, or face cards, showing a young man in jaunty yellow-and-red trousers, hanging upside down by one foot from a tree, his free leg crooked at the knee, foot tucked up against the opposite leg, so that his body made the shape of an upside-down four. The Hanged Man.

"Symbol of sacrifice and prophetic wisdom," said Eircheard over my shoulder.

The figure on the card looked more like a boy than a man — a jester even, with particolored trousers of red and yellow, his face oddly serene. In his hand he held a knife with an angled back and runes on the blade.

"Look at the knife," I said.

"Aye," said Eircheard, gently taking the card from me. "But it's not just the blade that's overfamiliar. It's the tree as well." It was an ancient spreading oak, its scalloped leaves minutely detailed. Crutches held up its massive lower limbs, giving it a distinctive silhouette. "It's the Birnam Oak," he said.

Dunsinnan must go to Birnam Wood.

I looked up sharply. "Is that part of Birnam Wood?"

"Part?" scoffed Eircheard. "It's all that's left. That and two sycamores. But they're bairns — children — by comparison. The oak, now, he was already mature in Shakespeare's day. There's an outside chance he was a sapling when Malcolm's men were stripping branches for their march on Macbeth."

Lady Nairn had finished her phone call and was stepping around toward us, a look of annoyance on her face. "We're not to touch —" She stopped in her tracks, her face going white. "The card," she said, her

181

voice rasping. "It's Lily's."

You'll like my deck, she'd said to me. *It's a* Macbeth *deck.*

"There's writing on the back," said Ben from the other side of the trench. I turned it over. The design on the back was a tangle of Celtic knots. Across it, someone had scrawled a phrase in red ink: *Blood will have blood.*

Lady Nairn's words, as we'd first seen the blood.

Macbeth's words.

The image of Lily naked and bound beneath the blue gown flashed across my mind. And voices in the darkness: *She must die.* "Where is she?" I asked.

"Still in bed," said Lady Nairn, already calling Lily's cell.

"Did you see her?"

"I —" This call went to voice mail, too. Lady Nairn's eyes grew wide. "No."

I began to walk down the hill. And then I started to run.

14

Lady Nairn had started out with me, but I was younger and faster. At the base of the summit, she tossed me the keys to her car and said, *"Go."*

Back at the house near the top of the stairs, I startled a maid, who pointed out Lily's room. The bed was unmade, the duvet half hanging to the floor. But Lily was not there. For a moment I stood panting on the threshold, and then I turned on my heel and went down the hall to my own room.

Someone had tossed it. The mattress had been pulled off the bed, the bedding left in forlorn heaps on the floor. Pillows had been slit and every drawer pulled out and turned over.

The drawer where I'd hidden the knife was at the top of the heap. The pillow I'd put over it was still there, and the towel in which I'd wrapped it, but the knife was gone.

Had there been enough time, after I'd left for breakfast, for someone to take it and get up the hill before us? And use it?

Just barely.

Whether or not it had been mine, some knife had certainly been used up there. *She must die, she must. . . . A most unspotted lily shall she pass to the ground, and all the world shall mourn her.*

Where the hell was Lily?

The Hanged Man of her tarot deck had pictured not only the knife, but the oak that was, according to Eircheard, all that was left of Birnam Wood. *Dunsinnan must go to Birnam Wood,* Sir Angus had said.

I turned on my heel and went back downstairs. Just as I was climbing back into Lady Nairn's Range Rover, she and Ben pulled up in his car. "I can't find Lily, and the knife's gone," I said as the passenger window zipped down. In the car, her eyes met Ben's.

"Have you searched the whole house?" she asked.

"No. But I'm going to that goddamned wood."

"I'm staying here," she said. "You two go."

"Do you know the way?" Ben asked.

I shook my head no.

"Then let me drive," he said. "It'll be faster."

I got back out of Lady Nairn's car and slipped into Ben's. "Why aren't you with Sybilla?"

"She had a shock and she fainted," he said shortly. "But she's safe."

"Which is more than can be said for Lily," I said, buckling up.

"Or you, Kate."

I glanced over at him, but he was watching the road, his expression inscrutable as we pulled out of the drive and headed down the lane.

Last night, he'd stopped me from going back up the hill, more or less pointing out that I'd been a fool. "That card was Lily's," I said a little defensively. "And it points straight at Birnam Wood. I mean to follow the trail."

"Yes. But not alone. Is it a trail only, Kate, or also an invitation? Especially since you've already heard what might amount to a death threat, twice."

"If you mean 'She must die,' that's aimed at Lily."

"Maybe," he said with a shrug as I explained the context. "But it was you they spoke to."

I looked out the window, my heart thudding as we sped along in silence between hedgerows lining close-shorn golden fields.

"About the knife," he said after a while. "It's gone from your room, but not exactly gone."

I turned sharply. "That was you? *You* took it?"

"Lady Nairn has it."

"You tossed my room?"

"I didn't exactly toss it, Kate. Didn't have to. It was the first place I looked." His faintly amused calm was infuriating.

"You complete fucking bastard," I burst out.

He looked across at me, startled. "*Has* someone tossed it?"

"Of course somebody's tossed it. Bedding in tatters, every drawer emptied."

"Good thing I got there first, then. Though I am sorry about the room."

That he was right did nothing to lessen my fury. Nor did the fact that he was having a hard time keeping a smile off his face.

"Come on, Kate. It's fair enough to be angry. But not so much with me. . . . Tell me about the tarot card. What do you know about the Hanged Man?"

For Lily's sake, I had to set aside my anger. "Not much," I said tightly. "She had the deck last night, though. Offered to read

186

my cards."

He raised one eyebrow. "How much of a twist have your occult studies taken?"

"I put her off."

"So you don't actually know if that card was still in the deck."

"No." Tarot wasn't something I knew very much about. I phoned Lady Nairn and put her on speaker.

"Lily's not here," she said, her voice tense with worry.

"We'll find her," said Ben.

"The tarot card is hers," she said. "The deck's spread out on her bed, and the Hanged Man is missing." She'd found nothing else missing and no further clue to where Lily had gone, but she could tell us a fair amount about the card's meaning.

"The Hanged Man," she explained, "symbolizes sacrifice and prophecy — not death, as novices often assume. He's a reference to Odin, chief of the Norse gods. A divinity of war and wisdom who wrested secret, possibly forbidden knowledge from the underworld."

"How?" asked Ben.

"By sacrificing himself to himself, hanging nine nights on a tree, pierced with a spear, until he'd sunk deep enough into the realm of death to seize runes and, screaming, pull them up into the world of light."

"Got to love the Norse," said Ben, shaking his head.

The Hanged Man, Lady Nairn went on, always had a serene face. He symbolized the surrender and acceptance that led to clarity of vision, and to wisdom. Unless he was reversed, and then he symbolized passivity, or the tendency to get lost in a labyrinth of idle dreams.

"Where'd Lily get that deck?" I asked.

"From Corra bloody Ravensbrook," she snapped. "Who else? Ordered it off her Web site."

"How did the card come to have the Birnam Oak on it? And the Nairn knife?"

"No idea. All I care about is finding Lily." Her voice cracked as she hung up.

We drove awhile in silence. On either side of us, fields stretched into the distance, stacked with cylindrical bales of hay. Now and then the road shot through thinning archways of russet and yellow trees. Halfway across the plain of Strathmore, we headed west and wound into the foothills of the Highlands.

"Who would do this?" I asked suddenly.

"Do *what*? Do we actually know what's been done?"

I took a deep breath. "Lily's missing, for

one. And yesterday, I saw a body I thought was hers."

"Yes. But it wasn't her. And whoever she was, she wasn't there when we went back, and she isn't there this morning. We don't even know that the blood is human, Kate."

"There's the knife."

"Which was clean yesterday and has been in either your possession or mine or Lady Nairn's ever since."

"And there were the voices, both on the hill and in the stone circle. Which told me, more or less, in the circle, to put the damned thing back, or else." *Or else she must die.*

"Auld Callie told you that straight out, didn't she?"

We looked at each other. She was supposed to have met us up on the hill that morning.

"Did you see her?" asked Ben.

"No."

That made three missing people. What was going on?

"There's also Sybilla's card," said Ben.

The Hal Berridge card. I sighed. "At the very least, someone's doing a damned fine job of trying to sabotage Lady Nairn's production. Is that why you're here?"

"She's spoken to me. She has some legitimate concerns."

"Do they have names?"

"A Reverend Calvin Gosson. On the far, fire-and-brimstone fringe of the Kirk. The Church of Scotland. Currently filling in as minister at the Cathedral of Dunkeld, while the regular man recovers from heart surgery. I'm told that he believes we're all engaged in a great battle between good and evil, only most people can't or won't see the battlefield any longer. Which, in his view, means the odds have tipped in favor of the forces of darkness."

"Would he have any connection to Effie Summers?"

"Yes. He's said to favor the quotation *Thou shalt not suffer a witch to live* in his sermons, for one."

"Charming. Is there a 'two'?"

Ben looked sideways at me. "Gosson found his calling late, it seems. He used to be an actor. He was in Lady Nairn's famous *Macbeth.* Played Fleance."

"The boy who got away." Banquo's son, the young boy who escapes Macbeth's murderers — played in many productions by the witches, or at least by the same actors who played the witches.

"The boy who lived," said Ben with a wry smile. "Like Harry Potter, he's dedicated his life to the war against evil. Unlike Harry, he counts witches among his enemies."

"Even the stage variety?"

"He warned Lady Nairn off the play. Told her it gathered dark powers strongly around itself, especially in the hands of gifted performers."

"A compliment in reverse, I suppose. . . . If Effie's under his spell — so to speak — why would she take the role of a witch?"

"Dunno. Maybe she's only recently been swayed by him. Maybe she's a mole."

"A spy? Are you serious?"

He smiled. "Admittedly not a very good one."

"Did Lady Nairn mention anyone else?" I asked.

"One other. Lucas Porter."

"The film director?"

He nodded.

Lucas Porter was a Hollywood legend — all the more mythic for his reclusiveness. He'd been a great film director, auteur of a dozen or so classic films from the fifties and sixties. Cult films, most of them. Four or five of them, including two starring Janet Douglas, perennially showed up fairly high in lists of the greatest films of all time.

Janet Douglas — Lady Nairn — had left the stage for Sir Angus. She'd also left Lucas Porter.

"Her next project," said Ben, "would have been a film version of *Macbeth,* directed by Porter. He was furious, apparently. Told her she'd ruined the picture he'd meant to make his magnum opus, the crowning achievement of his career."

"Jesus. There must have been any number of actresses who would've killed for that part," I said.

"That's what she told him, but he wouldn't make the picture with anyone else. He told her that he'd ruin — personally — any production of *Macbeth* that she got anywhere near."

"But that was over forty years ago."

"That's what I said. She said, 'You don't know Lucas.' She and Sir Angus apparently kept watch on him from a distance."

"He scared her that much?"

"Mmm. Two years ago, she says, he faded from view. Not that he was ever flash. More like a recluse. But he just quietly disappeared. They waited for a year and a half —"

"And then they figured it was safe to mount their show?"

He nodded. "And then Sir Angus died. And you know the rest."

Coming through some trees, we turned down through the tiny, ancient town of

Dunkeld, which clung to the River Tay as it tumbled out of the hills. Far away, at the bottom of the steep main street, I glimpsed a graceful bridge of stone arches curving over the river, deep blue and swift, rushing its way toward the sea. On the far side lay the village of Birnam and the wood from which it took its name. From Eircheard's description, I'd thought there were only the oak and two sycamores left. But the riverbank was thick with trees, their canopy orange and red, yellow and russet, all the colors of fire.

At the bottom of the road, just before the bridge, the light turned yellow. Walking toward it, two people broke into a run, crossing just as the light turned red. One was a tall man with black hair; he was pulling along with him a girl with long flame-red hair that seemed to float about her of its own accord.

I leaned forward, pointing. "That looks like Lily."

We drew to a stop several cars back from the light, which seemed interminable. As long as Lily and her companion were on the bridge, we could at least keep tabs on them from a distance. Once they reached the other side, they could scatter in any direction. They neared the other side, and the light still showed no signs of changing. Ben jerked the car out of the line. One wheel up on the sidewalk, we careened around the cars in front, shooting through the morning traffic on the cross street and onto the bridge. At the far end, the man pulled Lily into a run, disappearing into the woods on the left.

We skidded to a stop just past the foot of the bridge and leapt out of the car, following in their wake. The bank here was still far below; steep steps led downward from the road into dimness. "Lily!" I called, but got no answer. With a glance at Ben, I chased after her.

The chill of dawn still lingered beneath the eaves of the wood, though the sun was well up in the world beyond. Deeply carpeted in coppery leaves and roofed by the arching trees, the path was a long tunnel lit by a scattershot sun. No one was on it. "Lily!" I called again as I ran, glimpsing flashes of the river through laced branches. Save for our footfalls and breathing, and the rush of the water, however, the wood was silent and seemingly empty.

Stirred by our passing, leaves swirled up in eddies that looked, from the corner of the eye, like small animals herding us onward. Rounding a bend, we came to an enormous tree, green with moss, its trunk gnarled into the silhouette of a giant's bulbous face staring sadly at the ground. "The sycamores," said Ben as we passed another, equally immense.

Beyond that, I looked up to see the ancient oak, unmistakable in its majesty. There was no sign of Lily, or of anyone else. I bent down panting, hands on my knees, gazing at the tree, an aged emperor asleep in the watery morning sun, crutches propping up low branches thicker than most of the other trees in the wood. "It" was not a pronoun that came to mind. He was recognizably the same tree as the one pictured on Lily's tarot card. Around him, the air was golden and heavy and silent, thick not only with a strange heavy sleepiness, but with something old and anguished, even angry, despite the sweet haze of autumn.

Three trees left, from the primordial forest that had once covered much of central Scotland. Three trees, set apart from their fellows by something more than sheer size. *Like creatures from an elder world,* I thought, and caught my breath as I recognized the phrase. It came from Holinshed, Shakespeare's source for *Macbeth,* talking about the weird sisters.

There had been three of them, too.

"You really think it was her?" asked Ben.

I nodded.

"Who was the bloke?"

"Don't know."

Where could they have gone?

As Ben scanned the ground for tracks, I gazed at the tree. What about this tree — or this place — had drawn Sir Angus?

Wind stirred its branches, which creaked and groaned. I slid down the bank and put a hand on the tree, trailing around it; its trunk must have been at least ten feet in diameter. A hollow gaped in the far side, opening into a room I could stand up in. It smelled of damp and decay.

As I ducked out, I felt a drop on my hand and looked down. It wasn't rain; it was red. A splatter of blood.

Backing from the tree, I looked up and my voice caught in my throat. Glancing over, Ben slid quickly down toward me. All I could do was point. Twenty feet overhead, just where the trunk began to branch and entirely invisible from the path, a body was hanging, swaying a little in the wind, which made the branch creak.

It was an old woman with wild gray hair. Auld Callie.

Someone had clearly looked at a tarot deck before arranging her. Auld Callie's hands were tied behind her back, and her left foot had been tied up behind her right knee, making the shape of a 4. But she was not the Hanged Man, upside down, with a mask of serenity on her face. She hung by her neck. Her abdomen had been slashed through her dress, dripping blood in slow, heavy drops, and her face looked as if she had died cursing all the demons of hell. She was Odin, pierced with a sword and screaming.

"Call the police," said Ben, brushing past me and hoisting himself into the tree. He reached her in what seemed like no more than three moves. Holding himself to the tree with one arm, he felt for a pulse. But from the crook of her neck, it was pointless. She was dead.

15

I called the police and told them about Auld Callie and her link to the mess on Dunsinnan Hill as well. We were told in no uncertain terms to stay right where we were.

And not to cut the body down.

Which was just as well, as we had no knife that would cut that rope.

The knife from the hill would do it, I thought suddenly. But it was in Lady Nairn's safekeeping.

The day before, Auld Callie had pulled me from the hill as I'd run down the path with the knife in my hands, and seconds later the dark-haired man had cantered by. She'd quite possibly saved my life. And now she was dead.

No one, surely, would kill Auld Callie just to torment Lady Nairn. That seemed to rule Lucas Porter out, at any rate. What about the Reverend Mr. Gosson?

Thou shalt not suffer a witch to live.

"There's a paper here," said Ben quietly. "Clipped to her dress." He pulled it loose. It was a single sheet, folded loosely in quarters. He let it go, and it floated slowly downward, eddying and bouncing a little in the air like an oversized butterfly, landing gently in the dying bracken at my feet.

I stared at it warily. There was a smear of blood across it, already dried to brown. Beneath that, someone had written my name. *Kate Stanley.*

I bent and picked it up, my fingers shaking a little. It was a single sheet of thick buff-colored paper. My name was written on the otherwise blank reverse. Inside the folds, the front was thick with ink. The top third was covered with tiny writing in old ink faded to brown. The bottom was blank — or had been, until someone had filled it with a drawing in pen, deep black ink, and wash: A fierce-looking Shakespeare in doublet and hose reached in a fencing lunge toward a kilted Scottish King. Both figures wielded leafy branches instead of swords.

Beneath the picture, in the same ink as the drawing, someone had scrawled a line from *Macbeth:*

Who can impress the Forrest, bid the Tree unfix his earth-bound root?

The impish curves of the drawing and the proud folly of the expressions were one-of-a-kind. I was staring at a Max Beerbohm caricature, an original by the looks of it, probably penned sometime during the nineteenth century's fitfully wanton fin de siècle. For all that, it was the cramped writing above the caricature that riveted me.

"What is it?" Ben asked quietly.

"A page from a diary, I think."

"Can you read it?" asked Ben.

"Not easily." The hand was seventeenth-century, at a guess, and the messy scrawl of a voluminous writer on top of that: someone who wrote too much and too fast to bother with neatness. A magpie who recorded everything as he heard it, without any attempt at organization or culling.

At the top of the page a single legible line stood out:

I once heard Sir William Davenant say that the Youth who was to have first taken the parte of Lady Macbeth fell sudden sicke of a Pleurisie and died, wherefor Master Shakspeare himself did enacte in his steade.

I was staring at a page from the notes of the prattling seventeenth-century antiquarian John Aubrey. A page that scholars had never found, but Max Beerbohm had. A page that said the origin of the play's curse was not a hoax after all.

A page on which someone had written my name. Who? And why?

I glanced up at Auld Callie, thinking of Odin hanging for nine nights from his tree. Not for love or release from death, like Christ, though he was sometimes compared to Christ. For knowledge. All for the sake of knowledge, in the shape of runes. I looked back down at the page trembling in my hands. What had Auld Callie been so brutally made to toss back, screaming, from the underworld?

Ben dropped beside me, and I became aware of a whirl of sirens in the distance and booted feet pounding down the path.

What are you trying to tell me? I asked Auld Callie silently. And then I folded the page and shoved it into the pocket of my jacket. Someone meant for me to see this; I had no intention of handing it over to the police till I'd had a chance to do so.

Ben raised one eyebrow. "I take it we are not mentioning the knife, either."

We, I thought. Was this what it took to bind Ben and me together into the first-person plural? Murder?

Aloud, all I said was "Not yet."

"And Lily?"

"Leave her out of it."

"Do we know she was in it?"

He wasn't really looking for an answer, and I didn't give him one.

16

The wood was quickly teeming with police. Forensic officers in white suits and blue gloves tented off the tree as best they could, while uniformed officers cordoned off the path for a long way in both directions. Plain-clothes detectives from CID, or the Criminal Investigations Department, weren't far behind. A sergeant took down our names and information.

Detective Inspector Sheena McGregor arrived from Dunsinnan House, marching straight for us with a face of cold contempt. In her late thirties or early forties, she had short brown hair, a wiry build, and brittle eyes; she smelled of cigarettes and coffee. She already knew who we were, and her questions were blistering. Why hadn't we waited, as asked, atop Dunsinnan Hill, and what in God's name did we think we'd been doing tramping into a crime scene at the Birnam tree?

"We didn't know it *was* a crime scene, Detective Inspector," said Ben, all solemn contrition.

"What sort of fool do you take me for, Mr. Pearl?" she said coldly. "You took one look at the slaughterhouse arrangement on top of that hill and drove straight here. Why?" She looked from him to me.

She must have seen the tarot card. She couldn't be asking, "Why Birnam Wood?" She's asking, "Why you? Why come?" I felt my chin going up. "We thought we were looking at an ugly prank. We didn't expect to find murder."

"A prank," she said, her face tightening in displeasure. "That's a lot of blood for a prank, Ms. Stanley."

"We were up there to read *Macbeth*."

Her eyes narrowed. "A bloody prank for a bloody play, eh?"

"It's said to be cursed. I don't expect you to believe that, but a lot of actors do. Someone had already tweaked the cast's jitters on that subject. I thought this was another . . . tease."

Her foot tapped impatiently on the ground. "Come with me," she said suddenly, striding down the bank.

A forensics squad had shielded much of the tree from the path, but the way the body was placed, there was no way to tent it entirely from view. From the riverbank, Auld Callie was still plainly visible, dangling from a high branch, her crooked knee bumping against the trunk, her grizzled hair lifting, now and again, in the wind. A wide streak of reddish-brown blood spilled down her dress, falling in a long vertical stroke down the trunk of the tree. With camera flashes going off and white-suited crime-scene officers swarming up and down ladders, the scene looked like a surreal film shoot.

"That doesn't look like a prank to me," said DI McGregor. "That looks like ritual murder."

What's a ritual knife for *but ritual?* Lily had asked the night before. Only, the ritual knife had not been anywhere near Callie; it had been under my pillow, or safe in Ben's and then Lady Nairn's possession.

Lily, on the other hand, was another story. Was it her I'd seen scurrying into this wood? What was she doing here, and where had she gone?

McGregor was looking at me with a strange mix of distaste and grim triumph. Ritual murder was probably what she lived for. Solve this case quickly, and she'd move up from detective inspector to detective chief inspector in a blink.

One of the white-suited forensics officers approached, pulling McGregor aside for a moment. They were ready to remove the body. Turning back to us, she motioned over one of her underlings. "I'll have more questions for you presently, but in the meantime you will wait, please, with my sergeant. But I should like to have one thing straight, first. I've heard a bit about you. Both of you." She took a step toward me. "If you know anything — anything at all — about what happened up on that hill or in this wood and are withholding it, you will do time for it. I will see to it personally. Is that clear, Ms. Stanley?"

The page from Aubrey's diary seemed to tingle and flare in my pocket, the letters of my name scrawling across the page in lines of fire.

"Yes, ma'am," I said.

There wasn't much we could tell them about Auld Callie's death beyond the time when we'd found her and the eerie emptiness of the wood when we had. Other witnesses told of a man and a woman ducking into the trees before us; there was no point in denying that. The police didn't find any more trace of them than we had, however.

About Lily, both Ben and I remained mute. If McGregor and company wanted to draw the same inference that I had based on reports of a redheaded woman, there was nothing I could do about it. Meanwhile I saw no need to point them in her direction. Not yet.

She was fifteen years old. Whatever she was up to, it couldn't be murder, I told myself. It was one thing to relish the beauty and power of ancient pagan ritual. It was quite another to participate in a ritualized kill.

Was it a sacrifice? Who had clipped the page from Aubrey's diary to her dress and marked it "Kate Stanley"? The urge to look at it was so strong that at times I had to find something else to do with my hands, to keep them from drawing it out of my pocket of their own accord.

DI McGregor had no intention of letting us go easily or soon, however. The sun rose in the sky and curved toward the west again before she would release us. Only the obvious fact that Auld Callie had been dead a few hours before we arrived stalled her from arresting us both for the murder, I thought glumly. Even then, we were sent home like naughty schoolchildren. She'd declared the entire verge at the end of the bridge, including Ben's car, part of the crime scene. It was a stretch, but not one Ben was willing to contest. "Let her look," he said quietly to me. "There's nothing for her to find, and it won't do us any harm to cooperate." We were driven back to Dunsinnan House in the back of a police car.

It was a quiet ride.

17

Late slanted light had fired the battlements of Dunsinnan House to gold by the time we arrived. We were ushered into the hall, where the police, under the orders of DI McGregor, were still working their way through what seemed like interminably thorough statements from everyone in the company. Apparently, the statements Ben and I had given at Birnam Wood were not going to excuse us being last in line at Dunsinnan. Two crime scenes, McGregor said briskly. Two statements. We were asked, politely but firmly, to remain in the hall until we'd been seen to.

Lady Nairn had fresh tea brought in, serving it herself from a pot of Georgian silver. "I thought I saw Lily earlier," I said quietly. "Going into the wood. I don't know what she's up to, but she's not safe."

For an instant, her hand stilled. Then she nodded. "Point taken," she said, leaving me with a rich, steaming cup of tea.

She'd canceled the trip into Edinburgh to see the Samhuinn Fire Festival. Sybilla, Jason, and Eircheard, as the three leads, were still going, as were one or two others. Most everyone else had given their statement and quietly departed for home; raucous celebration did not have quite the right ring to it in the face of murder.

Jason had driven off before we returned. Sybilla, however, was waiting for Ben. As dusk draped blue shadows across the lawn, she began to get restive. Scudding across the room, she came to a stop before the table where McGregor sat. "I have a *performance,*" she announced.

"And I have a murder," said DI McGregor, glancing up from a clipboard. "In any case, no one is stopping you."

"You are stopping Ben. And he is driving me."

"Find someone else."

"He's my bodyguard," said Sybilla.

I almost choked. *Who did she think she was, Whitney Houston?* I glanced over at Ben. A lot of men would have been mortified; he clearly thought the whole scene was funny.

Sybilla never wavered. "There are ten thousand people massing along the Royal

Mile in Edinburgh," she said, her voice low and silky, "waiting to see the Samhuinn Fire Festival. Stopping it in its tracks, I assure you, will guarantee you publicity you do not want."

McGregor was irritating and driven, but she wasn't a fool. Sybilla was playing diva to the hilt, but she was right. Setting her jaw, McGregor sent Ben on his way.

Watching from the doorway, Eircheard hobbled over to me, shaking his head. "Born diva, that one. Would you like me to try something similar for you?"

"Are you in need of a bodyguard?" I asked acidly.

"Ah well, I seem to have mislaid my vulnerable side. But I'm sure I could find it, would it come in handy."

"Thanks," I said with a smile. "But I'm running on about three hours' sleep as it is. I think I'll stay here and collapse." *Kate Stanley,* whispered the paper in my pocket. All I wanted was to be alone so I could figure out what this page meant. It would never happen in a crowd of ten thousand.

Eircheard laughed. "Sweet dreams, lass."

McGregor motioned me over, and we went through a set of questions remarkably similar to those I'd already answered. Finally, I was free.

I fairly ran up the stairs toward my room. Would anyone have put it back together again? So long as there was a single working lamp, I didn't much care.

As I came up to the top landing, I heard a wail through the corridor and stopped. "Bollocks!" burst out Lily. "Jason, Sybilla, and Eircheard are going. Why can't I?"

So she was back. Relief eased through me as I heard Lady Nairn's voice reply. "For starters, Jason, Sybilla, and Eircheard have the lead roles. The festival won't go on without them. Like it or not, the same can't be said for a torchbearer. Furthermore, none of them grew up with Auld Callie in and out of their homes. She was murdered this morning, Lily. You will pay your respects."

"Eircheard knew her. Better than me."

"Eircheard is not my granddaughter."

"Auld Callie, of anyone, would *want* me to go."

"I'm sorry, Lily," Lady Nairn said firmly.

"No, you're not. You're a . . . you're a . . ."

"Secret, black, and midnight hag?" prompted Lady Nairn with a sigh.

I heard a quick intake of breath. "That's a quote."

"The taboo is in effect for the hall, darling. Extending it to the entire house does seem

212

a bit excessive."

I stifled a chuckle, but Lily clearly didn't see the humor in the situation. "You are trying to live up to your part in that bloody play, aren't you?" she cried. Footsteps ran down the hall, and a door slammed.

Lady Nairn appeared around the corner.

"Is it safe?" I asked.

"So long as you avoid the dragon's lair," she said with a rueful smile. "Third door on the left, that would be." For the first time since I'd met her, she looked her age.

I hesitated. On the one hand, I really just wanted to read the page in my pocket. On the other, I needed to know who had directed it to me, and for that, I needed Lady Nairn's help. She was gliding past me, heading down the stairs, when I heard myself call her back.

"Today on the hill, you said *Blood will have blood.*"

Two steps below me, she turned.

"You asked me to help you. But I can't unless you tell me what's going on. Where has Lily been, for instance?"

"You think I know?"

"You know more than you're telling."

She said nothing, but her hand tightened on the bannister.

"Lady Nairn, Lily's been threatened three

times in two days."

"*Three* times? You've heard another?"

"Effie."

"Thou shalt not suffer a witch?" She shook her head. "Effie's harmless. She's got nothing to do with this."

"Lady Nairn, there is a long, bloody history of Christians killing witches."

"You think I don't know that?"

"Like it or not, Effie has fallen in with a radically conservative arm of the church."

She looked down. With a deep breath she looked back up. "What I am going to tell you is private. Not for other ears. Not even Lily's. *Especially* not Lily's."

I nodded. Coming back up the stairs, she led me to the little sitting room off the landing. It was empty; even so, she beckoned me to some chairs in a far corner, settling into one of them with a sigh.

"Forty-odd years ago now, when I left theater and film to marry Angus . . . it wasn't just my career I left behind. I also left a man."

"Lucas Porter."

She raised an eyebrow.

"Ben told me a little," I said.

She clasped her hands together in her lap. "I felt I had to tell him about my decision in person. We'd been lovers for three years;

I would not send him a 'Dear John' letter, or the Hollywood form of it, a call from my agent. So I flew to New York and told him myself. Lucas was furious. I've never seen anyone that angry before or since. As I left, he made — well, he called it a promise, but it was a threat. Any production of *Macbeth* that I got anywhere near, he said, he would ruin.

"For many years, I didn't mind. I was in love; I was raising a child and building myself another life in which playing a blood-soaked queen did not figure into my priorities. But in the last few . . . well, Angus and I had collected some remarkable pieces, and one night we had the notion that it would be interesting to see them in use, you know. Not just displayed like so many butterflies on a placard.

"But the specter of Lucas was worrisome. Through the years, you know, there'd been times when Angus was very near purchasing something for the collection, either at auction or through a private deal, and suddenly, the object would be bought out from under us at an outrageous price. We never knew who it was . . . or even that it was one person — these things happen, at times, in the life of a collector. But we both found it odd, and we both suspected Lucas."

She cocked her head. "I like to think that neither one of us is — was — particularly cowardly, but we shelved the idea because of him. And then, two years ago, I read a small article in the paper. Lucas Porter had disappeared. He'd gone sailing one day in waters north of Boston and never came back. I'm sorry to say it, but I read that article with hope. We waited a year, Angus and I, to see whether he'd reappear. Walk into some police office and tell a strange story of dodging taxes or fighting sharks, or something. But a year went by, and he was still missing.

"Neither of us was getting any younger. So we decided to put together the show. But then Angus died, the Hal Berridge card showed up, and the blood on the hill . . . and now Auld Callie. My God, Kate, I've known Auld Callie since I married Angus. How could anyone do that to her?"

The fire crackled, and I watched her face slowly line with tears.

"Blood will have blood," she said, brushing the damp from her face. "It was a phrase Lucas used that day in New York. He referred to what I was doing to his picture as an abortion, in rather graphic terms. As a stillbirth. Murder. I'd killed his picture and his career."

"You really believe he's capable of this? The card, the blood, Auld Callie?"

She rose and crossed to the fireplace, staring into the glowing embers. "Just before I left him to start rehearsals for *Macbeth* in London, we'd been talking about children. He wanted them right away; I wasn't ready. One day I was looking through some things at his studio, and I found a picture I hadn't seen. One of those Victorian photos of dead children dressed in their Christening robes, laid out in their cribs, just before burial. At least, that's what I thought it was at first. But then I realized it wasn't Victorian, it was one of his own staged photographs. He used to like to do that, you know. Mimic photographs or paintings from other periods. He might have had a stellar career as a forger, except that he always marked his work. He'd put in some little detail, buried in the background, that pinpointed the year he'd made it. In this case, it was a bolo tie slung over a mirror in the background. The clasp of the tie was a political button that read *Let's back Jack.* With a stylized line portrait, almost a cartoon, of JFK's face."

"So when you found it, the photograph was recent?" I asked.

"The button was from the 1960 presidential election. This would have been 1964. . . .

The thing was, he'd also made a film. It documented the child's death from what looked like fever. It showed the mother rocking him, holding him through chills and then a seizure, and then stillness."

"So he staged a child's death?"

She sniffed. "There was a copy of a death certificate pasted to the back of the photo."

I stared at her for a moment. "You mean the child actually died?"

Her voice was almost a monotone. "I mean, Kate, it was a snuff film." Her eyes met mine. "I have no proof, of course. But I knew it then, and I know it now. He arranged that child's death as a work of art, and he filmed it happening."

I could hear the blood pulsing in my neck.

"So you see, after he threatened me, I avoided *Macbeth* for forty years," she said. "He's capable of anything."

18

"Have you told this story to the police?"

"Yes. They did not seem overly impressed with the notion of forty-year-old vengeance on the part of a missing and possibly dead ex-lover. Even so, you should leave Lucas to the police, Kate. Just find the manuscript. Because if it is him, he'll be after it, too."

I nearly showed her the Aubrey; perhaps I should have. But it had my name on it, not hers, and I wanted to think about it in private first, uncluttered by other reactions. So I let her go back down the stairs without saying anything.

As I turned into the corridor leading to my room, I saw Ben and Sybilla coming out of his room and froze. I thought they'd left ages ago. Glancing down at me, she leaned in and drew him into a deep kiss, her whole body rippling with the force of it.

Desire and jealousy and anger — at her, at him, and maybe most of all at myself —

shot through me in a blinding flush of red and I stumbled backward. There was a door next to me. Groping for the handle, I ducked inside.

A narrow stairwell led upward. Wanting to be anywhere but where I was, I took it, following it up two stories, where it opened onto the roof.

Night had fallen while I spoke to Lady Nairn. I stood in the darkness, feeling as if I'd left my skin behind. Up ahead, the battlements carved up the starlit sky. Atop them hunched a gargoyle whose head slowly twisted to face me.

"Oh," said Lily dourly. "It's you."

"Come down from there."

"Bothered by heights?"

"By the possibility of you going splat, yes."

She shrugged. "I like it up here." She pulled her knees in even closer to her chest. "I don't suppose you have the knife, do you?" Her voice was taut with wistful eagerness.

"On me?"

She sighed. "I suppose not. But I'd like to see it again. I'd come down for that."

"Your grandmother has it."

She made a sour face. "That's that, then. I won't see it till I'm eighteen. She'd keep me a child till I'm eighty, if she could.

Hey . . . *you* could head down to the Fire Festival if you liked. I bet she'd even lend you a car. And I could stow away —"

"I'm heading to bed, Lily." The adrenaline flush I'd felt downstairs was draining away, leaving me hollow with exhaustion.

"How boring. Or is it that you're taking her side?"

"I'm staying out of it."

She sighed, laying a cheek on one knee. "I thought you were *way* cooler than that."

"Sorry to disappoint."

"He's going to be at the festival," she said petulantly. "And I'm not."

"Who is?"

"Ian." Her eyes glittered in the moonlight. "Ian Blackburn. He's an artist."

"Is that who you went off with today?"

She nodded.

"I thought I saw you at Birnam Wood this morning."

"That's ridiculous." She held my eyes as she said it. No flinching, no flickering. "I'm supposed to meet him at the festival. *Please,* won't you go?"

"Lily. There's been a murder. A fairly brutal one. And some strange threats."

She leapt down onto the roof. "That was you? *You're* the one who fed Gran that bollocks about threats against me?" She turned

221

around and slammed both hands down on the stone. "You have no idea what's going on, do you?" She twisted back around. "You know, it could be amazing tonight. A ritual knife and a ritual fight such as hasn't been seen for *centuries*."

"Lily — where's this coming from? That knife is a lethal weapon, for Christ's sake."

"From Corra," she said defiantly.

"Corra Ravensbrook? You told her about the knife?" Just last night, she'd stood in front of me and promised not to say a word to anyone.

Lily went still. "She's brilliant."

"Bullshit." I was tired and frustrated and filling with an undercurrent of dread, and I finally snapped. "You could roll the full moon through the holes in her logic, not to mention the evidence in her so-called scholarship, and if that's the advice she's giving you about the stage, then she's dangerous."

I watched angry frustration rising in Lily as I spoke, her hands tightening into small fists. "You're . . . you're . . . you're just like Gran," she burst out.

A secret, black, and midnight hag, I thought with grim hilarity.

"So damned focused on facts, facts, facts, and all the possible things that could go wrong, that the beauty and power and poetry the world throws at you fly straight by. I thought — I thought you might be different. But you're so caught up in your precious Shakespeare and your stupid stage traditions — fake exorcisms! God! How stupid was that little ritual last night? — that you can't see real magic under your nose. Wake up, Kate. Theater is dead. Jesus, even film is dead. It's spontaneous performances by real people that matter. Happenings like the Samhuinn festival."

It was all I could do not to laugh out loud. She'd been spoon-fed some self-righteously radical theories about art, and she was spouting them with all the passion of adolescence. It was oddly endearing, at the same time that it was infuriating.

"I'll take Ian over you any day," she flung at me. "He *gets it.* Mixing up theater and film with video games, the Internet, Twitter, music, painting, books, all rolled into one . . . He'll change the way stories are told, stretching them into new technologies to make a new kind of art altogether. Something interactive. *Shared.*"

"But with his name on it, I bet," I said sardonically.

Her eyes flashed. "Something *real.*" She snorted with derision. "It's what Shakespeare would be doing if he were around today. I mean, he didn't mess around with writing, like, manuscript books or carving hieroglyphs, did he? He spent his life shaping the newest, coolest art form there was. Putting his stamp on it." She threw up her hands. "Don't you see? You're wrecking *everything* for a whisper of dead, boring Shakespeare heard on the wind. Or maybe in your dreams. And not just wrecking it for me. For *everyone*." She burst into tears. "I hate you," she cried, brushing by me and heading for the stairs.

I stared after her, seeing my fifteen-year-old self. And wondering, deep down, how much truth there was to some of her accusations.

19

Drawing in a deep breath of clean, pine-scented air, I glanced over at the hill.

Lie still if you don't want to get the both of us killed, Auld Callie had said in my ear on its slopes just yesterday. And later, *Put it back.*

Put the knife back. I hadn't, and now I couldn't. I didn't even know where Lady Nairn had stashed it.

Did it matter anymore?

Lily thought it did.

Pushing those thoughts aside, I at last pulled the Aubrey from my pocket. Nearly full, the moon poured silvery light across the page. I could make out Shakespeare sparring with Macbeth in Beerbohm's fin de siècle drawing, but it was too dark to read Aubrey's cramped seventeenth-century writing. And I was shaking, with more than just cold.

Nine nights, Odin had hung on his tree,

wrenching the knowledge of runes from the otherworld with a scream of agony and triumph. Runes represented secret knowledge. Hidden, arcane.

Occult.

Kate Stanley, someone had scrawled. That much I could read, even in the moonlight.

The need to read the rest was suddenly overpowering. I rushed down the stairs, peering cautiously out into the corridor. It was clear; I hurried to my room.

Lamplight glowed on the Chinese dragons roiling on their silks. The bed, turned back, gleamed with smooth white linen and a neat swell of pillows; a fire shimmered in the fireplace. Lady Nairn's staff must have spent all day putting it to rights.

I dropped into one of the armchairs by the fire and began to read, skimming quickly over the lines I'd read before: *The Youth who was to have first taken the parte of Lady Macbeth fell sudden sicke of a Pleurisie and died.* And then I let my eye slide down the page.

On this occasion, 'twas told me that Mr. Shakspere was a man torn between two masters. Lord Salisbury would have a play to shadow forth a witch, while old Dr. Dee would have him draw her sting.

I went still, barely breathing. Salisbury and Dee. Robert Cecil, earl of Salisbury and secretary of state. Most modern historians referred to him as Cecil; King James had called him "my little beagle." The brilliant, hunchbacked toiler in the shadows who ran the kingdom while the king played in the sun. One of England's great spymasters.

And John Dee, the greatest magus of the Elizabethan age. A brilliant mathematician, but also an astrologer, alchemist, conjuror of angels and demons. A man whose shadow stretched long and dark across the subject of the occult — and not only in the narrow sense of secrets. One of the foremost practitioners in England — indeed, in all Renaissance Europe — of learned magic.

I swallowed hard. What was Aubrey suggesting, naming these men as Shakespeare's masters? I read on:

Dr. Dee begged Mr. Shakspere to alter his Play lest, in staging curs'd Secretes learned of a Scottish Witch, he conjure powers beyond his controll. But Mr. Shakespere wuld not, until there was a death, whereupon he made the changes in one houre's time.

Aubrey's tale backed Ellen Terry's, that

Shakespeare had changed the play. And the Nairn family legends, too, in the matter of the Scottish witch.

I have heard it whisper'd that the Youth Hal Berridge dyed not of a Pleurisie but of mischief on the part of this selfsame Witch, but if so it was quieted.

I sat back, staring at the words swimming on the page in the firelight. If Aubrey was right, behind the curse was not just a death but a possible murder. The killing of a child. One of the players' boys, probably about Lily's age.

The first Lady Macbeth.

Was it the original Lady Macbeth — the historical Elizabeth Stewart, Lady Arran, Lady Nairn's ancestress — who'd been the Scottish witch whose secrets were stolen? Lady Nairn would think so, I was certain of it. It fit her family's legends. But then one also had to ask: Was it Elizabeth Stewart's "mischief" that killed the boy who'd first played her on the stage?

In the grate, a log collapsed, and I jumped.

What did Robert Cecil, earl of Salisbury, have to do with this tale? His involvement was surely unlikely. On the other hand, his predecessor and teacher as spymaster, Francis Walsingham, had employed Christopher Marlowe as a spy. In earlier years, it had been Walsingham who'd centralized England's acting companies into a few closely controlled networks; there was circumstantial evidence that he'd deliberately meshed these with his network of spies. Licensed to roam the country and prowl the halls of the great, who better than traveling players to act as London's eyes and ears in distant parts of the realm? So it wasn't entirely preposterous that Cecil might reach out to Shakespeare. But why? Against whom, and for what end?

Macbeth was widely believed to be a sort of zeitgeist response to the horror of the Gunpowder Plot, in which some radical Catholic gentlemen had planned to blow up the Opening of Parliament in 1605, hoping to kill the king, the entire royal family, both houses of Parliament, and most of England's top judges, lawyers, and prelates to boot. Sort of the equivalent of terrorists flying planes into the Capitol during a State of the union address. It hadn't come off — just barely. But it had sent paroxysms of fear through the English consciousness, setting off a fearsome spidering of manhunts and executions. Those horrors had burned themselves out fairly quickly — but a wary, watchful suspiciousness had lingered for years. Cecil had spent the rest of his life searching for the plot's kingpin, who he believed had escaped justice.

Had the king's beagle somehow tried to use *Macbeth* in his search? I shook my head. I couldn't recall anyone suggesting that the Scottish Play was, among other things, a piece of political hackwork. Political, maybe — it was popular to see all Shakespeare's work as political, in the sense of being about power — but propaganda? What was the message? Fear witches? It didn't sound very like dry, rational Cecil, bureaucrat extraordinaire.

In any case, it was Dee who was in many ways more disturbing.

What did Aubrey mean by saying that Dee was Shakespeare's master? Dee was an expert in fields as far-flung as navigation, geography, history, and mathematics. It didn't have to be magic for which Shakespeare owed him mastery. But it was magic that Aubrey clearly had in mind.

The magic in *Macbeth,* however, was the dark magic of witchcraft. Not Dee's cup of tea at all. He was an intellectual, a strenuous defender of ritual or ceremonial magic as a learned and difficult process of invoking angels. There was a big difference between the intuitive, folklore-bound customs of witchcraft, or "low" magic, and the precise, complicated ceremonies of "high" magic. Even if *Macbeth*'s magic was a memory of some ancient pagan religion mislabeled as witchcraft, as Lady Nairn seemed to believe, why would that concern Dee?

I began to pace the room, thinking of the magic in *Macbeth*.

Double, double toil and trouble,
Fire burn and cauldron bubble.

The great cauldron scene involved witches cackling over a revolting brew of body parts. Not Dee's sort of thing at all. On the other hand, the witches weren't old village scolds, as witches on the English stage had always been before. Eerie and unearthly, they weren't human at all. They were condensations of evil whispering on an ill wind. "Creatures of the elder world," Shakespeare's source had written. The weird sisters. The fairies. The witch-hunters, including King James, had believed such spirits to be demons.

Maybe *Macbeth* was about demonic magic after all.

Come to think of it, just as the witches

finished stirring their grisly brew, Macbeth arrived and launched into one of his greatest speeches. *I conjure you,* it began. Rummaging about, I found my copy of the play and opened it to that scene. Macbeth's words were usually taken to be metaphorical. But what if Shakespeare had meant it literally? What if Macbeth were donning conjuror's robes, casting a circle? Enacting onstage the kind of rite Dee spent his life performing for real? No stage direction specified it, but stage directions were notoriously absent from Shakespeare's plays.

Secretes learned of a Scottish Witch, Aubrey had written. Legend made Elizabeth Stewart, Lady Arran, a witch, but Lady Nairn had called her ancestress a serious student of magic. In the Renaissance, that meant conjuring, not casting love charms, much less worshipping a pagan goddess. The "Great Art" of conjuring had been thought of as an almost exclusively male pursuit. But surely not entirely: There had to have been women who'd tried their hand at it. Had Lady Arran? What if the rite Shakespeare had learned from her — if he'd learned one at all — had been high magic, not toads and newts in a stew?

I read through the speech.

I conjure you, by that which you profess,
Howe'er you come to know it, answer me.

The room felt suddenly icy. I made myself read on, the speech rising in passion and power as Macbeth worked himself up to challenge winds whipping the sea into a devouring monster, ripping out trees by their roots, hurling down churches and castles. *Even till destruction sicken,* he roared. *Answer me.*

He was conjuring, all right. And what he wanted was what Odin wanted: knowledge. If Macbeth's words were the remains of some magic rite, it was a rite demanding knowledge — ripping it at gale force — from demonic powers. What if the missing or altered magic in *Macbeth* wasn't witchcraft at all, but a dark version of Dr. Dee's wizardry?

Dee had spent his life battling popular suspicions that he was a master of demons: that he invoked evil, not angels. All the more after a Scottish king with a penchant for witch-hunting had ascended the English throne. Surely, he'd have disapproved of this Scottish play, seeing it, perhaps, as a reflection of himself shadowed in a dark and possibly dangerous mirror.

Pacing the room, I caught sight of my

reflection in the dressing-table mirror, hands on my hips, forehead furrowed, my hair standing on end where I'd run my fingers through it. I looked like a witch myself, for heaven's sake. This was ridiculous. Last night, I'd gone to bed wondering whether Shakespeare might have recorded some long-forgotten ancient rite. Tonight, I seemed to be flirting with the possibility that he was a spy and a magus. A man with two masters. And maybe a mistress.

Call me Corra Ravensbrook.

I laughed darkly at my mirror-self. Aubrey, after all, wasn't dependable as a historian. He'd been a great collector of anecdotes, but his stories — though fairly reliable as gossip — weren't trustworthy as *truth.*

All the same, my other self seemed to say, his note *did* harmonize with every other bit of evidence I'd run across: not only the Nairn family stories, but Ellen Terry's letter. She, too, had heard about the rewrite that altered the magic. Aubrey just included more details — and why not? The page was undated, but most of his diary was from the late seventeenth century. He was closer to Shakespeare than Terry by roughly two centuries.

The thought struck me: If Terry's informant had been right about the revision of the play . . . had she also been right about the survival of a manuscript?

I picked Aubrey's page up from the table where I'd left it. What did any of this have to do with Birnam Wood and the deaths of Sir Angus and Auld Callie? At the bottom of the page, Shakespeare drove at Macbeth with his tree branch, glancing out at me with a sly, mocking smile: *Who can impress the Forrest, bid the Tree unfix his earth-bound root?* It was a phrase from the same scene of conjuring. Macbeth's solution to one of the witches' riddles: that he should never be conquered until Birnam Wood came to Dunsinane.

Sir Angus had turned the phrase around: *Dunsinnan must go to Birnam Wood.* Still, he'd focused on the same subject of trees and forests and woods. Was this page what he had found? What he'd possibly been killed for? If that were the case, how did it come to be pinned to Auld Callie's dress, with my name on it? More important, where was it pointing?

It had to be pointing somewhere.

Whatever secrets this page was hiding, they had to have something to do with that goddamned tree. But mid-joust, Shakespeare remained stubbornly mute.

A loud, insistent knocking cut through my thoughts. Slipping the Aubrey into my copy of the play, I opened the door to find Lady Nairn, her face white with fear.

"It's Lily," she rasped. "She's gone." She gripped my shoulder. "And so is the knife."

20

"You think she's headed to Edinburgh, for the Fire Festival?"

She nodded. "I've called Ben. He's got people out looking for her. But I'd like you to go, too. She likes you."

Not after tonight, I thought.

"And you think Lily took the knife?"

"She's the only other person who knows how to get in the safe." She set the edgeless knife in my hand. "She left this in its place. Take it. Maybe whoever wants the knife will take this in its stead."

I doubted it. Whoever wanted it wanted the real thing: *What's a ritual knife* for *but ritual?*

"Please," said Lady Nairn, her heart in her eyes. "I'm an old woman. I'd just be in the way. But you and Ben . . . you have a chance to find her." Her voice, shaky to begin with, dropped to a whisper. "I can't lose Lily, too."

Ben was the last person I wanted to be anywhere near, tonight. But I had no choice. Grabbing my jacket and dropping the knife in its pocket, I took the keys she held out and hurried down to the car.

It was a little over an hour's drive into Edinburgh. Following directions I had from a brief, brisk conversation with Ben, I drove into the old city's confusing warren of streets, turning left as we came to the Grassmarket, a wide, tree-filled, shop- and pub-lined boulevard. Up ahead, a line of sharply gabled stone buildings came to an abrupt end. I pulled up beneath the last building.

Two men detached themselves from the building's shadow, stepping quickly toward me. Ben and a shorter sandy-haired man. Ben opened my door; as I got out, pulling my jacket from the passenger seat, the other man ducked behind the wheel.

Ben led me swiftly up a stairway clinging to the side of the building, bordered on the other side by a steep grassy slope. Far overhead, atop a ragged, jutting cliff, perched the castle, shining golden in the night, never taken, across a thousand years, except through treachery.

"What's the point, if you'll pardon the expression," asked Ben, "of slipping the real knife into the performance?"

"Authenticity, according to Lily. She said it was Corra Ravensbrook who put the notion into her head, though I'm not sure I trust her. The question is, just how authentic are we talking?"

Something strange happens to blades that have drunk blood, Eircheard had said. *They wake. . . . And some of them want more.*

"You brought the stage copy?"

I patted my pocket. "She won't want to take it."

"She won't have a choice."

He'd had people out canvassing the performers for Lily, but no one could recall seeing her. On the other hand, the torch-bearers painted their entire faces in bold black and gold, greasing and braiding their hair into outlandish shapes or tucking it into extravagant jesters' caps. Our footsteps clattered on stone and cement, punctuating a thick ooze of worry. How far could one fifteen-year-old get along one several-block stretch of an old city? Even with a black-and-gold face, she shouldn't be that hard to find.

"The way Lily told me the story, it's the Cailleach who's supposed to carry the knife," I panted. "My guess is that she's probably sticking close to Sybilla."

"Hurry," was all he said.

Halfway up the hill, we came out onto another street angling slowly upward, left to right. Cutting across it, we ran up another stair, steeper and narrower. Sounds drifted down from above: flutes and drums and horns, cut by laughter and the occasional shout. And singing. At one point, I thought I heard soft footsteps behind and stopped, looking back.

Below, I saw nothing but shadows moving in the wind.

The Esplanade was writhing with revelers. There were fire breathers and fire dancers twisting batons of flame through the darkness, and drummers dressed in green crowned with wreaths of ivy and holly. Acrobats, jugglers, and leering devils milled about. The Winter Court stalked the fringes, cloaked in black, faces hidden beneath long-snouted wolf masks, howling at the swollen moon hanging high overhead.

In the sort of simple color coding common in folk plays, the Summer Court was recognizable in greens and reds, all the colors of growth and harvest and fire. The Winter Court was mostly in black and gray. The Cailleach was blue and her ice maidens white.

Where the street opened out of the parade ground, leading downward from the castle into the city, hundreds of people had lined the way, swaying and chanting: *People are returning to the ancient ways.* Lily's phrase. Into this funnel, the players were slowly pouring themselves in a chaotic procession down the hill. Between the buildings and the police barriers that kept the onlookers out of the parade, both sides of the street were packed as far as I could see. Pushing our way through the crowd down to Parliament Square, where the main show would take place, would take hours, if it could be done at all. My heart sank.

"Hurry," said Ben again.

"How? With wings?"

"*An angel is like you, Kate, and you are like an angel.* But if you're feeling less than celestial, we could try going as wolves in wolves' clothing."

Instead of heading toward the street, he began edging around the back of the milling crowd, between the merriment and the castle. I called to him once, in confusion, but he didn't hear. There was nothing for it but to follow.

We skimmed around the back of the Esplanade in a gigantic half-circle. In the corner on the opposite side, we came to a low wrought-iron fence in front of a white-and-black half-timbered house. A policeman stood in front of the gate. Seeing Ben, he opened it and stood aside, and we ducked along a short pathway and into the house.

A scullery opened into a large old-fashioned kitchen. In the middle of the room, two piles of clothing lay on a long table once painted blue. Atop each pile perched a long-snouted papier-mâché mask: the head of a wolf.

"How'd you get these?"

Ben shoved one pile toward me. "Everything has its price. Even a place in the festival. Just ask Sybilla." Pulling off his shirt, he started to dress in the clothes from the other pile.

We each had a long-sleeved shirt, trousers, and a cloak, all in black. Just before donning the mask, I drew Lady Nairn's unsharpened knife from my jacket pocket and tucked it into my belt beneath the cloak.

21

By the time we emerged transformed into wolves, the Esplanade had largely cleared. The Cailleach and her ice maidens had gone before we arrived. Now Eircheard and his Summer Court had gone as well, and the Winter Court, led by Jason, was well on its way. I could just see antlers in the distance. As we stepped outside, Ben leaned over to me. "If you find her, or you run into trouble, come back here. Or to the front entrance off Ramsay Lane . . . you know where that is?"

I nodded, and my three-foot snout nearly upended me.

"That's where the car'll be," said Ben.

"Are you planning on skipping?" I asked.

In answer, he threw back his head and howled a challenge to the night, loping into the crowd. The road was lined with torch-bearers. Ben took the one side, and I took the other, scanning their faces. Behind the barrier, the crowd was twenty deep in places, swaying and chanting so that the whole street reverberated with their words: *People are returning to the ancient ways.*

Except for taking videos on their mobiles and posting them to Facebook, I thought.

I searched every black-and-gold face on the way down but saw no sign of Lily.

What had she got herself into? That she was involved in Auld Callie's death I would not believe. That she'd been swept up by others whose passions were less innocent was entirely possible. Corra Ravensbrook, for one. Lily had told her about the knife, and it was Ravensbrook who seemed to have convinced her that inserting it into this festival would be a fine turn of events. Who was she? A bored housewife, Lady Nairn had scoffed, but I doubted it. Could she have some connection to Lucas Porter?

Around us, other members of the Winter Court were infiltrating the crowd from behind, as winter creeps gradually into summer, sneaking through the crowd and out into the procession from the closes, the narrow, winding alleyways that cut steeply down between buildings from the top of Castle Hill all the way to its feet.

Ahead, to my left, a wolf howled behind the crowd, and the crowd eddied and seethed, people turning in all directions, as the separation between performers and audience melted. At the edge of the scrum, I thought I saw a flip of red hair above a black-and-gold torchbearer's costume, and then the crowd closed around her.

I pushed my way over, and the crowd enveloped me, too. It was densely packed; I caught snatches of German, Spanish, and something that might have been Russian, along with broad Scots. Three women on stilts ducked through the close behind, their costumes the pale flowing blue and white of ice, glittering with crystals and sequins. Behind them, a puppet fifteen feet tall unfolded through the doorway: a wraith with a twisted face, its skirts of white and silver silk whirling over the crowd like a billowing veil.

A voice cold as winter spoke in my ear. "Walk away, Kate."

Who knew me, in this mask? Who knew my name? I twisted the wolf's head to see an old man watching me with watery blue eyes. He was gaunt and a little bent; what remained of his close-shaven hair was gray.

"Who are you?"

His dry laugh faded into a cough. "A messenger. You're better at giving direction than taking it, aren't you?"

Suddenly, I recognized him. In the flaring darkness, his body ravaged by illness, he looked more like a figure of Death than the golden man I'd seen in pictures from his glory days in Hollywood.

"Lucas Porter," I said, stepping toward him, but hands caught me from behind, pinning my arms at my back, holding me where I was. One of the stilt-women bumped into me. As I stumbled, my mask was lifted off and passed into the whooping crowd, bobbing from hand to hand like a trophy.

Lucas stepped close, and for a moment I thought he'd seen the knife at my belt and meant to take it. Instead, he slid his cheek in along mine in a sensual move that made me flinch. "We've taken what you would not give." His voice in my ear was harsh and rasping as a sibyl's, devoid of emotion, which somehow made the light touch of his skin against mine worse. "Now she must die."

"Who?" I jerked back, but the hands behind me only tightened their grip. Around us, the crowd jostled and milled, the stilt-women danced, and the puppet wraith whirled, its skirts twirling overhead like a huge parasol.

"Begin to doubt the equivocation of the fiend that lies like truth. . . . Either Lily will die, or

you will." He stepped back, a serpent's cold smile on his face. "Walk away, Kate. This isn't your story."

"It's not Lily's, either."

His eyes were dark pools of hatred. "She was born into it."

There was a crack and a sharp cry, and the puppeteer stumbled and fell to the ground. Fifteen feet of puppet sighed and collapsed, its silver skirts slowly settling over the crowd like the fall of a parachute. As it slipped over my face, the hands holding me let go.

By the time I worked my way free, Lucas was gone. Someone else grabbed my elbow and I spun, jerking away. It was another wolf, holding my wolf's head in its hands.

"Jesus, Kate," said Ben's voice. "What happened?"

"He's here," I panted. "Lucas."

"You saw him?"

"He delivered a message." It stuck in my throat. "Either Lily will die. Or I will."

Ben gripped my shoulder, steadying me. "Are you all right?"

I grabbed my mask from him, settling it back on my head. "We have to find Lily."

We reached the main stage down in the square before St. Giles' Cathedral just as the revels of the Summer Court reached their climax: red and green people gyrating around each other in squealing decadence, tumblers bouncing through the air, giants swaying on stilts, fire batons swinging flame through the night.

In the center of the stage Sybilla sat enthroned, veiled head to toe in deep blue, almost like a burka, except that in the center of the veil covering her face was painted a single staring white eye. In a grand gesture, she rose, slowly raising her arms skyward. From every side, horns and drums and flutes swelled into a great crescendo until with a single motion downward, she silenced it, and with it the chatter of the crowd. For a moment there was no sound in the square save wind whipping through banners and, in the distance, the cry of a frightened child.

When she brought her hands back up, she was holding a knife.

It rippled in the firelight. I took one step closer, peering at the blade. Down its center ran a line of runes.

Ben had seen it, too. Lily had delivered the knife.

And Sybilla had accepted it? What the hell was she thinking?

Beside her, Eircheard sat wrapped in some kind of fur that made him look more than ever like a bear. Draining a flagon in noisy gulps, he tossed it away. It rang on the pavement in the silence. He pushed himself to his feet and lurched across the stage, grabbing at the knife in Sybilla's hands but coming up empty. He yelled with frustration. Around him, his court tittered with drunken laughter.

At the edge of the stage, the wolves of Winter rushed into the open space, cornering Eircheard and scattering his revelers. Through it all, Sybilla stood motionless at the center.

As the last of the Summer Court slunk whining away, Jason strode toward Sybilla, sweeping into a great bow. As he rose, she extended the knife toward his breast. One thrust would send it piercing into his heart. I wondered whether he'd yet seen that the knife was sharp, but behind the visor of his horned helmet, it was impossible to tell.

A deep drum began to pound out a slow beat. Sybilla offered Jason the knife, and the wolves howled in triumph. The queen had chosen her champion.

From his corner, Eircheard bellowed with anger and lurched over to Jason, who let him come, stepping aside at the last instant, slashing out at him as he stumbled by. A piece of Eircheard's cloak fluttered to the ground, and the crowd clattered with laughter. Eircheard turned, a puzzled look on his face, and trundled back. In another graceful arc, Jason sliced a second bit off his opponent's cloak. The crowd warmed to it, the handsome young outsider showing up the boorish old king. It was a brilliant routine, bombast versus finery, light catching and flickering on armor and silk and fur.

I heard Ben's voice in my ear. "Watch Eircheard."

He stood blinking and swaying, unsteady on his feet, his eyes glazed. I frowned. This wasn't an act. He was having trouble staying upright. "He looks drunk," I said quietly.

"Or drugged."

Lowering his head, Eircheard went at Jason again. Another arc of the blade sliced through his cloak, and this time it caught skin. A rivulet of blood flowed down his arm and he bayed in fury.

Glancing over at the Winter King, I saw something that sent a floe of ice running down my spine. Jason's hands were large, a workingman's hands that could handle a broadsword or a horse, a pick or a hoe. But the hand that held the knife had long, tapered fingers, more suited to the piano or the rapier.

Whoever was behind the Winter King's

mask, it wasn't Jason.

Ben's head jerked around; he'd seen it, too.

Eircheard charged again. This time, he was tripped and fell sprawling on the pavement, subsiding into unconsciousness. The Winter King strode toward him, knife gripped in his hands, and the crowd roared with laughter.

"Kill him," a woman screamed, and the Winter King raised his head, as if sniffing the bloodlust in the air. His knife rose. Pulling off the wolf mask, I began to run, but the knife was already slashing toward Eircheard's neck.

Just before the blade reached Eircheard's throat, another hand rose and parried the blow. Pulling off his mask, Ben had stepped forward. His knife was black, of some dull material that caught little light, hard to see in the night. There was a long *aaaah,* and the crowd silenced, leaning inward.

Alone in the center, the matte-black blade and the pattern-welded blade swayed this way and that. And then both blades flew into the air, clattering to the ground, and both men fell heavily to the pavement, rolling over and over. The Winter King dove for his knife, and as he did, Ben caught his helmet, twisting it up and away, so that it came off. The face beneath was painted entirely white, and it took me a moment to recognize him: the dark-haired man from the Esplanade.

Holding the helmet by the horns, Ben was off, scooping up the pattern-welded knife as he went, dancing about with both of them. And then he clapped the Winter King's horned helmet on his own head.

The dark-haired man charged and Ben ducked, scampering about the square, using a large statue as a shield. Drawing him, with each move, farther away from Eircheard.

Once, Ben ran behind me, using me as a shield, spinning me a couple of times so that my cloak swept outward, enveloping us both.

"Trade," he said under his breath, thrusting the knife from the hill into my hand and plucking the stage dagger from my belt. And then he was off again, the crowd cheering him on as he led the dark-haired man in a merry chase, prancing about, juggling with the stage knife while the Winter King, no longer looking regal, lunged for it.

Across the way, Eircheard stirred. He sat up, squinting. And then I saw him recognize the antlers. With a yell, he pushed himself up and lurched across the stage, plowing into Ben's back. There was a sickening thud and Ben went down on one knee, the knife skittering across the pavement, stopping not far from the dark-haired man's feet. Eircheard skidded after it, catching himself on his knees just in front of the Winter King. With a slow smile of victory, the man scooped up the weapon and raised it over Eircheard's head.

It had no edge and a rounded point, but it was steel. Driven hard into the chest of an unarmed man, it could still be lethal. Again, a lone woman's shrill voice filled the square: *"Kill him."* This time, the crowd took it up. *"Kill him, kill him."*

Within the chanting crowd, the four of us might as well have been alone on the moon.

"Strike now," said Ben, "and it will look like what it is. Murder. And there will be ten thousand witnesses."

"It will look like an accident."

"Is it worth the risk, with the wrong knife?"

The dark-haired man looked up at the blade in his hand and his smile died. The crowd's chant died away and silence blanketed the square, broken only by flames crackling in the cold wind. "You bloody fool," he snarled, thrusting the knife down viciously. Eircheard subsided with a groan.

Someone screamed. I stepped forward.

There was no blood. And then I saw the blade, lying jagged and broken on the ground. The dark-haired man had driven the knife into the stone pavement.

Throughout the fight, Sybilla had stood motionless. Now she stepped forward and gave Eircheard her hand, pulling him to his feet, and the crowd sighed in relief at the Cailleach's resurrection of the old king.

At the back of the stage, sparks spurted and a pyrotechnic display shot flames into the night. Around the edge of the square, a troupe of fire dancers began spinning fiery batons, and the drummers pounded out a quick rising beat of anticipation.

Slowly, Sybilla reached up and unpinned her robe. The drumming grew more insistent. The blue cloak and hood fell to the ground.

Surprise stopped a cry in my throat; beside me I saw Ben do a double take. The woman beneath was not Sybilla.

She was Lily.

22

But if Lily was the Cailleach . . . if she'd been there beneath the Cailleach's blue veil all evening, where was Sybilla?

Lily held a pale hand out to the Winter King, who stepped forward and was presented to the crowd. The Cailleach's consort.

Before the crowd could cheer in approval, a single voice rose through the square: *"Thou shalt not suffer a witch to live."* From near the back, a burning baton streaked straight toward the stage like an arrow, catching the edge of Lily's robe, which caught fire in a quick whoosh.

I reached the stage in two steps, tossing her to the ground, smothering the flames. Ben was not far behind.

It was over in an instant. Lily sat up. The fire had torched one side of her robe and singed her hair, but other than that she was fine. Around us, chaos erupted.

Ben turned back to the spot where the dark-haired man had stood, but he was gone. I gripped Lily's arm, as if she might also disappear. "You're hurting me," she whimpered.

"Who was he? The Winter King?"

She glared at me in mute fury, and I shook her. "*Lily*. He tried to kill Eircheard. And someone's just tried to kill you. Where are Jason and Sybilla?"

"Do you have to ruin *everything*?" she wailed.

"Get her out of here," said Ben tersely. "And that goddamned knife, too." And he pushed into the crowd.

Still gripping Lily, I began weaving through the crowd, but she made no move to resist.

"Where are we going?" she asked grudgingly.

"Ramsay Lane," I said. "Just under the castle."

Loosed into a spontaneous dance party on the street, the crowd made the going frustratingly slow.

A little way up, Lily motioned to a doorway opening onto one of the closes that ran down the side of the hill. "Shortcut," she said sullenly, "if you want it."

I hesitated, looking from the chaotic street

to the quiet close. "Jesus," she said, pulling me through. "This'll take sodding days."

Inside, the sound of the crowd cut to a distant hum, and our pace quickened. Twenty yards in, a raucous party of drunken spectators erupted into the small space from a side door, whirling us apart as they folded us into their dance. It was a moment before I realized what they were singing:

> The master, the swabber, the boatswain, and I
> The gunner and his mate,
> Loved Mall, Meg, and Marian, and Margery,
> But none of us cared for Kate.

Glimpsing Lily, I reached for her, but she was spun away. I heard light laughter and someone shoved me against the wall. There was a scream and then the crowd was running off, half uphill and half downhill, and I could not see her in the fray. "Lily!" I shouted, turning about wildly, but in a matter of seconds, I was alone in the dark in an Edinburgh close.

"Lily!" I called again. But she was gone.

The crowd had scattered in both directions, so I had no idea which way to head in pursuit. Knowing it would be futile, I tried them both. Above, the royal Mile still surged with a dancing crowd. The lower street was mostly empty.

My mobile buzzed. *It must be Lily.*
Thank God.

It was a text, and therefore succinct:

Lily 4 knife. Hilltop. Midnight. Alone.

I stared at it, dread sinking through me. Up on the hill, Lucas Porter had laid out a stark choice: Lily or me. Someone must die. But that was when they thought they had the knife.

Now it seemed they were willing to trade Lily for the blade.

Or was I part of the trade as well?

There was only one way to find out: alone on a hilltop at midnight, with a ritual blade a thousand years old.

My call to Ben had rung twice when another text came through, from an unrecognized number. I cut off my call to Ben and pulled it up:

Contact anyone & deal off. Watching & listening.
Car @ bottom of hill. Keys under floor mat.

I looked up. The windows lining the small space all seemed curtained and dark, even opaque. But suddenly they seemed like staring eyes. Canceling the call to Ben, I made my way quickly down the hill.

As promised, there was a car just at the end of the close, where it came out on the main road that wound down the hill toward New Town. A black Mercedes. The driver's door was unlocked and the keys were under the mat. As I started the car, I found that the GPS was already programmed for Dunsinnan. Shaking, I pulled out into traffic.

Ben called four times on the drive north, but I didn't dare answer. *Watching & listening.* The car was probably bugged, and for all I knew, they were monitoring my cell calls. But I couldn't turn the phone off, in case I heard from Lily or her abductors. From that direction, though, there was silence.

What was Lucas up to? Why engineer Lily bringing the knife to Edinburgh only to pull them both back to Dunsinnan? How did the Winter King, the dark-haired man, figure into it? Where were Sybilla and Jason? *What happened to Lily?*

I looked at the knife on the leather seat beside me, gleaming now and then in the lights of the motorway. *Nothing is but what is not,* it seemed to whisper.

Other words kept playing through my head:

She must die:
She must, the saints must have her; yet a
  virgin,
A most unspotted Lily shall she pass
To the ground, and all the world shall
  mourn her.

Behind that, oddly, I heard Ben's voice: *"An angel is like you, Kate, and you are like an angel."* Whatever had possessed him to say that, it seemed heavy with irony now.

I drove north as fast as I dared.

23

I pulled into the lay-by at the foot of Dun-sinnan Hill with no more than fifteen minutes to spare before midnight. Slipping the knife from the seat, I headed quickly up the hill.

The path seemed longer and steeper, the stand of pines more ominous, in the dark. My footsteps thudded softly on the grass along the field and into the heather, my breath shortening as I ran. The moon hung high overhead, dimly lighting the way. Just below the summit, I paused, my heart thudding wildly in my chest, and not only from the climb. In my hands, the knife was cold. *Stupid not to have a backup weapon,* I thought suddenly. Though where I would have gotten one, I didn't know. When I handed it over, I'd be unarmed.

What choice did I have?

I set my shoulders and peered over the rim. The cairn seemed to have grown. Then

I realized that it was not the cairn I was looking at; it was wood, stacked into a high cone. Other than that, the summit was empty.

At the base of the stacked wood, a red gleam kindled into life. And then a breeze lifted, and the bonfire caught with a whoosh, orange and yellow flame licking upward through the cone. From behind it, a lone figure stepped into the light. A woman with pale hair falling to the middle of her back, her face lined with the fine-china crackling of fair skin in old age. Lady Nairn, in a shimmering blue gown. In her right hand, she held a knife with an angled back and a blade that seemed to ripple in the firelight.

What was she doing here? Where was Lily?

In a low voice, she began to hum, walking in a wide circle with the knife pointing outward and down to the ground, stopping at each of the cardinal directions to cry out in words drowned out by the wind and the roar of the fire. Slowly, she walked to the center, raising her arms to the moon. Her voice rose into a strange keening that soared into the night and seemed to wrap around the moon like a slender cord, drawing it down toward the hill.

On the far side of the summit, horns rose over the rim, branching into antlers, as if she were pulling a stag up from the deeps of the earth even as the moon dipped down. The head that followed, however, was not that of a stag, but of a man. He rose over the lip of the summit, naked and in his prime, his member erect, and strode down toward her carrying a cup, which he held high. It was his eyes I could not look away from. Fringed with feathers, they were the unwinking golden eyes of an owl.

What I had seen in Edinburgh was a play, a good-natured performance. This was the real thing. It wasn't Lily who was the witch in the household, it was Lady Nairn.

I must have made some sound, because they both turned toward me, Lady Nairn's eyes meeting mine. *She is Artemis,* I thought, *Diana, the Lady of the Hunt, and I will be torn apart by her hounds.*

Even as that thought crossed my mind, a cry of loneliness condensed and distilled rose in waves toward the moon. To my right, a wolf leapt onto the rim of the summit, its throat arced back in a howl. To my left, others answered. And then other figures rose into view. One of them was the dark-haired man. The Winter King.

From the startled anger on Lady Nairn's face, he was as much an intruder as I was. *"Run!"* she cried in a deep voice, looking straight at me.

As if blocked, somehow, from entering the bowl of the summit itself, the wolves and dark figures who stood with them began to pour around its edges, heading toward me, erupting into a cacophony of yipping and howls. I stepped back, stumbling and falling, scrambling up and away. Something nipped at me from behind, and I turned, knife in hand, as someone lunged at me. I was hit on the head, and the world went dark.

24

It was the cold I became aware of first, dimly and far away, as I slid back into consciousness. A clinging damp cold. A throbbing ache in my head. And grass prickling my cheek.

For a moment, I lay still. Hearing nothing but wind, I opened my eyes. I lay in the bowl of the hilltop, just near the rim. Thin fingers of steely light pierced a cloudy sky. This far north, in November, dawn came late. I must have been here for hours.

Lily. Her name tore through me in a silent, white explosion.

She'd disappeared after the Samhuinn festival, and I'd come here with the knife. Where was it? Where was she?

I sat up. I seemed to be alone. Off to my left, a pile of gray ash, thinly smoking, was all that remained of the bonfire. In the grass, my hands were sticky, and a musty and metallic scent rose thickly around me. *Blood.*

I looked down. I was red up to the elbows with it.

Just before blacking out, I'd slashed out with the knife. What had I done?

In panic, I began to wipe the blood from my hands on the grass when I heard a shout from over the hill, and then thudding footsteps. I stumbled backward, but there was nowhere to hide. A man rose over the rim, stopping as he saw me.

It was Ben. "Kate — *Jesus.*" He crossed the grass in three strides. "Where are you hurt?"

Words would not come; I just shook my head. It hadn't occurred to me to think about that. Was the blood mine?

Gently, he opened my jacket, and I saw that it, too, was covered in blood. His hands slid down my front and around my back.

"You're in one piece," he said. Taking a bandanna from his pocket, he wet it in the dew-soaked grass and began to wipe my hands and wrists clean. "What happened?"

Brokenly, I told him what I could remember — Lily's disappearance, coming up the hill with the knife. And now, the knife missing.

"Let me look," he said quietly.

So I sat there, holding my aching head and once again watching him comb the hillside for me. This time, though, he would not find the knife. I was certain of that.

Lily.

My pocket began to vibrate and then to dance with a light, catchy drumming, pierced by the unmistakable scream of Mick Jagger and the shake of maracas: the opening of "Sympathy for the Devil."

"Your phone, presumably," said Ben.

I shook my head. I had never put that ringtone into it. Besides, I had switched it to vibrate last night, before coming up the hill.

Ben shoved his hand into my jacket pocket, pulled out the phone, and handed it to me.

The phone recognized the call as coming from Lily. But I had never programmed her number into my address book.

"Put it on speaker," said Ben.

With shaking hands I answered it. "Lily?"

"You didn't come alone." The voice was full of reproach. I recognized it, though I'd only heard it in a snarl before. It belonged to the dark-haired man. The Winter King.

"Where is she?"

"Think of the knife as down payment. Reference to a certain manuscript. You will find it and deliver it in two days' time. And then we release Lily."

267

"*Two* — that's not enough time."

"It's what there is."

"And if it can't be found?"

"Ah. I think you already know. *She must die*."

"We have to know that she's still alive and well," said Ben.

"Still not alone," came the reply. "Be careful about that." But he put Lily on the line.

"Kate?" Her voice was wobbly.

"Are you all right?"

"I want to come home."

"We'll get you out of there as soon as we can."

Her voice sank to a whisper. "I'm sorry." With that, the phone went dead.

I was still staring at it in mute anger when a siren spiraled upward from the valley floor, piercing the quiet. Ben walked to the edge of the summit and quickly returned. "Police, coming toward the hill," he said.

"How would they know? Who else —" But even as I looked at him, we both knew who could have sent them. The people who'd taken the knife. Who'd taken Lily.

The traces of blood still on my hands seemed to burn with cold fire. Even if DI McGregor believed the manuscript-for-ransom story, she'd lock me up and look for it herself. But she wouldn't find it. And

Lily would die. "We have to go." I started for the path, but Ben caught my elbow.

"Not that way. Unless you mean to wave and say howdy as we pass the police on the way down."

"There is no other way."

"This hill has other sides."

"Have you *looked* at them?"

In answer, he strode across the shallow bowl of the summit to the southern rim. For an instant, he looked back. And then he disappeared over the edge.

Following in his wake, I saw a narrow ledge of grass just below the rim. Beyond that, a cliff sheered away into a tumble of gray rock far below. But the grassy ledge sloped down to the east, and Ben was already following it. At the end of the rock face, we found a narrow trail leading steeply down through the grass edging the western side of the cliff. "Where the sheep goes, there go I," said Ben with dark hilarity, plunging down the path.

It curved this way and that. In places, we slid more than walked as the path dropped a hundred feet or more. At last we neared the bottom of the cliff, turning into a wide meadow halfway down the hill. The trail dipped and rose again, and then Ben stopped so suddenly that I ran into him.

Three ravens rose screeching into the air, wheeling angrily overhead.

"Don't look," he said sharply. But I already had.

Just ahead, beneath a length of blue silk shimmering like snakeskin, someone lay sprawled in the shadow of a fall of boulders at the base of the cliff. The rocks were smeared and splattered with blood. I'd seen that gown before. It was Ellen Terry's, or a copy of it. I'd seen it last on Lady Nairn, her arms raised in wild praise to the moon.

Brushing past Ben, I stood over her for a moment. "She was the Lady of the Hunt last night," I said. "I thought it was me who was going to be torn to shreds."

I twitched aside a corner of the gown. It lifted with a light clatter as the dried husks of a thousand beetle backs shifted upon each other.

She lay with her head flung back, her hair cascading over rock thickly splattered and pooled with blood. Her throat had been slashed so savagely that the head had very nearly come off and was twisted at an impossible angle. But the hair was not a smooth pale blonde. It was dark gold, falling in ringlets.

Sybilla.

Beside me, Ben had gone still as the stones

around us.

On my hands, the blood still lining my nails and the deep grooves in my knuckles burned like acid. I glanced down, seeing them once again as I had seen them on waking: sticky and thickly smeared with Sybilla's life. Or her death.

What had I done?

INTERLUDE

May 1, 1585
Dirleton Castle, Scotland

She stood on the battlements and watched them come.

It had been a long time since Scotland had been ruled by a monarch of mettle. The young king, not quite nineteen, who rode toward her was a coward, and his mother, long imprisoned in a remote English castle, was a fool. If the countess had her way, however, that blight would soon come to an end.

Between them, she and her husband possessed all the right qualities to rule: ruthlessness, daring, intelligence, and, so far, the golden smile of the gods. Their blood claim — the blue blood of royal Stewarts — might not be the strongest, but it was undeniably present. In her case, it was written all over her face and the bright copper of her hair. In combination with their other qualities and the possession of the crown, it would be enough.

Long ago, dark powers had pronounced that one day she would be queen, and she meant to help them, if she could. After the death of her first husband, helped along by one of her cordials when she tired of waiting for him to take her to court, she had ridden south as a still-young and beautiful widow, shining with the red beauty of the royal Stewarts. Though nearly twenty years his senior, she'd intended to take the young king in hand, as Diane de Poitiers had once taken Henri II of France in hand, with almost exactly the same spread in age. She did not need the title of queen; she wanted the power.

She thought she had made her choice of second husband well: an elderly cousin of the king, old enough to leave her alone yet trusted enough to give her access to the boy. But the old man had not left her alone, lusting after her youth and beauty, and the young king, it soon became clear, though undeniably fascinated by her, reserved his deepest passions and trust for men. Deciding to cast off her second husband, she looked about for a third, a man who would rouse the king's admiration but respond to her seductions. A man who had royal blood, yet would need her backing to gain access to the halls of the great. A man with enough sense and sophistication to put aside petty jealousy and welcome any attentions the king might be induced to pay her, as she would welcome any attentions paid to him.

She'd found just the person she needed in the gallant and adventurous captain, now earl, who'd become her third husband. Their rise had been swift and sure. The day he had been handed the keys to Edinburgh Castle, she had swept into the storerooms that housed the wardrobe of the king's mother, Queen Mary, and shut the doors against everyone else save her old nurse. Breaking open the chests herself, she had riffled through the royal jewels and silks, furs and satins, alone.

Some of the jewels she had pawned the next day; others, along with the gowns that could be recut into current fashions, she had taken for her own use. That evening, she had appeared in royal splendor high on the battlements of Edinburgh, overlooking a crowd gathering in the open space below, aware of both their wonder and their fear, but ignoring them, looking out over the city and the country that she meant to rule.

To do it, she had to rule first and foremost over the king now riding toward her, a boy who might have the coloring of the Stewarts but not the heart. Bandy-legged and pasty-faced, he was a poor excuse for a man, never mind a king. Not that one could blame the boy, if you stopped to think about it. He'd known nothing but betrayals, assassination attempts, abductions, and rivers of blood since before he'd been born, all topped off with severe Calvinist schooling in cold castles in the years since, his boyhood alarmingly devoid of warmth in either the sense of human kindness or of weather. His mother's private secretary and possible lover — some still whispered his real father — had been slaughtered in front of her eyes by her husband while she was seven months pregnant with the boy. When he was not quite eight months old, the killer, the prince's publicly recognized father, had been strangled and his house blown up around him to disguise the murder. When James reached the grand old age of thirteen months, his mother was dethroned in favor of his own ascension, and he had never seen her again. A year later she was imprisoned by his "dear cousin," the English queen Elizabeth, with whom he nonetheless had to curry favor, in hopes of one day inheriting her crown. Or, at the very least, of avoiding yet another full-scale English attempt to annex Scotland by force.

And those were just the memorable punctuation points before he'd reached the age of two. If anyone had earned the right to fear naked steel and hidden plots, it was James. All the same, it was disconcerting to watch him, a month shy of nineteen, flush like a girl at the jingle of armor or walk in tight circles like a wandering top as he fretted over a minor slight or a major dilemma.

At least he could sit a horse.

He was sitting a horse now, in the center of a mounted knot of his most trusted men, her husband at his right hand as she watched them approach. They looked for all the world like a cheerful party out hawking, perhaps, bells jingling, ribbons streaming from the horses' manes, and shouts of laughter lacing the bright spring wind off the Firth of Forth as they rode. But if you knew what to look for, no doubt you could see hints of something darker. The tight hunch of the king's shoulders and his tendency to use the crop with a hard hand, for instance. A certain shrillness in his voice, perhaps. But the clearest sign was their speed. They were traveling much too fast for a party of leisure.

To be fair, this time it would not be just the king who was afraid. Most men were afraid of the Black Death, and two days ago it had broken out with a vengeance in a village to the west of Edinburgh. By yesterday afternoon, it had scaled the cliffs and entered the castle that loomed over the queen of Scottish cities. That had proved enough for the king, who had no wish to wait for the infection to roll down the hill and knock at the door of his pleasure palace of Holyroodhouse, scattering dark, foul-smelling buboes hither and yon, without respect for rank or piety.

She might have been frightened herself, had she not known that it was not yet her time to face death, black and bubo-swollen or otherwise. As plague season had approached, she had plotted with her husband to offer their newly acquired home of Dirle-ton Castle, a safe twenty miles east of the pestiferous city, as a refuge, where the king could find safety and a certain sophisticated beauty that enchanted him. For it was important to keep the spell of attraction strong and bright.

So she'd called in servants and laid in cartloads of food for several weeks at the approach of plague season. Hearing words of a traveling troupe of English players, she'd diverted them from the road to Edin-burgh, sweetening their palms with enough money to make sure that their alternate route took in Dirleton. After a dour childhood, the king was fascinated by music, dancing, and plays.

And then Lord Henry Howard had come with a different proposition, one that twisted all her deep-woven plans to another shape entirely. A smile of satisfaction on her face, she went down to welcome the king.

Unaccountably, her husband, who had thrilled to the idea of taking the crown in the cold morning light, balked at it amid the music and laughter of the night. With a suddenness that even the king noticed, he rose and left the great hall in the middle of the feast. She knew where to find him: on the battlements outside her aerie, looking out toward the sea.

He flinched at her touch. "We will proceed no further in this business," he said. "He has honored me of late."

"He's a boy, and fickle. It will not last."

"He's a boy. As you say. And frightened. And he's here in double trust, as kin and king."

A spurt of anger and annoyance shot through her. "I love our boys as much as you do. And yet, if I had sworn it, as you have sworn yourself to this, I'd dash their brains against the wall behind you."

He walloped her across the cheek at that. A stinging blow, not bruising. A warning. She let the mark of his hand redden her cheek, disdaining to hold it, and pulled herself under control. The point was to persuade him, not to win a petty row. Sidling close, she began once more to paint visions in the air for him, running light fingers down his arm, lifting it high. "He has brought the crown within our reach tonight. Put out your hand and pluck it down, before we are plucked ourselves."

He jerked away from her.

"Another opportunity may not come."

"No more." Turning on his heel, he strode off.

She watched him go as she might watch a recalcitrant child. He'd grown to like the boy, or at least to pity him; well and fine. He would have to be schooled to see that the king, despite his liking, was still a pawn. She had worked too hard to let the chance of a crown slip away now.

A shadow detached itself from the opposite doorway and Lord Henry Howard materialized before her eyes, contempt curdling his face. "If you cannot handle a husband, my lady, how will you control a kingdom?"

She tossed her head with impatience and distaste. "Husbands, like horses, occasionally require to be given their heads."

She was brushing past him when he caught her. *"Put out your hand and pluck it down, before we are plucked ourselves,"* he said in light mockery, and then his voice hardened. He pushed her backward, pinning her against the wall. "If I have come here on a fool's errand, I will see that both of you are plucked directly. I swear it." Around them, the tapestries rippled and moved, and in the gap where one ended and another began, they saw the eyes. Another watcher in the night.

In an instant, Lord Henry had drawn his sword and thrust it through the cloth, but it had rung impotently against the stone as the watcher slipped sideways. Ducking out from his hiding place, the other man skittered across the room, putting her heavy oaken table between himself and Lord Henry's blade.

He was the player, she saw. The player with the half-moon brows. Come back for more of what he'd found last night, no doubt, artless, addled fool that he was. Though she felt a thrill, truth be told, at this proof of her power. For a moment, the countess remained leaning against the wall, exultation and dismay tangled in her throat. Who else had been watching in the shadows? Was the king himself lurking in a corner?

A blow thundered against the table and she pushed herself up. Unless she stopped him, Lord Henry would kill the boy, which was a waste. She'd seen him at his work earlier, prancing about in a Robin Hood play as one of the merry men. She'd found herself laughing.

Nobody was laughing now. She caught at Lord Henry, but he flung her off. Tasting blood on her lip, she pulled down a tapestry and went at him again as she had learned to stop her father's drunken men-at-arms from killing each other, whirling the heavy brocade like a net over his sword arm. The cloth wrapped around him, unbalancing him, bringing him crashing to the floor on one knee. "Let him go," she commanded. "He is not your concern."

The boy needed no further prompting. Flashing her a cheeky grin, he scampered out onto the battlements and down the stairs. No doubt he'd disappear into the hills before dawn.

Lord Henry disentangled himself from the tapestry and rose, ramming his sword back into its scabbard in disgust. She'd expected to see rage in his eyes, but there was only coldness. "Not my concern. Then I take it he is yours. Did you rut with him last night?"

"Did you?" she shot back, still looking after the boy, the memory of his heat playing at her breasts and groin.

Lord Henry's eyes hooded. "I would kill a man who said that."

"You will not kill me."

He laughed aloud at that, but it was not a sound of merriment.

"He's nothing but a poor player."

She had expected derisive laughter. But the man went pale and deathly still, his olive skin blanching with cold anger and something she had not expected to see in his face: fear. He took a step toward her, his hands clutching like claws, and for a moment she thought he might attack her. "What have you done?" he cried. *"Nothing but —"* He began pacing, his hands running through his salt-and-pepper hair. "Was he here last night?"

"That is not your concern."

He grabbed her, shaking her with a force she had not felt since her first husband had been on a tear. *"Was he here?"*

She laughed in his face. "He was. All night."

For a moment, she thought he might squeeze the life out of her, but he put his mouth close to her ear and spoke with a low, quick urgency.

"You do not know young Robert Cecil, then. Lord Burghley's son and Walsingham's protégé."

She went still. Burghley was Queen Elizabeth's secretary of state and lord high treasurer. The quiet, conniving man who ran her kingdom. Walsingham was her master of spies. She did not know the son, but his connection to these two men made him someone worthy of caution.

"Misshapen as a changeling," Lord Henry went on, his voice low and urgent with loathing, "with a mind as twisted as his body. But precocious. A few years back, at his recommendation, every troupe of players in England surrendered their best actors to the queen's own company. The rest were redistributed, and many were recruited." He ran a long, cool finger down the line of her jaw. *Nothing but players.* They are Elizabeth's eyes and ears at a distance. *They are spies.*"

He flung her off and backed away, and at last the scornful laughter ripped from him. "Within three days, Elizabeth will know everything that has passed within these walls. If she finds it to her advantage, she will pass your treason on to your king." He brushed the sleeves of his doublet as if the very air of her room had soiled him. "I must ride for England and attempt to control the coming storm. As for you, madam, do what you will; I fear you will never be queen." With that, he strode out the door.

"You are wrong," she'd whispered defiantly to the empty room. "I have seen it."

■ ■ ■ ■

MIRROR

■ ■ ■ ■

You go not till I set you up a glass
Where you may see the inmost part of you.

25

Ben took the blue robe from me, laying it back down across her face.

"What have I done?" I whispered.

He frowned, as if hearing me from a great distance. "You did not do this."

"You don't know that. *I* don't know that." Hysteria was rising in waves.

There was a shout overhead.

"Kate, you have to go. I can't leave her, and you can't stay." He made a move toward me and stopped, as if he could not bear to touch me. A look of blank horror filled his face. "Listen to me: You're the only person who can save Lily right now. Go down to the house. Make sure the police aren't there. I doubt it: They have no reason to be, yet. Clean yourself up, get a change of clothes. Get money. Get whatever you need to find Lily. And then get out. Get as far away from here as you can."

I was staring at him stupidly.

"Go."

I turned and stumbled across the meadow. At its edge a thick row of pines skated down another steep stretch of the hillside, tumbling to the road. Bracken cracked and rustled beneath my feet, small rocks tumbling and sliding around me. The wood was eerily silent.

At the bottom, the trees ended abruptly at the road. I edged forward to look up and down the pavement. The sun had not yet made its way this far down the hillside, and the road was a ravine of gray ghosts. Thinking of Sybilla rustling behind me in shimmering blue, I slipped across the road and floundered up the slope on the opposite side, toward the house. What had I done?

Sybilla was dead and Lily had disappeared. I had forty-eight hours to find the manuscript and ransom her.

If I did, if I found her, I might — just might — learn what had happened up on that hill last night. Learn what I had or had not done.

Forty-eight hours.

I had to tell Lady Nairn.

The house was dark. On the terrace, I looked up. There was only one light on, high in a corner tower. Lady Nairn's treasure room.

With my hand on the front door, I paused. Lady Nairn had been on the hilltop last night, her arms raised to the moon, a knife in her hand. She was a witch, a Wiccan priestess; that much was clear. But what other role had she played? I'd thought her a victim when I first saw the body covered in her blue beetle-wing gown. Was it possible that she'd killed instead? Or seen me kill? Swallowing back dread, I opened the heavy door and slipped inside.

It did not feel like a sleeping house, filled with the sense of slow breathing and dreams. It felt empty, even derelict. I fumbled my way up the dimly lit stairs. One floor up, just outside the hall, a vase lay smashed on the floor. The room beyond was dark save for the far corner, where faint light oozed from the door to the stairs up to the tower. Hearing nothing, I crept across the room, pausing again to listen before pattering up the steps.

At the top, the door to Lady Nairn's room was ajar. Through the crack, I saw that the chest beneath the window had been smashed, its splinters scattered across the floor. The last time I'd come, the room had been singing, the air filled with wind chimes and the quiet burble of a fountain. Now it was silent. Holding my breath, I pushed open the door.

It wasn't just the chest that was broken. Around it, the once beautiful room was a shambles. Ashes had been scattered across the floor, and the chimes ripped down and savagely bent and broken. The small bookshelf had been overturned. Some of the books smoldered on the hearth; others had been tossed into the fountain, clogging its flow. Nearby, the two armchairs had been slit. Within the circle inlaid in the tile floor, a pentacle had been drawn in what looked like blood.

Maybe it was the pentacle. Maybe it was the memory of Lady Nairn on the hill, her arms raised to the moon. Looking around the ravaged room, I finally realized what it was: Fire to the south, water to the west, chimes to the east, for air, and the window framing the hill to the north, for earth. It was a Wiccan temple. Or the ruins of one. A temple desecrated with a fury, a pointed and extreme hatred that was frightening even in its aftermath.

Through the open door, I heard the shuffle of a step on the stair below, and then silence. Whoever was out there did not want to be heard. Why? The pentacle on the floor suggested that the place was ready for some rite — missing only the celebrants. Was that who was rising up the stairs? Had the light in the tower been a lure?

The room was at the top of the tower, with only one door; the stairs were the only way out. I was trapped. Picking up a stout board torn from the chest, I slipped behind the door. Moments later, I heard a step on the threshold and an intake of breath. I gripped the board like a bat, and the door was flung shut.

Eircheard stood facing me, knife in hand, horror spreading across his face. "What's happened, lass? Are you all right?"

I looked down. I'd forgotten my blood-soaked clothes. Dropping the board, I began to shake. "It's not my blood."

Behind him stood Lady Nairn in dark trousers and a thin sweater, her face drawn. "Where's Lily?"

"It's not hers, either."

"Where is she?"

I took a deep breath. "We found her last night at the festival. But she was taken again. From me, Lady Nairn. It's why I came back up the hill last night. . . . I'm sorry."

As I spoke, she raised a hand to her mouth, stifling a cry. Now she turned away. As quickly as I could, I recounted all that had happened from seeing Lucas up through the phone call from Lily's captors.

"Who are they?" demanded Lady Nairn.

"I don't know. I saw Lucas at the festival. But he told me to walk away. On the hill last night, I saw the Winter King. It was his voice, on the phone."

"The bastard who first slipped me a mickey and then tried to kill me?" asked Eircheard.

I nodded. "I don't know who he is. None of this makes sense."

"What do they want?" Lady Nairn snapped.

"They took the knife. Now they want the manuscript of *Macbeth*."

She wheeled about the room. "How do they even know about it?"

"I don't know. They gave me forty-eight hours. . . ."

She stopped at the window that had once sung with chimes, fingering a shard of mother-of-pearl and crystal from the sill. "The mirror, the knife, and now the manuscript," she murmured.

"The mirror?"

She turned and surveyed the room. "This . . . this isn't just hatred for me and my religion. Though it's both of those things." She shook her head. "It also covers a theft. Whoever did this also took the mirror."

Dim and spotted with age within its heavy silver frame, the mirror she'd kept in here had once belonged to the King's Men; it was said to have been used as a prop in the first performance of *Macbeth*.

"I've been wrong, Kate," she said, her face grim. "It isn't sabotage we're dealing with."

"They're stealing your finest treasures," I said bleakly. *Including Lily.*

She shook her head impatiently. "They're gathering tools." She crossed her arms, her eyes dropping to my jacket. "Whose blood is it?"

"Sybilla's. She — she's dead," I faltered.

"Dead how?"

"Her throat was cut."

Eircheard snorted with outrage while Lady Nairn cried out, putting a hand down on the sill to steady herself. Briefly, her eyes met his. "Then they've consecrated it — the knife," she said. "And probably the mirror as well."

"Consecrated?"

" 'To make holy.' " She exhaled in sardonic disgust. "In Wiccan practice, we mostly consecrate with light, usually moonlight."

"So you are one, then. A witch."

"I prefer the term 'priestess.' "

I didn't care what term she used; why hadn't she told me?

"There are older, darker rites, though," she went on, "still whispered about in corners, that use other forces. The most powerful — and the most dangerous — is blood."

Rubbing her forehead, she stood staring at the pentacle smeared on the white floor. "Like I said, this isn't sabotage. It's a hijacking. It isn't just Lucas trying to ruin my show. He — and others, maybe — are taking it for their own. To work the magic . . . Black magic," she added. "Blood sacrifice."

26

Nausea rippled around me as I thought of Sybilla sprawled on the rocks, Ben's bleak face staring down at her body. "Sybilla was killed in a rite of black magic?"

"In preparation for one," said Lady Nairn.

"Preparation?" My voice was hoarse. "That was *rehearsal?"*

"It was a rite of consecration. Not the Great Rite itself, whatever that's intended to be."

"What were you doing up there?"

"Our Samhuinn rite. A ceremony of celebration and thanksgiving."

Staring at my hands, I began to shake. "I woke covered in blood. And missing hours . . ." My voice dropped to a whisper. "I might have done it." I looked up. "I might have killed Sybilla. Or helped to."

Eircheard took both my hands, his face solemn. "You've got blood on you, maybe. But not killing."

I twisted to look at Lady Nairn. "Did you see it? Did you see what happened?"

Her jaw twitched. "No. I lost sight of you in the chaos, and then I left as quickly as possible. I thought you'd done the same. So, no, I didn't see."

"Then you don't know," I said, pulling away from Eircheard in despair. *"You can't."* From the way my head felt, I was pretty sure I'd had a concussion. It would explain the amnesia and the headache, but not the action. What had I done in the hours that I'd lost?

"You saw something horrible, there's no doubt about that," said Lady Nairn. "No one deserves that kind of death." She shook her head slightly. "You said that Lily's captors wanted the manuscript. Did they ask you to deliver it?"

"Yes."

"Then I'm afraid there's another possibility, Kate. They consecrated the knife with blood. They may also have consecrated you."

I went still, the air slicing against my skin suddenly sharp as a million small knives. "For what?"

"Blood sacrifice, lass, requires a death," said Eircheard.

She must die, Lucas had intoned. Lily

would die, he'd said. Or I would.

I looked down. Did the blood on my hands mark me as killer or as victim?

Lily had been taken on my watch, her hand literally slipping from mine in that wild, dancing crowd in the Edinburgh close. She was my responsibility. Furthermore, if I'd killed Sybilla, or participated in any way . . . if I'd just *been* there . . . saving Lily was the best shot at redemption I'd ever be likely to manage.

And her captors were the only route I had toward finding out what I'd done.

Whatever the cost, I had to find Lily.

Lady Nairn was looking out the window, one toe tapping against the floor. "Forty-eight hours, you said?"

I nodded.

Again, her eyes sought out Eircheard, who'd begun to pick up the pieces of the smashed chest and stack them carefully against one wall. "Even the timing fits," she said. "In two nights, the moon will be full."

"Aye," said Eircheard. His eyes were bloodshot and bleary; a livid bruise was darkening across one cheek. "There's to be a total eclipse, as well."

"Rare enough to begin with. Even rarer on the Samhuinn moon. The Blood Moon,"

Lady Nairn said softly. She folded her arms. "They'll need the cauldron, too."

Having neatly stacked the remains of the chest, Eircheard righted the bookshelf and began filling it with whatever books he could find that weren't sodden or singed. "This mess maybe sprang, in part, from frustration at not finding it."

"The great silver bowl?" I asked. "It's downstairs. I saw it as I came up." Hard to miss a gleaming vat of silver three feet wide and two high, really.

"That's a copy," said Lady Nairn. "They'll need the original, and that's in the vault. Though I suppose I ought to check that as well."

"It'll be the manuscript they'll be wanting most of all," said Eircheard.

"They need to know what to do, don't they?" I said. "The earlier version of the play . . . it's supposed to lay out a real magical rite."

Gathering up bits of shattered wind chime, Lady Nairn sighed. "It may be more than a general description they're after, Kate. In witchcraft, at least the way I practice it day-to-day, spells are intuitive and improvised. Lived in the moment. Power, whatever there is, inheres in the witch, as a vessel of the Goddess."

She smoothed her hair back from her face. "But other practices are different. In ceremonial magic, precision matters: Spells depend upon using exactly the right tools in the right way at precisely the right time. Most of all, ceremonial magic requires the right words said in the right order, with the right pronunciation." She turned to look at me. "In witchcraft, as I said, power inheres in the witch. The speaker, the spell maker. But in ceremonial magic, power inheres in the language of the spell, in the words spoken.

"Most great rites, whether white or black magic, are at least in part ceremonial. So you see, to get it right —"

"They want the manuscript as a script for murder," I said. *They meant to use Shakespeare to shape murder.* In the last few minutes, Lady Nairn seemed to have grown smaller, somehow, and harder. As if Lily's disappearance had burned away everything but a single cold, ruthless purpose. "The lone bright spot is that they don't yet have everything they need. And we must make sure they never get it. We need to rescue Lily, Kate, so we have to find the manuscript. *But we must also see that they never get hold of it.*"

Eircheard was watching me. "Why are

they assuming you can find it in the first place, in that kind of time?"

In my mind's eye, I saw my name scrawled on a bloodstained page: *Kate Stanley.* "Come with me," I said, heading down the stairs.

Lady Nairn and Eircheard hurried in my wake.

Back in my room, I put Aubrey's notes in Lady Nairn's hand. As she read, Eircheard looking over her shoulder, I grabbed some jeans, a black turtleneck, and black Skechers and went into the bathroom to change. I looked longingly at the shower but didn't dare take the time, settling for scrubbing my face and arms in the sink.

Walking back out, I set out on the desk Lady Nairn's other evidence: the Xeroxed entry in the household account book, dated 1589, and the letter from Ellen Terry to her mysterious Superman, dated 1911.

Lady Nairn set the Aubrey down. "Where did you get this?"

"Ben found it on Auld Callie."

She looked up sharply. "It was left there on purpose? For you to find it?"

"I can only assume so. Could it be what Sir Angus found?" I asked.

"Possibly." Her eyes were shining. "It

backs the family legends."

I nodded. "It also links Shakespeare to Dee. To conjuring — to ceremonial magic — as much as to witchcraft." Quickly, I told her what I'd worked out the night before on the subject of Macbeth conjuring for the sake of knowledge.

"I'm no expert on Dee," she said with a frown. "If that's the direction things are going, we'll have to consult Joanna Black, down in London."

I'd heard of Joanna — had been told I ought to meet her for years, actually. She, too, had left academia for practice. But where my study had been Renaissance drama, chiefly Shakespeare, hers had been Renaissance magic. She had a D.Phil. from Oxford in the history of religion and science. I'd headed into the public world of theater; she'd headed into the reclusive world of magic and the exclusive world of occult collectors. I knew where her shop was, but that was about it; I'd never met her.

"I've never met her in person myself," said Lady Nairn. "But she's quite lovely on the phone and in e-mail, and that's all we'd need."

"Bollocks!" said Eircheard, looking up from the desk. "What matters right now isn't who made Shakespeare change the sodding play or why. What matters is where it got to, so we know where Kate needs to go. And Dee's got bog-all to do with that. The last known whereabouts of anything useful have to do with Ellen Terry's Monsieur Superbe Homme. Who is he, do you suppose?"

Lady Nairn shook her head.

"Look," I said, skimming through Terry's letter with one finger to point at the last line: *As it is, I am hoping that you can glimpse the Forest through the Trees.* "And then here," I said, sliding over to the Aubrey, to Beerbohm's cartoon of Shakespeare brandishing a leafy branch at Macbeth, with its caption of a loosely scribbled line from *Macbeth: Who can impress the Forrest, bid the Tree unfix his earth-bound root?*

"It's got to have something to do with that goddamn tree," I said.

"Superbe homme," murmured Eircheard. *"Sous* pear bum. Under the pear-shaped arse."

"Focus," I said shortly. "Both Terry and Beerbohm yammering on about forests and trees can't be a coincidence. Especially in light of Sir Angus's last words. *Dunsinnan must go to Birnam Wood.*"

"That isn't what he said," grumbled Eirc-heard.

"What?"

"Birnam Wood. That isn't what he said."

Lady Nairn rolled her eyes. "He'd just had a stroke. It was what he meant."

Eircheard looked at me. "What he said was 'Dunsinnan must go to the Birnam tree.' Not the wood. And if you're wanting to put a really fine point on it, it wasn't 'Birnam' he said, either. 'Birble,' or 'burble,' or 'bourbon,' or something."

" 'Birbam,' " said Lady Nairn curtly. " 'Dunsinnan must go to the Birbam tree.' "

"Pear bum, bare bum," Eircheard chanted under his breath, back to puzzling out Ellen Terry's correspondent. "Beer bum, burr bum."

"Will you be quiet?" snapped Lady Nairn.

"No," I said suddenly. "Say it again."

" 'Beer bum, burr bum'?"

I felt a flicker of excitement. "Did he say 'go to *the* Birbam tree'?"

"No. Just 'to Birbam tree.' "

"You're a *superbe homme* yourself," I said, kissing him on the cheek. "It's not 'Birnam,' and it's not 'Birbam.' " I pointed to the drawing. "It's *'Beerbohm.'* "

"The cartoonist?" asked Eircheard. "Max Beerbohm?"

"Beerbohm, yes. Max, no. His older half brother, Herbert.

Lady Nairn's eyes lit up. "Herbert Beerbohm *Tree*."

"*Tree?*" hooted Eircheard.

"One of the great Shakespearean actors and theater impresarios of the late Victorian and Edwardian eras," I said. "His family name was Beerbohm, but when Herbert went on the stage he felt it didn't sound English enough, so he translated the last syllable, *bohm* or *baum,* from the German to get Tree. As it happens, one of his greatest roles was Macbeth."

"Monsieur Superbe Homme," said Eircheard with satisfaction.

I smiled. "A cross-language pun of sorts. At a guess, the name 'Beerbohm' is pronounced something between 'pear bum' and 'bare bum' in French. He's supposed to have been superb, too. Tall and handsome. Witty. Gallant. He started RADA — the Royal Academy of Dramatic Arts — and was knighted. Also *superbe* in the French sense: splendid, magnificent, proud. Though apparently not arrogant . . ."

"But dead, I take it," said Eircheard.

"Quite."

"So how was Sir Angus going to go to him? Do we know where he's buried?"

"I don't."

"Where he lived?"

"No — yes." I stood up and sat down again. "*Yes.* Lady Nairn, was Sir Angus a fan of *Phantom of the Opera*?"

"Angus hated musicals," she said. "Fairly sniffy about them, actually. He preferred Verdi and Wagner. But after his stroke, I found two tickets to *Phantom* in his wallet. I assumed he meant to take Lily."

I stood still in the center of the room, adrenaline surging through me. "He wasn't going to Birnam Wood. Or the Birnam tree. He was going to Beerbohm Tree. And Tree lived at the theater. *His* theater. The theater he built and ran. Her Majesty's Theatre, in London."

"Oh, good Lord," said Lady Nairn.

"What?" asked Eircheard. *"What?"*

"Where *Phantom*'s been playing for nearly three decades," I said. I turned to Lady Nairn. "Do you have anything of Tree's in your collection?"

She was skimming out of the room when the sound of sirens floated through the window.

Coming back to the desk, Lady Nairn slid the papers back into the folder, which she stuffed into a tote and handed to me along with the tight bundle of my blood-soaked clothes. "Time to go, Kate."

27

"My place," said Eircheard. "We'll burn those clothes in the forge and get you on your way for London."

Lady Nairn led us swiftly to a back stairway. At the bottom, we came to a postern door opening onto a walled garden. The trees of the surrounding pine wood marched right up to the garden wall. Lady Nairn unlocked the small, stout oak door that led through it.

"I have something of Tree's you should see," she said with quiet urgency. "I'll be ten minutes behind you. If I'm longer than that, don't wait. Now go."

As two police cars rolled up the gravel drive, Eircheard and I slipped south through the trees. After a while, we turned back westward, Eircheard's rolling gait giving our footsteps a kind of jazz syncopation; other than our footsteps, the woods were quiet. High wispy clouds raced across the sky. Past the road that turned off toward the hill, we cut back to the main road. Edging through the dry bracken, Eircheard found a place dappled with dark shade and beckoned me forward. We quickly crossed the lane and entered the woods on the opposite side.

Five minutes later, we walked into the smithy. I prowled about, feeling exposed, until Eircheard said, "Make yourself useful," and showed me how to work the bellows as he stoked up the fire. The fire blazed up from red to orange and yellow that paled into white. He had just fed my bloody jacket into the flames when Lady Nairn scurried in, her cheeks pink and her breath coming in short gasps. "McGregor," she gasped. "On a mission. Headed this way and looking for Kate."

Eircheard thrust the rest of my clothes into the fire, and Lady Nairn grabbed my hand, pulling me back outside. As we ran across the field toward the woods at the side of his house, I heard the clang of a hammer on metal. Eircheard was forging. We ducked into the trees, and a car turned into the drive behind us.

Crouching beneath some dying ferns, we watched the police car pull to a stop, its doors flashing in the sun as they opened. DI McGregor and her sergeant got out and went into the forge. Eircheard's hammer beats never paused.

"Kate —"

I shook my head impatiently. "I need to hear what McGregor has to say."

"Eircheard will tell us. I need to tell you who's behind all this." My eyes locked on hers. As she caught her breath and the pink in her cheeks subsided, she looked ashen. I let her draw me deeper into the trees, into a clearing where pale light and the odd bird-call drifted down through lacy branches whose last clinging leaves were dry as paper. I blinked, realizing where we were: back in the stone circle. In the morning sun, the standing stones looked squat and sleepy. Stones that had seemed to loom taller than I in the darkness rose only to my shoulders; half of them had tipped and fallen. Even so, it was a place of brooding power. Asleep, not drained or dead.

We crouched in the shadow of one of three big stones fallen together, where I could still see the smithy and the car.

"I'm sure Lucas is involved. He has to be. But with him, or behind him, is someone far worse." She swallowed. "It's my niece, Kate. My sister's child. Her name is Carrie Douglas. I'd rather face Lucas any day. His hatred may be thick, but it's standard flesh-

and-blood wickedness. Jealousy and greed: things you can understand in a visceral way. But Carrie —" She paused. "Her evil is uncanny. Fey."

She ran a hand over her mouth. "After my sister died, when Carrie was twelve, Angus and I took her in — my sister had never identified the father. We gave her a home and did our best to love her, but she was . . . cruel. Not in the normal small ways of children still learning to be civilized. She enjoyed causing pain, and her eyes always looked as if she were seeing more than she ought to be. Frankly, she frightened me. And she'd frightened her mother, though my sister was too loyal to say so. But she was bright and curious, especially about the craft."

"Witchcraft?"

"It's in her blood. In our family, it's a tradition passed down from mother to daughter. It's in her name, too: Carrie's short for Cerridwen . . . a Welsh triple goddess famed for cauldron magic. But her mother was dead, and I would not teach her." She sniffed. "Walling her out was not, I've thought since, the right response. She went off and found other masters.

"On her seventeenth birthday, I found her on the hilltop with my daughter. There was a cauldron. In it was a dead adder and the head of Elizabeth's pet cat."

I grimaced.

"Next to it, Elizabeth was bound and naked. Carrie had . . . cut her." She put a hand out to the stone, as if she needed steadying, though we were both sitting down. "She likes to mark things — and people — with the old Pictish symbol of a cauldron. A large circle with two tiny circles on either side, a line running through the center of all three." With one finger, she traced the design on the rock:

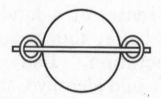

"It's a cauldron seen from above, hanging from a bar over a fire, with the two lugs, or handles, on either side." Her eyes narrowed as she looked out toward the smithy. "She'd carved it right over Elizabeth's pubic area. Elizabeth was ten."

She gave a little shake, pulling herself loose from the memory and turning her attention to me. "Angus wouldn't prosecute her. More because he did not want to drag our daughter through the consequences than out of any family loyalty. But he banished her from our house and our lives then and there. . . . This was almost thirty years ago."

"And you think she's back?"

"I've just spoken to Ben, Kate. He saw a symbol carved into Sybilla's belly." My stomach tightened with revulsion. "A large circle with two small circles on either side. It seems to have been scratched into Auld Callie's shoulder as well. McGregor asked me about it. I told her I had no idea what it meant."

"Jesus."

"It makes sense, of a kind, of Callie's murder, even before they needed blood for ritual consecration," Lady Nairn said bleakly. "She could identify Carrie, you see."

"Does Lily know any of this?"

Her face clouded. "No. I've never told her about either Lucas or Carrie. I probably should have, especially when she got so taken with Corra Ravensbrook. All that stuff about Dunsinnan in *Ancient Pictland* —"

"You think it may have come from Carrie?"

"She's not a bored housewife." Her lips twisted in disgust. "The Scottish counterpart of Cerridwen is a crane goddess named Corra. And 'Douglas' is Gaelic for 'dark water.' "

"Ravensbrook," I murmured. "So Corra Ravensbrook *is* Carrie Douglas."

She nodded. "I started to tell Lily, more than once. But somehow it always seemed like taking a hammer to her innocence."

And what's happened to her innocence now? I thought. "What's Carrie after?" I asked aloud. "I mean — Macbeth works his magic to gain knowledge. But the ability to play the stock market or manipulate Vegas . . ." I shook my head. "It seems too mundane, anticlimactic even, for someone who'd . . ."

"Hang Auld Callie and carve up Sybilla?" Lady Nairn said softly.

"Yes."

"Don't be distracted, Kate, by Aubrey or Dee or even Macbeth himself. Ellen Terry's source, my family's legends, and now Aubrey all say that what Shakespeare altered — what's missing — isn't something to do with Macbeth conjuring. It has to do with the witches' magic. . . . *What is it you do?* Macbeth cries as he enters. And the witches answer as one. . . ."

My voice slid through the words along with hers: *"A deed without a name."*

"That's the rite that's missing," said Lady Nairn. "That's what Carrie wants."

"But it's not missing. The witches are there, dancing around a cauldron."

"Oh, there's cauldron magic present, but it's the stuff of nursery rhymes. Or nursery nightmares. And if Macbeth could see and hear what they're doing, *why ask?*"

She had twisted her hands together. "Celtic myth is scattered with cauldron magic, Kate. Cauldrons of plenty and prophecy, mostly. But the goddess Cerridwen's cauldron is also, quite specifically, about poetry. Shorthand for inspiration of all kinds. For genius. The charismatic ability to conjure up shared dreams so bright and so strong that they move people to action. No amount of hard work or study or card-counting can buy you that. Nothing can *buy* it. It's a flash of fire from the gods that you are given, or you are not." Her eyes met mine. "But if there was some promise of manipulating such a flash of power? Of directing or luring the thunderbolt of the gods to land where you wished? That, I think, someone like Carrie might well kill for."

Lily had boasted that her beau would reshape storytelling, as Shakespeare once had. I pushed that thought away. "What promise?" I asked shortly. "This is the twenty-first century. What *promise* could

Carrie convince herself of?"

Lady Nairn drew in a deep breath. "There are those who say that the play itself is proof. More specifically, the playwright."

"Shakespeare?"

Her famous turquoise eyes, holding mine, seemed fathomless. "Some say he was able to record such a rite because he witnessed it, Kate. And having witnessed it . . . that he benefited from it."

I jumped to my feet, my breath coming in short bursts as if I'd been running. "Are you suggesting that Shakespeare's genius came from a rite of magic? *That's absurd.*"

Lady Nairn rose beside me. "Is it? He was a poor boy, a glover's son, from a provincial backwater. He left behind no record of education. No records at all, really, save that he sired three children and then disappeared for seven years, after which he showed up in London, his pen flowing with astonishing brilliance."

"It's extraordinary, I'll give you that. But to explain the inexplicable by totting it up to a moment of hocus-pocus —"

She was as calm and cool as I was exasperated. "Did what you saw last night look like hocus-pocus?"

I was silent, remembering the sweep of moonlight and starlight on the hill, the strange rise of the keening voice. And the horned man with the eyes of an owl. "Who was he?" I asked tightly. "The horned man?"

"Eircheard."

"No." It was not Eircheard I had seen. It wasn't possible. I'd seen a younger, fitter man who'd had no limp.

But Lady Nairn was adamant. "He's been a member of my coven for a number of years, Kate. After Angus died, he stepped into the role of priest. I had a driver collect him after the festival and drive him back here directly. He was — worse for wear, let's say, but he was here. Just before you saw him, he'd called down the god. . . . Why? Who did you see?"

I stared at her, feeling the world sway beneath me. The very air playing over that hill seemed to make me see things that weren't there. I didn't want to think about that. "You meant to work magic with this production as well, didn't you?"

A couple of leaves had stuck in her hair. She looked like a dryad.

She smiled. *"There are more things in heaven and earth, Horatio, than are dreamt of in your philosophy,"* she said lightly. "What you or I can or can't believe, Kate, doesn't matter. It's what Carrie believes that matters just now. However he came by it, it seems that Shakespeare wrote a dark and terrible rite of cauldron magic into *Macbeth* and later withdrew it. If Carrie believes, as I think she does, that she can use it to manipulate divine inspiration, then if she gets hold of it, she will perform it."

Beyond the wood, the hammering stopped. Presently Eircheard emerged with the two detectives, walking around to the back of the smithy. While McGregor stood talking to Eircheard, the sergeant peeked into the bedroom and opened the back of the van, apparently with Eircheard's permission.

Silently, I drew forward to the edge of the wood. Their voices floated thinly across the field. "What makes you think Kate was up there?" asked Eircheard.

McGregor's smile was cold. "Fingerprints tentatively matching those in her room are all over a car at the base of the hill. And there's blood in the trunk. A lot of it."

Bile rose in my throat. Had Sybilla been in the car as I drove? Already dead — or even worse, still alive? Had I driven her to her death?

"Give her up," McGregor said silkily, "and I'll go lightly on you."

"Kind of you," said Eircheard, his hands

in his pockets. "But I don't have her to give."

McGregor sniffed, surveying the smithy and the heap of scrap metal behind it. "Be careful, Mr. Kinross. A knife like some that you've made seems to have been involved in two homicides." She turned back to him. "I know your history. If you had anything to do with either of them, I'll see to it that you never see the light of day again."

There was a stiff moment of silence. "Good day," said McGregor. And then she turned on her heel, her mouth still curved in a serpent's smile, and left, her sergeant trotting alongside.

Eircheard watched her go and then went back around and into the smithy. As the police car pulled out, he began hammering again.

It's what Carrie believes that matters just now. Whatever other madness was twisting the world, that at least made terrible sense. If she believed she could draw down divine inspiration by a rite of black magic, she'd perform it. And that would mean more death.

It seemed like an age, though it was probably only a few minutes, before the hammering ceased again and Eircheard came back around the building. Opening the door to the van, he leaned against the vehicle's side. He was holding the bag with the folderful of papers. Lady Nairn pressed something into my hand. I looked down. It was an iPod. "When you have time, just pop it off 'hold' and push 'play.' "

"Lady Nairn" — I faltered — "forty-eight hours isn't much time."

She put a hand on my shoulder. "Find Lily," she said. "But Carrie can't be allowed to have that manuscript."

"How —"

She shook her head. "I'll do everything in my power to help you."

"Get the police in on this, too," I said. "The more people looking for her, the better."

"No," she said vehemently. "That woman will crucify you, given half a chance, and get Lily killed. There's no good that will come of going to the police, I'm afraid. If anyone can find her, Kate, you will." She passed her hand over my head in benediction. "Blessed be," she said, and smiled. "It's the witches' farewell."

I turned and walked toward Eircheard. "Into the van with you, then," he said. "Dunsinnan must go to Beerbohm Tree."

I glanced back as I slid into the passenger

seat. Under the eaves of the beech trees, Lady Nairn looked like a small shadow that had lost its body. The next time I looked, she had melted into the woods.

28

Shorn fields and autumnal woods slipped by in a blur. In the hedgerows, the haw-thorns were bright with berries. I seemed to be staring out at the world through a veil of shadow. "What did McGregor have to say?" I asked after a while.

"If you heard her outside, you got the gist of it. She wants your bonny hide, and she's willing to knock other heads together to get it. Mine especially."

"I gathered."

"Bit of a checkered past." He leaned back comfortably against the seat, one hand spread over the steering wheel, the other fidgeting with a small twisted bit of iron the size of a large marble. "Did some time a while back, for robbery." He shrugged. "Feedin' a habit. But there was a brawl afterwards, and another bloke got killed. With a knife. I didn't do it, but I was present. McGregor'll make hay out of that, given half a chance."

My stomach turned over. "Eircheard — you can't do this. Get me to the railway station in Perth," I said. "I'll be fine from there."

"Do you have any idea how many surveillance cameras there are in those stations? McGregor'll have you before you reach Edinburgh, never mind London. No. I'll drive."

"If she finds me with you, she'll have you, too."

"Then we'll just have to make sure she doesn't find us, won't we?" He drove as if he were at the wheel of a Ferrari on the autobahn, so fast that the battered van shook; even so he looked relaxed, as if he had all the time in the world. He slowed down only for speed cameras, whose locations he seemed to know by some sixth sense.

"It's not all for you, lassie," he said with a wry smile. "Though it's true I've taken a liking to your smile. But don't be taking the sins of the world on your shoulders. I owe the Nairns a great deal. . . . Met Lady Nairn in prison. She's a chaplain with the pagan prison ministry, did you know? Saw something in me that I couldn't. Or wouldn't. To this day, I can't tell you what. But she latched on and wouldn't let go." He shrugged. "I suppose I'd always been something of a pagan. But talking to her, the cycles of things just began to make some sense. Afterwards, she and Sir Angus helped me apprentice to a blacksmith. And then they gave me a hand setting up my own forge.

"That was when Lily was no more than a wee mite." He shook his head. "So you see, I'd be hard-pressed to forgive any bastard as harmed a hair on her head.

"But it's not all for her, or for them, either." His mouth twisted. "Bloody eejit down in Edinburgh tried to kill me. I'm no saint, Kate. I did my time. Wouldn't mind seeing that he does his." The van careened along the shores of a shimmering blue lake. "So you've had my story. What about yours? What did Lady Nairn come running to say to you?"

I told Eircheard what Lady Nairn had told me, watching his face go taut with disgust at Carrie's history. "I knew of her," he said. "But not about the cutting."

"How could she think that — that what she did to Sybilla and to Auld Callie would in any way contribute to a flowering of genius?"

I thought of Shakespeare, of the ease with which bright and dark worlds flew from his pen, bubbles blown carelessly on a breeze.

What made his genius so luminous was partly his range, I mused aloud: his moods stretching from silly to tragic, sometimes spinning from one to the other on a dime, his characters ranging from innocent girls to aged kings, from rollicking drunkards to ferocious queens, from sly and cynical bastards to hot-tempered youths chasing dreams of heroism. He gathered as his raw material all the fundamental experiences of being human, from birth to death, and all our passions in between: love and lust, hatred and hilarity, greed, jealousy, wrath, and murderous revenge.

But there were other great writers who had done all these things. What set Shakespeare apart, for me, even from other greats, was his generosity: his invitation, even insistence, for others to join him in the act of imagining. His words had the power to conjure up bright worlds, but Shakespeare did not claim that power all for himself. Far from it; he scattered it like petals or glittering confetti. Unlike Shaw or O'Neill, who'd left stage directions that ran to entire pages, or the Beckett police, who insisted on licensing productions to ensure that they adhered to the master's vision, Shakespeare did not specify much about interpretation or setting or action, about political or moral message, or the lack thereof. His reticence made his works wonderfully elastic. It also made them demanding — sometimes maddeningly so — for directors and actors who had to figure out at every turn why these words and no others needed to be said right here and now. But Shakespeare was also demanding of his audiences: "Yes," you could almost hear him say, "you are sitting in a fairly barren wooden theater. But dream yourselves to France. To a seacoast in Bohemia. To a magic-haunted island in a tempest-tossed sea. *I dare you.*"

And for four hundred years, in every corner of the earth, people had taken his dare and sailed into imagined worlds — together. For the art that Shakespeare had shaped was communal, shared in a way that books and even films never are. It was a singular gift: the infinite and unceasing invitation to crowds to come together with half-cocked brows of skepticism, a fair dash of rowdiness, and most of all, sheer delight, and collectively imagine worlds into being.

"To suggest that all this had its source in some lightning bolt that struck while watching a rite on a Scottish hill," I said, "strikes me as not only preposterous but insulting to whatever forces of creation produced him."

Eircheard had remained mostly quiet through my rant, a little smile playing on his face from time to time. "Only if you're insisting on a narrow definition of magic," he replied. "As narrow, in some ways, as the sniffy productions that drive you mad."

I bit my lip. "Lady Nairn gave me Crowley's definition: 'the science and art of causing change to occur in conformity with will.' "

"Ah, well, there's a nice double meaning there, for a man named Will." He gave me a sly sideways grin. "Never liked Crowley much, myself, or his definition, either. He equates magic with change. Willed change, but change all the same. I'd put it a wee bit differently. 'Making,' for instance. Did you know that the Anglo-Saxons used to call poets 'makers'?"

"So did the Greeks," I said, feeling suddenly exhausted. "The word 'poet' comes from their word for 'to make.' "

"Well, there you are, then." He turned the bit of iron in his hand. "Whatever you want to call it, some people seem to be able to tap into it strongly. Shakespeare, Michelangelo, Beethoven. But it isn't the moment of tapping — even if you could pinpoint it — that's important for any of them, or for any of us, if you see what I mean. It's the unfurling, the blossoming. Do you count conception, now, as the single miraculous moment of a life? Or are the nine months of growing curved in the dark, the bursting out into light, and, after that, the long unfolding of a life in the world all equally miraculous?"

"By that light," I said quietly, "all life is magic."

A gruff rumbling of assent rose from him. " 'Creation,' I think, is the word I'd use. But, yes, that's the deepest magic. Making whole shared worlds, like Shakespeare — maybe that's one of the highest forms. Very nearly divine in its power. But some of the most profound magic is fairly simple. Cooking, I'd say, and gardening, or farming. Rearing children. But you can also find it in making cabinets or clocks or quilts."

"Or swords?"

"Definitely swords." He grinned. "As for being annoyed about a rite glimpsed on a hill — well, ritual is just a way of celebrating certain snapshot moments. Turning points. Making you really see them, focus on them. Not making them *happen*." He shrugged. "Course, that's just my opinion, and I'm not a scholar or anything. Just an ex-con who enjoys banging on steel." He stretched and shifted in the seat. "What did Shakespeare think about magic, now?"

I shook my head. "It's hard to pin him down."

"Try."

It was no longer a question that was merely academic. Two lives might hang on it. One of them mine.

I stared out the window at the fields of Scotland rolling by. "His plays are laced with it, from first to last." In my mind, I went over the great conjuring scenes, from the *Henry VI* plays right at the beginning of his career, around about 1590, through to *The Tempest,* near the end, twenty-odd years later. "He was definitely a cynic about the capacity of politicians and prelates to use witch hunts for their own ends. And I'd say he was a skeptic," I added slowly, "about the ability of humans — either witches or conjurors — to control supernatural forces just by casting a circle, waving a wand about, and uttering a few odd words. But, you know, in the few actual scenes of conjuration he wrote, the demons or spirits always come. Within the world of the play at hand, they're real. They make prophecies and promises that always turn out to be true, though often in some tricky way — Macbeth says that the dark powers lie like truth. But you might just as well say that they tell the truth like a lie, I suppose.

"Oddly enough, if anything, there's more magic, more deeply wound into his plots, in his final works than his first efforts. Prospero, in *The Tempest,* is the real thing: a white wizard, imagined, I've always thought, with some affection. Very possibly a fictional version of John Dee, though it's also popular to see him as Shakespeare himself: poet as magician. Earlier, he was less reverent. In the first part of *Henry IV,* written in the mid 1590s, during Shakespeare's first great flowering of genius," I said, giving Eircheard a little jab, "the Welsh leader Owen Glendower is another Dee figure, but he's a proud, prickly, and somewhat empty boaster. *I can call spirits from the vasty deep,* he claims, but he's undercut by the equally proud and prickly Hotspur, who cares for swords more than spells and who shoots back, *Why, so can I, or so can any man; but will they come when you do call for them?*

"And then there's *Midsummer Night's Dream.*"

"Full of fairies, eh?"

"English fairies, not Scottish. Flower imps, mostly. Cobweb, Moth, and Mustard-seed. But there's a shadow of Scottish witchcraft, already, almost a decade before King James forced Scottish notions of witchcraft down English throats. In Titania, queen of the fairies."

"Up here," mused Eircheard, "the queen of fairies is also the queen of witches."

"Exactly. And Titania's great comic scene has her kissing a weaver named Bottom, magically given an ass's head."

"One way to kiss ass," said Eircheard with a shrug.

Sybilla's voice hung between us: *Titania waked, and straightway loved an ass.*

"It's a parody of the Black Mass that so enthralled King James and the Continental witch-hunters," I said after a moment, "but which the English more or less scorned. The central rite of that Mass was supposed to consist of the witch kissing the devil's bottom." I shook my head. "Talk about generosity of spirit. Shakespeare took a belief that was being used to torture and kill thousands and made of it one of the great comic scenes in all of drama."

"While up here we were saddled with King Jamie lighting fools the way to dusty death, burning them at the stake," said Eircheard. "Jesus."

"Far as I can tell, Shakespeare had no respect for witch-hunters, and he suspected most conjurors as either con men or fools. But he believed in spirits and demons, and maybe fairies and ghosts. One of his earliest plays shows it best. *Henry VI, Part Two.* Wretched title, that: All it does is slot the play into others that were written later. Its first title was *The First Part of the Contention of the Two Famous Houses of York and Lancaster.*"

"That's a blooming mouthful."

"More accurate, though: It was the first history play he wrote, right around 1590. One of the plays that made his name. In it, a duchess is wild for her husband to pluck the crown from the king's head and don it himself. Her husband's enemies lure her into consulting a conjuror, to see whether what she wishes will come to pass, and when she does, they use it to disgrace and banish her, and ruin him. As far as they're concerned, she's shown up as a silly woman, while the conjuror is unmasked as part quack, part political hack. But the thing is, the conjuration, which Shakespeare specifies should be staged as the casting of a circle, pulls up a real demon. Real, at least, in the world of the play. The audience can see him, and he utters prophecies that work out to be true through the whole series of his Wars of the Roses plays. It seems to work out like that a lot; in Shakespeare, humans can call spirits from the vasty deep, but they can't control them. It's pretty much the other way around."

Maybe Lady Nairn was right, I thought suddenly. Maybe Macbeth is a dupe. Led to believe in his furious passion that he's conjuring, when all along it's the witches around him who are invoking the spirits. I shook my head. If there was anything that Dee would have liked less than a play that made a conjuror the master of demons, it was a play that made a conjuror their dupe. Their puppet.

"A duchess who wants her husband to take the crown and who's willing to listen to evil spirits," mused Eircheard. "She sounds a lot like Lady Macbeth."

"She does, doesn't she? I've always thought she was a practice run. That she stayed with him, gestating in some dark corner of his soul, until he knew what to do with her."

"If Lady M is Lady Nairn's ancestor, you think this duchess is, too? You think she's another fictional version of the Scottish witch?"

"I don't know." But Elizabeth Stewart, Lady Arran, was rumored to have lusted after the crown. I knew that. "I can't see how he could have known her story; she fell from power in the mid-1580s, for heaven's sake. What would have kept him drawn to her for so long? And what would have made it spill out in *Macbeth* when it did?"

"So what was he thinking when he wrote *Macbeth*? In between the early skepticism and the late acceptance?"

I pulled out the page from Aubrey and read it once again:

Dr. Dee begged Mr. Shakspere to alter his Play lest, in staging curs'd Secretes learned of a Scottish Witch, he conjure powers beyond his controll. But Mr. Shakespere wuld not, until there was a death, whereupon he made the changes in one houre's time.

What had William Shakespeare, laughing skeptic that he was, made of the magic he was jotting down and the request to remove it? Had he been parroting it for fun and found that he scared people, like Orson Welles reading *War of the Worlds* over the radio? There were tales of productions of Marlowe's great conjuring play, *Dr. Faustus,* emptying theaters when audiences thought they saw one too many devils appear on the stage at the magician's call. Had Shakespeare been playing with something a lot of people around him thought was fire — even if he didn't — and found that the real-world

333

consequences were too great?

Or had he been experimenting with magic himself? He was "a man torn between two masters," Aubrey had written. And one of those was John Dee. Had Shakespeare played the sorcerer's apprentice behind his master's back?

The only way to find out was to find the manuscript.

And to hope that the finding — or failure to find it — did not result in either Lily's death or mine.

I pulled my knees up to my chest, as if I might squeeze this whirl of thoughts and the terrible possibilities that danced around them out of my body altogether.

29

"Are you going to do something with that?" asked Eircheard, stealing a glance at my hands.

I looked down and realized I was still clutching the iPod Lady Nairn had given me. I flicked off the "hold" button, and it glowed into life. I pushed "play."

The screen went black, and then the high wavering chords of Bach's Toccata and Fugue in D Minor swelled into life, spilling into their grand downward swoop. Gradually the black screen lightened to swirling silver clouds that cut to a title in white curlicued letters: *Macbeth, by William Shakespeare.*

Beneath that, in roman numerals, was a date: *MCMXVI* — 1916.

"What?" asked Eircheard.

But I shook my head in stunned silence. The tiny screen oscillated light and dark as the camera closed in on the jackbooted star in a dark tunic. His dark wavy hair was long and his mustache very nearly longer. His eyes grew impossibly wide, his face twisted in triumph, as he killed an enemy with a flourishing sword thrust.

"That's him," I said. "Beerbohm Tree. As Macbeth . . ." I held it up on the steering wheel so that Eircheard could steal a glance.

"Looks like a low-budget haunted house video," he said doubtfully.

"In some quarters, this alone would be enough to kill for."

"You're joking." He looked over at me. "Jesus. You're not, are you?"

I shook my head. "It's Tree's *Macbeth* of 1916. One of the great lost films from the silent era. From any era, I suppose. One of the great lost productions of Shakespeare."

And the Nairns possessed it in a digital copy.

Dunsinnan must go to Beerbohm Tree. Had Sir Angus seen something in this film?

The set was monumental Hollywood, an odd combination of medieval Scotland and Mycenaean Greece. As the film went on, thick black blood spilled across the stage, and the white flickering eyes of the actors grew wider and wider with horror.

I fast-forwarded, watching the actors rush about like Keystone Kops until the screen

336

cut to black again. Gradually, light rose, though the scene remained dimmer and a little fuzzy. Up to this point, Tree's costume of high black boots and a black tunic criss-crossed with a wide black leather belt looked more Prussian than medieval Scottish, maybe more Hells Angels than either. Now, though, Tree walked in wearing chain mail, a long dark cloak, and a winged silver helmet somewhere between Viking and proto–*Lord of the Rings.* And he was no longer in a castle, either Scottish or ancient Greek. Instead, he looked entirely out of place in a cozy paneled room with a small graceful fireplace set a little left of center on the back wall. Or a room that might have been cozy, at any rate, if three witches had not been cackling in glee over a cauldron hanging over the fire.

It was the room, though, rather than the witches or the bloody-minded warrior, that sent prickles running up and down my skin. "I know this room," I said. "I've been there." It was Tree's private retreat, tucked up under the dome at the very top of Her Majesty's Theatre. The Dome Room, it was called. It was rented out as rehearsal space. I'd spent hours up there a few years back, running through *Othello.*

The camera cut from the witches to Tree's

startled eyes, and then to a black title screen with fancy lettering in white:

HOW NOW, YOU SECRET, BLACK, AND
MIDNIGHT HAGS!
WHAT IS IT YOU DO?

The witches cavorted with evil delight.

A DEED WITHOUT A NAME.

The camera cut to a close-up of the bubbling cauldron and then pulled back to reveal the entire wall beside the fireplace, before cutting across to Macbeth again, who was swelling with pride. Advancing slowly toward the camera, he raised his arms.

I CONJURE YOU, HOWE'ER YOU COME
TO KNOW IT:
ANSWER ME.

The witches recoiled, as if in terror, but Macbeth kept advancing. The camera pulled back once more. In the paneling to the right of the fireplace, a rectangle of darkness had appeared, the smoke of hell billowing from its depths.

I hit "pause." In 1916, I thought, that recess in the wall wasn't just a trick of light. There was a cupboard there. A cubbyhole in the paneling.

But there wasn't. Not in the room I knew. I rewound to an earlier shot of the wall. I was right; there was no door visible. Not so much as a crack.

"What's happening?" asked Eircheard.

I let the film roll on. Macbeth — Tree — strode to the hell-mouth. Plunging in his hand, he plucked from the darkness a book — Odin pulling wisdom from the under-world. With a flourish, he opened it and began to pronounce a spell.

> Though you untie the winds,
> Though trees blow down and castles
> topple,
> Though palaces and pyramids do
> slope . . .

The Shakespeare had been drastically cut for the title frames, but its power was still recognizable. Filmmaker and actor alike had no doubt intended viewers to focus on the concentrated fury on Tree's face as he commandeered the forces of the hell. But it was the book that captivated me. It looked old, a leather-bound tome with one word just visible on the spine: *Dee.*

I let the iPod slip onto the seat beside me and began riffling through the folder for Ellen Terry's letter. On the seat, Bach's Toccata and Fugue in D Minor sounded tinny and distant through the headphones. Skimming through the letter, I came to the sentence I wanted: *I think the book queer enough, but it is the letter inside that you will find most curious.*

In 1911, she'd sent Beerbohm Tree — Monsieur Superbe Homme — a book to do with Macbeth . . . on the eve of his theatrical premiere. By 1916, he could have spliced into his film an older version of the conjuring scene. One that had him reading from a volume by Dee.

A volume he had pulled from a hidden cupboard in the wall of his theater.

"So the room's still there?" asked Eircheard.

"Yes." Whether or not the book was, though, was another question.

An image of Lily floated up in my mind, as I had last seen her: wrapped in the blue Cailleach's veil, her hand slipping from mine in the dark Edinburgh close. Lily rising in fury in the hall, red hair gleaming in the firelight. The image flickered and shifted to the ghostly sight of her lying bound on the hillside, a thin red line across her neck. And a symbol of one large circle and two small ones, carved into flesh.

Forty-eight hours.

"Drive faster," I whispered.

30

The sky condensed to sodden gray wool as we slipped down out of Scotland and into the steep hills and fells of northwestern England. We stopped once, for sandwiches, at a service area somewhere outside Preston, in Lancashire.

Lily's parents had died on the motorway outside Preston. The chicken-and-bacon sandwich went tasteless in my mouth, though I knew it wasn't.

Soon after we got back on the road, the shimmying of the van lulled me into fitful sleep. When I woke, London had swallowed us, and the gray afternoon was thickening toward early nightfall. The thought of driving in London soured my stomach at the best of times, but Eircheard drove like a gleeful madman through streets clogged with the evening rush and spattered with rain. We parked in a garage near Leicester Square, and I slipped a flashlight from Eircheard's glove compartment into my bag, along with the iPod and the folderful of precious papers. Huddling together under a single lopsided umbrella, we hurried up a dank, narrow street. Stepping into Haymarket, which was lined with grand buildings, was like walking into a completely different city. Just down the street sat Her Majesty's Theatre, lit like a dowager in diamonds, its blue-gray square dome in the French baroque style as imposing and intricate as a Marie Antoinette coiffure.

I pointed at the dome. "That's it. The room we want is just under the cupola."

"And just how do we plan to get there?" asked Eircheard.

"Same way that Sir Angus meant to, for starters. We buy our way in."

We bought two tickets for the Royal Circle, as close to the exits as possible, and headed up the stairs. It wasn't long before the houselights went down and the iconic white mask of the Phantom began to glow from the covers of programs scattered through the audience. I wove my way through cluckings of disapproval back out to the plush corridor, followed by Eircheard. When the lone usher disappeared, leading another late soul into the Phantom's lair, I veered to the end of the corridor and pulled back a curtain to reveal a nondescript door.

"Fingers crossed," I said under my breath. I pulled the whole door upward and turned the knob slightly, and the lock clicked open — a quirk long known by everyone who knew someone in the cast of *Phantom,* which was pretty much everyone in the theatrical world.

We found ourselves in an entirely different place from the gilt and red plush of the front of the house. As the entire theater hushed, leaning toward the stage, we wound into the labyrinth of corridors behind. I closed my eyes, trying to remember my way around. Rattling up to the top floor in a tiny pale blue elevator, we hurried down a narrow hall with threadbare red carpet and peach walls punctuated by white doors, all closed.

Up a few steps, around a corner, I paused by an old radiator. Behind it, a large barrel key hung on the wall from a tassel. Down one more short corridor and up a half flight of steps we came to a wide landing before an immense arched door whose medieval look was faux but whose studded oak solidity was not. WELCOME, it read, in Old English letters.

I inserted the key into the lock.

The door opened, exhaling the scent of rehearsal rooms: dust, old sweat, wax for the linoleum. And dreams. One wall of the outer room was lined in mirrors, like a dance studio. On the other, high windows looked over Haymarket. From beams crisscrossing the dome overhead hung massive circular iron chandeliers — the kind that burned real church candles, though their sockets were empty and drear.

As Eircheard slipped in behind me, I shut the door and locked it from the inside, leaving the key in the lock. And then I switched on the flashlight.

"Jesus," he said. "Could you get more cliché for a phantom's lair?"

"He lives in the dungeons," I said absently. "This is more like Quasimodo's tower. Though old Sir Herbert would be put out by both comparisons. He's supposed to have given fab dinner parties here. Lived here, as much as he could. Didn't much care for the niceties — or the narrowness — of Victorian home life, apparently."

I'd spent long wonderful hours here away from home, too, rehearsing *Othello.*

A wide archway led through to a more intimate room, paneled in warm Jacobean squares and filled with an oval table probably built for the room. Beyond was an offset stone fireplace.

"That's it," said Eircheard quietly.

I nodded. "The room in the film. Which means that that part of the film didn't belong to the original, which was shot on location in Hollywood."

"You think it was shot later?"

"Or earlier. The costume he's wearing in this room looks like the costume from his stage version of *Macbeth,* which premiered here. In 1911. The same year that Ellen Terry wrote Monsieur Superbe Homme."

I slid past the table to the opposite wall. The door in the wall, if there really was one, should be to the right of the fireplace. But even close up, I could not see it, or even its seams, much less a latch.

I stood back, biting my lip. Had it, after all, been a trick of light? The magic of film? Slipping the iPod from my pocket, I brought up the cauldron scene. Just before the cupboard opened, the camera lingered in close-up on the cauldron.

I went to the fireplace. There was no obvious chain or lever from which to hang a cauldron now. But it wouldn't be a working fireplace anymore, in any case. Not in a theater. I leaned in and looked up. A small slice of sky was visible far above.

I ran a hand up the stones. Nothing. I felt

around all four sides . . . wait, one stone jutted out. It was loose. Carefully, I pried it out. Behind it, folded up, was a lever. I pulled it down. At its end was a hook.

A thunderous knocking exploded on the door behind us. "Desmond, you sodding wanker," said a deep voice. "It's my turn to use the roof." He tried a few more times, and then he went grumbling away.

I turned back to the film. The witches bent around the cauldron, stirring it. Something had been *in* it. Weighting it down. My heart in my mouth, I pulled the lever even farther, putting some force into it.

There was a pop, and several panels in the wall next to me pushed outward and over the wall in a sort of sliding wooden door. Behind was a cupboardful of shelves, bowed and bent with books, their titles obscured beneath a duvet of dust a century thick.

I hovered above it, loath to disturb it. Finally, I ran a finger across the spines, and glimmers of tarnished gilt appeared in partial words.

Secretor — and — *catrix* and *Daemono.* They were, at a guess, some of the oldest printed grimoires. And a few, even older, in manuscript.

This time I swept my palm across the books, dust cascading to the floor. The titles leapt out: *Secreta Secretorum. Aristotle,* read one. *Picatrix,* said another. And *Daemonologie. King James I and VI.* Weyer, *De praestigiis daemonum.* And Bacon, *The Mirror of Alchimy.*

"You think Tree was a wizard?" asked Eircheard.

"Doesn't fit the general picture of the man," I said. There was no way of knowing if he *used* these books. But he was certainly a connoisseur of magical books. I wondered, fleetingly, if the owner of the building had any idea what was hidden back here. From the thickness of the dust, he did not.

It would be the project of a lifetime to work through these books, figure out just what was there. With regret, my hand passed over rare volumes that even the British Museum and the Bodleian might well not possess. Occult esoterica was one subject in which private, hidden libraries were still better stocked than the great repository libraries, which had gotten a late start on officially banned books.

There were books claiming to be by Roger Bacon, Aristotle, Agrippa, Hermes Trismegistus, Solomon, and Trithemius. But nothing so short and sweet as Dee.

At last I came up with what I was looking for: *The Monas Hieroglyphica.* Dee's treatise on symbolic language, in which he devised a single sign, or sigil, supposed to contain all knowledge within it. The monas was a curious stick figure, like a little man wearing a horned hat. Heart in mouth, I opened it and riffled through the pages.

No letter.

Damn. Replacing the volume, I skimmed on down through the shelves. There. At the bottom. A thin book, almost a pamphlet. "DEE" was stamped lengthwise in gold on the narrow spine. I looked closer.

DEE and the Theatre, it read.

I pulled it out and opened it. On the flyleaf was a neat inscription: *Herbert Beerbohm Tree, 1911.* The year he had opened *Macbeth.* The year that Ellen Terry had sent him a present.

I flicked through the pages. It was not a printed book. It was, for the most part, a notebook full of geometrical drawings. Bound in front of that, however, was a letter. In an italic hand. I skimmed down to the signature. Arthur Dee. John Dee's eldest son and favorite child. Heart in mouth, I moved up to the beginning.

My dear Sir Robert:
Apologies for the tardyness with which this will no doubt find you, but news must

take a while to travell to Muscovy and back. I am apprised that you are interested in ferreting out certaine Books and Papers once in my Father's Library. You possess, I know, a number of them already, and admiring your esteem for Books and for Learning, as I do, I cannot think of better hands to protect them.

Those which you propose to find, however, are of a different nature. You may discover, after perusing them, that it is you who needs protection, rather than the Books. My Father, at any rate, felt so.

The moon flitted through a cloud, sending a shadow over the lines. I looked up at the windows but saw nothing.

You aske, in particular, after any with connexions to a Witch my Father called Medea. This was the Lady Elizabeth Stewart, sometime Countess of Arran, and also of Lennox and March.

There was a small ping somewhere in my abdomen. Lady Nairn was right. Her ancestress *was* mixed up in this, somehow. With a nickname of Medea, for heaven's sake. Possibly the most infamous worker of cauldron magic in Renaissance myth.

Another woman with a penchant for carving the life out of people.

My Father possessed, at one time, two Manuscripts concerning this Quondam Countess. One, a Work as wicked as it was ancient. The other, borrowing wholecloth from the first, was a sly piece meant to shadow her forth on the stage. . . .

Was he talking about *Macbeth*? If so, the letter backed Aubrey, and Shakespeare had stolen Lady Arran's magic, but not just that. He'd also stolen her person, and he'd set both on the stage. Had she killed in response? Had she murdered the boy who played her? If so, *why?* Why Hal Berridge and not Shakespeare? Did it have to do with his scrying? Or with the rite of magic? "Aubrey says that Dee begged Shakespeare to alter the play," I said, thinking aloud. "So Dee must have seen the early version. *Maybe he kept it.*"

Eircheard whistled. "Does his son say?"

I skimmed through the letter, my finger coming to rest on a sentence that I could not read aloud.

Looking over my shoulder, Eircheard read it. *"Deeming that their pages might tarnish even the noonday Sun, my Father buried these and other Workes of Darkness where they belonged, in the dark at the bottom of his garden."*

For a moment, we both stared in silence at the book shaking a little in my hand. Buried in Dee's garden. Where the hell was that? Mortlake. I'd always thought it the perfect home for a wizard: *Dead Lake. Lake of the Dead.*

But it was little more than a word to me. Somewhere west on the Thames, on the way to Hampton Court, I knew, but couldn't get much more precise than that. In Dee's day, it had been a quiet village, well out in the country, but the chances that his garden on the Thames had remained undisturbed in the booming centuries since were virtually nonexistent.

What if Dee's works of darkness had been destroyed long ago?

I pushed that thought aside. They had to exist.

"We need someone who knows about Dee." In London, as Lady Nairn had pointed out, that meant one person: Joanna Black, of Joanna Black Books and Esoterica, in Covent Garden. The problem was that Joanna was elusive. I'd been told I must meet her, and I'd been to her shop once or twice, the public part of it at any rate. But I had never laid eyes on her. It was said that somewhere in the back was a small door that opened onto a labyrinth that only the wealthy and well-connected could penetrate. Beyond that lay inner rooms that not even money would open, where only serious students of Dee's Great Art were granted entry.

I knew only one person who might gain me quick access to Joanna. Without waiting to read the rest of the letter, I texted Lady Nairn.

I had just pushed "send" when I heard a small click and whirled around. The key was turning in the lock.

31

Switching off the flashlight, I stood in the moonlit darkness, watching as the key continued to turn. I looked quickly around the room. The only other way out was the fire escape, a wide wooden ladder that led up to one of the high windows. Eircheard was looking at it in dismay. We had no time to wait. Slipping the book into my bag, I dashed up the ladder.

The window opened with a groan. Outside, a peaked roof sloped steeply to the left. The rear of the building stretched away, long and narrow, into the distance. Slick with rain, it would be treacherous going for me. It might well be impossible for Eircheard.

I turned and ran back down the ladder, pulling Eircheard with me to the door. When it opened, we'd have to hope its angle would hide us while the open window drew the picklock forward. With luck, we'd have just long enough to slip around the door and out before the intruder turned around.

The key clattered to the floor, and the door slowly pushed open. A man stepped inside and stopped. He was dressed all in black, down to gloves; the long barrel of a pistol with a silencer extended from his right hand. In the darkness, I couldn't see his face. A gust of wind sent rain clattering through the window, and he looked sharply up at it.

He was halfway across the room when I moved out from behind the door. At a small squeak in the linoleum he spun, and I found myself gazing down the barrel of the silencer. The face above it belonged to the Winter King. The dark-haired man.

"Put it down, Kate," he said.

Beside me, I felt Eircheard flinch. "You're the pile of shite from the festival," he grunted.

"This time, the reach of my arm is longer," said the dark-haired man. The high whine of a bullet whizzed past my ear, thudding into the oak door behind me. "Step forward to the table and set the book down," he said.

"Not worth dying for," said Eircheard, giving me a nod.

Slipping the book from the bag, which I handed back to Eircheard, I did as I was told, rage pressing around me. As I set the book down, he motioned me away again with the gun, and I walked stiffly back to the door. Stepping forward, he flipped the front cover open, revealing the letter, and then he scooped the book under his arm.

"Step outside," he said, "and close the door." Presently we heard him approach the door from the inside, and the key fumbled in the lock. If he locked us out, he'd escape out the fire exit and disappear into London without a trace. "He can't get away with that letter," I said. "He can't."

Eircheard moved back three steps and hurled himself like a battering ram against the door, which flew open, knocking our stalker halfway back across the room. Both gun and book skidded away from him. The gun slid somewhere under the table, amid a welter of chair legs. But it was the book he went after and came up with.

He also came up with a knife. I thought of Sybilla on the rocks, and my insides turned to water.

He backed up the ladder, holding us both at bay with the blade, and ducked out onto the roof.

"Go," said Eircheard tightly. "I'll be hobbling a bit behind you, but I'll be there. With some firepower, too, if I can reach the bloody gun."

I raced up the ladder and into the night.

Overhead, the clouds were washed a dull and dirty pink, reflecting the city's lights. Crouched low, the dark-haired man was running down the spine of the roof. Some way up, he half slid, half ran down the slope to the left, and I followed, mostly on my rear. At the bottom, a low access door hung open. A narrow ladder disappeared into the darkness within. Somewhere below, footsteps pattered downward.

And music twined upward. A sweet, romantic duet: the first act of *Phantom,* crooning to its climax.

I stepped onto the ladder, feeling my way as fast as I dared, suddenly aware of vast space beneath me. I'd gone maybe twenty steps when I heard Eircheard's voice above. *"Kate?"*

"Heading down," I said.

Somewhere below I heard a chuckle that might as well have come from the Phantom. I picked up speed. A couple of stories down, I at last came to the fly floor, the narrow ledge to the side of the stage and high above it, used by stagehands to pull the ropes controlling stage equipment and scenery. But the dark-haired man had disappeared up ahead into an intricate netting of ropes and pulleys and weights, though I could hear snatches of teasing laughter. I stilled for a moment, trying to hear him through the billowing music, pinpointing his whereabouts. Eircheard landed with a heavy step beside me.

Then we saw him, weaving back among the ropes toward the catwalk that crossed from stage left to stage right, along the back wall. I began to run. Up ahead, he reached the catwalk even as the music swelling up from below darkened and picked up speed, cascading into heavy minor chords.

His voice cutting through the music, Eircheard bellowed at the fleeing man to stop, but he only quickened his pace. I saw a kick of dust hit the wall in front of the dark-haired man and he skidded to a stop. I glanced back. Eircheard had taken a shot and was prepared to take another. Turning, the dark-haired man crossed his arms, waiting.

I reached the end of the catwalk and started across toward him. When I was ten feet from him, he said, "Me or the book, Kate. Not both." Around us the Phantom's manic laughter cascaded through the space. And before I knew what was happening, the dark-haired man tossed the book into the air, sending it tumbling in a high arc back over my head. I had no choice. I turned and raced back in the direction of its fall, catching it just before it plummeted over the rail to the stage below. Below, people in the wings began glancing up. I turned back to the dark-haired man. At the other end of the catwalk, three stagehands appeared, starting out toward us.

"*Go,*" screamed the Phantom, and the dark-haired man loosed a coil of rope over the balcony. As the gigantic chandelier that had been cinched to the ceiling all through the first act now swooped down across the theater at the Phantom's command, swaying over the stage, the dark-haired man stepped over the side of the catwalk's balcony and, gripping the rope, slid three stories down to the stage, landing with a reverberating thud and running off stage right. Already rising into their end-of-the-act applause and escape to the bars, the audience gasped, and here and there a woman shrieked. Moments later, the stage door opened and the dark-haired man pushed his way out and melted into the crowd.

On the far side of the catwalk, the stagehands, looking none too pleased, set out in my direction. I didn't wait, fleeing back to the other side.

"Jesus," said Eircheard as I reached him. "Do you think he thinks he can fly?"

"He damn near can, apparently," I said. "Just now, it might be helpful if we could too."

Eircheard was already wiping down the gun. "I don't fancy being caught with this, now that he's gone," he said, sliding it behind some ropes. "God only knows what it's done." We took off back across the fly floor. Coming to the narrow stairs, we pounded down them.

Why? I kept thinking. *Why take the book at gunpoint and then throw it back?*

At stage level we darted through a gathering crowd of actors staring up at the now empty catwalk and out another door leading to the house. As we funneled our way up the aisle toward the exit, I searched every face in the crowd for the dark-haired man, but he'd vanished.

In my pocket, my phone, set to vibrate, began to buzz. It was a message of two words: *Joanna waiting.*

32

Outside the theater, we darted across Haymarket at the first break in traffic, heading back up the narrow lane we'd come down. On a rainy November night, it seemed more like an alley.

Twice, the ring of footsteps on the pavement gave me pause, but once it was a woman in high heels, head down against the damp, and then an older gentleman who might have been a banker; both of them turned off into the parking garage. Clutching Dee's book, I felt exposed, as if every window, every shadowed doorway and corner, held prying eyes.

Eircheard could move surprisingly fast with his odd rolling gait; I had to trot to keep up with him. Passing along the back of the National Gallery and the National Portrait Gallery, we emerged onto Charing Cross Road, still bustling with crowds looking for pubs or restaurants or bookshops open late. One block up, we turned into a small pedestrian street lined with bow windows and hung with carved and gilded signs; it looked as if it hadn't changed much since Victoria sat on the throne. "Cecil Court," I said. The heart of bibliophile London. Five doors up was a simple sign in black and white: JOANNA BLACK BOOKS AND ESOTERICA.

The window was filled with small white lights; inside, the shop looked dark. Eircheard pushed open the door and we hurried inside to the shimmering of small silver bells. It was warm, after the chill damp outside, and fragrant with a spicy incense. The high ceiling was painted a deep midnight blue, and small lights like stars seemed to float and spin like fireflies overhead. Momentarily, I had the impression of standing on a windy hill on a moonless night.

But the horizon was made of tall shelves of books, each dimly lit so that you could read its titles without the light ruining the overall effect of the room. Up ahead, behind a carved wooden ledge sat a man with long, lank hair and a top hat. At the sound of the chimes, he looked up. His right ear, I saw, was oddly folded over, a quirk he accentuated with a pierced earring of dangling silver in the shape of a pentangle. His eyes were ringed with smoky black eyeliner. "Kate Stanley?" he asked, leaning forward intently, as if murmuring a secret password. When I nodded, he rose, unfolding a body as lank as his hair. The fingernails on his right hand were long and slightly pointed ovals. His handshake, though, was firm. "Joanna is expecting you. She'll be right out. Make yourselves at home," he said with a sweep of his arm.

In the center of the room, on a round marble-topped table, gleamed a wide silvery cauldron. On its front, in raised relief, was the figure of a horned man sitting cross-legged, a serpent in one raised arm. Below, the space from tabletop to floor had been glassed in, making a cylindrical terrarium. Inside this, on a free-form tree made of antlers, a boa was coiling in slow gleaming spirals. Off to one side, a black cat with emerald eyes sat on a long velvet sofa watching the snake.

"Meet Medea," said the man behind the desk.

"The cat or the snake?"

"The cat is Lilith. She will introduce herself, if she pleases."

She swished her tail but did not look away from the snake.

I was too wound up to do anything but

wander restlessly. The bookshelves bore titles like *Divinatory Arts, Shamanism,* and *Goddess Spirituality.* But books were only part of what the shop had to offer. An open hutch was stacked with candles of all colors — VIRGIN BEESWAX, read a placard, TOUCHED ONLY BY A SOLITARY CANDLE-MAKER IN SUSSEX, A HEDGEWITCH. There were ritual soaps and bath crystals for various kinds of cleansings; goblets of blown glass, pewter, and carved wood; blown eggs of various sizes and colors; wands — BLANKS, TO BE PERSONALIZED BY THE OWNER; and blank books bound in tooled leather and marbled paper, to be used as Books of Shadows — a witch's or coven's private diary/collection of spells. The tiny drawers of an antique spice cabinet held herbs — ORGANICALLY GROWN, PICKED AT THE FULL MOON IN DORSET — as well as spices I'd never heard of and aromatic resins and gums: frankincense, myrrh, aloe, and bright red dragon's blood.

"Look at these," said Eircheard. Hands behind his back, he was bending over a bow-fronted Victorian display case. On its upper shelf lay a varied collection of knives with handles of black bog oak; beneath that was a shelf of smaller white-handled knives. "Some of them are beauties," he said gruffly.

"Quite a compliment, from a master swordsmith," said a woman's low voice with some amusement.

We both straightened to see a slight woman, about my height, with long curly black hair and wide dark eyes barely hatched with laugh lines, standing in a doorway behind one of the tall bookshelves, which had hinged outward from the wall. She wore a low-cut tunic of some rich tribal material that showcased her necklace, an intricate Afghan collar of silver mesh set with lapis. Heavy silver bracelets clinked on her wrists. Something in her stance and her wary amusement reminded me, a little, of a younger version of my old mentor at Harvard, Roz Howard.

"Joanna Black," she said, stepping forward to shake hands. "Lady Nairn has been singing both your praises. What can I do for you?"

My grip on the book under my arm tightened. "John Dee's garden," I said anxiously. "Where is it?"

She raised one brow. "Mortlake. About seven miles west. Halfway to Heathrow, more or less. Right on Mortlake High Street. Only, I'm afraid the question ought properly to be past tense. It's under concrete, I'm afraid. A block of flats called the

365

John Dee House. Used to be council housing. 'Projects,' I suppose Americans would say. It's been privatized, but it's still 1960s ugly."

Lily. A lump rose in my throat. If the play lay entombed beneath a block of flats, it was unreachable. If it had been moved — well, I had no trail to follow.

She looked from me to Eircheard and back. "From what Lady Nairn said, you're not just looking to spend some quiet hours in an Elizabethan garden."

Having lost the last string through the labyrinth, I had nothing to lose. I held out the book. "We're looking for some of Dee's papers. Not his plants."

She ran a finger along the spine, its gilt lettering winking up at us. *DEE and the Theatre.*

"Come with me," she said, turning back through the door behind the shelves. We hurried after her down a long passageway, passing half-glimpsed rooms and other corridors as we turned this way and that, going up five steps, turning, and then down three again before coming to a stair that took us up two stories to a landing with a heavy arched door, ajar. Pushing it open, she ushered us inside.

Candlelight played on paneled walls, and

two deep windows lined with old-fashioned shutters overlooked the street below. Beside the fireplace stood a tall gray stone covered with Celtic knots; on the mantel was a carved African mask. A long, empty library table was surrounded by several high-backed chairs upholstered in deep green brocade. Unlike the rooms below, this room was spare, a setting for displaying rare treasures.

Pulling a red velvet cradle such as archival libraries use from her desk, Joanna set the book down on the table. One finger on the cover, she looked at me. I reached across and opened it. Her breath caught in her throat, the tip of her tongue between her teeth, as she saw the letter.

"Read it," I said.

As she did, her fingers twining in the mesh of her necklace, I let my mind play back through Arthur Dee's words. How had he put it? A sly piece meant to shadow Lady Arran forth on the stage? Surely that was *Macbeth*, borrowing from an earlier manuscript of dark rites. Lady Arran and her husband eerily echoed the Macbeths, from their ambitious scheming and their interest in witchcraft right down to their deaths. Lady Arran had died miserably, according to some Scottish chronicler. Fading out in torment, well off the world's stage, as Lady Macbeth does. And her husband had been ambushed, his head struck off and raised on a pole.

If the play was indeed *Macbeth,* then it *did* contain a rite of black magic. Surely that was the implication of the younger Dee's letters — that bits had been copied wholesale into the play from a work of wickedness so dark it had frightened even Dee.

Dee senior had called Lady Arran Medea, a sorceress who had a habit of carving up aging kings on the promise of making them young again — a promise she did not always feel bound to keep. She was also said to have poisoned her husband's mistress and to have killed her own children, feeding them to their father in revenge for his desertion. What had possessed Dee to liken Lady Arran to Medea? Was her magic, like Medea's, bloody cauldron magic? Aubrey, for one, implied that she had blood on her hands.

What would Carrie Douglas, carver of cauldrons, make of that?

And what was her relation to the Winter King?

Joanna looked up as she finished the first page. "Do you know what you have?"

"Some idea," I said.

368

She rose, pacing before the fireplace. "The manuscripts — you're after the missing rite in *Macbeth,* aren't you?"

I hesitated, but I needed her help. After a moment, I nodded.

"Do you think that's wise?"

"Probably not."

Beside me, Eircheard snorted. "*Wise!* It's about as daft as things get. But we're after it nevertheless. Can you be of any help, madam, other than telling us that they're buried under a building?"

"Not yet," she said. Lifting the page, she glanced at me, the question in her eyes. I nodded, and she turned it over. Eircheard and I drew in around her, so that we all read it together.

The Manuscripts, should you find them, are yours. There is *One Object,* however, that I would reserve for myself. I am not at all certaine that it is there to be found: The Howards wanted it, and I do not knowe whether my Father kept it from their greedie grasping.

The Howards! One of the most powerful and ruthless families of Renaissance England. I'd met up with them before, clashing with Shakespeare on another subject.

And here they were, pursuing Dee — in a matter that I hoped also included Shakespeare.

It is a Mirror.

Many years before I was born, when Lady Arran was almost still a child herself, she presented herself to my Father in Antwerp, asking to be taught his Art. When he refused on account of her tender years and her sexe, she flew into a furie. That night, she stole the Mirror, knowing that he set great store by it, and fled awaie.

Years later, it was returned, from an Unexpected Quarter, along with another Treasure, this one hers: a Manuscript of words *so evil* that my Father himself quaked to read them, and indeed woulde not until urged to it by his Angels. I never learned how he came by them, but with these gifts, Mr. Shakspeare established himself as one of my Father's Schollars.

There it was: Shakespeare, Dee, and Lady Arran in a triumvirate linked by the study of magic and an evil manuscript. And also a mirror.

Could that be Lady Nairn's mirror, which had once belonged to the King's Men? The one stolen from her tower? My breath caught in my throat as I hurried on:

> An Honour which he rather trampled in the muck than burnished bright, not only in word, but most appallingly in deede. In later years, he asked to borrow the Mirror back, along with the Boy who was then my Father's Scryer, for use in a play before the King. My Father was reluctant, but the Boy was talented — he had fore-seene the Powder Plot — and the request came from a Quarter impossible to refuse. When he understood, however, that the Boy was not to play a Scryer, but to be prinked and powder'd as a Queene, and a Witch Queene at that, he grew fiery with rage and demanded to read the play.

Dee's boy had been set to play a part . . . the part of a queen. *Had he played Lady Macbeth? Had Hal Berridge, the boy who died, been John Dee's scryer?*

"A boy?" asked Joanna in some consternation. "His scryer was a boy?"

I nodded, and she began drumming her fingers on the table. "All Dee's scryers were grown men. But there is an ancient tradition — one that Dee certainly knew — that boys were better: The purer the vessel, the clearer the sight. Which put youth and virginity at a premium. And we don't know *who* he was using in 1606, around the time of *Macbeth;* the diaries of his last years are lost."

"We do know," I said quietly, pulling out the page from Aubrey and handing it to her.

While she read Aubrey, I went back to Arthur Dee.

It was Worse than his *Worst Imaginings.*

I was not surprised about the Boy. I had warned my Father against him. Neither Virgin nor even Chaste, he was a Ganymede who corrupted the house, but my Father was besotted with his powers, with his clarity of Sight.

The Poet, however, was another and more dangerous matter. For hee was ever a sly watcher in corners —

Shakespeare? Was he the poet? A sly watcher in corners? What had he seen in Dee's household?

— and it was not just the Mirror that he borrowed, but a Rite that out-Medea'd Medea, stolen in parte from my Father's translation of the Witch's Manuscript. Father warned the Poet against such folly. Mr. Shakespeare, tho', would not listen until the Boy was dead.

So Aubrey's sources on that tale were solid, at least as far as the boy's death. And surely Arthur Dee was at least implying that the death was not accidental.

You will knowe the Mirror by its black surface, and by a Posie around its edge:
  Nothing is but what is.

Eircheard started.

"You recognize the saying?" asked Joanna.

"Young Dee got it wrong," said Eircheard. "Left off a word. 'Nothing is but what is *not*.'"

"It's a round," I said quietly. "Carved around the perimeter of a circle. The first three letters of the first word and the last word overlap."

"An infinite circle linking being with not-being, life with death," said Joanna, a smile of satisfaction slipping across her face. "Powerful magic."

"It's from *Macbeth*," I said. Whatever else this mirror was, it wasn't the one stolen from Lady Nairn, which was silvered glass. It might be spotted with age, but it had never been black.

Rising, Joanna switched off the light, leaving the room in candlelight. From a drawer in her desk she pulled out a hard circular case; inside lay a black velvet bag. From this, she withdrew a disc of glimmering darkness, laying it on the table.

"Polished obsidian," she said.

I bent over it. Within its surface swam a world of shadows.

"Is this it?" I asked. "Dee's mirror?"

"God, no," she said with a laugh. "But it's a fine copy."

"And the original?" asked Eircheard. "Are you going to tell us it's under cement out in Mortlake?"

"No," said Joanna. "As I said, I can't tell you about the manuscripts, or the rite that's in them, either. More's the pity, believe me. They'd fetch an astronomical price at auction. But I can take you to the mirror." She looked at her watch.

I put both hands on the table and rose. *"Where?"*

"Just up the road," she said with a mischievous smile. "At the British Museum. Open late tonight. If we hurry, we can just get there before closing." She ran a finger lightly across the surface of her mirror. "I've been trying to get the curator to open the bloody case and let me examine that mirror in person for three years. I think you may just have delivered the key." Deftly, she slipped her own mirror back into its bag and then into the case. "But I'd have to call and tell him at least part of what you've found."

"Call," I said hoarsely.

As she made her call, I sat staring at the mirror case, my mind spinning. The manuscripts were out of my reach. But whoever had taken Lily also wanted the mirror: *Blade, mirror, cauldron* . . . On the score of the mirror, as of the knife, they were surely resting quietly.

Lady Nairn's mirror had supposedly belonged to the King's Men. But this one, if Arthur Dee were right, had not only passed through the hands of Dee, Lady Arran, and Shakespeare, *it had been the original mirror in Macbeth.* If so, it was this mirror, not Lady Nairn's, that Carrie and her friends would want — no, *need* — for their ritual. Which made it the key to more than just a case in a museum, I hoped tightly. It might be the key to Lily's release.

If I could not take the manuscript to ransom Lily, I would take the mirror.

Across the room, Joanna had reached the curator. She had her back to us, staring out the window at the shops along the street below as she spoke to him in quick, clipped tones. Before I could think about it, I opened the case, slipped out the velvet bag with the mirror, and dropped it into my bag.

Eircheard stared at me in openmouthed astonishment.

"I mean to play bait-and-switch. I'll need your help."

"At the British fucking Museum?" he hissed. "Are you mad?"

"Just gallus, I hope," I shot back. "Don't you think a piece of black stone is worth Lily's life?"

He shut his mouth in a tight line, his fist closing around the smooth bit of iron he'd been toying with all day. "Do you trust her, about the manuscripts?" he whispered. "Or do you think she's having us on, meaning to go after them herself later?"

"She's a respected antiquities dealer. Not a position you can reach or keep if you scoop finds from your clients or their friends. In any case, do we have a choice?" I pointed at the bit of iron in his fist. "Hand that over."

He let it slide from his hand to mine, and I set it inside the case. At least it wouldn't feel entirely empty. I shot Eircheard a bleak smile. "Besides, at the moment, I'm the one who's not trustworthy."

"Tonight," Joanna said firmly into the phone. "Yes, that's brilliant, thanks." Ending the call, she came back with a smile. I felt a momentary pang: She was going out of her way to help us, and I was stealing her mirror. *A stone for a life,* I told myself. It had to be done.

In five minutes, we'd put on our coats and were hurrying north up St. Martin's Lane, toward Bloomsbury. The rain had stopped, but the air was still damp and the streets slick and gleaming.

33

"You think he'll really let us see it?" I asked as we wound through Seven Dials, ringed with restaurants and pubs, jazz spilling through a briefly opened door and bouncing along the wet pavement at our feet. "Why?"

"Because up to now, there's been no proof that it's actually Dee's mirror. Though the museum so far has gone out of its way not to say so in public, seeing as it's touted among the cognoscenti as one of its great British objects."

"But it might not be?"

"Walpole said it was Dee's."

"*Castle of Otranto* Walpole?" I squeaked. "The inventor of Gothic fiction?"

"Good old Horace," she replied with a smile. "He of the creaking doors in the night, the distant scream, the bats fluttering about the moonlit tower. All the great clichés of ghost stories and horror films. Yes, that Horace. He gave us Dee's magic mirror, too. Unfortunately, there's suspicion in some quarters that his tale about the mirror's history might be as fantastic as his fiction. Not quite fair, really. He was a true collector, a connoisseur of esoteric art and occult objects. And the provenance he gave the mirror winds plausibly back through eccentric aristocrats to a man who patronized both Dee and his son."

"Arthur?" I asked. In the bag on my shoulder, the weight of the stolen mirror seemed to grow heavier.

"Arthur. Physician to the czar of Russia. Son of an English wizard. And most important, at least tonight, correspondent of Sir Robert Cotton — maybe the most significant collector of ancient books and manuscripts in Britain's history."

For a ways we walked in silence, our footsteps ringing on the pavement.

"Right now, the mirror has pride of place in the Enlightenment Gallery, under the aegis of Owen Knight, head of European collections. A curator who's half-Welsh and wholly fascinated by Dee. Steeped in British history. But there's a struggle brewing behind the scenes between Owen and his counterpart in charge of the Americas. Because the mirror may or may not be

Dee's, but it is most certainly Aztec."

"Aztec?" I exclaimed.

"An attribute of the god Tezcatlipoca. Dark twin and eternal rival of the better-known Quetzalcoatl. The mirror is supposed to have been fixed to his leg after a sea monster bit off his foot in a titanic battle at the dawn of creation. The Aztecs believed the mirror worked two ways. Priests could see in it visions of whatever the god cared to show them — things near or far, past or present, or yet to come. But the god also used it as a window through which to gaze out on the world he had helped to create, watching the people he sometimes chose, on a whim, to destroy. Lord of the Smoking Mirror, his name means. God of poetry and jokes, he was. Sounds bright and beautiful, doesn't it?" Her eyes twinkled with mischief. "But he was also the god of night and mockery, of disease and sorcery and death. The Enemy, he was called by those who worshipped him. The Trickster. The Spanish missionaries had another name for him: the Aztec Lucifer."

"How did such a thing fall into Dee's hands?" asked Eircheard, rolling along on the other side of Joanna.

She shrugged. "Nobody knows. It's not like it's the only one. Tezcatlipoca was a major god, and most of his statues had these mirrors attached to them. The conquistadors hacked up the statues as evil idols, but trinkets like these mirrors tended to be slipped out of the carnage by the foot soldiers when the priests weren't looking. A number of them were floating about Europe in the sixteenth century. Dee made several extended visits to the Continent, where he had rock-star status as an intellectual, though he was shamefully ignored at home. It's not implausible that at some point he picked one up from a Spaniard in the Low Countries. He was in Antwerp, for instance, in 1563, in search of rare manuscripts.

"We know he had one. The question has always been, is it *this* one? Your letter — assuming it's genuine — offers proof. And since Owen's locked in a territorial battle over the thing, he'll probably kiss your feet, never mind letting you hold the damned mirror. You'd think it was one of his own balls, the way he protects it."

We turned a corner and the museum soared into sight, its colonnade and grand sculptured pediment glowing gold in the darkness. Behind its high wrought-iron fence it looked like an immense beast, a hoarder of knowledge. Late on a rainy autumn night, its grand stairway was eerily deserted. We followed Joanna up the steps, our footfalls echoing in the night.

We ran up the steps and in through the dim echoing entry hall, into the blinding white space of the Great Court, mostly empty. It was dizzying, like walking through a hard, cold, echoing egg turned inside out. In the center was a circular tower, the old Reading Room of the British Library before it had moved to its new digs farther north a decade earlier.

Joanna marched us toward a grand pedimented doorway leading off the court to the right. Inside was a long, narrow gallery, dark after the brightness of the court. I stood blinking in the entryway for a few moments until my eyes adjusted to the dimness, aware only of the room stretching far into the distance on both left and right.

"Enlightenment Hall," said Joanna. "A tribute to the seekers of knowledge. Displayed in their fashion." Which meant lots of classical statuary, apparently, and display cases packed chockablock like curio cabinets with objects gathered by abstract ideas — justice, geography, religion, magic — rather than by the time or place of their making.

We turned left, past a lion-headed Egyptian goddess in black stone — Sekhmet, goddess of chaos and destruction, noted Joanna — and stopped at a case that held magical objects of all kinds. The antithesis, I thought, of the Enlightenment and its proud rationality. In one corner was a small black disc of polished stone, about a quarter-inch thick. It had a handle with a hole drilled through it.

"Tezcatlipoca's foot," said Joanna.

"That's it?" asked Eircheard, clearly unimpressed.

Nothing was visible around its rim.

Joanna pulled out her phone to call the curator, and casting a baleful glance at me, Eircheard limped off for the men's room. But I stood entranced by the dark mirror. A blank bit of darkness. It seemed preposterously small to hang a human life upon.

Its reflections were dim shadows. It was like the night sky, except that the more I stared into it, the more light seemed to recede from the surface, almost as if I were pouring into it. Clouds skidded across it, growing and dissolving. Barely discernible, without stars in the distance.

And then I saw a shadowy reflection. The face of a man over my shoulder. With dark hair and pale, wolfish eyes. The Winter King. And then I saw the gleam of a knife.

I whirled, my heart knocking against my

ribs. But I was alone in the gallery, save for one shadowy figure at the far end, too far off to have cast the reflection.

"Kate?" It was Joanna. "Are you all right?"

Dumbly, I nodded.

"Owen's waiting for us at the restaurant."

34

We crossed back through the court to the stairs at the base of the Reading Room. Wide steps spiraled up around it to the museum's upper level, where a chic post-modern restaurant was tucked in behind the Reading Room, prickling with the muted clink of cutlery. The few patrons left looked to be an even mix of obvious tourists and well-heeled Britons. It was an airy space, the steel netting overhead now dark.

A man with a shock of dark gold hair and a finely cut suit rose as we approached, and Joanna introduced Owen Knight, curator of European collections. He gave Joanna a cool kiss on the cheek, his smile faintly lascivious. "I took the liberty of ordering already, as the kitchen was closing. I hope you like calamari."

There was a mound of them on a plate in the center of the table. I realized I was ravenous.

"How are things with Gloria?" Joanna asked.

He leaned back in his chair, grimacing. "Greedy Gloria." He had a soft "r" that sounded more like a "w."

"Gloria Moreno," explained Joanna. "Curator of the Americas. She has an interest in Dee's mirror."

"If she'd put it like that, I'd be ecstatic," he grumbled. "But she won't admit it's Dee's. Says it belongs in her rooms as indisputably Aztec."

As they talked, Eircheard and I ate, content to listen to their sparring.

"No one *knows,* actually, if it's Dee's mirror at all," said Joanna.

Owen colored a little. "It's Dee's."

"But you can't prove it." Joanna leaned forward. "Yet."

He went still. "What have you got?"

"A letter from Arthur Dee," she said. *"You will knowe the mirror by —"* She stopped with a sweet smile.

"By what?" Sweat had sprung up on his upper lip.

Joanna leaned back. "Hard to tell from the display. It will have to come out of its case."

He sat back. "Impossible. You know that."

Joanna set her drink down on the table.

"Pity. As Ms. Stanley's adviser, I've told her that the best price will come via select auction among occult collectors. As I've said, this might mean it could disappear from view for centuries. Such a secretive set." She rose.

"Wait." He ran a hand through his hair. "Come back to my office."

She unfurled a wide smile. "With pleasure."

I took one more piece of calamari for the road, and then we clattered down the stairs and back into the Enlightenment Gallery, this time turning right, away from the mirror. At the lower end of the gallery, we passed into another, smaller room, turned left into a long hallway of offices and study rooms, and then right.

The office had high ceilings and two windows that looked out over a narrow side yard cluttered with a few cars. Beyond that, a black iron railing fenced off the tree-lined street that ran along the eastern side of the museum. A large desk and a long table cluttered with papers and bits of statuary faced each other across the room. Every available surface seemed to be filled with body parts in cold, beautiful stone. Most of them female. A lioness head torn from another statue of Sekhmet, goddess of chaos, pestilence, and bloodlust. A white marble foot. A single, impossibly perfect breast. Did Owen fancy himself Pygmalion? Or Dr. Frankenstein?

He sat on the edge of the table, arms crossed. "What have you got?"

Joanna put both hands on the table and displayed her prodigious memory, quoting a sentence she'd seen only once before. *"You will knowe the Mirror by its black surface, and by a Posie around its edge."*

"You'll have to do better than that," said Owen, retrieving a piece of paper from his desk and laying it on the table. "Second inquiry in as many weeks, as it happens, about lettering around the perimeter."

The page was a Xerox of a daguerreotype. A man with Victorian sideburns in a kilt and an immense tam-o'-shanter with a cockade and a tall pheasant plume. He stood holding a dark circular mirror like a trophy. At the bottom was scrawled a date: *May 10, 1849.*

I started and then stopped myself, hoping Owen hadn't seen it.

He was staring at the photo. "Nothing for years, and then two inquiries in two weeks. Odd, don't you think?" He looked up. "Unfortunately, unhelpful. It was ground down at some point. Nothing legible left."

"No marks at all?" asked Eircheard.

"Nothing useful unless you know what it says."

"But we do," said Joanna.

Owen's fists clenched involuntarily, his voice tightening. "What?"

"It comes out of the case first."

We had to wait, he said, none too graciously, until the museum emptied of patrons for the night.

"I'll need some help," said Owen, looking pointedly at me.

Beyond him, Joanna gave a slight shake of her head. *No.*

"I'll do it," said Eircheard.

We hung our jackets in his closet, and I set my bag with Dee's book on the floor. And then we all sat on the floor in the dark, out of sight from the windows, watching the moonlight slip over the walls.

I thought of the black velvet bag inside my bag. I had no idea how I'd manage the switch. But Eircheard was a clown. No doubt he'd improvise some distraction when the time came.

Half an hour ticked slowly away before Owen rose and beckoned to Eircheard, and the two of them disappeared into the hall, the door closing quietly behind them.

Through the windows, the lights of Lon-

389

don bounced off the clouds, giving the sky a strange pinkish glow. The wind rattled against the panes in gusts that sent leaves whirling about.

"He's not telling all he knows," I said.

"Neither are we," said Joanna. "Particularly you. That picture startled you." She went to the desk and picked it up.

"It's the date: the day New Yorkers rioted over *Macbeth*." I laughed at the look on her face. "Sounds absurd now, but it remains one of the worst riots in U.S. history. Twenty thousand people in the streets, and New York's National Guard firing into the crowds. A lot of people died."

"Over Shakespeare?" Joanna's voice cracked.

"*Macbeth* was the trigger. Class warfare was the chronic rumbling that fueled it. That, and the sheer delight that some of the big street gangs had in fighting. But it was sparked by a personal and stylistic clash between two actors: an American named Edwin Forrest, and a Brit named William Charles Macready. Brawn versus elegance. In their sensibilities, it was a little like a contest between John Wayne and Laurence Olivier."

She held the photo before us. "Bound to be one of them, don't you think?"

"Let's find out which." Taking the page from her, I went to Owen's desk. His computer was on; the screen saver was a finely painted Renaissance portrait floating around against a black background. A disappointed-looking man with long nose and dark, reproaching eyes under a black skullcap, a long white pointed beard flowing over a compact Elizabethan ruff. He might have been scowling. It was hard to tell beneath the beard and mustache.

"John Dee," Joanna said softly. "Still the archetype for our ideas of what a wizard should look like."

We were in London, so I Googled Macready first. It wasn't him. Just to make sure, I typed in Forrest's name. The picture was different, but the man was the same.

Where had he come from? Who else had known to ask about a posie?

The keyboard was under my hands. I pulled up Owen's e-mail and glanced at the subject lines. "Look what we've got here."

Dee's mirror.

The e-mail was brief. *Could you tell me whether John Dee's mirror has any lettering engraved around the perimeter? I attach a daguerrotype that might feature this mirror. If you have further information, or would like to know more about the image, please contact* me at this e-mail address or the cell number below.

The signature was an automatic one: *Professor Jamie Clifton, Department of English, College of Mount Saint Vincent, New York.*

I pushed "print," and the printer hummed into life. As I was picking the page up from the printer tray, the computer cut out, and the lights in the room flared once and died.

35

I went to the window. As far as I could tell, the whole museum had gone dark, though the buildings across the street still had power. The room, however, was not entirely black. Light from the streetlights, from the ambient light of London, drifted through the windows.

Eircheard and Owen should have been back by now, surely. I listened at the door but heard only silence. I folded the copy of the daguerrotype and the e-mail together and shoved them in the pocket of my jeans. "I'm going after them," I said.

Joanna did not care to sit alone in the darkness, so we slipped out of the office together. With one hand on the wall, I turned right, counting three more doors before the corridor turned left. Up ahead, a faint light spilled into the corridor from the galleries leading off to the right, more like paler darkness in a shade of gray, rather than actual light, like the mysterious light in Rembrandt's gloomier paintings. I sped up, heading for it. Behind me, Joanna kept up.

I paused at the wide doorway leading into the Enlightenment Hall. The glow of London's lights washed in through the high windows up along the gallery, bright enough to cast faint shadows of the trees and branches swaying outside, so that the whole hall seemed to be moving, dancing around the space amid lashing branches. The movement of the trees made the statues — Cupid, Pan, Hermes, Sekhmet — look as if they were moving, swaying to some silent music.

"I don't hear anything," said Joanna.

"That's the problem," I whispered back. "We should hear *something*."

"What have you dragged me into?" Joanna said with more than a hint of accusation.

"Sorry, but we have to find Eircheard."

Keeping to the deep shadows in the narrow lane between the long wall of books and a line of exhibit cases, we crept forward across the room. As we came to the wide-open space in the center, where the grand doors led out to the Great Court, we stopped.

The court seemed to be empty, save for the white lion-legged vase. More disturbing, we heard and saw nothing in the northern end of the gallery, where Eircheard and Owen should be.

We darted across the open space, sliding back into the shadows between the books and the exhibits until they came to an end, guarded by Sekhmet, sitting stiffly upright on her black throne.

"Kate." Joanna was pointing. Something was draped across the goddess's lap. A man's tweed jacket. She stepped out and picked it up. Beyond I saw something flicker on the floor. A crystal ball. And beyond that a thick circle of wax lay on the floor, broken in two. I looked up at the case.

It was gaping open.

I drew forward, filling with dread. The mirror and its case were gone. And at the exhibit's foot a body lay in a heap. Owen, with a bullet hole between wide-open eyes. I looked around for Eircheard, but saw no one else.

The glass of the exhibit, though, was smeared with something. *Blood.* On the floor at my feet was a small pool of it; a trail of smaller droplets led straight on through the gallery. My stomach twisted in a sudden twinge of fear.

Coming up behind me, Joanna made a small squeak. At a quick motion from me, she went silent. I stood, hands on hips, thinking. We'd heard nothing, though this was an echoing space. That meant a gun with a silencer. Such as our stalker at the theater had possessed. Though it couldn't have been that one.

Pulling Joanna forward, I followed the trail of blood.

At the end of the gallery, it led into a grand echoing stairwell. Beyond lay a smaller gallery, muffled in almost total darkness. A small spattering of drops crossed into the dark.

My eyes adjusted. Two more cases were open.

A cry rose from depths of the museum, rising in waves of agony and anger, and then cut to silence. It entered the small gallery from both ends and seemed to wind through space, bouncing off walls and cases.

Eircheard.

I turned back, peering out into the Great Court. It looked and felt like the ghost of some ancient snowstorm, pale and ethereal and cold. It was entirely silent, as if that cry, and perhaps all other sound, had never been. Against the far wall, faint in the distance, I thought I saw a trail of dark petals dropped haphazardly across the floor. Blood?

Somewhere above, we heard the clatter of hard shoes on marble, the spat of radio static, and a man's voice barking orders. Security.

The mirror, I thought, suddenly afraid. It was the one remaining thread, fragile as it was, that led somewhere through the darkness toward Lily. Pulling Joanna forward across the court, I ducked into a postcard shop, roped closed, as the security guard passed at a trot.

The trail of blood by the wall curved around the Reading Room, following it around to the front, stopping at the double doors facing the museum's main entrance. One of them was ever so slightly ajar. Fear coiling around me, I pushed it open.

It was darker here than in the Great Court, but not so dark as in the galleries. High rounded windows circled the space three floors up, before the ceiling bent inward in a dome I knew to be blue and gold, the blue of robins' eggs and the Virgin Mary, though now it looked nearly black.

"A temple of knowledge," my aunt Helen had said. She'd brought me to study there for a week the moment she heard the British Library had been slated to be moved. The wheel of learning where Virginia Woolf and Karl Marx and Charles Dickens had toiled. With the departure of the national library up to new digs by King's Cross, the space had been divided like a cathedral, the front third an empty, echoing nave where unhallowed tourists were allowed to wander. Separating the profane from the sacred, a long curved line of desks swept across the room. Beyond lay the museum's private library.

"Eircheard?"

In answer, I heard nothing but a steady, slow drip.

Up ahead, there was a gate through the black granite-topped information desk, like the little gate in an altar rail. Beyond curved a line of low shelves. Above these flickered two points of light. Candles.

In a library? The candles stood atop the line of shelves, as if on some high altar.

With mounting dread, I crossed the room and stepped through the gate. Just inside, a stench of sewer thickened the air, and I stopped again, so suddenly that Joanna bumped into me. A little way off to the left, two white pillar candles stood six feet apart on the shelf. Between them, a black velvet shroud veiled a body. Just beyond it, a wide-eyed face leered at us, fangs bared.

I stepped back, hearing someone gasp, and the candles guttered.

My heart thudding against my ribs, I realized that the face was a human skull inlaid with wide stripes of black and turquoise stones, its eye sockets filled with large gleaming gray discs. Without lips, its teeth looked like bared fangs.

"The mask of Tezcatlipoca," whimpered Joanna. The Lord of the Smoking Mirror.

Dee's mirror. I glanced along the body, but the black mirror was nowhere to be seen. Beneath the closest candle, though, lay a stone knife, its blade a pale milky green.

Stepping forward, I lifted a corner of the shroud. Beneath lay a man with ginger hair. *Eircheard.* His face, which had so quickly come to seem dear, was contorted beneath his red beard, his eyes wide and staring. He was dead.

I reached out and brushed his eyelids closed; he was still warm. A sound scraped in my throat, and I gripped the edge of the counter to stay upright. What had they done to him?

I gave the shroud a small tug, and velvet slid to the floor with a small whisper that made the candle flames dance.

They'd stretched him naked on his back, his body arched over arms bound beneath him. Blood had pooled and thickened on the shelf top, dripping in slow, steady drops. Just below his rib cage, a wide slash gaped across his abdomen like an obscene mouth. Above that, a mark had been carved into his skin: a circle flanked by two smaller circles, all cut with a horizontal line. Carrie's mark.

She'd killed him to consecrate the mirror.

For a moment, everything went black before my eyes, and my ears filled with a thunderous rushing as fury spread through me. I looked wildly around the room.

"Carrie!" I heard myself cry. *"Cerridwen Douglas!"*

My voice echoed around the dome and died away. A rasping voice scraped through the darkness to my left. *"Nothing is but what is not."* I spun toward it, but the light of the candles did not penetrate deep enough into the shadows.

From the other side came another voice. *"She shall be queen hereafter."* And then laughter sputtered down from above. I looked up. Ringing the room were two catwalk galleries lined with bookshelves, the upper one lit faintly by light drifting in through the high arched windows. A dark figure stood there, spread-eagled at the balcony as if embracing the night. Three more words echoed through the dome. *"She must die."*

At the back of the room, the double doors flew open. Joanna grabbed me and dove for the ground, pulling us under the information desk, clamping a hand over my mouth as several pairs of footsteps strode forward across the floor.

INTERLUDE

Summer, 1590
Shoreditch, north of London
For the first time, Dr. Dee walked into the building that he had helped old Burbage, the famous actor's father, design: the Theatre, in the fields of Shoreditch, north of London. At least, it had been set among fields when it was built — almost fifteen years ago, that was now. In the intervening span, though, a hodgepodge of vaguely and not-so-vaguely disreputable taverns, brothels, and tenements had sprung up around it until it seemed to be pretty much an extension of the city.

It would be interesting, he supposed, to see his design at work. He'd drawn it partly from the inns and great halls that players had long been accustomed to playing in, as Burbage had insisted, and partly from drawings of old Roman theaters. Less well known, he had also drawn on a different tradition of performance entirely — which, were the truth to be known, was the reason Burbage had come to him in the first place.

The crowd streaming in around him was boisterously jovial. By the time he reached his seat, he'd been propositioned at least three and possibly four times by ladies of questionable virtue — the last of them wearing a concoction of orange feathers on her head that would surely annoy whoever had the misfortune to sit behind her. In fastidious black scholar's gown and skullcap, Dr. Dee found her plumage alarming enough seen briefly from the front.

He had come to see the first public performance of young Master Shakespeare's new play, *The First Part of the True Contention Betwixt the Two Famous Houses of York and Lancaster*. An extravagant title on the part of a little-known upstart, though possibly the most prodigal thing about it was the promise implied by the word "first." What, after all, had a mere player, a glover's son from provincial Warwickshire, to say about the mighty ones of the kingdom?

On the other hand, Master Shakespeare had the backing, it seemed, of the earl of Derby's charming scamp of a younger son, the Honorable William Stanley, with whom he was much of an age, though their stations in life could hardly be more different. Dr. Dee bit his lip, considering. If anyone could tell the Lancastrian side of the "contention" in question, a long and bloody dynastic war that had lasted generations, it would surely be the Stanleys, who'd acquired their earldom by decisively backing the correct side in the last battle, setting the crown on the queen's grandfather's head.

It was not, however, the politics or the history of a war of roses — the Lancastrian red against the Yorkist white — that had captured Dr. Dee's curiosity. In general, he cared little about what young men more prone to revels and riots than to study might say about matters best left to the wise. But this play, he had heard, strayed into territory altogether more dangerous and more dear to his heart. Mr. Shakespeare had dared to conjure a demon on the stage.

He was not the only one who'd heard the whispers. Most of the mob, he reckoned, seemed to be there for the same reason that he was — to watch the magic — though more out of prurience, to be sure, than a learned and professional attachment to the subject. Stuffed to its rafters, though the day was hot and sticky and the sky threatened to dump rain, the whole place was abuzz with wonder and a deep thrill of fear:

Would the play — *could* the play — raise something more in its circle than a stage demon? Would the spirits of hell know the difference between a proper conjuror and a player-conjuror? Would they care, even if they knew?

Dr. Dee did not, as he had feared, have to sit through wearisome hours of warriors' bombast before arriving at the magic. It appeared — or at least the dark promise of it did — almost as soon as the characters began speaking and the crowd's chatter subsided. Young as he was, Mr. Shakespeare, thought Dr. Dee, knew how to stick bums to seats.

A short time later, however, when the magic itself arrived, Dr. Dee was no longer so sure about that. Onstage, two Jesuit priests, a witch, and a fool of a duchess gathered in the company of a conjuror. Somewhere, someone began rippling a thunder sheet, the sound of it so low at first that it was felt more than heard. The conjuror began to move, casting a circle around himself using words and motions and even props that lifted every tiny hair on Dr. Dee's body. Up on the stage, the man gathered speed and force, and around him the rumbling of thunder rose. Through the commotion, a deep voice roared *"Adsum!"* — "I come," in the Latin tongue favored by the denizens of hell. There was a small puff of smoke; when it cleared, a demon stood growling on the stage. A player, of course, but it had to be admitted that his entrance, no doubt through a trapdoor, was unsettling.

"Asnath!" shrieked the player-witch, naming the spirit. As her cry died away, there came a bright flash and a great crackling of sound that no thunder sheet could ever make. With a sudden stench of sulfur, lightning hit the flagpole rising from the building's tallest turret. The banner that hung there burst into bright fire even as the skies opened up in a thick downpour that drowned the flames.

As one, the audience rose, the seated to their feet and the standing to their toes, and a long "oooooh" spiraled around the stage. Behind the player-demon, a shadow thickened and stretched skyward. Dr. Dee, a tall man, pushed himself up to stand on the bench and pointed a long finger at the darkness. *"Void,"* he bellowed in a voice that might have quelled the waves.

On the point of dissolving into trampling chaos, the crowd suddenly stilled. Even the actors froze, and the rain blew over as quickly as it had started, until the only movement was the trembling of the old wizard's arm. He stepped down from the bench and walked solemnly down the aisle, people parting a way for him. Down the stairs he went, and back into the street.

In the theater, a tucket of trumpets broke out at Burbage's insistence, and the play went on, fighting to be heard over a great murmuring among the audience. Heading back toward the city on foot, Dr. Dee did not notice, the world having closed into a dark tunnel around him.

He did not, like most of those in the crowd, ask what had happened up on the stage. He knew what had happened. What he wanted to know was how the boy had done it. How had he learned what he'd put on the stage?

He had first come to Dr. Dee's attention last December in the company of Derby's son, at one of the lowest points in his life, returning after several years on the Continent to find his precious library in his home out at Mortlake ransacked: four thousand books — the collection of a lifetime — gone, the precious glassware in his alchemical laboratory smashed or taken, the two globes Mercator had made especially for him stolen, even the shelving stripped from the walls. Into this mess had walked Master

Stanley with Master Shakespeare, a mirror under one arm and a manuscript under the other.

Master Shakespeare, Derby's son had explained, after introducing them, had recently returned from Scotland, where he had come into the possession of certain objects Dr. Dee might welcome. As the boy set the round mirror of polished black stone in his hands, Dr. Dee had looked up sharply. This, too, had been stolen from his library, but not this library, and not recently. He had last seen it in Antwerp twenty-five years or so before, in the hands of a young witch with red hair and a Scottish accent.

Without a word, the lad had laid atop the mirror a manuscript. It was old, in an antique form of Welsh that even Dr. Dee found difficult to read. So far as he could make out, it concerned a Welsh witch who lived in a lake and wove strong spells with the aid of a cauldron.

On the subject of exactly how he'd come by either mirror or manuscript, Mr. Shakespeare remained coy. Dr. Dee, however, let the question slide, as collectors often must, he told himself. He was intrigued. He was enthralled. And he was happy to start his library anew with two such rare finds at its heart. He had welcomed Mr. Shakespeare to visit when he pleased and make use of his library how he might.

That had all been well and good. The books trickled back, and with them intellectuals from all corners of the kingdom. His home once again became a gathering place for scholars of all sorts, hashing out questions of all kinds. How many ships could the emperor of Cathay command? What was the proper title and style of the czar of Russia? How did geese navigate their migrations? Was there such a thing as an unbreakable cipher? And what was the hierarchy of hell?

It was the last question that a small coterie of his best and brightest students — the most daring thinkers of the kingdom — pursued, among others. His scholars of the night, they called themselves. It was among these, William Stanley and his protégé included, that he'd shared a summary of his deep studies of Mr. Shakespeare's manuscript.

Not even among this select group, however, had Dr. Dee shared the information that he intended to attempt one of the rites described in the manuscript. Cleaned up, of course, polished into something acceptably Christian. He had shared that, in fact, with no one save Arthur, his eldest son, ten years old, who was currently serving as his scryer. It had taken three days to prepare the room and the properties, and one more to fast and bathe, to make the two of them ready. A month or so ago, this had been. They had retired at nightfall to his innermost study, beyond the double sliding doors, with the black mirror and a candle, and they had set to work.

How someone else came to be there, he still could not understand. Surely he had seen that the room was empty before they started. He could not quite remember, but it was force of habit: How could he have failed on this occasion? But it seemed equally odd to suppose that someone could have entered after they had begun, without their knowledge. He had purposely left a creak in the doors for just such an eventuality, but no sound had disturbed either him or his son.

But someone *had* been there. A shadowy presence he became aware of as they finished the rite, not knowing how long he had been there or what he had seen. Not knowing, indeed, who he was, though Dr. Dee and Arthur had both given chase through the maze of his library and out into the street.

In the rite, they had been equally disappointed. It had promised clarity of both sight and thought, but neither he nor his son had noticed a change. Dr. Dee had long been resigned to the fact that he would never see the spirits for himself, save on the rarest of occasions, and then only dimly. But for Arthur, this blindness to the spirit world was still a raw hurt that the boy strove to heal, and the failure of this ceremony had seemed a hard blow. It had, however, been a private disappointment.

Until this afternoon, when he saw it, mimicked and even parodied, lifted on the common stage. How had the player known, unless he had been the watcher in the shadows? Knowledge, though, was for sale the width and breadth of the kingdom. The watcher need not have been the boy himself, Dr. Dee thought.

Except that there had been one or two details in the casting of the circle that not even a glimpse of Dr. Dee's private ceremony could explain. Details available only in a singular manuscript in a crabbed and antique form of Welsh that he would not believe the young man had at his command. And if he had acquired these details neither from Dr. Dee nor from the strange manuscript, *where had he got them?*

And the only answer Dr. Dee could light

upon was the possibility of the player having glimpsed, in some other place, a different version of the rite from his own.

Mr. Shakespeare has recently returned to us from Scotland, Mr. Stanley had said upon introducing them. Words that now haunted Dr. Dee. Where in Scotland, and when? With whom? *And to what effect?*

At the start of the afternoon, the player's unprecedented rise in poetic power and popularity had seemed no more than a curiosity. Now there suddenly seemed to hang around his reputation a faint stench of sulfur such as Dr. Dee had scented on the air in the playhouse.

His fine black gown bespattered with mud and grime, the old wizard reached the Thames without much awareness of having walked right through the city. Treading heavily down some stairs and into a waiting barge, he bespoke a row upriver to Mortlake.

Leaning back in his seat, the cool pull and slip of the water rushing by his ears, Dr. Dee shuddered. Young Master Shakespeare had written what he should not; he was sure of that. How he'd come to know it perhaps not even heaven knew.

■ ■ ■ ■

CAULDRON

■ ■ ■ ■

Double, double toil and trouble,
Fire burn and cauldron bubble.

36

Huddled in Joanna's arms beneath the desk, I twisted to look back up at the high balcony. The mocking figure was gone.

Below that lay Eircheard. As the footsteps moved steadily toward us, I made him a silent promise. *I will kill her. I will find Lily, and then Carrie will die.*

Near the little gate, the footsteps slowed. Stepping through, two pairs of shiny black shoes stopped, so close to us that I could have reached out and plucked at their trousers. Overhead, radio static scratched the darkness. Security guards, then.

"Jesus," said a male voice. Farther back, a third person spun away, and I heard the sound of heaving. Then another sound cut through it. Somewhere at the back of the room, a door creaked.

"Bastard's still here," growled the closest guard.

"Hey!" shouted the second. "Stop!" They

took off running, the third stumbling after.

Joanna and I wasted no time. Scooting out from under the desk, we ran in the opposite direction, sprinting through the main doors into the Great Court, our footsteps ringing against the marble floor as we turned back toward the Enlightenment Gallery. Behind us, someone shouted, pattering down the stairs curving around the Reading Room.

We didn't look back. Skidding through the gallery, we crouched behind an exhibit case as scattered footsteps ran into the room after us, stopping just inside the door. There was a slight jangling of keys and another burst from a radio. Guards, again.

What had happened back there in the library? What door had opened? There must be an emergency exit, presumably out to the Great Court level we were on. But there were also doors, somewhere, that led down into the warren of rooms beneath the Reading Room — the old stacks of the British Library. Where had the killers gone? Was there a floor between us, or had they, too, headed back this way? How many of them were there?

And how many guards?

Somehow, we had to avoid all of them and

get out of the museum before the police arrived.

Whoever had killed Eircheard and Owen had taken the mirror. Would the killer, as we had done, go looking for more information? In Owen's office? Jesus, his office. I'd left Dee's book, my bag with all our other papers, my jacket — everything — in Owen's office.

Flashlight beams sliced through the darkness. There was a fifty-fifty chance that our pursuers would go left instead of right. If they glimpsed the open case, that chance went up to a certainty . . . and once they saw the trail of blood, they'd surely follow it as fast as we had. It would give us a chance.

Fishing in my pockets, I found a pound coin and lobbed it high. It clattered down somewhere in the distance, and the lights instantly swept that way, catching on the open case. As the guards stepped down toward it, Joanna and I sped in the other direction. As we reached the staff corridor, I caught her hand, stopping her. After the gallery, the windowless corridor was utterly dark. I did my best to still my breath, listening for sounds up ahead.

Behind us, the museum had become a tangle of echoing shouts and footsteps, but ahead, I heard nothing. Guiding ourselves with hands on the wall, we plunged into the void. The corridor seemed to have stretched to a mile or more, so that it took forever to come to the turn leading right and begin counting the doors. At the fourth, we stopped and I put my ear up to it. Had anyone else got here first? Hearing nothing, I flung it open.

The room was empty, but one of the windows had been opened wide, so that gusts of chill autumn air swirled around the room, moaning lightly in the corners. A handful of leaves scraped and swirled across the floor.

Grabbing a war club from a shelf, I yanked open the closet. No one was there, but our jackets still hung inside. On the floor sat the bag with Dee's book and the folder from Lady Nairn. I looked in the bag. Everything was still there.

Gathering our things, we went to the open window. Whoever had been here had gone through it, but it was still our best bet for getting out unseen. I leaned out. The night air was tangled with sirens, but I saw no sign of a person.

Climbing out, I let myself drop to the ground. Joanna dropped beside me. We were in a narrow graveled and tree-lined side yard — essentially a private roadway used as an employee parking lot, separated from the public street by a wrought-iron fence. Joanna pointed off to the left. Twenty yards up stood a narrow gabled guardhouse the size of a telephone booth. Beyond that a gate opened onto the street. We edged forward.

The gate clanked in the wind. Drawing up to the guardhouse, I glanced inside. The guard was slumped back, a bullet hole between his eyes. He'd died the same way that Owen had.

At the bottom of the road, a siren screamed along Great Russell Street heading for the museum's front entrance. In the other direction, it looked as if there wasn't another cross street for a half mile. Row houses, many of them converted to hotels, lined the road on both sides. Lights began to flick on in their windows.

Taking my hand, Joanna darted through the gate and across the street, dragging me up a little way to a spot where the row houses ended and a brick wall, twelve feet high and covered in ivy, began. She started to climb. Slinging the bag over my shoulder, I followed. The brick was old, scarred and pitted from centuries of urban air, which made for easy climbing. We were up and over, landing in a spiky pile of conkers, just as a siren veered around into the road behind us and a car squealed to a stop.

We stood in a garden fronting two houses set back from the street; between them and the last row house, a path led back into shadows. Joanna pulled me toward it.

The path led back to a narrow tree-studded garden stretching left and right the length of the entire block, surrounded by buildings on all sides. Around us, dogs were beginning to bark, and more lights winked on.

Eircheard. I felt bile crawling upward again and swallowed hard against it. I needed to think.

Beside me, Joanna was trembling, her face taut with horror. "The mask of Tezcatlipoca, the knife. Even the cut. It's how Aztec priests sacrificed: cutting just under the rib cage and up through the diaphragm to reach the heart."

Tezcatlipoca, I thought. *God of mocking laughter. God of night and sorcery and death. The Aztec Lucifer. Lord of the Smoking Mirror.*

"Jesus, Kate, that was an Aztec sacrifice. Owen was right, that woman is insane. . . ." Her voice was rising toward hysteria.

"Listen to me." I took her by both shoulders. "It wasn't Aztec. But it was a sacrifice."

"Not —"

"The mirror was missing. If Eircheard's killers had really been Aztec devotees, they'd have taken all three objects. Not just the mirror." *And they wouldn't have quoted Macbeth.*

"Why the mirror?"

"It was being consecrated. With blood."

Her eyes widened. "But the only reason for that —"

"Is to work black magic."

Joanna took a step back. "You *knew* how dangerous this was, and you still involved me?" she asked thickly. "Without warning?"

In my pocket, my phone drummed to life. "Sympathy for the Devil" again. *Lily.*

It was a picture message. A photo of Lily, bound as I'd seen her in my dream on the hill, except this time, she was also blindfolded. Beneath the photo were two words: *24 hours.* "What's going on?" demanded Joanna.

I shook her off, frowning at the phone. The manuscript they'd asked for looked to be untraceable, and they'd taken the mirror. What else did they want? What was I supposed to do now?

How had they known? I wondered suddenly. How had they known to come to the museum? To go after Dee's mirror? Possibly, they'd followed Eircheard and me. Or had

421

they somehow bugged one of us? I stared at the phone in my hand — the phone whose ringtone they'd reprogrammed. What else had they done to it?

It gleamed in my hand, a mocking and treacherous magic mirror of an all too modern variety. Suddenly I wanted nothing more than to throw it as far as I could, to drown it in some fathomless deep, but it might as well have been chained to my bones: It was the one frail link I had to Lily.

I began to shake.

Think.

They'd taken the mirror. But they hadn't yet given up on the manuscript.

Which meant I couldn't, either. But what other leads did I have?

Owen's snide voice slid through my mind: *You'll have to do better than that. Second inquiry in as many weeks, as it happens, about lettering around the perimeter.* He'd held up the old photograph. A page that I'd shoved into my pocket, just after the lights had died.

I fished it out.

Holding the dark mirror, Macbeth glared out at me beneath his preposterous hat. Edwin Forrest, on the day of the riot he'd helped to instigate, or at least had done nothing to quell.

Forrest.

As Joanna stared openmouthed, I crouched down, setting the bag on the ground and scrabbling through the folder to find Ellen Terry's letter and Aubrey's diary. *I am hoping that you can glimpse the Forest through the Trees,* wrote Terry. And at the bottom of Aubrey's page, Max Beerbohm had quoted *Macbeth: Who can impress the Forrest, bid the Tree unfix his earth-bound root?*

Both of their "trees" referred to Beerbohm Tree. Did both of their "forests" also point to a man? Either Max Beerbohm had misspelled "forest," or he'd spelled "Forrest" correctly. Was Terry's "forest" — with one "r" — also a reference back to the American actor? And if so, what did her reference mean?

Her letter said nothing of the mirror. But it did speak of the manuscript. And the "poor soul" who believed herself the guardian of its whereabouts was *a fellow denizen of the drama whose personal tale is as tragic as any role she might encharacter on the stage.* Was she someone who'd known Forrest? Who'd been caught up in the gunfire and screaming and blood of the riot?

I slid the e-mail from behind the photo. The Xeroxed photo — or maybe "scanned" was a better term — had been e-mailed by Professor Jamie Clifton of New York, who'd somehow known to ask about the posie around the mirror. How? What did the original daguerrotype reveal that the copy did not?

It was a thin filament to follow through a dark labyrinth. But it was all I had. I phoned Lady Nairn to tell her what I knew and what I needed: a meeting with a man and a daguerreotype in New York.

37

"Eircheard?" Lady Nairn exclaimed with a strangled cry when I told her he was dead. "They killed Eircheard?"

I spared her the details for the time being; I didn't trust my voice to deliver them without quivering, in any case. Instead, I told her what little I knew about Jamie Clifton. "I need to make sure the man's there, before I get on a plane." I rubbed my temple as if I might squeeze out a coherent plan. "He'll be expecting news from Owen Knight, the curator he'd contacted at the museum. Let's set up a meeting between Clifton and Knight for tomorrow morning, early. With the implication of passing on news about the photo and its mirror that will leave the professor panting."

"Will Mr. Knight go along with this?"

"He's dead. And since Carrie and company killed him, I like to think he won't mind us taking his name in vain."

"And you'd like me to arrange it?"

"Not you. Ben." His very name tasted bitter with guilt and sadness.

"Would you like to speak to him?"

Yes, some part of me cried in silence. *More than anything.* But I couldn't, not with Sybilla's blood on my hands. Aloud, I said, "No. But you need to."

"Leave it to me, then," said Lady Nairn, suddenly all brisk business. "In the meantime, head for Farnborough. I'll have a private plane waiting. As soon as we confirm that Professor Clifton's at home, you can take off."

"And if he isn't?"

"We'll cross that bridge when we come to it."

I felt suddenly drained. "Carrie's killed for both the knife and the mirror, Lady Nairn. She'll come after the cauldron too — within the next twenty-four hours, if Lily's captors aren't lying about their timing."

"Let them," she said darkly. "They shan't have it. Now go and hail a taxi."

As I hung up, Joanna glared down at me, hands on hips, her earlier hysteria condensed to anger. Her long dark hair lifted a little in the wind; moonlight glinted on the silver mesh around her neck, rising and falling with each breath. "The knife, the mirror, and the cauldron? Plus three dead bodies, one of them a sick ritual killing? *What insanity have you pulled me into?*"

I had the time neither to answer in detail nor to babysit her. "Kidnapping and murder. I'm sorry," I said, shoving the papers and the phone into the bag. "But a fifteen-year-old girl's life hangs in the balance. Your client's granddaughter."

"Lily? Lady Nairn's Lily?"

"You know her?"

"Not personally, but I know a bit about Lady Nairn and her family."

"I'm trying to get her back. So was Eircheard." I rose. "The manuscript of an early version of *Macbeth* is her ransom."

"Jesus, Kate. So you really do think it still exists?"

"Someone thinks it does. Strongly enough to kill in anticipation of delivery. As you saw. I have twenty-four hours remaining, more or less, in which to find it."

"And if you don't?"

"Lily dies. Or maybe I do. They're being cagey on that subject."

"*You think someone means to perform the missing rite from* Macbeth?"

"You saw what happened to Eircheard. Do you think they'll flinch at witchcraft?" If

427

Carrie could rip out a man's heart just to prep a tool, what was she capable of in the grand rite itself?

"They'll call it witchcraft, won't they?" She took a step toward me, her hands balling into fists. "Everyone will. They have to be stopped."

I lifted the bag to my shoulder. "That's what I'm doing. Or trying to." I sighed. "You should go. Now."

She touched my arm. "I can help."

"No." My breath came out close to a sob. "I let Eircheard help."

"You didn't kill him, Kate."

"I let him come with me when I shouldn't have. I let him get killed."

She clasped my arm just above the elbow. "I've spent my life working to restore respect to the pagan way of life. To witchcraft and ceremonial magic. These people — they're beyond fringe. They're psychopaths hiding behind a sick fantasy of paganism. They don't represent who we are. But the instant this story hits the news, everything I and a lot of others have worked for . . . it will crumble like so much dust. In two days, they'll have destroyed a lifetime of labor. The only way I can see to right that particular wrong, at least partially, is for a witch to be part of stopping them."

"I won't have your blood on my hands."

"My blood, my hands," she said quietly. "You want to save a girl, Kate. I want to save an entire religion."

Who was I to argue with that?

"Who's there?" called a voice off to the left, and footsteps headed toward us.

"Come on," said Joanna. Cutting to the right, she wound around trees and bushes until we came to another narrow path between buildings, fronted by another high wall, this one with a door in it. It opened onto a road one street over from the museum. *Head straight into the thick of things,* I heard Ben's voice say in my head. *It's what innocent people do.* So I turned right, back toward Great Russell Street, Joanna at my side. On the curb, we stood blinking in the whirl of headlights and sirens. In a lull, we crossed the street and hailed a cab heading west.

38

We stopped at Joanna's flat in Chelsea just long enough to retrieve her passport; I waited in the cab. Just as she was returning, Lady Nairn called back. "Board the plane," she said, "the professor's at home and waiting — from what I gather, probably standing on a ladder beneath a clock, speeding the hands around."

While Ben had arranged the meeting, she'd looked up Clifton on the college Web site. According to the faculty list, he was a scholar of drama and theater history, she said. His dissertation had been about Edwin Forrest and the growth of celebrity culture in nineteenth-century America; he was currently at work on a book about the Astor Place riot. The *Macbeth* riot, whose date was scrawled beneath the photograph. "Which makes his home address intriguing," she added.

"Where's that?"

"Astor Place."

Around me, the world flushed cold and then hot.

"It would appear that the professor's interest is not only professional, it's personal," said Lady Nairn. "Bordering on the obsessive, I'd say, but living in a house called Dunsinnan, that might be the pot calling the kettle black. . . . Did I mention that Clifton's invited the curator round to his condo for breakfast? Seven-thirty?"

"That's brilliant, Lady Nairn. Joanna Black will be with me."

"Find Lily," she said as she hung up.

The taxi drove right up to the plane, where a sleepy customs official was waiting. All he wanted was a flash of valid passports. And then we were up into the plane and on our way. During takeoff, I sat looking at the photograph of Forrest. "Tell me what you know about him," said Joanna.

"Not much. He was one of the great tragedians of the nineteenth-century American stage. Maybe the greatest. A man's man. Worked his way up from nothing, which endeared him to the masses. He played heroes, and Americans loved him: He was all noble strength and innocence. The British thought him uncouth and extravagant, which he was."

431

"Macbeth doesn't quite fit, does it? Was it a sort of side specialty?"

She was right. "I don't think it was considered his greatest role. But it was dear to his heart. His parents had emigrated from Scotland. For all I know, he considered it his birthright. He certainly considered it a vehicle for competing with Macready.

"They started out as friends. But when Forrest got a cold reception in Britain, he blamed Macready. Took to following the older man about, watching his performances, or scheduling his own to conflict with them. In Edinburgh, once, he stood up in an otherwise rapt theater and hissed Macready at some tense moment in the middle of *Hamlet.* Everyone saw and heard him. He might as well have called his rival out in a duel — and other men would have settled the score at dawn, in a barrage of pistol fire. But Forrest and Macready fought their battles by proxy, on the stage."

"And let other people do the dying, apparently," said Joanna. She ran a finger over the date: May 10, 1849. "Why date the photo with a day of infamy?"

I shook my head. The play's curse was beginning to seem more real than I liked to admit. What had been Forrest's role in the riot? And what about the mirror? Was it

Dee's mirror, in Forrest's hand? Was it the same mirror the museum had? Or used to have?

Those who'd taken it would need a scryer, just as Dee had. The purer the seer, Joanna had said, the clearer the sight. Lily had been learning to scry, I thought suddenly. What if they'd taken her as a seer? Hal Berridge had not survived the experience of scrying in that mirror.

Eircheard had not survived its theft. I rubbed my temples, trying to press away the prick of tears. Whatever Clifton knew, I prayed it would be useful. I had twenty-four hours, and the flight to New York would eat seven of them. Fourteen, if I had to fly back.

She must die. Shakespeare's words ran through my mind like some imp of the perverse.

Did they point at Lily? Or me?

I'd promised Eircheard I would save her.

Twenty-four hours.

As the plane leveled out, I moved to a sofa, laying out the evidence on the coffee table and walking Joanna through it. She'd risked her life coming along. She might as well know what and who we were up against.

"So you think it'll be a cauldron rite?" she asked, peering up over her glasses.

"Lady Nairn's convinced of it."

"Makes sense of Arthur Dee's Medea comment."

"Makes sense of a hell of a lot more than that." I told her about Carrie — Cerridwen — Douglas and her penchant for carving people with the Pictish cauldron symbol.

Joanna's eyes crinkled with revulsion.

"Lady Nairn thinks she's become a writer. Maybe you've heard of her: Corra Ravensbrook."

"Ravensbrook?" She took off her glasses and ran a hand through her dark hair. "I'm sorry to say so, but in that case, the cutting and the killing both make more sense than I'd care to admit. I won't stock her books. She sends parents frantic. Not that I usually pay much attention to parents' whining — but they have a point about Ravensbrook. Teenagers who are easily led have gone, well, badly astray under her influence. I imagine the police have a file on her. But she's very clever. She never quite comes out and says *kill.* On the other hand, she preaches the beauty of folding death into life and life into death. And she brings ancient rites of sacrifice alive quite uncannily. She talks about the bog bodies, for instance, with ghastly relish."

"Bog bodies?"

"Ancient bodies, many of them victims of violent death, who've been discovered ritually buried in peat bogs, mostly in Britain, Ireland, and northwestern Europe. They're decent evidence for fairly regular human sacrifice among both the Iron Age Celts and Germanic tribes, though the scientists keep insisting they might be the victims of capital punishment. Hard to see how so many young children and older women were thought to have committed crimes meriting execution, though.

"Ravensbrook, as I recall, is especially taken with the Kayhausen Boy, who was found in a peat bog in northern Germany with his feet tied together, his hands bound behind his back; another length of cloth was wrapped around his neck and passed lengthwise around his body through his groin. The ghoulish woman rabbits on for what seems like pages about how similar that binding is to the binding a lot of modern covens use in their initiation rites."

It was how Sybilla had been tied. How I'd seen Lily tied. I pulled up the picture of Lily on my phone and set it down before Joanna. "Like that?"

She leaned forward to look. "Jesus. Is that Lily?"

I nodded. "You think it's some kind of

initiation?"

"Are you joking? Ravensbrook scorns modern covens as namby-pamby pablum. Not exactly the opiate of the masses — 'the watered-down wine of starry-eyed fools' was how she put it once." Her mouth pursed in distaste. "She has not made herself warmly welcome among the pagan community."

If Lady Nairn was right, it wasn't initiation Carrie was after. It was inspiration. Genius. The thunderbolt of the gods, Lady Nairn had called it. Carrie would kill for it, she'd said. I ran my tongue around dry lips. She *had* killed for it. Eircheard had been carved into an Aztec sacrifice, Auld Callie hanged and pierced like Odin, and Sybilla bound like an Iron Age bog body, before having her throat slit. *Why?* What was this leading up to?

Across from me, Joanna suddenly looked up from the Dee book. "Do you know what this is?" she asked in a strangled voice, smoothing it open. Beneath her hand, the pages were strewn with diagrams in blotted ink, as if drawn in a hurry: circles and triangles, separate and apart, some of them fitted together in octagons and even more elaborate structures. They made no sense to me.

"Plans," she said. "For the Theatre, with a

capital 'T.' Burbage's Theatre, 1576."

"The round wooden O," I murmured. The first sole-purpose theater built in Europe since the fall of Rome, I explained to Joanna, as we both stared at the wizard's manuscript. The Theatre had been the home of Shakespeare's company, in the fields of Shoreditch, north of London. Twenty-odd years later, when they'd had trouble with the landlord, they'd sneaked in and pulled it down, board by board, on a single cold winter's night at the end of 1598. Quietly shipping it in pieces across the Thames, they'd rebuilt it in Southwark, on the southern bank of the river, and renamed it the Globe. *Dee* had designed it?

"The magical community has long suspected so," said Joanna, tracing one of the circles with her finger. "But I don't know about 'sole-purpose.' I've seen these same diagrams elsewhere among his papers, I'd swear it."

"Where?"

Her gaze was faintly challenging. "In notes showing how to cast circles of power."

The darkness and cold outside the plane seemed to press inward. "For making magic?"

"For invoking demons. Or angels," she added with a small smile. "Depending on

437

your point of view."

I pushed back from the table and rose, unable to sit still. "What are you saying? That the Theatre — the foundational structure of English drama — was designed as a place to work magic?"

"To invoke spirits." Her eyes were shining with excitement as she held up the book. "This is proof, Kate. Proof positive."

There wasn't much room on the plane, but I paced wildly through what there was of it. Had Shakespeare known? *One of my Father's schollars,* Arthur Dee had written. True, men had sought out John Dee in pursuit of all kinds of knowledge. His library had been one of the finest in all Britain, bettering even the queen's on certain topics, and far outstripping anything Oxford or Cambridge had to offer. But according to Arthur, Shakespeare had bought his way into Dee's coterie and his collection of books with a strange mirror and an even stranger manuscript. Begging the question, a scholar of what?

I conjure you, by that which you profess . . . answer me. What was it that Shakespeare had professed? I came to a stop before Joanna, my voice cracking. "The Theatre was built for conjuring?"

"Conjuring and performing were closely

linked, at least in some minds, in the Renaissance. You must know that."

"Raising spirits in a circle," I said. It was what conjurors did. It was also what companies of players did. Shakespeare said as much, near the end, in one of his finest speeches, given to his great magician, Prospero:

Our revels now are ended. These our
    actors,
As I foretold you, were all spirits, and
Are melted into air, into thin air:
And, like the baseless fabric of this vision,
The cloud-capped towers, the gorgeous
    palaces,
The solemn temples, the great globe
    itself,
Yea, all which it inherit, shall dissolve
And, like this insubstantial pageant faded,
Leave not a rack behind.

Had Shakespeare meant the globe, as in the earth, or had he meant the Globe, the theater in which the actor playing Prospero would have pronounced the words? Or both? And if he'd meant both, just how closely did he link theater and magic in his own mind?

I exhaled sharply. "Of course he also made

'raising spirits in a circle' refer to sex."

Joanna rolled her eyes. "He made *every-thing* refer to sex. The man had the libido of a lovesick seventeen-year-old boy crossed with a bull, permanently. That doesn't mean he couldn't be serious about a subject on occasion, as well."

I dropped back onto the couch. "What was the point of conjuring? What was Dee looking for when he invoked his angels?"

Joanna stretched, crossing her hands behind her head. "He spent decades at it, Kate. Not fair, really, to demand a single burning focus." She leaned forward, her dark eyes gleaming, a thrill running through her voice. "But ultimately, he was searching for the lost language of God. A tongue that carried such force that one could say *fiat lux* — 'let there be light' — and light would appear. Dee and other Renaissance magi believed that the languages they knew and spoke and studied were descended from that divine original, but that they'd dwindled in power, though there were still flashes of it left in certain combinations of sounds. Especially in Latin, Greek, and Hebrew rites of magic, closely guarded as precious and dangerous secrets."

Her reading glasses dangled like a pendulum from one hand. "It's not entirely far-fetched, you know. There *are* certain phrases, in every language, that don't merely describe the world but make things happen."

I nodded. "Speech-act theory. One of the few corners of literary theory I could make sense of, once upon a time."

She leaned back. "The doctorate that got away?"

"I like to think that I was the one doing the escaping." I'd left the ivory tower for the theater with all the eagerness of an eloping bride; the only regret I had about it was the lasting rift it had opened between me and Roz Howard, my academic mentor. Whom Joanna was reminding me of more and more.

"Quite. Well, then you know that in what's called performative language, uttering phrases like 'I do' at a wedding, or 'I promise' and 'I bet' bring certain states of affairs into being."

I bit my lip. "Words with the force to change the world."

"In Shakespeare's England, the phrase 'I conjure' was widely thought to have such force."

If the point of conjuring was a search for the language of God, language that could create worlds with words, it was tied even more closely to theater than I'd thought.

"I've always thought that's one reason the Puritan preachers hated theater so," said Joanna softly. "They ranted on about loose morals and whore-mongering and people being lured away from church. But idol-worship was one of their most serious charges, and beneath that, I think, lurked a recognition of theater's power. They saw in it the same thing that Dee and Shakespeare saw: the shadow of the language of God." Her voice gathered into dark intensity. "And I think it scared the shit out of them."

She leaned back over the book. "And they weren't the only ones worried. In conjuring, circles of power are cast for one reason: protection. They keep the demons at bay. Often, there's a triangle off to the side: that's meant as a kind of unbreakable holding cell for whatever spirits should arise." She pointed at the diagrams, full of circles and triangles. "Maybe the Theatre was designed to raise spirits in safety."

Maybe. "If so, it wouldn't have worked for *Macbeth*. Not for the premiere, anyway, which took place at Hampton Court, in the rectangle of the Great Hall."

"Maybe that's why it was so dangerous," said Joanna.

For a moment we stared at each other,

not speaking, the only sound the drone of the plane.

Modern theaters, for the most part, were no longer built in the round, on Dee's plan. They hadn't been since the Restoration. Could that be why the play had grown a reputation for being cursed?

Good grief, what line of thought was I allowing myself to be drawn down? I stood up quickly, as if I might shake off all this talk of magic like a dog shaking off water.

"It makes the play a catch-22," said Joanna. "Play it to the hilt, capture the essence of the conjuring, and even without the exact rite, you'll half-wake forces beyond most people's control, without any safe place to contain them. Fail, though, and you invoke Macbeth's curse."

I frowned.

"End of the cauldron scene," said Joanna. "*I will be satisfied,* the king screams when the witches warn him off pursuing more knowledge. *Deny me this, and an eternal curse fall on you!* So you see, in the hands of the untrained, either the magic half-works, in a terribly dangerous way, or it doesn't, and the production pulls a curse down on its own head."

"If you believe in magic," I said.

"If it exists," said Joanna, "it doesn't matter a toss whether you believe in it or not."

Lady Nairn had said something very similar. "No," I said. "What matters is what Carrie believes."

"If she's Corra Ravensbrook, she believes in magic. Death magic."

I pulled my knees up to my chest and buried my head in them. Dee had spent years and most of his treasure invoking angels, trying to rediscover the language that could bring force to a statement like "let there be light": *Fiat lux.*

Now someone was out there grasping toward something much darker. *"Fiat mors,"* I whispered. "Let there be death."

Was that what she wanted? And meant to have, via some ancient rite of cauldron magic?

It was a power she'd already grasped. Images and sounds slipped through my head. Auld Callie in the tree, the rope creaking against the oak. The blue gown pattering down across Sybilla's body, tied and bloody. My own hands, smeared with her blood. Killer, or consecrated victim? For all I knew, she'd foisted some of the killing off on me.

And Eircheard. Rollicking, irreverent, kind Eircheard, his face twisted in agony, his heart, for Christ's sake, ripped beating from his chest. The bitch had torn out his heart.

And now she was toying with Lily.

If she'd been present, I think I might have torn her limb from limb like a Maenad. If I'd been on the ground, I might have run screaming into the night sea, or crowds, or wide empty fields spreading under the moon. Somewhere large enough to hold the grief and anger pent-up within me. In the tin can of a plane, all that passion had nowhere to go but into tears. I wrapped my arms more and more tightly around my knees, trying to hold it in, but the sobs welled up and out all the same.

Beside me, Joanna gathered me in her arms and let me cry.

Somewhere over the Atlantic, I slept. I woke in darkness to Joanna's gentle shaking. We'd arrived at Teterboro Airport, on the New Jersey side of the Hudson. It was three in the morning, local time. The meeting wasn't till seven-thirty, but I saw no point in waiting; I had no hours to waste.

I glanced in a mirror. My eyes were bleary, still rimmed with red, but nothing that someone who didn't know me might not chalk up to being awake at a preposterous hour. I ran cold water over a couple of washcloths and brought them with me, to cool down my face. It was the best I could do.

"You think he'll just invite us in at this hour?" asked Joanna.

"I don't intend to give him a choice."

A limo was waiting at the foot of the stairs. We drove through suburban New Jersey, into the glazed glare of the Lincoln Tunnel, and up into the cement canyons of midtown Manhattan. Past the Empire State Building, past the darkness of union Square, down toward the Village, and left into Astor Place, where the cab drew up to a graceful Romanesque building in terra-cotta brick, its windows soaring up six stories to curve in semicircular arches. Up ahead, a few giggling tourists were spinning the famed Cube sculpture on its axis, but at half past three the open space — not quite a plaza, though it seemed to aim in that direction — was otherwise mostly quiet.

In the lobby, the doorman was hunched over a computer screen, watching a third-rate horror film, judging by the soundtrack. Hearing that we were old friends of Clifton's, he glanced up with heavy-lidded eyes. "The professor's expectin' ya?"

I gave him a wide, giggly smile. "With shots of tequila."

He waved us on with a smirk.

I phoned Clifton from right outside his door. "God, this better be good," said a luxuriant voice into my ear.

"Come to your door and you tell me." Reaching into my bag, I pulled the mirror I'd taken from Joanna from its black velvet wrapping and held it up before the peephole.

Behind me, Joanna stirred. "Is that mine?" she whispered.

I nodded.

"This will drain its power," she hissed.

"I'm sorry," I mouthed. "I owe you." If I had to lie naked in a field with the disc of cold black stone lying on my belly at every full moon for a year to recharge it, I would. Meanwhile, if it could help show the way to the manuscript and Lily, it would be magic mirror enough.

A few moments later, I heard an intake of breath over the phone. In the door, bolts turned in their locks.

39

The door opened on a willowy woman with short dark hair tousled with sleep. She wore a silk robe of multicolored stripes that made me think of Joseph and his Technicolor dream-coat. In one hand she held the phone on which she'd been talking to me. I stood in the hall, blinking in surprise. Jamie Clifton was a woman.

The promise, dangled before her, of learning more about the mirror whisked us inside, where we perched on an uncomfortably low but doubtless very cool leather sofa, while Jamie padded around the kitchen, making coffee. The condo was a model of sleek urban chic, a loftlike space with high ceilings, exposed brick walls, and a lot of gleaming steel and granite. Almost one entire wall was a window overlooking the plaza below. The glass coffee table before us, though, was piled with papers to grade, and the kitchen island was scattered with takeout cartons, which cluttered the image.

"How'd you know about the lettering around the rim?" asked Joanna as Jamie set mugs of coffee down in front of us. "There's nothing visible in the image you sent Owen."

"He showed you?" she shrilled in annoyance. "Asshole." Sinking cross-legged into an armchair in a cloud of striped silk, she breathed in the steam rising from her mug. "Explain to me again why I should help you?"

She could play coy all she wanted, but she'd let us in at a ridiculous hour of the morning. She was interested. I leaned back against the sofa. "Because you'd like to know what it spells."

"You've seen it?" There was an eager catch in her voice.

I smiled. Knowledge, the oldest temptation.

She disappeared down a hall and came back with a hinged frame, folded closed. "The image I sent . . . it was only half the picture. Not quite aboveboard, maybe, but I wanted to give the Brits a reason to take my inquiry seriously without giving the game away. The daguerrotype you've seen — it's freakin' gorgeous, of course, but it's the companion shot that's really fabulous.

Taken at the same sitting. They're both by Matthew Brady, the Civil War photographer. He had a studio in New York before he went down to Washington. Did you know that? He did society portraits. Very solemn, most of them. But he convinced some of his clients who were actors to experiment with emotion and action."

She'd hardly taken a breath since she started, her words tumbling out in a quick staccato patter. Opening the frame with a flourish, she set it down on the table before us. On the left was the daguerrotype she'd sent Owen. On the right was another, again showing Forrest in the same kilt and plumed bonnet. But this pose was more akin to a still from a silent film than to the Victorian solemnity of the other portrait. A woman, turned away from the camera, faced him, holding the mirror as he leaned back in exaggerated horror. What he saw in the mirror remained unseen. But in the woman's hand, a few letters were visible in reverse around the rim of the disc:

UꓭƧIꓕИ

"Daguerrotypes flipped images left to right, like mirrors," said Jaimie.

Reversed back, the letters read NGISBU. They were from the middle of Arthur Dee's identifying phrase, NOTHING IS BUT WHAT IS NOT, minus the first five letters of "nothing" and everything after the "u" in "but." I glanced up at Joanna.

"It's Dee's," she confirmed.

Jamie looked from me to Joanna and back. "No shit? You can tell? Just like that?"

My voice raspy in my throat, I quoted Arthur Dee: *"You will knowe the Mirror by its black surface, and by a Posie around its edge: Nothing is but what is . . . not,"* I added. "It's the mirror that was originally used in *Macbeth.*"

"The mirror that originated the curse," said Joanna.

"Well, then it came into play on May tenth, 1849." Jamie shook her head. "He had it the day of the riot. Did you know that? *Forrest carried it the day of the riot.*"

"But it was Macready who was acting at the opera house, wasn't it? Forrest's fans were on the outside, throwing stones."

Jamie shrugged. "Some say he *was* there." She walked to the window. *"There,"* she snorted. "*Here.* It was here. This building rose from the ashes of the Astor Place Opera House. . . . Imagine twenty thousand people down there, throwing paving stones and oil-soaked torches. And then cavalry and infantry marching in behind, squeezing them ever closer into the building, filled with a standing-room-only crowd."

Her voice seemed to people the night with the cries of men and the screams of horses, the roaring of flame and echoing volleys of gunfire. "Who knows where Forrest was? He might have been in the crowd, or even in the building. Probably idle speculation. But the suspicion was there."

I tried to keep my mind on the photos. "Who's the woman?" I asked.

"I don't know," said Jamie. "At first I thought she might be his wife, Catherine. She was an actress herself, you know. But this can't have been her. They'd already parted by the riot. Sad story, that. Forrest could be a real bastard. With regard to his wife, he became a character out of one of his plays. Henry the Eighth, maybe. Or even worse, Othello."

The person Ellen Terry had her story from had been a woman, *a fellow denizen of the drama,* she'd written, *whose personal tale is as tragic as any role she might encharacter on the stage.*

"What happened?" asked Joanna.

"Catherine Sinclair was beautiful and vivacious, the daughter of actors, and Edwin swept her off her feet when she was very young and he was already an international star. For twelve years, they had a blissfully happy marriage — as happy as one can be, at any rate, that endures the death of every child born into it. She bore four children to full term, but none of them lived more than a week."

"Jesus," said Joanna.

"In the spring of 1848, he took Catherine on tour with him. One afternoon he returned unexpectedly to their hotel room and found her in what he regarded as a compromising attitude with another actor, a known ladies' man. Then, in the early months of 1849, he went snooping among Catherine's things and found a letter from the same man. A ridiculous letter, really. Completely over the top in declaring his passion for her — and no proof that she returned it. But that was it for Forrest. He decided his wife was a fallen woman and he was a wronged man. There was one bitter fight that went on all night, apparently, and then six icy weeks of silence. And then he threw her out.

"Beyond all understanding, she seems to have still loved him. She jumped through all kinds of hoops for him and signed some really humiliating letters that he dictated. It wasn't until he tried to cut her off without enough money to live a respectable life that she began to fight back. In an era both phobic of publicity and fascinated by it, any sensible person would have settled matters out of court, for his own pride, even if he couldn't muster the tiniest crumb of sympathy for a woman he'd adored for twelve years. But Edwin had become a vengeful god. He forced Catherine into court for a divorce trial and accused her, in open court, of adultery with numerous men. It became one of the sensations of nineteenth-century America."

Had Ellen Terry's "poor soul" who regarded herself as the guardian of a *Macbeth* manuscript been Catherine Forrest? *I am hoping that you can glimpse the Forest through the Trees,* she'd written to Herbert Beerbohm Tree.

"What happened to her?" I asked, gripping the edge of the sofa.

"Remarkable woman, actually," said Jamie. "After the divorce, she went west to run theaters in gold-rush California: San Francisco, Sacramento, the gold camps. Toured Australia, then London, and then traveled through Scotland on her own. Her parents were Scottish by birth. Same as Forrest's."

"She went to Scotland?" I asked. "You're sure?" Sir Angus had believed that Terry's informant was the dark fairy of Dunsinnan legend.

"Twice, that I know of," said Jamie. "Can't pinpoint the date of the first trip, but the second was 1889. She saw Ellen Terry's *Macbeth*."

Plucking the frame from the table, I examined it, but there was nothing to be seen that we hadn't seen already. At the back, both sides were sealed with brown paper. Picking it up, I walked into the kitchen, found a knife, and slit one side open.

"What are you doing?" cried Jamie. "They're sealed in the original frame. It's half of what makes it valuable."

"Not so valuable as a life," I said, lifting the daguerrotype plate from the glass. It was the one with the date. There was no other inscription. No mark of any kind. I slit open the other side of the frame.

To the back of the plate, someone had fixed a note written from Hells Delight, California, in 1855:

Mr. Forrest,
Not for your sake, but for posterity's, I
must beg you to read one further missive

from me.

When you were in Edinburgh last, a singular opportunity came my way regarding Macbeth, the very play that you and Mr. Macready had chosen to make your battleground. I acquired a curiosity I intended as a surprise for you, but never delivered.

Tho' wonderful, it was a dark gift that I trembled to look on. More than once, I have wondered whether its presence, even in secret, may have poisoned our love, as I believe the mirror did.

You will find it beneath our sweet fountain on the hill. Or, if you do not, it is at least safe, under the watchful eye of heaven.

Farewell,
Mrs. Edwin Forrest

At the last sentence, Jamie rose in excitement. "The fountain hill. Fonthill. The castle on the Hudson that Edwin built for Catherine."

"Does it still exist?" I asked.

Jamie laughed. "It does. He sold it, in 1855, to some nuns."

"Under the watchful eye of heaven," said Joanna.

"They originally ran a school in what's

now Central Park. After the nuns moved their school north to Fonthill, it became the College of Mount Saint Vincent. . . . Where I'm on the faculty. The building's just called the Castle now. It's where I teach."

I had no time to wait for bells to ring. "We have to go now!" I fairly shouted at her.

I could see, though, that there would be no hesitation. It took Jamie no more than five minutes to throw on jeans, a sweater, and a jacket. Downstairs, we stepped out into the cold darkness of early morning. I looked at my watch as we slid into the car. It was a quarter past four.

40

We headed west through Greenwich Village, winding through tree-lined streets that sprouted at odd angles. At the tail end of a cold night at the edge of winter, the streets that refused to sleep looked either sad or seedy, even in Manhattan, the haunt of garbage trucks and revels gone on too long. At the drive lining the island's west side, we turned north.

Fonthill, Jamie told us as we drove, had been named in homage to Fonthill Abbey, in England.

"A church?" asked Joanna.

Jamie laughed. "Sounds like it, but no. It was a preposterously grand home erected by one of the wealthiest Brits of the eighteenth century. Inherited money from Jamaican sugar — slavery, in other words. Damn near bankrupted himself, though, building Fonthill." She shook her head. "He was one strange dude, was William Beckford. Wrote a weird Gothic novel called *Vathek,* about demons and human sacrifice and the unbridled need to know everything. He said it was a response to some things that happened to him at Fonthill one Christmas. So maybe it shouldn't be too surprising that the Forrests' little Fonthill is at least as much in line with the occult as with the church."

"Do you think the Forrests knew that?" I asked.

"Don't know if Edwin did. But Catherine almost certainly knew. Ran with a Bohemian crowd, when occult investigations were all the rage. She was into Spiritualism later. Trying to contact her dead babies. And she seems to have forged a psychological link with Lady Macbeth. Did a lot of research on Elizabeth Stewart, at any rate."

Elizabeth Stewart, the original Lady Macbeth.

I pulled my jacket tighter around me. Off to the right, the city's skyscrapers clawed upward into the sky and then subsided again. The George Washington Bridge swooped off left to New Jersey. Trees lurched up and swallowed the road. In the darkness it seemed as if we were gliding through some primordial forest, in a world made only of road, trees, and the shimmering waters of the Hudson.

The parkway crossed a small, ordinary bridge as it emptied into the Bronx, and the city slipped into view, battling back the trees. After a while, we shot past a long low stone wall edging tall trees to a traffic light, where we turned in. "Welcome to the College of Mount Saint Vincent," said Jamie. We wound back to a gatehouse, where a guard looked up sleepily from his book, saw Jamie, and waved us on.

The road carved through trees, between brick buildings, mostly dark, and back to a wide expanse of lawn out of which rose a small knoll topped by a castle. A toy castle, next to Windsor or Caernarvon or Edinburgh. But for all that, a castle: octagonal towers of rough-hewn gray stone huddling together, raising battlements like fists into the night.

"Our sweet fountain on the hill," said Jamie. "Fonthill."

The driver stopped the car at a tall pointed archway filled with double doors, and we got out. Wind whistled around the building. Jamie avoided the steps up to the great door, darting off into the darkness to the right. Skirting some rhododendrons, we came to a steep stairway leading down. In the wall, half aboveground, was a door.

Unlocking it, Jamie beckoned us inside.

I found myself in a bare hallway smelling of earth and damp, though the walls were a utilitarian white. We went up some stairs and down a hall to find ourselves in a domed octagonal room on the ground floor, lit only by the moonlight drifting down through a skylight far overhead at the dome's apex. A dark wooden balcony ringed the room at the level of the second story. At ground level, rounded archways led into other rooms. This central room, though, was bare of furniture save for a few stiff armchairs against the wall. At our feet, a cross was inlaid in green and burgundy tile on the floor.

"When he first saw the cross," Jamie said, "Forrest said he thought it looked like he'd built the place for the Roman Catholics. And then he sold it to the nuns before he could ever live here. A little ironic. Especially since the cross with equal arms is Greek, not Roman."

"Not just Greek," Joanna said softly. "Celtic. Babylonian. Pre-Columbian American. Inside a circle, it's one of the oldest symbols of all."

"The oculus," said Jamie. She was staring down at a thick quartz-like slab of translucent glass set into the middle of the cross, where the arms intersected. "Early renewable energy: It's supposed to light the basement with the sunlight from the skylight overhead."

" 'Oculus' is Latin for 'eye,' " said Joanna with a sharp glance at me.

"Under the watchful eye of heaven," I murmured, glancing from the skylight to the floor. I knelt down. The oculus fit tightly into the floor. There seemed no way of prying it loose. I sat back on my heels, thinking. And then I rose and hurried back downstairs. The others followed.

At the end of the dank white basement hall was a thick metal door. On the other side, the building morphed into a cave. It was lined with furnaces that probably hummed all day, but at night the room, was silent and cold, colder than the night outside.

"Carved right into bedrock," said Jamie.

The eye in the ceiling lit the room with a faint greenish glow. A little off to the side, what I'd taken at first for a table wasn't: It was an immense slab of bedrock like a bier. The entire room seemed to have been chipped out of rock. If Catherine Forrest had hidden something at Fonthill, *under the watchful eye of heaven* . . . you'd think it would be there. But where? There seemed no way of hiding anything underneath the eye.

I trotted back up the stairs, glancing morosely at the eye, and then turning to take in the whole of the room. On the walls were four carvings in shallow bas relief. Joanna was standing before one of them. "Strange art," she murmured. It showed Macbeth staring horrified at hands curled like claws, dripping with gore. In the background, Lady Macbeth disappeared through a doorway, a dagger in each hand. Gilt letters beneath picked out a quotation from Shakespeare:

What hands are here? Ha! They pluck out
   mine eyes.
Will all great Neptune's ocean wash this
   blood
Clean from my hand?

I moved to the next scene. It was Othello the Moor, eyes starting from his head, his hands around Iago's neck; Iago's face, twisted away, wore a cruel smile. In the background, a young woman walked alone in a walled garden, a handkerchief on the ground, her maid bending to pick it up.

O, beware, my lord, of jealousy;

It is the green-eyed monster which doth
    mock
The meat it feeds on.

I looked back at Macbeth. His face had the same features as Othello's, though not the same expression.

"It's Forrest," said Jamie. "They're all portraits. His favorite roles," she added.

"They're all eyes," said Joanna. "Hamlet's across the way, attacking his mother in her bedroom, turning her eyes into her black and spotted soul."

The fourth scene wasn't a tragedy. It was from *Twelfth Night* — one of the great comedies. Dressed as a boy, the young heroine Viola faced the gaunt and priggish hauteur of the steward Malvolio, pointing at a ring lying on the ground between them. Malvolio's whole body seemed to be pointing — long finger, long nose . . . he had even extended a leg with pointed toe at the offending ring. But what seemed suddenly strangest was that he wasn't a portrait of Forrest — either in body type or in facial features.

"Three for Forrest," said Jamie. "One for Catherine. That's pretty much how their marriage seemed to work, even when it *did* work."

"So it isn't him?"

"Not Forrest, no. At least, not *Edwin* Forrest." She pointed at Viola. "But that's Catherine as Viola. A role she never played onstage, though she maintained it was her favorite."

It was everybody's favorite. Viola was one of the greatest roles ever written for a woman, full of sexual passion for both a man and a woman, romance, hilarity, and music. Longing and fear, too. I looked at Mrs. Forrest's face. She was beautiful. Fragile somehow, with high cheekbones and small pursed lips.

But it was the gilt inscription beneath the scene that caught me. Not poetry, as the others were, but prose, all run together on one line:

If it be worth stooping for, there it lies, in your eye; if not, be it his that finds it.

Malvolio's words to Viola, or Catherine's to her husband?

I looked down at the oculus, the eye in the floor. *If it be worth stooping for, there it lies, in your eye.* I turned back. The ring was very nearly life-sized, in deeper relief than the rest of the carving.

I put a finger into the ring. Nothing happened. I pushed, and faintly, I heard a grinding noise and an exhalation of breath long held. I turned to see the oculus lowering and sliding under the floor.

Would it still be there — whatever Catherine had found? Was she right? Was it — could it be — a version of Macbeth? Whatever she'd found, she'd thought it evil.

Crossing to the hole in the floor, I dropped to my knees. The green stone had moved down, leaving an open space between the floor and the ceiling of the basement below. Sitting on a ledge in a coat of dust a century and a half thick lay a small packet tied in faded ribbon, addressed with two words in a woman's hand:

To Edwin.

Be it his that finds it, I thought. With shaking fingers, I pulled it out, dust cascading down through the open hole onto the stone and into the basement below. The ribbon crumbled as I touched it, but the wax seal was intact, pressed with what might have been a signet ring. Two trees. One for Catherine and one for Edwin. A fine and private forest.

I broke it open. Scrawled on the inside of the cover sheet was a letter in handwriting

I'd seen before. I glanced at the signature to be sure. *Catherine.* I handed it to Jamie.

Inside was another sealed packet, the paper darker and finer, its seal already broken. It had no address.

I heard a small squeak behind me. *"Be it his that finds it,"* said a deep voice.

I turned to look. A man was standing just inside the room with one arm around Joanna's neck, clamped over her mouth. With his other hand, he had a gun to her head. He was gaunt, his hair white and close shaven.

Lucas Porter.

41

"Hold it up," he demanded. "Where I can see it."

I did as he asked, my eye on the cold hard lines of the gun.

He skimmed the page, his lips moving as he read. Caught in the crook of his arm, her face wide with fear and fury beside him, Joanna's eyes flickered. She was reading along.

Reading what?

"Next," snapped Lucas, and I shifted the pages. *"Ha!"* he burst out, and then his voice fell to rhythmic chanting echoing around the room.

Double, double toil and trouble,
Fire burn and cauldron bubble.

"Then it's the *Macbeth* manuscript?" Without realizing what I was doing, I stepped forward.

His grip on Joanna tightened. "Get back," he growled.

Joanna's brow pinched, and ever so slightly she shook her head. I stepped back.

"Stay there," he ordered, and went back to reading. "The key lines are there," he crowed after a few seconds. "The heart of the witches' ceremony." His voice cracked in exultation. "The collection of parts around it in the First Folio, that's rubbish. Ghoulish nursery rhymes, not to mention cliché. But *Double, double* . . . that's different. What, for instance, do you suppose that it means? What's the double toil?"

"Can't you just let me see it?" I pleaded.

"Maybe in another life. *What's the double toil?*"

"Nobody knows," I said shortly. It was the truth, but it was also the answer he was looking for, I surmised. He wanted to talk, it seemed. I wanted him gone and the rest of us safe. Mostly, I wanted the damned manuscript I held in my hands. A *Macbeth* manuscript, for Christ's sake.

Tightening his grip on Joanna, he laughed drily. "Sex and death, Kate. The two great rites of passage. Death and birth. Or at least conception. They're very powerful moments. Make them simultaneous, for one man, and you create a whirlwind of energy, a dark vortex, allowing a spirit to drain, like Odin's, into the underworld, while making a channel through which it can veer back directly."

"What are you talking about?" I was watching him for an opening, the least moment of dropping his guard.

"The deed without a name, Kate. Putting a man back into the womb."

"*What?* How?"

"That's the great mystery, isn't it?" he chortled. He was *enjoying* this, the sick bastard. "But I've worked it out, with a little help from Shakespeare and Ovid. Did Janet tell you that I used to beat her and her bearded fool of a husband at auction from time to time? Once, I scooped a copy of Arthur Golding's translation of Ovid out from under them. *The Metamorphoses.*"

Possibly Shakespeare's favorite book. He'd mined it for plots and subplots, for themes and vocabulary and phrasing. Golding's Ovid was laced through Shakespeare.

"It wasn't the Ovid I cared about," said Lucas, "so much as a single note in the margin next to the story of Medea. *A deede without a name.* In a hand that looks like Shakespeare's."

"How do you know what that looks like? All we have is six signatures, for Christ's

470

sake. And those are all different."

"It's his phrase and his hand. I had it confirmed. *Which suggests that the missing and unnamed deed, you see, was based on the rite next to that notation.* The witch Medea slitting an old man's throat to pour his blood into a cauldron, from which he springs forth young again."

"That's not what happens," I said. "She puts in an old ram and pulls out a lamb, but it's pretty clear she's pulled a bait and switch. What makes the old man young again is the liquor she brews up, poured back into his empty veins."

"It's a mythic substitution, and a sexual myth at that: an old man's life spurting into a cauldron, from which he emerges as a youth. The old man dies, to be born again." His eyes glittered, his voice dropping to a half chant. "The blade for the death, the cauldron for the birth."

"And the mirror?"

He shrugged. "So much crossing rips a wide passage between the living and the dead, and those with the gift of sight or the power of calling can summon other spirits through the void. Especially at Samhuinn, when the veil between life and death is thin to begin with."

His voice was eerily calm. Coupled with

471

images of Sybilla and Eircheard dead, his serenity suddenly seemed obscene. "You don't have the cauldron," I said hotly.

"Too literal, Kate," he sniggered. "A quirk that got Macbeth into trouble. The cauldron is a vessel, but not one of silver or bronze. A woman. And we've had her all along."

Lily? "Where?" I cried hoarsely. "Where is she?"

"Back where it all began." He smiled at my confusion. "Fifty years ago, Janet Douglas walked out on me. Destroyed the film that was to be my magnum opus. *Macbeth.*"

"There are other actresses."

"Not like her. She denied me her body and my children her bloodline." His mouth twisted. "Did she tell you? She's a direct scion, mother to daughter, of Elizabeth Stewart, the Countess of Arran. I plucked Janet from nothing when I discovered that, dreaming of my seed mingled with a bloodline of great power. Catherine Sinclair was another of Stewart's offspring, did you know that? No doubt why Forrest wanted her."

Beside me, Jamie stirred.

"Everything else I did with Janet was dry rehearsal for *Macbeth.* And then she left, on the eve of filming. I swore then that one day I'd take what she'd denied me, and now I am. . . . Taking Lily is a grand revenge, you have to admit. Worthy of Dante or Dumas."

"It's insane," I whispered.

"Cold, logical, perfectly rational, I assure you. If the magic works, I die and return, my blood mingled with hers. If not, then I take my revenge and go out with a marvelous bang." His laughter sputtered around the room.

I'd been so focused on Lily, I'd ignored the other half of his rite. "It requires a death," I said.

"We all owe one. In my case, quite soon. I am dying of pancreatic cancer. So I have nothing to lose. And everything to die for."

I stared at him in disbelief. "You mean to die —"

"Just as I come. The great death and the little death converging. One spirit draining into death, another rising into life at the same time." He was leaning into Joanna, as if he were imagining it already. Joanna closed her eyes.

"And how will you do that? Will your heart to stop?"

"That wouldn't contribute much to my grand revenge, would it?" he said softly. "No; I'll get Lily to kill me. And I'll get the whole thing on film. Do you see the beauty of it? Lady Nairn will find losing Lily to prison in some ways worse than losing her to death. . . . Now fold up those papers and set them on the floor."

I did as he asked, as slowly as I could. Somehow, I had to keep him talking. "I was bringing the manuscript to you. Why go to the bother of stealing it?"

"I didn't want you to succeed." He laughed at my surprise. "Carrie Douglas is almost as single-minded as I am. Not quite, or she'd be standing here in my place. But if she gets hold of that, she'll use it. And I have no intention of scrapping my script for anyone else's, not even Shakespeare's. Now turn and walk to the wall, please." He nodded at Jamie, too. "Both of you."

I had to pull her along with me. Knowing we were fast running out of time.

"On the other hand," he went on, "if I have the manuscript, Carrie will do exactly as I please, in order to get it. For the length of one ceremony, at any rate. But that's all that matters. They'll have other chances. I won't."

He sighed. "She's made things difficult. You, now, you'd be easy to control. With Lily, for starters. But I can also tell you what you want to know. . . . *Guilty or not guilty?*"

Of course. He'd been there. "Anybody can tell me," I said bitterly. "Can you make me believe it?"

His eyes were wide in the darkness. "I filmed Sybilla's death."

I started and stilled. He'd made snuff films before. He was planning to direct his own death, for God's sake. Why shouldn't he have filmed Sybilla's?

"I don't want you to think me ungenerous," he said. "Ask me one question."

Guilty or not guilty? I thought of my hands on the hill, smeared with dark blood, and the revulsion on Ben's face as he looked up at me from Sybilla's body. I thought of Lily.

"Where is she?" I asked quickly. "Where's Lily?"

He laughed aloud. "Altruistic to the last. Optimistic, too. Admirable, but also delusional, in this case. . . . Like I said, she's where it began. On an island in a boiling lake. Now, say good-night to the light, Kate."

Next to me, Jamie let out a sob.

I'd turned my head slightly, so I could just see him. The instant he pulled the gun from Joanna's head, I dove, pulling Jamie with me, hurtling as hard as I could into Lucas. A shot boomed through the space, and all four of us crashed to the floor.

INTERLUDE

October 1606
Mortlake, west of London

Dr. Dee lowered himself carefully into the high-backed green brocade chair at his writing table in his inner sanctum. Just shy of eighty and twisted with rheumatism, he no longer found it such an easy thing merely to sit down. He massaged his fingers, kneading enough looseness into them to hold a quill, at least for a while.

Though the afternoon was chill, he had the window open to the garden. He could no longer hear the songbirds well, but he liked watching them among the autumn leaves blushing red as the robin's breast. His eyes, at least, weren't failing. Not yet. For a man of his scholarly bent, that was a great comfort; at times, it even had the lift of joy.

Not at all times, however. His reading, yesterday, of Master Shakespeare's new play had seemed to dim, for a moment, all the brightness and color of the world. He dipped his quill in ink and set it to the page. And then he pulled it off again, tickling his nose with the bit of feather he'd left at the end. What to say to the impudent poet, and how best to say it?

Somehow, he had to make him see reason. Because this time, it wasn't books or sums or even reputations at risk. This time, lives hung in the balance.

What Robert Cecil, Lord Salisbury's hold over Shakespeare was he did not know, though he knew it extended deep into his past, to his boyhood in Warwickshire. In all likelihood, that meant Catholic plotting against the old queen; that part of the country clung stubbornly, obdurately, and most imprudently to the old religion. Dr. Dee sighed and shook his head. Poor man. He'd probably breathed easier since the queen's death three years earlier. The new king, just down from Scotland, could have no grudge against a player from the provinces. Far from it; His Majesty adored players and playing, and in short order had adopted Shakespeare's company as his own: the King's Men.

And then had come the Powder Plot, almost a year ago now, hatched among men

Shakespeare had surely known, or at least known of, in his youth. Salisbury's old leash, whatever it was, had probably tightened to a stranglehold.

It was Salisbury, Dee knew, who had demanded this infernal play from Shakespeare's pen. Not just a play about king-killing, nor even "just" a play about witches, but a play that would shadow Elizabeth Stewart and her husband, the quondam earl of Arran, on the stage. Favorites of the king in his youth. They had fallen from grace twenty years ago now, however, fleeing into exile in the remote mountain fastnesses of Scotland, no doubt hunching over peat fires among the wild clansmen of the north, conspiring their return to the glittering courts of the south.

So why this story, why now? Especially since their plotted return had not come to pass. A decade earlier, the earl, stripped of his title, returned to the status merely of captain, had been ambushed by his enemies as he rode through some hills, his head raised high on a pole and carried off in triumph, thus fulfilling a prophecy that his head should be higher than any of those around him. The lady had died the year before that, swollen mightily and thus fulfilling a prophecy of her own: that she might be the greatest woman in Scotland. Some said she had died in childbed, others said of the dropsy. Neither story was true, if Dee's source was to be believed: She'd been caught by a witch-hunting mob and torn to pieces.

He'd kept tabs on her from afar since the day she had arrived at his doorstep in Antwerp, her hair bright as flame, her eyes dark and sly. She was a mink, he thought, a strange slippery cross between serpent and cat, with tiny, sharp teeth and a streak of cruelty beneath her red beauty. And she had the sight that had eluded him all his days.

It was why, in the end, he had refused to teach her. He'd dreamed of Viviane, or Nimue, as some of the old manuscripts called her: Merlin's Lady of the Lake, who'd sat as demurely at her master's feet as Elizabeth was then sitting at his — until she'd learned all that Merlin could teach. At that moment, she'd raised herself up like a hooded snake and struck the hand that fed her, locking Merlin away in an enchanted palace of dreams, asleep in some still-hidden hollow in the Welsh hills. Dee had wakened in a cold sweat that night, unable to return to sleep until he could dismiss her.

Lady Elizabeth's response to his refusal — the theft of his mirror, the burning of a manuscript — only confirmed to him that his choice had been wise and that he had, indeed, made a narrow escape. He had kept a watch on her from afar ever since, aware of her growing power. Regretting only that in the wake of his refusal, she had gone back to the Highlands and found other masters. Or mistresses, to be more accurate.

That Salisbury — and his father — would have set their own watch on her made sense, after she'd made herself and her third husband powers to be reckoned with behind a king whom they'd rightly predicted might one day rule England as well as Scotland. But still, Dee could not fathom why it should matter now, with both of them long dead.

Still less could he fathom why the Howards should care, particularly Henry Howard, the king's dark spirit. His evil genius, whom the king had elevated from Lord Henry to the earl of Northampton.

It all seemed to revolve around the face that his scryer Hal Berridge had seen in the mirror. Who was she? Salisbury thought her a woman at court and set the boy to look for her. Northampton appeared to fear that she was someone whose identity might come home to roost, unpleasantly, in a Howard nest.

The upshot was that the boy's life was in danger, and Mr. Shakespeare's play was making things worse. Dr. Dee dipped his quill in ink once more.

Salisbury has commanded, and you have obeyed. Northampton will not command, he will kill. If you choose to put yourself in the Howards' way, so bee it, but I beg you: Find some way to leave the Boy out of it. He is a talented Child, almost as talented, in his way, as you once were. If hee should die in other men's quarrels, merely because he once looked into a Mirror for me, I will beare the burden of his death on my soule, but I will not beare it alone.

He lifted the quill once more, absentmindedly drawing marks on the tip of his nose. He had set down part of his worries, but only a part. The others were somehow more formless and shifting. Truth be told, Dr. Dee suspected that the boy had seen the redheaded witch. The lady Elizabeth Stewart. If that was the case, one must then ask *when?* Had he looked into the past, the present, or the future? Surely the past; she had been dead eleven years.

But it was the present that worried him.

Or perhaps "presence" was a better word. For if Dr. Dee were honest with himself, he would have to admit that he sensed her presence. A peculiar malevolence that had its own spiky, sweet scent.

And that he thought he understood. For in his new play of *Macbeth,* Mr. Shakespeare had done it again, had lifted a magical rite onto the stage. *Her* magical rite, drawn from her manuscript. But not entirely. Not only had Mr. Shakespeare filled in a certain detail that Dr. Dee had left out of the translation, but the playwright had filled in details that were not in the *original* manuscript. Perhaps they sprang from his imagination. But Dr. Dee worried that they sprang from memory.

What had he seen in his long-ago travels in Scotland? Dee had done some digging. He'd discovered another player who could remember a journey north out of Edinburgh, to Perth and beyond, in the company of Mr. Shakespeare. The fellow had remembered, too, playing at a castle called Dunsinnan that figured in the new play. They had been there, he said, at All Hallow's Eve and seen the heathen fires burning on the hills. Gave him quite a turn, it did, just thinking of it now, the old actor had said.

What sort of a turn had it given his companion?

If anything would call the witch back, even from the dead, it was the blasphemy of parading both her magic and her person on the public stage. If she were dead, for he would swear he could feel her. Once more, Dr. Dee set his pen to the page, scratching his final warning with a flourish: "Beware lest, like the Hydra hidden in the Lernaean spring, this serpent is scorch't, and not dead."

■ ■ ■ ■

A Deed Without a Name

■ ■ ■ ■

How now, you secret, black and midnight
hags!
What is it you do?

42

The gun clattered across the tile; I went scrambling after it. Behind me, I heard Joanna cry out and a confused welter of footsteps. I reached the gun and swept it back up, looking for Lucas. He was gone and so was Joanna. From the corridor, I heard footsteps pattering up the stairs.

Jamie was crouched by the wall, trembling. "Hide," I said, and left her there. In the corridor, an arched doorway opened onto a turret tower occupied entirely by a spiral staircase. At the bottom, I stood listening. The footsteps had stopped. I crept upward. Joanna stood on the first landing.

"Did he have it?" I asked quietly.

Seeing me, she put one finger to her lips.

"Did he have the goddamned manuscript?"

She nodded impatiently. Around us, the building was silent.

We were stepping into the second-floor corridor when we both heard the scrape of a door directly overhead. Two more flights up, near the top, a shutter banged loose in the wind. Running up, I found that it was more like a small door, leading onto the roof of the adjoining tower. The roof was empty. I stole to the edge, peering over. An easy drop of one story below was the roof of yet another tower, also empty.

From far below, another shot exploded through the night, the sound ricocheting around the building. *Jamie.* I'd left her alone and terrified. We pounded back downstairs.

In the octagonal hall, the arched double doors leading outside gaped open, bathing the room in moonlight. Jamie was nowhere to be seen. On the floor by the open oculus lay a single sheet of paper, pale in the silvery light. *Dearest,* it began. It was the cover page I'd handed Jamie.

I picked it up and strode across the hall to glance in each of the adjoining rooms. They, too, were empty.

"Kate," cried Joanna from just outside the arched doors, in a tone of urgency that made me run across the room to her side. "He's leaving," she said, pulling me down the stairs at a trot. "The bastard's leaving."

She pointed off to the right. The castle sat alone on a hill overlooking the Hudson. The closest buildings were several hundred yards off; even so, lights were winking on around us. In the distance, a siren rose into a wail. In the moving shadows under the trees, it was impossible to see clearly, but I thought I saw a man hurrying down the slope toward the river. "Two of them," said Joanna.

We ran down the hill in their wake, in and out of the shadows. At the bottom was a narrow private lane. On the other side, a fence overgrown with a thicket of brambles and spindly trees bordered a deep railway cutting. I glanced up and down the fence. Nothing.

"Two?" I whispered. "He's got Jamie hostage?"

She shook her head, her eyes gleaming wide in the moonlight. "Didn't look like it." She pointed. Off to the left the gate to an old wooden bridge hung open. It led across the tracks to a small spit of land ending in a narrow rocky beach. Beyond, three-quarters of a mile wide, spread the dark murmuring waters of the river. A private dock jutted into water. Around it, a number of small boats with outboard motors bobbed up and down.

No — one of them was moving more purposefully than the others, in a steady line away from the dock. The wind veered around, and I heard the whine of an engine. I could just see the hunched shape of someone at the tiller. Around the dock, the other boats began to bunch up and drift away from the dock, slipping into the river's current.

Lucas had cut them all loose.

Behind us, sirens spiraled toward the castle. We broke into a run.

The last of the remaining boats bumped around the dock's upriver corner just as we clattered out to the edge. I caught its line just as the river spun it clear, plucking at it, pulling it out toward deep currents. It took both of us to haul it back.

"How much do you know about Jamie?" Joanna asked as she stepped in the boat.

"Just what Lady Nairn told us: professor of theater, obsessed with *Macbeth* —"

"Are you sure that's her name?"

I looked back, my eyes meeting Joanna's. "Who else . . . you think she might be *Carrie?*"

"I think we have to consider it."

The motor sputtered and caught, and we headed out into the open water. Low in the west, the nearly full moon laid a rippling path of gold on the water. Well north of it, the other boat was a small moving speck of darkness on the face of the river. Their boat was more powerful than ours. As ours bucked and strained against the current, theirs pulled steadily ahead, making for the opposite shore.

"How much did you see back there? Of the manuscript?"

Joanna shook her head. "Not a lot. His arm kept getting in the way. But the first page was a letter; I saw that much. *The witch is not dead,* it read. *I can feel her presence. She is near. She is the red-haired woman my boy saw in the mirror, I know it. You, of all people, should know the danger that imports, and not for the king alone.*"

"Whose letter?"

"It was Dee's handwriting. I didn't see to whom he'd addressed it."

"You think it was Shakespeare?"

"Do you think it wasn't?" She held my eyes. "After that came the play. There's a death, Kate. The witches' brew isn't about body parts. It's about a body."

Staring balefully at the high line of cliffs, I leaned forward over the gunwale as if I might move the boat faster by sheer force of will. We were still little more than halfway across, though, when the other boat stopped among some boulders and headlights flashed once in the trees along the shore.

The boat, now empty, bobbed back out into the current.

The cliffs loomed tall and threatening as we neared. By the time we reached the shore, though, both boat and car were gone. In my pocket, my phone began to drum. I knew what it would be before I answered. Another photo of Lily, this time with a different message: *12 hours.*

This time, it seemed a cry of triumph.

Back where it all began, Lucas had said when I'd asked where he'd taken her. What would that mean, for him? The only person who might know was Lady Nairn.

On the phone, her voice sounded as if it were drifting in from the stars. "An island on a remote loch. Taken up mostly by a ruined castle. It was the first place he took me alone. I danced for him, under the moon."

I thought of Lily spinning under the moon on the lawn of Dunsinnan House. "What loch, Lady Nairn? *Where?*"

"I never knew its name. Up in the Highlands somewhere. It was a long time ago, and I wasn't driving. I was staring at a man I thought was a great artist, giddy with love, or what I thought was love —"

"He's got Lily, Lady Nairn. He's got the manuscript."

492

She stopped short. "We drove out of Inverness. . . . What does he want?"

"To take from her what he couldn't have from you."

"Find her," pleaded Lady Nairn.

Joanna had arranged for a driver while we were still on the river. All the same, it took him half an hour to reach us; by the time we clambered in the backseat, dawn was silvering the eastern shore. "Where to?" he asked.

Back where it all began. The Boiling Lake.

"Teterboro," I said. Teterboro and then Inverness. And from there, apparently, into the realm of fairy tales. In Scotland, that was not a comforting notion.

A little while later, the plane Lady Nairn had hired for us took off as an orange sun rose over the towers of Manhattan, glowering with the fires of Apocalypse.

43

On the plane, I switched on the computer and pulled a map of the Highlands off the Net. The white landmass was thickly speckled with blue water like some mad marbled egg.

"It'll have to be close to Inverness," said Joanna. "That'll cut it down some."

"Not enough," I said bleakly. By the time we landed we'd have no more than a few hours before the beginning of the eclipse.

"What about your other evidence?" asked Joanna. "Does anybody else mention a lake?"

I shook my head. Only the Nairns' dark fairy. And then I remembered the page I'd skimmed up off the floor at Fonthill. I pulled it, partly crumpled, from my pocket.

It was the letter from Catherine Forrest to Edwin that I'd handed to Jamie.

Dearest, it began:

While you have been gone these long weary weeks, I have had an adventure of my own — and what an adventure! And the best part is, there is a surprise for you at the end of it!!

A distant cousin had contacted her father, it seemed, requesting a visit from Catherine, whom she was close to settling on as her heir, and specifying that she must travel alone. In a private note to Catherine, she'd intimated that she wished to pass on a great treasure.

It was the first stirring of interest in the world that Catherine had felt since losing her fourth child. She'd taken passage on a ship up to Inverness.

Joanna drew close. "Go on."

At the dock, Catherine had been met by an immense black carriage-and-six driven by a coachman in old-fashioned livery and a top hat. No sooner had she settled inside than a whip had cracked, and the carriage had thundered along the sea, turning inland to wind up through pine forest and out into moorland, rumbling along the edge of a loch.

Some way out, castle walls rose from the water with the suddenness of Excalibur thrusting upward from the depths. The loch was so still that there seemed two castles, one shimmering in the black mirror of the water and another rearing its broken teeth into the sky.

The track ended at the loch's edge, but the horses plunged into the water without breaking stride, and for a moment she thought they would drown. But a shallow causeway lay just beneath the surface, and the carriage pulled up under wide arches and into a courtyard on a small island. The coachman had leapt down and helped her out, where, to her surprise, he had whipped off his cloak and hat and turned butler, escorting her inside.

As he led her upstairs, she saw that the place was half-derelict, its rooms empty but for echoes. High up in one tower, however, one large room was furnished in modern comfort.

Her hostess was an old woman in the black crepe of mourning, but she held out two hands to Catherine in greeting, and her smile was warm. "Welcome," she'd said, "to my home in the Boiling Lake."

"That's it," I said to Joanna. "It's not only the beginning of Lady Nairn's story, but of Catherine Forrest's, too."

After supper, the old lady had at last shown Catherine her treasure.

I could not take my eyes from it. The instant I saw it, I had to have it for you, though the price she named was staggering. She would use it, she said, to restore the castle to its former glory.

She told me that the pages had passed down for generations, mother to daughter, from the original owner, a countess reputed to be a witch and known, once, as the Lady of the Lake. A woman, furthermore, whom Shakespeare had known. Whom he had shadowed forth in the character of Lady Macbeth.

"My ancestress," she said. She sat back, eyeing me in appraisal. "Yours, as well."

"Is that why you have chosen me?" I asked.

"I did not choose you," she said. "I saw you."

I sat back. "It's Elizabeth Stewart's home, this Boiling Lake."

Joanna swallowed hard. "What do you know about Elizabeth Stewart that puts her in the vicinity of Inverness?"

I frowned. Her *Macbeth* years had been spent far to the south, near the king in Edinburgh and Stirling or at castles close by. But she was a Highlander by birth. Daughter of the earl of Atholl.

497

Joanna shook her head. "I know Blair Castle, seat of the earls and dukes of Atholl. Even in the nineteenth century, you'd have gone by train to Dunkeld, I reckon, and then north in a carriage. There's no way that south from Inverness would've been anyone's first choice of routes. And it couldn't possibly have been a single day's journey in a carriage."

At the computer, I typed in the words "Elizabeth Stewart Arran," and up popped an entry in the *Oxford Dictionary of National Biography.*

"It's her first husband," said Joanna, pointing at the screen. Another Highland lord and a great clan chief: Hugh Fraser, fifth Lord Lovat.

I skimmed down through the entry. After their fall from power, she and her third husband had withdrawn from the glittering world of the court, where many people wanted them dead, to her dower lands in the wilds of Inverness-shire.

"How about Lovat's castle?" asked Joanna.

But Beaufort Castle was not on a loch.

"It's near a river," said Joanna hopefully. "Do you think that counts?"

I shook my head. "Catherine was clear. Walls rising sheer from the water. Besides, according to this article, Beaufort wasn't

498

built until the late nineteenth century. Too late. And its predecessor was destroyed just after the Battle of Culloden, in 1746: too early."

Trying not to watch the time ticking away in the lower right-hand corner, I looked back at the biographical entry. The sources weren't much help.

"Not much out there on Lady Arran," said Joanna.

"We don't need books about *her*," I said slowly. "We need books about the Frasers. And clan histories were popular in the nineteenth century." I pulled forward to the keyboard and started typing. "It means they're out of copyright. It means there's a good chance they'll be searchable on Google Books. The largest library on the planet, in digital — and searchable — form."

It didn't take long to find her, scattered in venomous mention across a number of Fraser histories. "The Lady Jezebel." "An ambitious, avaricious, and ill-natured woman." A whore who consorted with witches.

And yet, in fear for her life, she'd gone back to these people who despised her.

It was a measure, I supposed, of the depth of the hatred she faced farther south and the thickness of clan loyalties in the north.

The Frasers might have reviled her, but she was the mother of their chief. So long as she lived among them, they'd allow no one else to kill her.

The details of her exile among them, however, seemed wrapped in a forbidding wall of silence. I'd have to sift through the histories one by one, wading through their thick Victorian prose from beginning to end.

The first turned up nothing. As did the second. The third wasn't really Victorian: a nineteenth-century edition of an obscure seventeenth-century manuscript called the *Polichronicon,* or the Wardlaw manuscript.

In the lower right corner of the screen, the time sped on.

Six hours into the flight, I sat up. Tucked away in a passage that mentioned neither her nor her husband by name — and thus slipped beneath the radar of word searches — I read that "the great, though not good lady" and her husband had whiled away their time in exile by hunting.

Being under continuall feare, their residence was in the Isle of Lochbruyach, a fort remoat from any roade. . . .

Lochbruyach.

"Loch Bruiach, in the Kiltarlity Hills,"

500

read a terse footnote. With shaking fingers, I entered it into Google Maps, and a Loch Bruicheach popped up, southwest of Inverness.

"Think that's the one?" asked Joanna.

"There's no island."

"There has to be." She toggled over to the satellite view, which showed a tiny white speck in the water.

I looked at the clock. We'd have one chance to find Lily. Did I trust it to a speck seen by satellite on a loch with a not-quite-right name? And why had people called it the Boiling Lake?

Out of curiosity, I searched "Loch Bruiach Place-Name."

"Look at this," I said softly. " 'Bruiach' comes from an old Gaelic word, *brutach,* meaning 'boiling or raging one.' It is, quite literally, the Boiling Lake."

"That's it, then," said Joanna.

I looked back at the map. It was still remote from any road.

"I'll arrange for a Range Rover," said Joanna. "How are you at backcountry driving?"

The last hour of the flight, perversely, was the hardest. We phoned Lady Nairn again, but there was no answer. There was nothing further I could do, save pace back and forth in the aisle, willing the plane to hurry.

By the time we finally landed, it was long since dark; the full moon had risen huge in the east. "Call the police," I said as we drove out of the airport in the Range Rover, heading west along the sea.

"Lady Nairn didn't —"

"She's not thinking straight," I said. "Call the goddamned police."

Joanna put in a call. "I need to report a kidnapping," she said.

As she began to go through the details, I heard her voice harden. "No, no relation. No, she hasn't been reported missing. At the Samhuinn festival in Edinburgh, I understand. . . . She's being held, we think, on an island in a loch. Loch Bruiach . . . Heard a threat of rape against her. In New York . . ."

She hung up pale and shaking. "Bastards. Clearly think I'm a nutter. But they promised to send a constable round to check the place."

Prickles crept over me. I hoped to God he'd be discreet.

"Drive like the bloody wind," said Joanna.

We drove briefly through the glare of city lights and then back out into country darkness. It had snowed that morning and was supposed to snow again that night; the slush on the road squealed against the car's tires. We left the sea, turning inland through snowy fields and then climbing into hills. The road narrowed, its curves tightening. Traffic, sparse to begin with, thinned and disappeared, until we were the only car I'd seen for miles.

The shrill of Joanna's phone made us both jump; she answered in half a ring and hung up with a sour face. "The police have checked. There's no one there." She gave me a sideways look. "And there's been no one there, apparently, for over a century."

"They're wrong," I said, tightening my grip on the steering wheel. "They have to be."

Soon afterward, we left the pavement altogether for a deeply rutted track. A forest closed around us, glowing an eerie blue and silver in the moonlight, and the track veered steeply downward. I thought of Catherine hurtling along in the black carriage. Hushed with the anticipation of snow, the world was utterly silent save for the grind and slip of the car.

Just beyond the edge of the forest, we came to a stop at a fence. Tracks in the snow looked as if another car had stopped here recently. I stepped out, shivering in a wind sharp with the needling tang of pines. Beyond the gate, open moorland rolled down and away, stark and strangely beautiful, about as blasted as a heath could get. No loch was visible, only the moor bound in the far distance by ancient, worn hills. The moon hung in the southeastern sky like an immense luminous pearl, but clouds were thickening in the west, fingers of darkness upon darkness.

There were no buildings and no lights. Save for a single set of tracks leading out and the same track coming back, there was no evidence that humans had ever walked here at all. Had ever existed, for that matter — as if not only my species but our history had been obliterated. Or had not yet occurred.

Back where it all began.

If Lucas and Jamie were here, there was no sign of them. Either we had somehow passed them or there was another way in.

The track wound down into a shallow fold between two slopes. Half an hour later, we curved to the right and struggled back up a slope. Beyond, the loch suddenly appeared, dark, cold, and menacing, lapping at our feet with greedy little slaps. Close to the opposite shore, a castle rose from the water.

Wind ruffled the loch's surface, however, so there was no reflection, no second castle in a dark mirror. And no sound, either, save the slap of the wavelets and the moaning of the wind.

And then a wolf's howl rose into the night, in a place where no wolves should be. I glanced over at the moon. A sliver at its edge had darkened to orange. The eclipse was beginning. I looked back at the island and caught a spark of light. Flame flickered and grew. Someone had set one of the turrets ablaze.

"They're starting," I said. I pulled out my phone. No service. Joanna had none, either. I put the car key in her hand. "Go back to the road. Drive if you have to . . . find somewhere with a signal. Call the police again and drag them here if you have to tell them you've witnessed murder yourself."

"Where are you going?"

"To find Lily."

I took off around the loch at a run.

44

The path skimmed the edge of the lake. Bent low, my feet slipping in icy mud, I ran until the cold air scoured my lungs and it hurt to breathe. On the island, the fire licked upward into the night. The shore curved in toward the island, and I came to a stop in a dark stand of trees opposite the main entry.

The place was ruinous, some of the towers half-crumbled away, but I recognized it all the same. It was Fonthill, writ large. Or rather, Fonthill was this place writ small and drawn from memory. Catherine Forrest had shown her husband the castle all right. . . . She had designed for him a copy, remembered rather than exact.

Behind me, another howl rose through the night. On the hill at Dunsinnan, wolves had heralded the attack that scattered Lady Nairn's rite and left Sybilla dead. I had no wish to wait and see what would emerge from the trees. I waded into the loch, hoping the shallow causeway Catherine had described was still there. The water was icy, and ten feet in, I could no longer feel my feet. I had to move slowly. But the water came no higher than my knees.

A stone drive sloped up from the water's edge, leading through the archway into a small courtyard. Icy snow crunched underfoot, the sound of my footsteps loud in the silence as I made my way through stones fallen from the surrounding towers. The shape of the castle's main doorway echoed the arch in the wall behind. The doors themselves were missing.

Around the main hall clustered battlemented towers of various heights, their walls pierced with windows like staring eyes. The hall was a great octagon; if it had once been domed, like Fonthill's, the dome had long since disappeared. It was open to the sky. For a moment, I stood in the shadow of some fallen stones in the courtyard, listening. The only sound was the crackling of the fire and the skittering of leaves across the ground. Easing the safety catch off the pistol, I stepped inside.

Around the floor stretched a circle of candles such as Lily had once danced within, except that these were enclosed by hurricane glasses. Even so, their small flames bent and fluttered in the wind. But there was no dancer here; the hall was empty. Directly across, a large window framed the moon, its disc being devoured by a deep orange shadow. The floor was paved with stone, not tile, but just as at Fonthill, there was a central stone different from all the others. An eye.

Stepping into the circle, I walked forward through the room. Cut into an octagonal stone in the center of the floor was a small circular groove with an irregular protrusion. In it — the groove clearly made for it — lay a handled disc of polished black stone. It was not, as at Fonthill, a translucent eye. It was a mirror.

Dee's mirror.

In its surface shone a small reflection of the dying moon.

Off to the side, I heard a small noise and turned. In a doorway stood Lily, a blue silk gown rippling around her, her eyes wide with terror. Behind her stood a hooded and cloaked figure with arms around her neck, a knife at her throat.

"Drop your weapon," someone said, and I whirled toward the voice.

In another doorway stood Lady Nairn. She wore her own clothes, but she, too, had a keeper with a knife at her throat.

"Drop," said another voice in a whisper.

Lily and Lady Nairn were both being used as shields; I had little chance of rescuing either of them by force and none of freeing them both. Carefully I set the gun down on the floor, cursing my own stupidity.

A shadow flittered over me and I looked up. Another gown of blue silk floated down toward me like wings. Blue silk shimmering with beetle's wings.

"Put it on."

Pulling it from the air, I wrapped it around me.

A deep, slow drumbeat boomed through the space. A high voice rose, twining up to the sky. As if drawn by it, from every door drifted figures cowled in black, their faces invisible. In their right hands, each one held a knife.

"Let her go," said a voice behind me. I turned. In the doorway to the courtyard stood Lucas. *"Lily is mine."* He stepped forward to the edge of the circle, flinging away one of the hurricane glasses, which shattered, and picking up the candle within.

"Enter two kings, old and young," said the figure holding Lily. *"Double, double toil and trouble* . . . Not one king and the double deeds of sex and death, but two kings, young and old. Shall we guess which of them ravishes the maiden?"

"I don't need to guess," said Lucas. "I have the manuscript." He raised the candle's flame near its edge. "As it happens, the answer is neither. Which is why we're not following the script. Not this time. Let her go."

Behind him, a shadow detached itself from the rocks strewn across the courtyard and slipped silently up the steps.

The figure gripping Lily did not move.

"She is mine," said Lucas, touching flame to the paper.

In a flash of silver, steel slashed across his abdomen. A deep scream burst from him as he pitched forward onto his knees, and the burning pages fell to the ground. The shadow darted from behind, smothering the flames.

On his knees, Lucas was holding his entrails in his hands, blood welling through his fingers. The figure turned, and the knife flicked out again, slashing his throat.

Stepping back from the blood spilling across the stones, the figure loosed the cloak and let it fall away, revealing a woman clad in another blue gown. She turned back toward the circle and I saw her face.

Joanna.

Still holding the knife, she raised bloody arms to the moon. In a deep voice, she called aloud to the darkness: *"Nothing is but what is not."*

45

"Meet my niece," said Lady Nairn in a voice of loathing. "Cerridwen Douglas."

Joanna? Joanna, not Jamie, was Carrie. Jamie was probably dead in a corner at Fonthill, while I'd brought Joanna with me every step of the way. Discussed every piece of evidence with her, shared everything I knew. Spilled my sorrow and my fury to her. Wept in her arms, for Christ's sake.

Left her to call for help . . .

In a wash of despair, I realized no help would come. There would be no police. There had probably never been any police — just one of her followers on the other end of the phone, someone who'd driven out to the gate and made believable tracks in the snow.

Why? The only reason to do that was to lure me on.

Which meant she still needed me.

Double, double toil and trouble, Lucas had

said. *One spirit draining into death, another rising into life at the same time.*

What role did she mean to hand me? Victim or killer?

Another voice slipped out from memory. My own, facing Eircheard's body. *I will kill her. I will find Lily, and then Carrie will die.*

Around me, the candles guttered in a gust of wind. I stepped forward, heart knocking against my ribs. "You have the manuscript. You have me. Let Lily go."

Joanna — Carrie — looked up from the manuscript. "When we are finished with her."

"That was the deal. I bring the manuscript, you release her."

"And we will. When you are finished with your role and she with hers."

"What role?" My throat was dry.

"Have you not guessed?" She folded the pages and slipped them into a pocket. "*Thou shalt be queen hereafter.* Hecate, queen of witches. Not the cackling fool added by some later hack. The triple Goddess: maiden, mother, crone. There and not there, as Ellen Terry put it, in the three witches. A girl to gaze, a mother to mate, and a crone to kill."

I frowned. "That's not how Shakespeare wrote them." *What are these, so withered and so wild in their attire,* Shakespeare had made Banquo say. *You should be women, and yet your beards forbid me to interpret that you are so.*

"Come on, Kate," Joanna chided.

Not Joanna, I told myself. *Carrie.*

"You of all people should know better than to trust what one character says. . . . In any case, there's a stage direction here that disputes Banquo's observation as illusion."

All was illusion, nought was truth.

"In any case, without Lily, we have no maiden. No one to see . . . Lucas was right about one spirit draining into death and another rising into life." She lifted her voice to a ritual cry. "The old king is dying. The new king must take his queen."

The drumming rolled out again, and the wordless song rose once more into the night. The figure behind Lily pushed her forward into the center of the circle. "Dance," he commanded.

The instant she was clear of him, a man hurtled down from above, landing like a cat in the center of the circle, pulling Lily close and hauling her to the door, sweeping the room with a gun. The cowled figures who'd begun to close in on him pulled back.

All but one. Lady Nairn had pulled loose

from her captor, wresting the knife from his hand.

"Let her go," said Ben.

It was only then that I realized he was talking about me.

In the confusion, a man had come up behind me. Now his arm snaked around me, pulling me back into the corridor from which Lily had emerged, using me as a shield for both himself and Carrie. As he dragged me into a spiral stairwell, I twisted and writhed, catching a glimpse of his face.

He was the dark-haired man. The Winter King.

I slammed his arm against the wall, and he dropped his knife, but before I could reach it, Carrie tossed him hers, which he brought up against my throat. Beneath the blood clotting the blade I saw runes and a pattern of blue-gray whorls.

Nothing is but what is not.

I caught one last glimpse of Ben's face before I was dragged backward up the stairs.

46

Up and up we wound, the blade cold against my throat, the stone wall on one side hot to the touch. It was the tower adjoining the stair turret that was burning. We passed floors opening onto rooms that were empty and others that were missing floors. On the fifth floor, all that remained of the corridor was a narrow ledge. I was pushed across it at knifepoint and shoved into a vaulted room holding a table, two high-backed chairs, and an unnecessary fire glowing in the grate. Two crumbling windows looked over the loch and the dark orange moon; wind moaned through the room.

"Strip," said my captor.

One spirit must die, another must rise.

"No." I slid around the table, backing against the far wall.

Tossing the furniture aside, he strode toward me, the blade gleaming dully in his hand.

"Ian." Carrie stood in the doorway. "She must be a vessel of the Goddess. She must consent." At the sound of her voice, he stopped, panting a little, his body still poised to spring.

"Consent!" I burst out. I was watching the knife in his hand. Somehow, I had to get it away from him. "You think I'll consent to a rape?"

Carrie looked at me coldly. "If you consent, it will not be rape."

Ian, I thought, backing into the alcove made by one of the windows. It was the name of the man Lily had talked about with shining eyes. *This* was her beau? The Winter King? "Have you touched her?" I asked, my voice thick with disgust.

His mouth curled in a faint leer. "Nothing that she did not want. And not as much as she wanted."

With scryers, Joanna had said, virginity was at a premium. *The purer the vessel, the clearer the sight.* Which meant he was toying with me. "She's fifteen," I said shortly. "She doesn't know what she wants. And I'll bet she didn't know what you were up to, either, or she wouldn't have let you anywhere near her. She probably still doesn't know."

"Do *you* know what you want?" He gazed at me with the calculating eyes of a cat, the

517

knife weaving in the air as he spoke. "It took two months to stack the tower next door for the bonfire. Nine sacred woods, three stories high. It will collapse eventually and bring down this whole tower and everything in it as well, in a cataclysm of fire. You'll want to be gone by then, if you want to survive. But to get out, you have to get past me. For a price." His voice lowered to a dark caress. "So what is it you want, Kate? How badly do you want to live?"

I glanced out the window. Five stories down, the wind whipped the loch to an angry froth. *The boiling lake,* I thought. *And the burning tower. Double, double toil and trouble, fire burn and cauldron bubble.* I knew how cold the water was. How deep was it?

"You'll die," said Ian. "I'm offering you life."

"It's not life that she wants," said Carrie, walking forward with another offer. In one hand, she held what looked like a necklace with a rectangular silver pendant and some papers. The manuscript. In the other, she, too, held a knife. The one I'd knocked from Ian on the stairs. "I can tell you what you want to know. Shakespeare's past, or your own."

I stilled, hearing my voice rasping on the hill. *What have I done?*

She'd known. She'd known the entire time she'd held me on the plane, like a mother holding a child. I realized that betrayal with the force of being slammed into a wall of cold stone. "Even if I were in the market," I said through clenched teeth, "what reason would I have to trust any word from your mouth?"

The pendant she was dangling was a flash drive. "Lucas's raw footage," she said. "He filmed Sybilla's death. Auld Callie's and Eircheard's, as well." She dropped it on the table, tossing the knife down next to it and spreading out the papers. "The fruit of the knowledge of good or of evil. Of innocence or guilt."

Looking at that small silver rectangle, listening to Carrie's voice, other certainties began to drop into place, pieces of a puzzle floating of their own accord into a picture that made appalling sense. Carrie may have masterminded much of the killing, but she'd been with me when Eircheard died. The hand that held the blade had not been hers. And even bound and on his back, Eircheard could have swatted Lucas aside like a gnat. I looked at Ian, rage making the very air around him seem to ripple, like the quivering of heat around a mirage. "That was you, wasn't it? *You* killed Eircheard." I could feel my hands pumping into fists. I'd promised Eircheard as he lay dead in the library that I'd kill Carrie, but that was when I thought she'd wielded the knife. It had been Ian, though, now standing before me with the killing blade in his hand, a mocking leer on his face.

Lunging for one of the chairs, I shoved it into Ian and darted toward the table, reaching for Carrie's knife. I almost had it when Ian caught me, dragging me to the floor and pinning me down with both hands.

I must have knocked his knife away with the chair, I realized, even as his hands clamped in a chokehold around my neck.

He leaned in as if for a kiss. *"Put out the light, and then put out the light."*

Othello's words, while killing Desdemona. The opposite of the language of God. Not *fiat lux,* "let there be light," but *fiat mors.* "Let there be death."

"You're beautiful when you're angry, Kate. Not smart, maybe, but beautiful. Wild cat, wild Kate." His face began to go dark. Around the edges of things, lights began to glow like fiery haloes. It wasn't my death that he wanted, though. Not yet anyway. It was darkness. If I lost consciousness, I realized, he'd do what he wished to my body and count it as consent when I didn't fight back.

In one last burst of strength, I hurled him off, rolling away, scrabbling for the blade that I knew had to be on the floor somewhere. Even as he pulled me back toward him by the feet, I saw a glint of steel, and my hand closed around the black hilt. . . . *Nothing is but what is not.*

I slashed out at him, and the blade caught his arm, trailing a bright line of blood. He flinched, and I scrambled to my feet, keeping the knife before me as Ben had once taught me. *In a knife fight,* he'd said with unusual seriousness, *the only defense worth having is an offense.*

"Ian!" Carrie cried, and once again I saw her knife soaring through the air toward his hand. I couldn't let him catch it. As he reached for it, I launched myself into him, hitting him square in the chest with the full weight of my body, unbalancing us both so that we crashed to the floor. With a thud, my knife drove into his belly up to the hilt.

The other knife clattered harmlessly to the ground, and a wild, deep cry split the room. For a moment he gripped me hard. Then he jerked away. I stumbled to my feet, the knife in my hand rippling red in the firelight.

Pushing himself up, Ian gripped his belly, blood welling through his fingers.

A loud rumble filled the room, and the floor lurched. Grabbing at the windowsill to stay upright, I dropped the blade. Ian staggered into the table. For a moment, there was silence. Then the wall behind him disappeared, collapsing in a sheet of flame. The floor rippled and bucked, dropping him to his knees, and the room began to tilt. Across the room, Carrie stepped back into the doorway, clinging to the door frame. In the center, Ian was still gripping the table. Another jolt, and the floor heaved again, tilting farther. Before I could reach it, the knife slid away from me, heading toward Ian. Bellowing with rage, he scooped it up and threw it. I ducked, and it sailed through the window into the night, plummeting down to the lake.

Ian began throwing everything he could lay his hands on. Papers, pens, books. There was a glint, and the flash drive on its chain snaked through the air. I reached for it, and it brushed my fingers. It clattered against the stone, but before I could grab it, it slid down the outside of the wall and disappeared.

Inside, the floor lurched a third time and disintegrated. With one last wail of fury, Ian slid backward into the flames, his cry lost in the roar of the fire. Where he'd stood, loose pages of manuscript floated on the heated air like slow butterflies bursting one by one into flame.

47

From the doorway opposite, a wail rose from Carrie. "What have you done?"

The heat in the room was intense; the cold wind sweeping over my back was all that made it bearable.

"Did you not think the spirit of Shakespeare worth calling forth from the deeps?" Carrie went on.

"That's what all this killing was for? To conjure *Shakespeare*?"

"Not the man," she said with contempt. "The spirit who possessed him. The man was dross, merely. Do you know what Dee wrote?" She held out a page from the manuscript. *You are a servant of the great, no more, a bit player who glimpsed the Great Rite not once, but twice: both times, uninvited, from the shadows, and both times, stole its fire for yourself.* She looked up. "Fire and power that was meant for me and mine: for Arran's daughter. For Dee's son. And it lit, instead, on the poor clay of a glover's son." A narrow strip of floor along one wall was all that remained of the room. She began advancing across it.

"You seriously mean to suggest that spying on some magical rite explains Shakespeare's genius?"

"I would have called it forth again. Made it light upon my son."

Ian was her son?

"He was an artist," she said. "A visionary. A conduit of power."

It was what Lily had said. A genius, she'd called him. *He'll change the way stories are told . . . make a new kind of art altogether.*

"He was a killer," I said aloud.

"An artist in flesh and blood," said Carrie. "A man who would shape the world by the force of his will. I thought you might have the imagination to help."

"You thought I would help?" I thought of Auld Callie, strung up in the tree. Of Eircheard, his body slashed in the darkness in the British Museum, his heart torn out. Of Sybilla with her throat cut and Ben's face looking down on her.

"You are no better than your petty-minded poet. *Shakespeare.*" She spat the name. "He took a gift of great power, the shadow of the language of God, and did what with it?

Wasted it. Exhaled it on the public stage, grabbing at pennies here and there in exchange for doling out cheap delight to the grubby masses." Her voice rose in contempt. "He could have shaped kingdoms and crowns. He could have seized wisdom from the deeps of time."

"He *did* shape kingdoms and crowns," I said quietly. "Not the everyday England of Elizabeth and James. Kingdoms of the mind. He made new and bright worlds from nothing but words. . . . *The shadow of the language of God:* your words. It wasn't angels or demons Shakespeare chose to conjure. It was people: audiences.

"He offered humans a brush with the divine. And he harmed no one doing it. . . . *An it harm none, do what ye will.* Isn't that the one rule of witchcraft?"

"A rule made by those afraid of its old powers. But to celebrate life, you must also celebrate death. To create life, you must create death."

"You don't create anything. You destroy only. But you can't even do that, not with words alone. You can only make it happen by finding someone to do it for you: a terrible shadow of Shakespeare's weird sisters getting Macbeth to do their dirty work by whispering on the wind." I shook my head.

"But you are also Macbeth. Your magic, your power, it's nothing but a sham. An illusion. You are no better than Shakespeare's bloody king, lured into acting as the robotic arm of evil."

She laughed aloud. *"Watch. . . ."* She began to raise her arms, her voice a low, throbbing chant. "I conjure you —" The wind buffeted through the window, tearing her words away, so that I heard them only in snatches.

Though you untie the winds . . .
. . . trees blown down . . .
Though castles topple . . .
Even till destruction sicken . . .

Outside, the storm slammed into the castle with a fury, buffeting the walls like some hammer of the gods, churning the water below into high waves clawing at the stone. Whipped to frenzy, the fire rushed upward in a thundering whirlwind of sparks and shooting flame.

"Answer me!" cried Carrie, and in a sudden gesture of triumph, she brought her arms down to her sides.

Behind her, the corridor imploded in a deafening roar. For a split second the fire darkened to glimmering red embers and then it billowed back, exploding skyward, almost, it seemed, in the shape of a raging man. With a wild shriek of triumph, Carrie turned, the blue gown floating out around her like wings, and walked into the flames.

The heat rolling off the fire was scorching. I slid down the outer side of the window, dangling from the sill, letting the tower wall shield me from the worst of it. For a moment, I hung there, fighting to cling to the damp stone, though it was heating up by the second.

No one would imagine I had survived that last cataclysm. I barely believed it myself. And if they did . . . what then? Between the storm and the fire, there was no way to reach me by land or air or water. Fire burn or cauldron bubble. I had a choice of deaths: water or fire.

From far away, I heard the wail of sirens, weak as the mewling of newborn kittens.

Even if I did survive, clinging to the stone till the fire died, what then?

What part I had played in Sybilla's death I did not know and never would; everyone else who had been there was now dead, and the flash drive with its footage had been swallowed up in the fire. All that remained was a trail of evidence that said, beyond the shadow of doubt, that I had been there.

Whatever I had or had not done to Sybilla, I had killed Ian. He had been cruel, a killer, and very likely insane, but it was still a death. Blood on my hands.

Around me, the wall began to steam, and I realized, as if from a distance, that my fingers were blistering where they dug into crannies in the stone.

In the sky, a sliver of white appeared at the edge of the moon as the shadow began to slide off. Somewhere, I heard singing, a lone voice, rising like silver in the night, joined a few moments later by another. As suddenly as it had hit, the wind now calmed. Below, the angry waves were subsiding, the water cold and dark beneath a surface of red and gold. Out over the loch, snow began to fall in flakes large and slow as drifting feathers.

Suddenly, I was aware of nothing but empty exhaustion. It was not physical; I could have clung to that wall for a while yet. But for what?

I let go.

It seemed to me that a silvery light rose around me, wrapping about me like a cool slip of silk. For a moment, I thought, it buoyed me up. Then I felt a shock of cold. And dark water closed over my head.

48

Darkness and cold swirled around me, smooth as glass, as if I'd fallen into the dark mirror. The next thing I remember is the shock of hands, a rushing, and air scraping across my body. I coughed and retched, and a face swam into view above me, ringed with the glow of the fire.

Dark, wet hair and green eyes. The planes of his face chiseled with damp and fire.

Ben.

"Kate," he said, his face very close to mine as he wiped wet hair from my eyes, wrapping his body around mine so that warmth flowed from him to me.

We seemed to be on a rocky shore. The singing had stopped, and the silvery light was gone. The moon laid a long glittering path of gold across the dark water. From the other direction, red and blue lights flashed over the water. *Emergency vehicles,* I thought. *Police.*

Behind Ben, other faces peered down at me. Lady Nairn, full of concern, and Lily, her face pale with relief and something I would not recognize till later: pride.

"How did you find me?" I asked Ben.

"I can call spirits from the vasty deep," he said lightly, his mouth tipping into a smile.

I frowned. "How?"

"Lily told me where to dive."

Just beyond him, she'd bent to pick up something among the rocks. A silvery rectangle dangling from a chain. "I saw you," she said, looking back with a smile. "In the loch."

But that is not possible, I thought, slipping back into unconsciousness.

INTERLUDE

November 4, 1606
Hampton Court Palace
Not long after the boy Hal Berridge had
come to Mortlake to serve as his father's
scryer, Arthur Dee had walked in on the
boy kissing Dee's younger brother Rowland
— a particularly deep and passionate kiss.
He'd reviled the boy as a catamite ever
since, a Ganymede corrupting his little
brother. He spat vile terms at the boy, aim-
ing hidden kicks and blows his way whenever he could. Not only because of the al-
lure he had for Rowland, but because
Arthur found himself also gazing at the boy,
tingling when he walked by. Deep down, he
knew it was not entirely the issue of sex that
rattled him, however, no matter how star-
tling he found the attraction. It was jealousy,
and not of his body. Of his sight. With the
possible exception of Edward Kelley, Hal
Berridge was the best seer his father had

ever employed.

Though his father had been crestfallen, Arthur, for one, had breathed more than one sigh of relief when the boy left Mortlake for Hampton Court at the invitation of Lord Salisbury. Then, on the eve of the play in which Berridge was to star as a queen, Arthur discovered that Rowland had made an assignation with him at the palace. Telling himself that he was protecting his little brother's reputation, Arthur had got Rowland stupendously drunk, left him snoring in the music room, and then gone downriver himself to keep the appointment.

The exact spot turned out to be deep in a deserted wing of the oldest part of the palace. Arthur had arrived early to find the otherwise empty room warmed by a fire of apple logs scented with lavender. He had laid Rowland's cloak on the floor and retired behind the door to wait.

The boy's blue velvet skirts whispered sweetly against the flagged floor as he entered the room. Arthur stepped swiftly behind him, closing and latching the door. The creature had turned, and Arthur had enjoyed the flash of fear on the boy's face.

"Arthur —"

"Don't foul my name in your mouth," he said, and lunged.

Berridge managed to duck, and Arthur's elbow hit his jaw with a glancing blow. The boy kept his feet, barely. As Arthur came back at him, he pulled a knife, which slid across Arthur's arm, trailing a bright line of blood. A scratch, really, no more, but it made him shout with rage.

He aimed another blow at Berridge's head and this time connected with more force. Winding a fist into the long hair of the boy's wig, he dragged him across the floor. When the wig did not come off, Arthur stopped and, with his other hand, tore at the gown, which ripped down to the waist.

As if Berridge had suddenly turned to a serpent in his hands, Arthur stepped back, his eyes widening, his breath seizing. "But you are not — you are not a boy," he stammered.

Naked from the waist up, the person in front of him was a woman. A beautiful woman with long red hair. "Would your father have taught me in this shape?" she charged.

Arthur's mouth opened and closed. "And Rowland — ?"

"Has known almost since the beginning," she said.

He blinked, still trying to process her transformation, and she stepped close and took his hand in hers. With a smile, she slid his hand up to her breast.

Suddenly all the longing that he had bottled up inside, twisted and questioned and tried to press out of himself for over a year, tumbled forth. An instant later, his arms locked around her, and she let him pull her down onto the cloak spread over the floor, where they mounted one another with a wild, rutting urgency.

Some time later, she lay atop him, her head in the small of his shoulder as the dark explosion of climax drained away. Hearing a sound, he opened his eyes to see an old man he did not know lunging at them, a knife in his hands. Arthur rolled, flinging Berridge — or whoever she was — away.

Stumbling with the force of his drive, the other man ran past them but turned quickly, leaping at them again.

How the knife — the one she'd cut him with, still marked with his blood, and with strange characters running down the blade — came into Arthur's hand, he didn't know. And what happened next happened so quickly that he could never quite remember it: As their attacker darted around him, clearly headed for her, Arthur's hand flicked out and slit his throat.

The other man dropped to the floor,

blood welling and spurting into pools on the flagstone. Arthur heard the knife clatter to the floor as well and stood staring at his hand in horror.

Moments later, the Berridge who was not a boy propelled him out the door, saying he must save himself and that she would clean up as necessary. And she'd added a strange request: Send Mr. Shakespeare.

January 1607
Castle Bruiach, Scotland
Well-wrapped in furs on a still and moonless night, she sat alone in an open window high in a tower, staring down at the dark ice of the loch. Once, her mother had ruled this castle. Just that morning, however, after a quick but decisive seduction of the young lord who now had charge of it, she had become the new lady of the lake. The way she sat, one hand resting protectively on her still-flat belly, might have made her new husband proud, thinking he had tilled his new field well. Inside her, though, another man's child was already growing, a fact she had not found fit to share with her new lord.

The night before, in a sudden bitter cold, the loch had frozen, its surface smooth as black glass. Still uncluttered by snow or the tramping of men, it glimmered faintly in the starlight. Letting her breathing slow and her body relax, she stared at its surface without really seeing it, and after a while, pictures began to form in her mind. At first, they were memories, though she saw the scenes with a detached clarity, not, as she'd first seen them, from within her body, but floating somewhere overhead.

She had always looked young and boyish, so it was easy to bind her breasts and dress like a boy five years younger than her true age. She had refused, however, to cut the bright hair that had always seemed, some-how, to be an extension of her soul, some part of herself more intrinsic than other, less unique features. So she acquired a wig and a large cap, and she experimented with various substances until she found one that could slick her long hair down inside them. And then she traveled south all the way to London.

West of London, to be exact. To a place called Mortlake. *From a boiling lake,* she thought with dark satisfaction, *to a lake of the dead.* There, she presented herself to the English wizard Dr. Dee, in order to steal the learning out of which he had cheated her mother.

Her mother had been dead for nearly a

decade, but the girl had forgiven neither the wizard nor the thief for their part in making her mother's life a disappointment. Though she had met neither man, the whole of her young life had been one long exercise in reviling them. Neither man, in fact, had any reason to know of her existence, though the thief, Mr. Shakespeare, had been present — as an illicit observer — at the hour of her making. During a Great Rite, her mother had told her, at the top of Dunsinnan Hill, in the light of a Samhuinn fire. Later that night, he had stolen away the mirror and the manuscript whose loss had made her mother howl at the moon. She had been born, the girl sometimes thought, with the express purpose of retrieving those two lost treasures. She had gone to London to hold true to that purpose.

Dr. Dee sensed her power at once and took her in. He had been in the dark, when it came to the spirit world, since his last scryer of real talent, Edward Kelley, had got himself killed in Bohemia. So he welcomed this new boy, Hal Berridge, with open arms and trembling delight, giving thanks to a gracious heaven. In the guise of a boy, she toiled for him dutifully, and he repaid her efforts, unveiling, layer by layer, all the deep learning of his long life. More than her mother could ever have dreamed.

She spent all her spare hours in the maze of his library in that rambling set of conjoined cottages on the banks of the Thames. It took her almost a year to find her mother's manuscript in his most closely guarded hiding place, behind the movable stone in the fireplace of his innermost study. She could not read the original, but she could and did read the translation, making her own copy sentence by sentence in the moments she could finagle alone with it. By the time she finished, she had engraved its tales of the goddess Corra — also called Cerridwen, Dee had noted — and her rites, word for word, into her memory.

It would not, however, be enough. For always, Dr. Dee taught her, learned magi left some crucial detail out of their written records of magical rites, lest they fall into the hands of the uninitiated. It was why apprenticeship was so essential and why Dee's refusal to teach her mother had rankled so.

Dr. Dee as good as told her that he'd remained silent on some key aspect of what she sought: the deed without a name. In all probability, the writer of the original manuscript had done the same. If she meant, as she did, to reenact the rite whose secrets had gone to the grave with her mother, then she would have to milk that knowledge from a witness. And she knew the identity of only one.

A man who had stolen, according to her mother, not only the mirror and the manuscript, but also something more precious: a thunderbolt from the gods. The first two she intended to take back. The third she intended to avenge.

And then vengeance landed in her lap. First, in the face of a redheaded woman she had seen in the mirror. The face of a woman with a knife. Dr. Dee, she knew, suspected that it was the face of her mother. It was not, but it was useful, nevertheless, in a way she had not dreamed. It took her, willy-nilly, to court, where she found herself lodged in Hampton Court Palace.

And then, in a strange chain of events, it had prompted the misshapen earl of Salisbury to call for a play from Mr. Shakespeare. An early draft had been sent out to Mortlake, which had brought the old wizard back to court in a quavering rage. At first, when she'd realized that it shadowed her mother, she'd thought she had yet another reason to wreak revenge on Mr. Shakespeare. And then she'd realized that it also conjured up something else: the memory she had been seeking, of a rite seen long ago on a hill in Scotland. A deed without a name. A deed Mr. Shakespeare had remembered, it seemed, without the guile of a wizard, recording it in full.

After that, she laid her plans well. The suggestion that she might be given a role in the play came from her, though it reached Salisbury's ears through a circuitous route. The play was to be offered before the king amid the celebrations around the anniversary of the Powder Plot. The Samhuinn moon fell just before the appointed day, and she chose that night for her revenge.

She'd found the empty wing of the palace and chosen the room with care, arranging an assignation there with Rowland Dee. Some time before, she'd gone fishing for Mr. Shakespeare's eyes; feeling them fall upon her, she'd done her best to keep them there. She'd sent a message to him, as well, begging his company.

And then she'd seen what she'd seen in that mirror, the moment it passed her by in that last rehearsal.

Dressed in her queen's costume, her real hair cascading around her in coppery waves, she left the rehearsal in the Great Hall, heading back to the buttery that served as a greenroom. She knew exactly where they kept the mirror in its chest. It was the work of a moment to pick the lock and take it, and then to slip back out, unseen by the rest of the company, who were riveted by Burbage in full-blown rant.

She made her way through the palace's web of corridors to the old deserted wing, but from there her deep-laid plans went awry. First, Arthur Dee had appeared instead of Rowland. And then the old man who'd been tailing her had died instead of Mr. Shakespeare.

She'd sent Arthur quickly away, telling him to send the playwright back.

As soon as he was in the corridor, she latched the door behind him and set about the work she needed to do. She had just drawn the blue gown over the body, stripped naked and bound, when she heard a tap at the door.

Mr. Shakespeare, at last. "You are late," she said as he took in the form of the body draped in blue on the floor. "That was meant to be you."

He looked up with horrified eyes. "And if I cry murder?"

She held his eyes coolly. "They will arrest the killer. Arthur Dee."

He would not consign his old master's eldest son to the executioner, and they both knew it.

She had quoted his words to his face, enjoying it: *"Look like the innocent flower, but be the serpent under it."*

As Arthur had recently done with her, she now enjoyed watching him realize who she was. "The Lernaean Hydra," he murmured. "Lady Elizabeth Stewart's child."

In exchange for her silence and her disappearance, they agreed upon a trade: He had brought, as requested, a folded wad of pages excised from the first version of his new play — a version that he said was now obsolete after he'd spent the last few hours revising.

He insisted, however, that she leave behind the mirror. She looked at it, briefly, with regret, for it was beautiful, and a thing of power. But she did not need it. There would be another, more powerful, where she was going. So she opened her fingers and let the dark circle drop; it rolled into the folds of the blue gown.

After that, they had both exited through a high window, leaving the door latched behind them. The way he had come, he thought, was being watched. In the garden below, they parted. She turned one last time before fading into the dark, a smile playing at the corners of her mouth. *The queen, my lord, is dead. And I shall be queen hereafter.*

■ ■ ■ ■

In the tower window, the memories went
dark. And then another picture arose, not a
memory, though whether it belonged to past
or future, she could not tell: the face of a
redheaded woman with a knife.

And in the background, the tower in
which she sat, in flames.

EPILOGUE

The following day, the remains of a body, blackened beyond recognition, were pulled from the smoking ruins of the castle. It proved to be Ian Blackburn. Though a police forensic team searched the ruins with a fine sieve, no trace of Carrie Douglas was ever found.

Their followers at Castle Bruiach were charged with the Scottish version of accessory murder in the death of Lucas Porter. A lot about Auld Callie's, Sybilla's, and Eircheard's deaths, however, would never be explained, because everyone who knew the details was either missing or dead.

At the hospital, they told me I'd recently had a pretty serious concussion. It explained my amnesia on the hilltop, along with the headache and sluggishness I'd wakened with. But not, I fretted, what I'd done. Or hadn't.

It was Lucas's flash drive, in the end, that

did that. He'd documented, in cold detail, three murders. On a sullen gray afternoon at police headquarters in Perth, DI Sheena McGregor summoned Lady Nairn, Ben, and me to view the film if we wished. "Wish" seemed a very odd choice of words; I would not wish that sight on anyone. But I needed to see with my waking eyes what I had done, or not done. So I sat with my hands tightly clasped in my lap, watching myself dip in and out of consciousness in the background as Carrie held Sybilla down and Ian raised the ritual blade. The cry from Sybilla as it struck was hair-raising even on a small screen. At the moment of its happening, it had roused me from my stupor. I'd stumbled to Sybilla's side as if drunk, trying to stop the blood, to pour it back into her body with my hands. As Carrie laughed, Ian had backhanded me so that I spun away, sliding once more to the ground, unconscious.

That was all I needed to see. I walked out of the room before the camera pulled away from me. I could not bear to see Ben either looking at me, his face a careful blank, or looking studiously away. And I had no wish to watch Eircheard die.

There are some things that, once known, cannot be un-known. Cannot be forgotten or erased.

I walked out of the building to find Lily sitting on a bench outside the door. She looked pale and very young, her face pinched with grief inside the bright halo of her hair.

"It's my fault," she said, swallowing back tears. "It's all my fault."

I sat down beside her. "You're not responsible for what Carrie and Ian did, Lily."

"I thought he was brilliant. I thought he was cool. I thought he *liked* me. I'm an *idiot,*" she wailed.

"He used you, sweetheart. So did Carrie."

"I went along with him," she said, her voice ragged with self-loathing. "I lied to you: It *was* me on the hill, that first day you were at Dunsinnan. I thought we were rehearsing a secret initiation rite. And I was with Ian the next morning, after they killed Auld Callie. I didn't know, but I should have. And then I went with him, after the Fire Festival. I thought it was a lark. And they almost killed you. And Eircheard — Eircheard is dead." She bit her lip, looking away as her voice dropped to a whisper. "I miss him."

"So do I."

"I'm sorry." Her face crumpled and sobs

racked her. I put my arm around her and let her cry. She'd been naïve, not evil, but she would have a hard time forgiving herself. It was one of the worst sins of evil, I reflected. Twisting naïveté and innocence to its own use.

Holding Lily, I sat lost in my own thoughts. That she'd been on the hill explained part of what I'd seen, but not everything; the image of her neck thickly smeared with blood was still vivid in my mind. Surely what I'd seen had been half dream, twining around reality, twisting its shape.

It took time to sort out everything we'd found, and some things that we'd lost.

The manuscript we'd found at Fonthill had vanished in the flames at Loch Bruiach. What little I'd heard about it came from Carrie and Lucas. Tantalizing as their hints had been, I could not trust a word of it — even, at times, the basic identification of a letter by John Dee, presumably to Shakespeare, and a manuscript of *Macbeth*. No one else would likely want to trust even the fact of the finding. I knew the sort of media storm that Shakespeare manuscripts stirred up. It was easier to wonder about what I'd nearly seen — and rue its passing — in quiet and let others blather publicly about just what Catherine Forrest may have found.

The mirror proved to be Dee's and went back to the British Museum — its exact fit into the groove in the floor of Castle Bruiach was noted, though no one knew quite what to do with that information. Marks on the side were consistent with the lettering identified by Arthur Dee — but they were also consistent, noted the lab, with random lettering.

It went on rotating display, half the year in the Enlightenment Gallery, half the year in the Mexican room, attached to a statue of Tezcatlipoca at the foot. Museum staff noted that every once in a while, in either place, someone would be found in front of it, shaking in terror, claiming to have seen visions of blood and fire. The guards avoided looking at it.

Lady Nairn's mirror was found in a ritual room deep inside the maze at Joanna Black Books, surrounded by black and purple candles, half burned away. Nearby lay a knife with traces of Auld Callie's blood. The only prints on the handle were Joanna's. Or Carrie's, I should say.

The loch, which had so easily cast me back out, kept close and secret hold of the knife from the hill, which remains unrecovered.

The owner of Her Majesty's Theatre was discreetly informed of the cache of magical books in the dome room; what he did with most of them remained still more discreet. Dee's book with Arthur's letter inside, however, he donated to the British Library, where scholars began to squawk over just what the phrase "one of my father's scholars" implied. No one was as certain as Joanna had been that the diagrams had anything to do with the Globe.

Aubrey's diary went to join the bulk of his papers at Oxford University's Bodleian Library, on permanent loan from Lady Nairn.

Plans for a private production of *Macbeth* using objects from her collection were scrapped. Instead, Lady Nairn opted for the first public exhibition of the Nairn collection, to open at the National Museum of Scotland, in Edinburgh, later traveling down to the British Museum. As part of it, she decided to include screenings of Herbert Beerbohm Tree's lost film of *Macbeth*.

She still wanted a production of the play to run in tandem with the exhibition, but thankfully she did not ask me to direct it. Instead, she asked me to direct as its counterpart, light balancing darkness, the comedy that told another story of witchcraft: *A Midsummer Night's Dream.* To that, I happily said yes.

Both Carrie and Ian died intestate; under Scottish law, this made Lady Nairn the sole heir of them both, as aunt and "sibling of a grandparent," respectively. So Lady Nairn found herself in possession of a Covent Garden bookshop and a fine collection of rare occult esoterica, including a black, staring cat named Lilith and an unimpressed snake named Medea, as well as the royalties of Corra Ravensbrook's book, which became an instant bestseller when news of the murders broke.

Jason Pierce surfaced in Australia. Two hours before the Samhuinn Fire Festival was to start, he'd received a call from someone purporting to be with the festival organizers, offering him an out via his understudy. Jason had never once rehearsed the role of the Winter King and had had enough of Scottish gloom. He'd been so relieved that he'd jumped into his car and headed straight for London and then the surfing beaches of home.

Jamie Clifton turned up alive at Fonthill. After hearing shots, she had pulled herself, terrified and quaking, into an adjoining room, huddling beneath a desk. At her suggestion, the College of Mount Saint Vincent, which had no archival library, loaned the letter from Catherine to Edwin Forrest to the New York Public Library for the Performing Arts, where it could be properly housed and studied. Jamie began a biography of Catherine Sinclair.

Eircheard had been mentoring a young man in Perth, trying to keep him out of the sort of trouble that had landed Eircheard in prison. The fires of the forge had barely gone cold when Lady Nairn offered the youth the use of the smithy; he had moved in the next day. He had a long way to go before he could touch Eircheard's mastery in the making of swords, but he had nothing but time on his hands. That, and determination, and a chance to do something with his life. To become a maker, as Eircheard might have said. Eircheard, said Lady Nairn, would have found that legacy enough.

The morning of Auld Callie's death, Effie Summers had been found on her knees in Dunkeld Cathedral. Thereafter, she'd endured several days of police attention as a prime suspect in that murder. She attributed the revelation of her innocence to divine intervention. Much to Effie's surprise, Lady Nairn agreed. "Of course," Lady Nairn told me brightly over the phone, "our opinions as to the identity of the deity doing the intervening differ markedly. But it did not occur to Effie to ask." When the cathedral's regular minister returned to work, the reverend Mr. Gosson took his fire and brimstone to another post, and Effie followed him.

Sheena McGregor was promoted to detective chief inspector. Lily went back to school.

In the spring, Lily called to invite me back to Dunsinnan, her voice both shy and excited. She was to be initiated into her grandmother's coven on Beltane: May Day. The other great festival of the Celtic year, the celebration of life and light, as Samhuinn was the celebration of death and darkness. Lily wanted me to present her to the coven.

"It's unusual for an outsider to do the presenting," said Lady Nairn after Lily had ceded her the phone and danced away. "But it's not entirely unheard of. It does complicate things a wee bit, though. There are parts of the rite, you understand, that you may not witness. I must ask you to honor that rule."

I laughed. "I won't hide in a bush and watch."

"There are no bushes," said Lady Nairn. "It will be on the hilltop."

I took a deep breath. If it had been anyone other than Lily, I would have said no in an instant. I was not ready to go back. As it was, it took all my willpower to hold my voice steady. "I won't go up the hill alone, then."

"Good girl. Though in this case, it'll be more a question of heading down it, on cue." Lady Nairn sighed. "I would have waited, you know. It's customary to require initiates to be at least eighteen. But she has seen the darkest side of the craft, and I've judged it more important to balance that darkness with a vision of the light than to hold to arbitrary considerations of age."

Balance. It was something I managed, in a fragile way, most days. But I still had to fight for it more nights than I cared to admit, when the smell of blood rose thickly around me.

"How's Ben?"

The question startled me. "We aren't in touch." *There are some things that, once seen, cannot be forgotten. Once known, cannot be un-known.* He would never be able to look at me without seeing Sybilla's blood on my hands.

"Never is a very long time," said Lady Nairn, as if I'd spoken aloud. "It will become bearable, in time. If you let it."

I'd said something similar once, to Lily. "How do you know?" I asked, my voice ragged in my throat.

"I've seen it," she said simply.

So, on a blustery day at the end of April, I took the train north once more, this time all the way to Perth, where Lady Nairn and Lily picked me up at the station and drove me back to Dunsinnan House.

On a table just inside the door, the silver cauldron was filled with yellow daffodils and bright purple thistles. Up on the bed in the room of pale blue silk and dragons, a dress the color of peacocks was laid out on my bed. Beside it lay a folder. "Open it," said Lily.

Inside was a single scorched page. It seemed to be a letter from a woman writing to an unborn daughter, telling a tale about a death that was not intended and a boy who was not a boy.

"Hal Berridge?" I asked, looking up sharply at Lady Nairn.

"So it would seem."

The writer went on to claim for the yet-to-be-born girl heritage from Elizabeth Stewart, Lady Arran, and the English wizard John Dee.

"What will you do with this?" I asked.

"Keep it," she said. "Keep it quiet. But we thought you had earned the right to know."

She and Lily soon excused themselves. Lily, however, hung back at the door, her fingers twisting on the doorknob. *"Look like the innocent flower,"* she said bleakly, *"but be the serpent under it.* I've been the serpent more than the lily."

"Not necessarily a bad thing; the snake is an old symbol of wisdom, you know. Female wisdom."

"That's what Gran says." She smiled wanly. "From a time when the Goddess ruled in harmony with the god, before men set him above her, crushing her serpent beneath his feet. But I've been anything but wise. . . . I'm sorry, Kate. Though I don't think I can ever say it properly. Or enough."

"It's not what you say that will make it have meaning. It's what you do. How you live your life."

She took a deep breath and straightened. "Right, then. I suppose I had better go and get on with it. Thank you. Again." With the brief flash of a grin, she disappeared.

A maid brought dinner to my room on a

tray, but I wasn't hungry. I stood at the window for a long time, watching the setting sun light the hill to gold, which deepened to pink and purple shadows, draining to gray as the sky fired to liquid sapphire and finally went black. At last I stirred and began to dress. This far north, dawn would come so early that it was pointless to go to bed. I was to leave early in the morning, directly after the ceremony, to make it back for a rehearsal in London in the afternoon. I could sleep on the train.

At three o'clock in the morning, Lily tapped on my door. She wore a dress of white with a long pointed bodice and tight sleeves that Guinevere would have envied. On her head was a wreath of creamy rowan blossoms that frothed with a heady sweet scent as she moved. In her dress, she might have walked out of a painting or poem by Rossetti, or Millais, or Burne-Jones. But the red hair curling loosely around her was that of Botticelli's Aphrodite.

Outside, a full moon was spearing itself on the trees to the west. In silence, we walked up the lane to the woods surrounding the stone circle, and I waited while Lily went in to greet her goddess alone.

She came back, her face alight with excitement, and we walked around the hill to the path that led up its northern slope. As we trudged upward, dawn began to silver the eastern sky. We crested the summit and this time I saw two bonfires piled side by side, framing a doorway opening to the east. On the narrow path running between them, someone hunched low, twirling a small stick inside a hole carved in another. A small red glow sprang to life, nursed to a tiny flame. Just as the sun crested the hill's eastern rim, the new fire was divided in two and fed into each stack of wood.

As the sun rose higher and the fire caught, a man stepped out of the darkness, silhouetted against the growing light. Tall. With curly hair and a way of standing that I would have known anywhere.

Ben.

Yellow and orange flames licked upward, crackling, through the bonfires, and he held out a hand to Lily. She took it with her left hand, drawing me forward with her right, and the three of us walked between the fires. Just on the other side, we stopped.

A white candle in her hand, the wreath of pale blossoms around her head, Lily looked like Saint Lucy. *Lux, lucis,* I thought. The Bride, the Maiden, the personification of light. Which was, come to think of it, exactly who Saint Lucy was: another aspect of the goddess that, like Mary, Christianity had taken in and hidden in plain sight, beneath the veil of sainthood.

In the center of the summit, a circle was marked out with candles, as yet unlit; inside waited a small knot of people. At their feet gleamed the cauldron. Lady Nairn, her hair pale above a shimmering blue gown, raised her arms and called Lily forward. "Lilidh Gruoch MacPhee. Do you enter this circle of your own accord?"

"I do," said Lily, dropping our hands and walking forward. As she crossed into the circle there was, ever so slightly, a nod from Lady Nairn. A sign of thanks, a sign of dismissal. Together, Ben and I turned and walked back through the fires.

Beside me, I could feel his nearness, though we did not touch. At the edge of the summit, I paused briefly, watching the sun unroll across the wide, sleeping valley below, birdsong rising like lace into air that smelled clean and new. Something brushed my hand. I looked down. Ben's hand, taking mine.

In silence, we headed down the hill. At the bottom, as promised, Lady Nairn's driver was waiting with her Range Rover. Ben opened the door for me, and I slid into the backseat, swallowing down sadness as

559

his fingers slipped from mine.

"I can call spirits from the vasty deep," he said quietly. The phrase from the loch. Glancing up, I saw calm on his face, and the ghost of a smile.

This time, I had a clear enough head to respond. *"But will they come when you do call for them?"* I said, returning his smile.

"Good-bye, Kate."

For a while, I thought as the car pulled out from under the shadow of the hill and into the sun. It was not time. Not yet. But it no longer seemed impossible that at some point, one of us would call, and the other would come.

I could see it.

AUTHOR'S NOTE

Macbeth opens with eerie, unearthly condensations of evil adrift on a dark wind, whispering words that gnaw at a good man's mind, propelling him into horrific violence. Belief in such terrifying supernatural malevolence was rife during Shakespeare's lifetime, but on the renaissance English stage, witches tended to be comic evil: village scolds or cackling hags dealing in grotesque potions. As different from the norm of its day as Stephen King's bone-chilling evil in *The Shining* is from the Disney witches of *Sleeping Beauty, Snow White,* and *The Little Mermaid, Macbeth* is one of the first great horror stories in modern literature.

What makes the "Scottish Play" different from other tales of terror is that its evil does not stay put in the story. It leaches from the stage, spilling into real life with catastrophic consequences for productions and people

— or at least it has been fervently thought to do so for a century. The story of a curse on the play, the theatrical taboos around quoting or naming it, and the ritual for exorcising its evil are long-standing traditions still current among many actors the world over.

The fact that the story of the curse began with a hoax is not very well known, even among Shakespearean scholars. As Kate notes, however, the fin de siècle bon vivant, wit, and caricaturist Max Beerbohm does seem to have concocted the story of Hal Berridge's death in 1898, at a mischief-provoking moment of boredom with his day (or rather, night) job: reviewing Shakespeare on the stage.

Beerbohm attributed his fib to the seventeenth-century antiquary John Aubrey, and Aubrey, happy magpie that he was, is manna from heaven for a novelist with a need to uncover lost documents and seed trails of evidence. An inveterate gossip with the inclinations of a scholar and the organizational skills of a distracted adolescent, Aubrey recorded historical fact, hearsay, and ludicrous gossip with equal relish, sometimes twining them in the same paragraph, if not the same sentence. His notes are a scattered and incomplete mess. If anyone might have written a long-lost, secretly surviving page recording strange and suggestive tales about Shakespeare and Dee, it was Aubrey. He made notes on both men, after all, within living memory of their deeds, recording details and vignettes preserved nowhere else. And he was a relation of Dee, who was his grandfather's cousin and "intimate acquaintance."

So this novel began, in part, with a "what-if": *What if Max Beerbohm really did find the tale of Hal Berridge in an Aubrey manuscript? What if Aubrey had told the truth? What if the curse of Macbeth extended all the way back to the beginning?* What then? What might be the source of *Macbeth*'s admittedly strange power to frighten both audiences and actors?

This set me to wondering about the magic in *Macbeth*. As first published in 1623 in the first folio — the first edition of Shakespeare's collected works — the play is uneven in its sinister vision. In addition to the three spectral weird sisters, the witch queen Hecate arrives to sing and dance with all the chortling glee that English audiences expected from stage witches: Think of Walt Disney and Stephen King competing for the soul of a single film. So sharp is the chasm between Hecate and the weird sisters that scholars have long suspected that Hecate — who makes no necessary contribution to the play's action — is a late intrusion.

The general scholarly consensus is that someone other than Shakespeare revised the original *Macbeth* at some point before publication, bringing it more into line with what audiences would happily pay to see, namely evil that was more amusing than horrifying. To do so, the reviser turned to *The Witch,* by Thomas Middleton, which also has a witch character named Hecate. The reviser lifted some silly songs from Middleton's newer play into Shakespeare's old play and wrote in a new version of Hecate (very different from Middleton's) in order to explain the sudden burst of song and dance amid the gloom. It's the sort of light-fingered patchwork that was then part and parcel of the quick-turnaround mill of the theater.

As time went on, this alteration was intensified. By the time *Macbeth* reappeared on the restoration stage in 1666, the witches had grown in number from three to an entire Ziegfeld chorus of hags, some of them zooming about overhead on wires. Even while noting that they were "a strange perfection in a tragedy," the diarist Samuel Pepys thought the witches' song-and-dance bits, or "divertissements" as he called them, the best part of the play. Interest in "authentic" Shakespeare revived across the nineteenth century, and major productions gradually pared the play back to the text in the First Folio . . . but that is the earliest version of *Macbeth* that survives. What did the witches and their magic look like in Shakespeare's original?

Many scholars and directors happily pluck out Hecate and her songs and leave it at that. It's possible, however, that the alterations were more extensive. For starters, the play's central scene of witchcraft, the cauldron scene — act four, scene one — is an odd cobbling of grotesque cauldron magic and the learned magic of conjuring demonic spirits. Furthermore, there are other scenes that appear out of order and garbled. Finally, *Macbeth* is remarkably short: one of Shakespeare's shortest plays in any genre and easily the shortest of his tragedies. Of the four great tragedies he wrote in the first five years of King James's reign, the others — *Othello, King Lear,* and *Antony and Cleopatra* — are all longer by roughly a thousand lines or more. *Hamlet* — written at the end of Queen Elizabeth's reign — is nearly twice as long. What, if anything, has gone missing from *Macbeth*?

It is impossible to say but intriguing to wonder about, and in the wide space of that wonder, this novel was born.

In this novel, the key objects of blade, mirror, and cauldron are all real, or based on real objects. With two exceptions, the places where I've set major scenes are all real places with links to the historical King Macbeth, famous productions and actors of Shakespeare's play, or historical people whose lives Shakespeare may have used in shaping his play. I have altered them, in some cases, to suit the fiction, however. The myths are real — as myths — and the magical traditions and ideas of both the "black" and "white" variety have been put forward, historically, as real magic, though not necessarily tied specifically to *Macbeth*. Save for Carrie's final attempt to invoke a demonic spirit, however, the specific rites of black magic concocted by Lucas, Ian, and Carrie are my own inventions. For the most part, the historical characters are fantasias on fact. The modern characters are all fictional.

Samhuinn is the Scottish Gaelic name for the ancient pagan Celtic festival better known in some circles by its Irish name of *Samhain* and certainly widely known across the world by its Christian co-opted descendant of All Hallow's Eve or Halloween. It is one of the two great fire festivals of the old Celtic year once celebrated across the British Isles and Ireland — and much of western Europe, for that matter. The other is Beltane, or May Day. Whereas Beltane celebrates fertility, sex, and new birth, spring and summer, and the return of light, Samhuinn celebrates — or at least acknowledges — death and the dead, autumn and winter, and darkness. In the Scottish Highlands, Samhuinn was celebrated into the early twentieth century with bonfires on hilltops. Various folk traditions suggest that once upon a very long time ago, the celebration may have included sacrifice, possibly human sacrifice.

Edinburgh's Samhuinn Fire Festival, run by the Beltane fire Society, is a spectacular yearly celebration of this ancient holiday. I have tried to be as faithful as possible to the carnival spirit of the actual performances, which change every year, though the basic story of the Cailleach and the two battling kings remains the same. I have had to alter some practices, however, in order to slot my characters into main roles. In particular, Lily is too young to be involved, and I doubt that the BFS would ever cast a film star like

Jason Pierce in a lead role in exchange for money. I hope the society's members will forgive me those lapses as minor technicalities and enjoy the festival's fictional appearance in a thriller.

Whether or not Shakespeare ever traveled to Scotland is unknown. In fact, we know nothing at all of his whereabouts between the christening of his twins, Hamnet and Judith, in Stratford-upon-Avon, on February 2, 1585, and 1592, when he had made enough of a name for — and by some lights, a nuisance of — himself on the London stage to be attacked by Robert Greene in his *Groatsworth of Wit* as an "upstart crow," a "Shake-scene" stealing other men's thunder. However, the Scottish geography in *Macbeth* is surprisingly accurate — I had no idea just how accurate, in fact, until I started to research this book. That he might have been in Scotland is as much a possibility as his being anywhere else; companies of English players traveled north of the border with some frequency.

In 1583, Queen Elizabeth's spymaster, Sir Francis Walsingham, forced a reorganization of England's theatrical companies by cherry-picking the best actors from each for a new company called the Queen's Men.

Why he did so is unclear; he was not a known patron or enthusiast of theater, nor were players part of his day-to-day concerns as a secretary of state. (Regulating the players was part of the lord chamberlain's duties.) Walsingham's motives may well have included weaving actors into his network of spies. Roving players, after all, offered perfect cover for watchful eyes and ears inside the far-flung houses of the great. At the very least, as scholars Scott McMillin and Sally-Beth MacLean have argued in *The Queen's Men and Their Plays,* from this point on, Elizabeth's spymaster used government licensing of traveling acting troupes to give the impression of a vast network of watchfulness. Later, Walsingham certainly used some playwrights, most famously Christopher Marlowe, and possibly Thomas Kyd, as spies. It is my imagining that the young Shakespeare might also, willingly or unwillingly, have been among his "intelligencers." It does seem likely, however, that any player caught in the dubious circumstances into which I set Mr. Shakespeare at Dirleton would have found himself suspected as a spy.

In the autumn of 1589, the Queen's Men were sent north to Edinburgh to join in the celebration of King James's impending marriage to Princess Anne of Denmark. The celebrations had to be postponed after storms drove the princess's fleet back from Scottish shores, all the way to Scandinavia, and the impatient king took ship in pursuit. (Eventually, those storms were blamed on witches, resulting in one of the worst witch-hunts in Scottish history, spearheaded by King James himself, but that is another story.) That same year, civic records show that a company of English players acted in Perth, about ten miles distant from Dunsinnan and within striking distance of Dunkeld and Birnam Wood. I am not the first to wonder whether a twenty-five-year-old actor named William Shakespeare could have been among them. The Dunsinnan House account book, however, is a fictional document.

Shakespeare's main source for *Macbeth* was Raphael Holinshed's *Chronicles of England, Scotland, and Ireland.* He did not rely solely on the history of King Macbeth, however, but pieced together a story using dramatic episodes from the lives of other kings. In particular, he had to fish about for the story of Lady Macbeth because the historical Lady Macbeth, whose name was Gruoch (Lily's middle name), is little more than a blank. It is usual to see Shakespeare spinning her tale from the brief mention of another nobleman's revenge-urging wife. Some scholars, however, have also noted the uncanny resemblance that her story bears to the near-contemporary history of Elizabeth Stewart, countess of Arran.

This lady was, as stated in the novel, the daughter of John Stewart, fourth earl of Atholl. The date of her birth is unknown, though it must have been after May 1547, when her parents married, and before April 1, 1557, when her father remarried following her mother's death. She was married herself on December 24, 1567, which would make her only thirteen by the birth year of 1554 sometimes proposed for her (without, so far as I can tell, any basis in fact); I have chosen to push her birth to an early point in her parents' marriage, mostly to allow for a fictional meeting with John Dee at a time when he was in Antwerp in 1563.

She went through three husbands: Hugh Fraser, fifth Lord Lovat, who died suddenly, and some thought suspiciously, in 1577; the king's elderly great-uncle Robert Stewart, successively earl of Lennox and then earl of March, whom she married in 1579 and divorced in 1581, on grounds of impotence while pregnant with her third husband's child; and the swashbuckling Captain James

Stewart, for a time earl of Arran, whom she married two months after her divorce from March was final. She did have royal, if also bastard, blood in her veins, as one of her maternal great-grandmothers was an illegitimate daughter of Scotland's King James IV. A Highlander both by birth and by her first marriage, she was said to frequent "the oracles of the Highlands" and possibly to be a witch herself. She was also said to lust after the crown.

She appears to have been both fashionable and sensuous, with a French-inflected sophistication of style, speech, and sexual morality that bewitched the king but made his Calvinist ministers come close to spitting with rage. The story of her breaking open Queen Mary's chests of gowns and jewels as soon as her husband was given the keys to Edinburgh Castle was recorded by the English ambassador to Scotland.

For a while in the early 1580s, she and her third husband were two of King James's most trusted courtiers, people he sought out for both policy and play. So quick and decisive was their rise to power that they aroused envy and fear on the part of almost everyone else around the king. After they fell from grace in late 1585, they took refuge, just as Kate discovers, with her eldest son by her first marriage, Simon Fraser, sixth Lord Lovat, in the lands of clan Fraser, south and west of Inverness, where they were said to live on a remote isle in Loch Bruiach. It is a place that is still surprisingly remote, a distillation of the stark beauty of the Highlands.

The earl's end mimics Macbeth's — though perhaps it was the other way around: As Kate says, in 1596 he was ambushed by enemies who cut off his head and flaunted it on the tip of a lance. With enemies like that, their long sojourn on a remote island becomes understandable.

Lady Arran's end is somewhat mysterious and at least metaphorically offstage, just like Lady Macbeth's. She was first reported dead in childbed in 1590. Elsewhere, she was said to have died "miserably" in 1595 up in the Highlands; perhaps that misery was a euphemism for the suicidal end that Shakespeare suggests for Lady Macbeth. Yet another, later tradition has her die swollen to marvelous size, thus fulfilling a prophecy that she should be the greatest woman in all Scotland. The possibility that she was attacked as a witch is my own addition to history.

How Shakespeare might have come across her story is also unknown, though a handful of English players working in London as he rose to fame had a fair amount of experience working in Scotland and might have told him her tale. Among these was the king's favorite English actor during his tenure in Scotland, Lawrence Fletcher, another of the original members of the King's Men. It seems equally possible, however, that if Shakespeare went up to Scotland in his youth, he might have learned of her — or seen her — for himself, and possibly even acted before her.

The Arrans are known to have entertained James with a sumptuous feast and a play of robin Hood when the king spent twelve days at their newly acquired castle of Dirleton, beginning on May 1, 1585 — as it happens, the old Celtic festival of Beltane. The king was not coming to celebrate either May Day or Beltane, however, but to escape a fierce outbreak of plague in Edinburgh. The earl is said to have fallen deathly ill after the banquet — perhaps he left abruptly in the middle. While the festivities at that castle are historical, Shakespeare's appearance there is of my making.

John Dee was one of the foremost intellectuals in England during Shakespeare's lifetime, though he was shown more respect on the Continent. His interests, whether focused on mathematics or magic, were both theoretical and practical.

He was in Antwerp in early 1563, copying an exceedingly rare manuscript of the *Steganographia* by Johannes Trithemius, a work nominally about using angels and demons to convey secret messages at a distance. In reality, it is a three-part book about codes, in code. Dee knew that about the first two parts; the code of the third part is not known to have been broken until the late twentieth century and was generally believed to be about demonic magic, as it claimed to be. Whether or not Dee possessed the secret of the third part is unknown. It is this manuscript that I have imagined him accepting the young Lady Elizabeth Stewart's help in copying.

Most of Dee's life is traceable through letters and diaries, including a spiritual diary that covers in detail many of his attempts to invoke angels. No diaries survive, however, from 1601 to his death in 1608 or 1609, the period that covers the discovery of the Gunpowder Plot and the writing of *Macbeth*. This may be because he had stopped keeping a diary; on the other hand, his diary may have been destroyed.

Dee was not adept at seeing spirits in his

mirrors and crystal balls himself; he almost always used a seer or scryer. His eldest son, Arthur, tried to fill this role for a time during his boyhood but apparently with no more success than his father had. For many years, Dee's most trusted scryer was a man named Edward Kelley — who seems, at this distance in time, to have been at least half con man, a fact that makes it very difficult to understand Dee. Kelley and Dee parted ways on the Continent, however, before Dee returned to England in 1589.

Beyond the close of Dee's surviving diary in 1601, we know very little about his scryers or his dealings with the spirit world. Persistent rumors repeated through the nineteenth century, however, said that he — or one of his scryers — foretold the Gunpowder Plot by seeing it in a mirror. Linking his scryer and his black mirror to the boy-actor Hal Berridge and the mirror in *Macbeth* is my fiction.

That Dee's papers are fragmentary should not, perhaps, be surprising. What's astonishing is that any of them survived. The first editor of his spiritual diary, published in 1659, claimed that Sir Robert Cotton, the collector of a library perhaps even greater than Dee's, dug up a number of Dee's manuscript diaries from his garden. Others were discovered in a hidden compartment in an old chest and partly used up by a cook looking for scrap paper to line her pie tins before her master realized what she was using.

Dee invoked angels into mirrors and "show-stones," or crystal balls. The black obsidian mirror stolen by the witches in this book is a real object, and its history as given is pretty accurate: It was once a ritual object related to the Aztec god Tezcatlipoca. Dee is thought to have acquired it during his travels on the Continent, when he would have had easier opportunity to come into contact with Spanish culture, including precious objects plundered from the New World, than he would have had at home, at least after Queen Elizabeth's Protestant reign set England and Spain on a course toward war.

That is, if Dee acquired it at all. The attribution to Dee comes from Horace Walpole's eighteenth-century identification, which is based on hearsay and does not clearly trace the mirror's passage back through time to Dee. Walpole's claim, however, is certainly seductive and has long been accepted as the likely truth. The mirror is on display — as Dee's — in the British Museum's Enlightenment Gallery.

The other mirror — Lady Nairn's mirror, which she claimed had been a prop used by the King's Men — is a figment of my imagination. So far as I know no known prop certainly belonging to that company has survived.

Lady Nairn's silver cauldron — and the cauldron in Joanna's shop, for that matter — are both based on the huge Gundestrup Cauldron in the National Museum of Denmark in Copenhagen, the most glorious silver object of Iron Age Celtic Europe. Probably made in the first century B.C., it shows, among other scenes, a horned man sitting cross-legged and holding a serpent, and another man being thrown into a cauldron: possibly a scene of human sacrifice.

The cauldron symbol that Carrie uses is a real Pictish symbol found on stone carvings in Scotland.

The knife that Kate finds is no particular real knife but a variant of the *seax,* a single-edged style of blade used by Anglo-Saxons, Vikings, and Scots — both men and women — throughout the pagan period. Several knives and swords of similar date have been found with runic inscriptions, some of which appear to have been magical.

In Wiccan tradition, a black-handled knife, or athame, is part of the ritual equipment used by each individual witch. Athames are not used for cutting, which is actually taboo; they are used for directing energy. White-handled knives, or bolines, are used when cutting, carving, or whittling is necessary. Carrie and Ian's willingness to use their knives not only for cutting but for killing sets them far beyond the bounds of any acceptable behavior in Wiccan practice.

The making of pattern-welded blades is an ancient and exacting art. There are still a few swordsmiths in Scotland and elsewhere forging blades that men like the real Macbeth would probably have loved to wield.

Dunsinnan Hill is a real place with the remains of an Iron Age hill fort at its top. Medieval Scottish chronicles say that Macbeth refortified it with great difficulty, and apparently with great irritation of his followers. It has been excavated twice, in the early and mid-nineteenth century. The trenches from those excavations still pock the summit, which has fine views of Strathmore and the Highlands to the north. Lower down the hill, a modern and still active quarry has significantly gnawed away the western side of the hill, though the summit with its fort is protected.

There are more legends and stories about this hill than I could include in this novel. The nineteenth-century excavations, for instance, found evidence of collapsed souterrains, or stone-lined underground chambers, of unknown — but possibly ritual — significance. One of them is said to have held three skeletons: a man, a woman, and a child with a battered skull. Other tales say that the hill was once the hiding place of the real Stone of Scone, or Stone of Destiny.

At the western foot of the hill is a small wood that hides the Bandirran Stone Circle. There is a cottage, or bothy, roughly where I put Eircheard's smithy. So far as I know, it has never been used as a forge.

In contrast to the hill and the stone circle, Dunsinnan House is a castle of my making; a farmhouse stands in roughly the spot where I situated it. There is an actual Dunsinnan House — which I discovered after I had already built my fictional one — but it is in a different place and has nothing to do with the building in this novel.

The Birnam Oak and its two companion sycamores are all that remain of the primordial virgin forest that once blanketed much of the lower Highlands. They do seem, as Kate muses, creatures from an elder world.

The island in Loch Bruiach is a crannog: a man-made islet probably first constructed in the Neolithic or Iron Age period. There is no castle on it, and I have my doubts about whether it could support such a heavy stone structure, other than in fiction. However, if the Fraser chronicles are to be believed, it must once have sported a suitable home for a dowager Lady Lovat. I based my castle on three buildings: the ruined Castle Urquhart on the shores of nearby Loch Ness, the rebuilt castle of Eilean Donan on Scotland's western shores, and Fonthill, in Riverdale, New York.

The current incarnation of Her Majesty's Theatre was built for Sir Herbert Beerbohm Tree; it opened its doors in 1897. It is the fourth theater to stand on the same site in Haymarket, which has been part of London's theatrical world since the restoration. Since 1986, it has been running *The Phantom of the Opera.* Beerbohm Tree's dome room is a real place, currently rented out as rehearsal space, though both the secret cupboard and its cache of occult books are my invention. With the exception of *DEE and the Theatre,* the titles of the books in that cupboard, however, are real — and each of those volumes is potentially quite valuable.

Joanna Black Books and Esoterica is obviously a fictional shop, but Cecil Court, the street in which it stands, is one of my favorites in all of London. Joanna's shop is a composite of actual occult bookshops elsewhere in London, descriptions of John Dee's library as it once existed out in Mortlake, and other details from my imagination. The name "Joanna Black" is a female and anglicized version of "John Dee," "Joanna" being a feminine form of "John," and "Dee" coming from the Welsh *du,* meaning "black."

In New York, Jamie Clifton's condo is in a real building that now stands on the spot of the Astor Place Opera House: ground zero of the 1849 riot. A large Starbucks on the ground floor gives the public access to at least a portion of the building.

Up in Riverdale, Edwin Forrest laid the cornerstone of Fonthill Castle in 1848 as a token of love for his wife, Catherine, but by the time it was finished, the couple had split in a scandalous divorce. The oculus and the cross in the floor of the central octagonal hall are remarkable design features. I have added, however, the Shakespearean scenes sculpted on the walls, as well as the secret hiding place in the floor. The name — and certain design elements — were indeed bor-

rowed by the Forrests from William Beckford's Fonthill Abbey in England. The castle
is now the admissions building of Mount
Saint Vincent College.

As Kate notes, the saga of Edwin Forrest
and Catherine Sinclair reads like a Shakespearean tragedy; his behavior toward his
once adored wife seems as irrational, unjust,
and toweringly egotistical as Othello's.
Forrest at least opted to end the marriage
in divorce rather than his wife's death. On
the other hand, his cruelty to her remained
implacable. He never seems to have experi-
enced even the small surge of repentance
and grace that Shakespeare granted to
Othello. Catherine Forrest, after losing four
children and then the husband that she
loved, took back her maiden name of Catherine Norton Sinclair and went west to
make her own way in the theater, leaving a
lasting mark of sophistication on the dramatic tastes of gold-rush California. After
touring Australia and then England, she
retired to New York, where she quietly lived
out the remainder of her days, first with a
sister and then with a nephew. She never
remarried. I know of no record that says
she returned to London to see Ellen Terry
in *Macbeth* in 1889, though she lived long

enough to have done so. Her earlier journey to Loch Bruiach and acquisition of a *Macbeth* manuscript are fictional.

By all accounts, Ellen Terry's Lady Macbeth was one of the finest in history. John Singer Sargent's monumental 1890 painting of her in her blue beetle-wing costume is one of the treasures of the Tate Britain. The original gown is housed in Terry's cottage of Smallhythe Place, in Kent, now run by the National Trust. She was a friend and colleague of Sir Herbert Beerbohm Tree, but her letter to Monsieur Superbe Homme is my forgery.

Beerbohm Tree's 1916 film of *Macbeth* is one of the great lost productions both of Shakespeare and of silent-era Hollywood. A few still photographs survive; it is from these that I took the descriptions of set and costume.

This book owes more than usual to the heroic ministrations of Brian Tart, my editor and publisher at Dutton; his assistant Jessica Horvath; and my agent Noah Lukeman. Together, they nursed and prodded it — and me — through a writer's block of cursed proportion; all that is good about this book owes its existence to them. Thanks, too, to David Shelley, Thalia Proctor, and Sphere for their patience and speed.

I had the great good fortune to have advice and help from numerous experts while researching places, people, and practices for this book. I would like to give special thanks to Wiccan priestesses Ashleen O'Gaea and Carol Garr, along with their covens, for their openness and generosity.

In Scotland, Helen Bradburn, Cailleach of the 2008 Samhuinn Fire Festival in Edinburgh, gave me invaluable insight into the workings of that spectacular celebration. Colin Campbell, a photographer with a fine eye for the Scottish landscape, along with his wife, Linda, and dog Cal, got me out to Loch Bruiach on a silent, snowy November afternoon. Jamie and Karen Sinclair gave me the great gift of a family paper on the history of the real King Macbeth, as well as the loan of their collection of books on Dunsinnan and its environs while I was in the area, traipsing up and down the hill. Inspector Paddy Buckley-Jones of the Tayside Police kindly enlightened me on some details of police procedure; any irregularities in police behavior in this book are my fault, not his.

In London, Chris Green, house manager; Paul Rotchell, assistant manager; and John Fitzsimmons, theater manager, all ensured that I learned what I needed to know about Her Majesty's Theatre; Chris gave me a much-appreciated tour of Sir Herbert Beerbohm Tree's dome room. Jamie de Courcey served as my eyes and ears at the British Museum at times when I could not drop in myself; Dr. Silke Ackermann, curator of the British Museum's European Department, helped with the workings of the museum and its collections, John Dee's mirror in particular. Christina Oakley Harrington and her staff at Treadwell's Bookshop identified useful books on various occult subjects.

In New York, Sister Carol Finegan, director of institutional research at the College of Mount Saint Vincent, gave me a long and detailed tour of Fonthill Castle in Riverdale.

On the academic front, Professor Dan Donoghue of Harvard University's English department undertook to translate some Shakespeare into Anglo-Saxon poetry and then transliterate it into runes. Chris Tabraham, principal historian for Historic Scotland, helped me with details of Edinburgh Castle and its environs as they would have been in the sixteenth and early seventeenth centuries. Stuart Ivinson, library assistant at the Royal Armouries in Leeds, provided much-needed research on Anglo-Saxon and

Norse knives and swords, and John Oliver, curator (fiction) of the BFI National Archive at the British Film Institute enlightened me on material aspects of silent-era films.

Others who helped with various angles of research are: Ilana Addis, Martin Brueckner, Brian Schuyler, Bill Fetzer, John Alexander, Eric Baker, Bill Kapfer, René Andersen, Liz Stein, Lauren Galit, David Ira Goldstein, Nick Saunders, Louise Park, Bill Carrell, Laura Fulginiti, Phil Varney, Sandy and Brian Stearns, Jill Jorden Spitz, Stephanie Innes, Pamela Treadwell-Rubin, and Assistant Chief Kathleen Robinson and Crime Laboratory Superintendent Susan M. Shankles, both of the Tucson Police Department.

Charlotte Lowe and Ellen Grounds both read parts of the manuscript and gave encouraging feedback. Dave Grounds has a special and much-appreciated talent for listening to me wander through tangled thickets of plot and then cutting straight through the chaos with sensible suggestions. My mother, Melinda Carrell, and Kristen Poole remain two of my most trusted readers.

Without my husband, John Helenbolt, this book would never have seen the light of day.

He and our son, Will, give me day-to-day proof that the world is indeed full of strange and wonderful magic.

ABOUT THE AUTHOR

Jennifer Lee Carrell holds her Ph.D. in English and American literature from Harvard University, as well as other degrees in English literature from Oxford and Stanford Universities. She taught at Harvard University and directed Shakespeare for the Hyperion Theatre Company. Jennifer's first thriller, *Interred with Their Bones,* is an international bestseller, translated into twenty-eight languages. She is also the author of *The Speckled Monster,* a work of historical nonfiction about battling smallpox at the beginning of the eighteenth century. She has written a number of articles for *Smithsonian* magazine.